Hotwife Office Adventures and Beyond

10 Freeuse and Wife-Sharing Collection

Switching It Up
Birthday in Paradise
Hot for Her Husband
the Freeuse Office Toy
Freeuse Gaming Night
The Freeuse Plaything
Freeuse Office Slut
Freeuse Office Games
Freeuse Office Hours
Freeuse Office Party

Lacey Cross

Twisted Rose
·Publishing·

CONTENTS

SWITCHING IT UP

HOTWIFE LET LOOSE

LACEY CROSS

CHAPTER 1

As soon as I get home from work, I drop a thick black invitation on the kitchen table and ignore it while I wash out my lunch container at the sink. Mr. Knight, one lawyer at the law firm where I work, gave me the invitation a few hours before the end of the day. His voice plays like a recorder in my head, and I shiver. God, the way he says my name is so fucking hot. All he said was, "Miranda, do you want to go to a party in a couple of weeks?" and my panties were immediately wet.

The problem is, I might be in love with Mr. Knight, or smitten at the very least. When he first mentioned the party, my heart raced and I blushed a bright pink because I thought he was inviting me alone. Then he added that the invitation included my husband, Jon, and I had to hold in a flash of disappointment. I would have said yes immediately if it was just me, but since it wasn't, I said I'd take the invitation home and talk it over with Jon.

My feelings for Mr. Knight are messy, and I'm still working through them. Several months ago Jon encouraged me to live out his fantasy of me screwing other guys, and I'm having a ton of fun. I ended up fucking my four bosses at work, and I've been living the hotwife life ever since and banging two of them per week. The hotwife agreement evolved and I became a birthday gift for several other people. This has all been a wild, erotic journey of exploration that both Jon and I enjoy.

I didn't learn I liked BDSM until I had a bondage session with Mr. Knight. Once I told Jon about being tied up, his gleeful attitude proved he also found it interesting. Now he does tons of research online and tries to glean whatever information he can from the sessions I have with Mr. Knight. Jon was out of town for a work trip over my birthday weekend, and I ended up spending my birthday night alone with Mr. Knight. The sex was incredible and I've been obsessing about him ever since.

After changing out of my office clothes and into my customary loungewear—yoga pants and a t-shirt—I decide to not bother with socks or slippers. Heading into the kitchen, I plop down into a chair at the table so I can stare at the invitation. What am I going to do? Do I really want to go with Jon and Mr. Knight? I could hide the invitation and tell Mr. Knight we're not interested. The company I work for is small and Jon sees my bosses fairly regularly, so there's no way I could lie, say he didn't want to go, and go without him. I could easily see Mr. Knight one day telling Jon it was too bad he couldn't go and that he missed a fabulous party.

Picking up the envelope, I trace the embossed outline of the leather manacles on the back flap and imagine what could happen at the BDSM party. I can think of a variety of scenarios and my tingling pussy likes every idea I come up with. Shifting against the hardwood chair, I press my hips down and rub my pussy on the surface, hoping to ease the forming ache.

I'm never invited to swanky shindigs and Master X, the guy who sent out the invite, supposedly has a stunning mansion of a house and throws amazing parties. Mr. Knight hinted I would regret missing this one. Dammit, now if only Jon would say he doesn't want to go, but I'd bet a million that he's going to be more excited about this invitation than I am. There's no way in hell Jon will pass up the chance for some real-life BDSM research. I already checked our joint calendar and neither of us have anything going on the night of the party.

I've been debating what to do all afternoon, and the answer eludes me. The yearning in my gut proves I want to go, but whenever I picture the three of us together at the party, it seems like a horrible plan. If I ended up in a sexual position with Mr. Knight in front of Jon, I might reveal my feelings for Mr. Knight.

Jon needs to be my top priority, and the thought of making him upset strengthens my resolve to decline the invite. I clutch the envelope and stand up, intending to go hide it in my purse, but a small voice in my head stops me and asks, "Don't you think you'd have fun?" *Oh shit, I've gone crazy and now I'm hearing voices.* I shake my head to clear it, and the inner voice nags at me again. "You know you'd have fun."

UGH, fuck, okay. I lay the envelope back on the table and plunk down into my chair again. Jon will be home soon and I really should get up and start fixing dinner. We're having grilled chicken Caesar salad tonight, but since it requires no cooking, I'm not very motivated to move.

Staring blankly out the kitchen window, I fantasize that Jon can't go to the party and it's just me and Mr. Knight together. In the daydream, I'm wearing a black latex bodysuit with a zipper down the front, like Catwoman wears, and kitten ears. Mr. Knight presses me against the wall with my wrists pinned above my head, and he grinds against me while whispering in my ear all the dirty things he wants to do to me.

I lean back in the chair and slide my hand into the front of my yoga pants and under the band of my panties. I'm already wet from thinking about the party, and the added fantasy with Mr. Knight has me soaking. My fingers slip between my folds, and I caress my clit and moan softly. A pang of guilt hits me because of how aroused I am, but it only makes me rub faster. Daydream Mr. Knight pulls down the zipper of the bodysuit and it's his hands petting me and making me throb instead of my own.

My thighs tense as the pleasure mounts and I'm just about to come when I hear the front door open. *Fuck!*

Jon yells out his customary, "Hey, Kitten. I'm home," while I pull my hand out of my pants quickly and reply that I'm in the kitchen. I hustle over to the sink to wash my hands.

Jon comes into the kitchen and chats at me about his day as he unloads his work lunchbox. Since he's home, I might as well get dinner started. I move about, pulling salad fixings out of the fridge while trying to ignore how wet and needy I am from my unfulfilled orgasm. *Shit, why couldn't he have been five minutes late?*

It doesn't take Jon long to spot the invitation on the table. "Hey, what's this?"

My head is in the fridge, and I keep my voice casual. "Oh, Mr. Knight invited us to a BDSM overnight party. It's the weekend after next and I thought it might be interesting."

"Ooooh, really?" Jon's excitement is obvious, and I hold back a sigh. *Yep, I called it.*

"Oh, wow. This invitation is fancy."

I stay quiet and unload the dinner supplies onto the counter. Jon studies the invitation and goes silent for a few moments.

"What does a person wear to a BDSM party?" Jon asks aloud, but he's obviously talking to himself.

Oh shit, I never thought of that. This party sounds like too much work. Trying to hide my feelings all night will exhaust me and now I have to plan my outfit as well?

"Kitten, can you fix dinner so I can do some research on what we should wear?"

Oh thank God. He can figure it out. "Yes, love. I'll call out when the salad is ready."

Jon practically skips out of the kitchen in his haste to get to the computer, and I finally relax. I hope that by the day of the party, I can be in a better frame of mind about it.

Chapter 2

Jon spurns my attempts to find out what he bought for us to wear to the party. He wants to surprise me, and knowing my husband, that isn't always a good thing. He gets enthusiastic about projects and goes overboard. Despite finding catsuits hot, I better not be wearing one with large cut-outs at my pussy and breasts for easy access. I don't even know if an outfit like that exists, but if it does, you can bet my husband will have contemplated buying it.

His refusal to show me or give me any hints about what he chose annoys me. Jon gets a gleeful, evil glint in his eye the crankier I am, so I've stopped talking about the outfits all together. I don't want to give him the satisfaction of knowing it bugs me. Based on the last few times I've gone domme on Jon, I'm convinced that I married a submissive man, but now I'm thinking I also live with a brat.

Part of me wants to let my domme out, snatch a wooden spoon, and tell him to lie across my knees. We'll see how long it takes my sweet hubby to beg to tell me what he bought while I spank him. Then I'll demand he stop talking about it because he had his chance already, and he kept it a secret. But Jon and I haven't discussed doing any painful punishment-type play together, nor do we have safe words. Pulling out a wooden spoon and pinkening his tender backside requires a bigger discussion. I don't get the urge to go domme often, but if Jon and I explore the punishment side of things, maybe that will trigger me to want it more.

Even if we incorporated more play with me as the dominant one, I'm uncertain how to manage my submissive yearnings while married to another submissive. Part of me wonders if that is why I'm attracted to Mr. Knight. If my husband was a dom, would I still feel a pull towards Mr. Knight?

All the angst about the party and Mr. Knight has me stressed and I have to repeat to myself like a daily mantra, "I will stop worrying about this damn party." Every night before bed, I imagine Count Von Count from Sesame Street repeating the number of sleeps before the party and striking them from a calendar like they are the number of the day.

The last few days before the party, I'm super distracted at work and when the big boss, Mr. Jacobs, calls me into his office because he found a missed punctuation in a memo I typed, I consider telling him I'm busy. But hey, maybe the distraction will keep my mind off the disaster this upcoming party could be if I can't modulate my reaction to Mr. Knight in front of my husband.

For the first time in months, I'm wearing a dress to work instead of my normal black skirt and white blouse. The party is less than a week away and this morning I wanted to cheer myself up by gussying up in my favorite sexy dress. It's a burgundy form-fitting number, with long sleeves and a deep V-neck. It fans out at the waist to swing around my legs and ends just below the knee.

Mr. Jacobs hadn't seen me yet today, so when I enter his office, he's taken aback when he sees the dress. He's quick to hide his surprise and his gaze warms up with an appreciative glint. I'm not inexperienced anymore, and I always make sure whatever is covering my bottom half is easy to remove or push up.

"Miranda, come over here and bend over my desk. We have things to discuss."

Oooh yes, let's discuss this. I might not have been totally in the mood when he called me in here, but I'm like a trained dog now whenever I'm close to his mahogany desk. He's bent me over it so many times. I just have to glimpse it and my pussy gets wet and needy.

Mr. Jacobs is still in his chair, and he wheels backwards so there's room for me to walk in front of him. I kick off my black ballet flats before doing what he asks. I leave everything else on and lean over the surface, tilting my ass towards him and giving it a little shake. I know what he likes by now, and he appreciates a teasing wiggle whenever I'm in this position.

The mahogany desk is cool to the touch, and I lower myself down to my forearms with my hands flat on the surface. There's no good way to get a grip when he pounds into me, but my hands and arms help slow the jostling down a bit. I expect him to shove his hands up my skirt immediately, but he surprises me when he caresses my fabric-covered ass instead. When he rubs my pussy through the dress, I moan and press back against him. My heartbeat speeds up and my stomach flutters when he slides his hands down my legs and slowly lifts my dress.

I'm wearing pink cotton panties, and I wonder if he can already see how wet I am through the cotton. His belt buckle clinks and I hear the rustle of his pants being pulled down. He's being more gentle than I expected, since he'd originally brought me in here for punishment. When he slides my panties over my ass and down my legs, I step out of one side so I can spread my legs wider. He takes a moment and fingers me, smearing my juices all around my clit while I moan. Since I keep expecting a sharp smack to my ass, I can't fully relax and enjoy what he's doing.

As if he heard me thinking, Mr. Jacobs speaks. "Miranda, I brought you in here to punish you."

I squirm against his hand, anticipating the coming pain. "Yes, and I'm sorry."

"I've decided NOT to punish you."

What's this? Mr. Jacobs removes his hand and the tip of his cock probes my slit. My head spins as he presses in slowly. I don't question what changed his mind as he holds onto my hips and leisurely fucks me. The abrupt shift from expecting pain to receiving slow, deep strokes spins me towards my orgasm quickly.

I'm repeating "Oh, my god," with every thrust and when I push back against him to force him in harder, he finally speeds up. I groan out, "Oh, god, yes," as he hammers into me. My hands aren't able to stop me from sliding on the desk and every time he whacks against my ass, I'm shoved forward on the surface. His hands on my hips pull me back towards him each time.

The room fills with his harsh breathing, and my vocal murmurs and gasps. I can't last much longer, and the pressure in my core mounts. I close my eyes, lost in the rapture and when I finally climax, I cry out and spasm as waves of bliss spike through my body. Mr. Jacobs rocks against me and grunts as he blows his load. He doesn't pull out immediately and keeps fucking me slowly until his cock softens too much.

I keep my eyes closed and lay my head against the desk while aftershocks of pleasure make my pussy clench. There's a wetness dripping down my leg and I don't know if it's his cum or my juices, but my dress is thin so I think I'm going to have to do more clean-up today than normal.

Mr. Jacobs bends down and pulls at my foot so I'll lift it up, and slides my panties back over my ankle and pulls them up over my ass. This signals to me it's time to leave, but before he pulls my dress down, he gives my ass a hard smack and I squeak from surprise.

He's got a stern daddy voice when he chastises me. "That's for the typo."

His tone makes me want to flirt with him and tease that his form of punishment isn't an incentive to not make typos, but I play it safe and apologize as he pulls down my dress.

"I'm sorry. I'll look things over more carefully."

His dismissive tone when he says, "See that you do," gives me a thrill. I like how strict he is with me and I try not to question why. His lack of warmth is one reason I enjoy our interludes so much. I slip my shoes back on and visit the bathroom to clean up. Sometimes I consider keeping spare panties in my purse, but I relish the sluttiness of spending the rest of the day in my soaked panties.

CHAPTER 3

The morning of the party, Jon finally pulls out our outfits and proudly shows me what I'm wearing that night. My stomach drops when I see black latex, but when it turns out to be a dress—a very sexy one—I have to admit my husband did a decent job of finding something I would like. It's halter-style, fastening behind my neck, while the top part molds to my breasts, and flares out at the waist. Jon likes it when I show off my breasts, so I'm not surprised by his choice. It's shorter than anything I'd normally wear, and I'm not sure I should bend over in it, but figure my black lace panties will cover most everything.

The shoes he picked out were the best part. He bought four-inch black shiny spiked heels that look treacherous to wear. They have thick ankle cuffs with two decorative silver locks attached to the side, and I'm in love with the entire outfit. I might wobble a bit, but I'll use it as an excuse to grasp onto Jon or Mr. Knight to steady myself whenever I want.

When Jon pulls out his outfit, I almost snicker. Oh, thank god he went tame for mine. My crazy man bought black leather pants and a harness for his upper body instead of a shirt. The harness is black leather, and the straps run over his shoulders, around his abdomen, and buckle in the center of his chest. He modeled it for me, and the little punch of pleasure in my gut sobered me right up. Okay, so maybe he can pull this off after all. He doesn't have washboard abs, but he's fit and I have to admit he's pretty sexy in a harness. I don't know if people wear harnesses to these parties, but he won't look ridiculous in it.

He lays our party clothes out on the bed for later and I spend the morning in self-care. I take a long, hot shower and almost shave my kitty bare, reminding myself that Mr. Knight prefers his women completely hairless. I decide to leave a tiny landing strip so Jon doesn't get suspicious, and feel like a complete shit for landscaping for Mr. Knight while I'm getting a tingle of excitement thinking of fucking him. Yeah, I think I'm messed up in the head.

I decide to stop worrying about it and just enjoy the night while I'm blow drying my hair. Jon always loves it when I leave my hair down because he enjoys playing with the natural waves. To make myself feel better about shaving for Mr. Knight, I leave my hair down in consideration of Jon and it mollifies my guilty conscience.

Mr. Knight is picking us up and I take so long fiddling with my outfit and putting on make-up, I'm barely ready when the doorbell rings. Jon lets Mr. Knight in and I hear them making small talk as I put the finishing touches on my makeup. When I join them in the living room, Mr. Knight is wearing a standard black suit like he wears to work, but seeing him outside of work in it makes me flushed and tongue tied. God, he's sexy in a suit.

Jon whistles at my appearance, and Mr. Knight sounds sincere when he compliments me. "Wow, Miranda, you look ravishing." I blush harder at his words and wish I could hide my reaction to him.

We stand around awkwardly for a moment before Mr. Knight takes charge. "There are a couple of things we need to cover before we leave. First, Miranda, are you wearing panties?"

Uh, what? I sneak a look at Jon to see his reaction, but he's smiling as if it's perfectly natural for my boss to be asking what I have on under my dress.

I'm hesitant when I answer. "Uh… yes?"

"Okay, take them off now and leave them here."

Oh fuck, that's hot. I want to answer, "Yes, Sir," but stop myself because of Jon. Shit, this is going to be a tough night. I turn to go to the bedroom, but Mr. Knight interrupts me.

"No, take them off right here and just leave them on the floor."

My eyes widen and I'm breathless. Excitement ripples through me, but I also cringe in embarrassment. I don't want to see what happens if I disobey, so I hike up the back of my dress, hook my thumbs into the waistband of my panties, and pull them down. I awkwardly bend over so I can untangle them from around my shoes without tripping. When I straighten up, Jon and Mr. Knight both have a devilish twinkle in their eyes, and I sense they're enjoying my humiliation.

"Okay, the next thing is that tonight I want you both to call me Nick. We aren't at work so I'd prefer to be more casual."

Oooh, ugh. That might be hard to remember, but I nod at him like a good girl.

Jon, all jolly, quips, "No problem, Nick."

"Okay, that's it. Let's go."

Jon locks up the house as I follow Mr. Knight—er, Nick—towards his black sedan. The cool night air swishes up my skirt and I shiver. Not wearing panties with a short skirt is an oddly vulnerable feeling. The thought of bending over already concerned me before when I had panties on, and now it's worse. I'll flash the entire universe with my pale ass and nicely shaved kitty.

I'm unsteady in my spiked heels and when Nick goes to the driver's side without helping me open the passenger door, I try to temper my immediate crankiness. I'm a strong independent woman who doesn't need a man, right? Nick says he wants Jon in the front, and I struggle to open the heavy door and almost tip over. Shit, I need to learn how to walk in these shoes, pronto. I'm barely in when I freeze because there's another woman in the car sitting behind the driver's seat. *Uh, who the fuck is this?*

Jon climbs in the front and I ease myself all the way into the car and shut the door. My stomach clenches and I'm feeling nauseated. *Did Nick bring a date?* As we buckle our seatbelts, Nick introduces us to the woman.

"Miranda, Jon, this is Elizabeth, my girlfriend."

Jon gives her an enthusiastic hello while my brain screeches to a halt. *He's got a motherfucking girlfriend?*

I barely mumble out my own hello when she giggles and tells us to call her Liz. Her voice is soft, charming, and incredibly feminine, and I immediately want to hate her guts. This night just went from stressful to downright awful. How long has he had a girlfriend?

Mr. Knight drives while my mind whirls. I'm silent while everyone chatters around me and I'm not tracking the conversation. The longer we drive, the more I notice little details about Liz. The first is that she's wearing a long black pencil skirt, chunky heels, and a white button-down shirt—pretty much my standard office attire. Her long brown hair adds to the illusion that she's oddly similar in appearance to me.

When she notices me glancing at her, she shifts in her seat to angle her body towards me, smiles and tosses her head so her hair falls back and reveals she's collared. How in the hell did he meet someone and collar her in the couple of weeks since my birthday? Was he even single when he stayed the night on my birthday? I may not know much about the BDSM scene, but Jon told me all about collaring in his research. Unless Jon was totally incorrect, her being collared is a big deal.

Liz's smile turns to a smirk when she can tell I am disturbed by the collar and I immediately realize she doesn't like me. What the hell am I going to do tonight? Sex with Nick seems like it's off the table, and I for sure as hell don't want to watch those two fuck. I'm alternating hot and cold and my stomach roils while I try to puzzle this all out. I just don't understand where she came from, because—wouldn't he have mentioned a girlfriend? And also, what the fuck is up with her outfit?

Jon saves me from wondering about one part of it. He turns in his seat and talks to Liz.

"How long have you guys been together?"

She giggles adorably before answering, and I want to slap her. I'm not buying the innocent, girlish shtick she's got going on, not with how she enjoyed my discomfort about her collar. Jon, of course, is eating it up and seems enthralled with her.

"Oh, we've been together for years, but we were long distance. I finally moved in with him."

YEARS! What the hell? Did she realize her boyfriend is—was—fucking me?

My lovely, sappy hubby finds romance in the situation and tells her, "Oh, that's sweet," and beams an even wider smile at her.

Wait, does Jon think he's got a chance of fucking her tonight? A rock forms in my stomach at the realization that Jon and I never discussed the rules for the party. In my head, I was going to do whomever I wanted while he observed because watching is his thing... right? It's possible his birthday threesome with Danielle opened the door in his mind to thinking he's allowed to play.

My domme stirs to life and I need to talk to him privately as soon as we get to the party. There is no fucking way I'm going to allow my sweet man to do anything with someone else. I recognize this is hypocritical of me, but an odd possessive fierceness hits me when I imagine Jon screwing someone else. Oh, hell no. Not happening. I don't know why the threesome was okay, but tonight, him touching someone else isn't. We need to discuss this before something happens that pisses me off.

Everyone else chatters the rest of the drive while I vacillate between cranky at Nick and territorial over Jon. I'm barely paying attention when we pull up to a large iron gate. Nick speaks into the intercom briefly before the gates open. He pulls the car around and when he parks and turns off the car, I clamber out as quickly as my spiked heels allow.

Once I'm out of the car, I hesitate because I want to stalk off and ignore Nick, but I expected him to guide us tonight.

"Liz, Miranda, come here."

Hmm... what's this? I glare at him and consider telling him to shove it, but when Liz practically prances around the car like an eager puppy, I don't want anyone to know I'm upset.

He waits in front of the car and when I join them, Liz and I are on either side of him.

"I want you both to pull up your skirts, bend over, and lean on the hood."

My first thought is "Oh hell no", while Liz sighs happily and responds, "Yes, Sir," as she tries to pull up her skirt and it gets stuck halfway up her thighs. I hide a smirk and watch her struggle, thinking of how I learned my lesson with pencil skirts at work when I tried to give my bosses access to my cooch.

You know what? Fuck it. Let's see where this is going. I've reached a point where this night seems ruined, so I'm just going with it. Flipping up my free-flowing short skirt easily, I bend over, resting my elbows on the warm hood. I wait for a few moments, my ass exposed to the chilly air while Nick helps Liz unzip her skirt and pull it down. He moves over to me as she settles in on the hood. I try to watch what he's doing over my shoulder. He wouldn't fuck us out here, would he?

He pulls something small and silver out of one pocket, and then a tiny bottle of lube out of the other. A thrill runs through me when I recognize a butt plug in his hand. I may be cranky at him, but my treacherous pussy gets wet at the thought of him messing with my asshole. She hasn't gotten the memo yet that we're unhappy.

Mr. Knight gets right up behind me and uses a finger to lube me up. Luckily, since the lube was in his pocket it's not cold and I almost groan with pleasure as he presses his finger into my asshole. A moment later, the buttplug replaces his finger as he pushes it into me gently. I wiggle my ass a little, experiencing an unfamiliar fullness that isn't unpleasant, but it will be hard to ignore all night. I've only used a butt plug one other time, so this is going to make for an interesting evening.

When he's done, he announces, "There. Now stay like that," and moves over and does the same thing to Liz. Her moans of pleasure are loud, and I feel stabby again when she coos, "Oh, Sir, press it in harder," with her, now, too-syrupy sweet voice.

When he's done with Liz, he calls Jon over. "Jon, come see how pretty they both look."

Jon dutifully trots over and he laughs at our exposed asses. "I like the different colored gems."

Wait, we have different ones? I'm curious what colors he gave us, but I refuse to peek at her ass to find out what hers is. I'll ask Jon about it later.

"Okay, straighten up and let's go."

Nick and Jon both head around the car and Nick puts something in his trunk—possibly the lube—while Liz and I stand up and adjust ourselves.

The men are out of hearing range and Liz keeps her voice low when she speaks to me in a very normal-sounding, unsweet voice. "Do you like my outfit?"

I blink at her while my mind races. How do I answer her? I can't really say, "Sure, I love it. It looks exactly like what I used to wear to work when I first fucked your boyfriend."

When I don't answer her quickly enough, she continues. "Nick picked it out. He has a fuck-the-secretary kink and always hooks up with the women he works with."

Oh, now that's interesting. I'm breathless as I tense up and avoid eye contact with Liz. Am I just one in a long line of women for Nick? I try to temper my budding anger because I can tell she's trying to goad me.

It takes all my willpower to give her a tiny shrug and sound casual. "Oh, I didn't know that."

She leans in closer to me and drops her voice even lower. "Whatever you've got going on with Nick ends now."

Um, okay. I'm about to laugh in her face that I'm pretty sure Nick does what he wants, when I realize she's borderline furious. Oh, shit. I instantly sober up. She and I don't have to like each other, but it would be bad if she hated me, since if she lives with Nick now, we're going to be seeing each other at all the social functions for work.

I stumble on my words in my rush to spit them out. "Hey, wait. I didn't know about you. I swear. He never said he had a girlfriend."

She gives her skirt a final smoothing, and she looks at me cheerfully. "Oh, I'm aware you didn't. He told me that himself. I'm just telling you it's over."

Suddenly, I am 100 percent on board with her. I have no desire to be any part of whatever mess those two have going on, and her sudden mood shift from angry to...happy—I don't even know what that is, but I've got a husband and three other bosses I can fuck. I don't need Nick, even if he can tie me up and thrill me. Jon can learn to do whatever Nick does, if I crave it in the future.

I'm serious and quiet when I say, "Yes, Liz. It's over."

"Thank you." Her sweet tone has returned, and I want to grab Jon and get the hell away from these two.

I teeter over to Jon, and snag his wrist to stop him from walking towards the mansion.

"Nick, Liz... Jon and I are going to do our own thing tonight. Thank you for bringing us."

Liz beams a smile at me, but Nick looks confused and asks, "You sure?"

"Yep, have fun!" I try to sound cheerful and Nick shrugs, saying he'll let them know at the door that we're with him so we can get into the party. He and Liz head off and I feel like I can finally breathe again.

Jon is staring at me while I said for them to get far enough away that there's no chance they can overhear us talking.

"Miranda, what's going on?"

A rush of relief and love washes over me as I look at Jon. Holy fuck, I almost potentially fucked up my marriage over a psycho couple.

"Um, Liz wasn't that nice to me and I didn't want to be around her all night."

Jon looks puzzled. "She seems like a sweetheart."

"Yeah, well, to you maybe, but she wasn't nice to me. I'll tell you about it tomorrow." I'm dismissive because I don't want to explain what went down until I process it a little better, so I continue on. "We need to talk about something before we go in."

"What's up?"

The interlude with Liz drained any domme energy out of me, so I'm not sure how to word what I want to say. I am probably going to fumble around, but I attempt it anyway.

"Uh... did you plan on doing anything with other people tonight?"

Jon looks momentarily shocked. "No. You don't want me to, do you?"

Some of the tension I was holding drains out. Oh, thank God. I didn't want to fight with him about it.

"Oh, no, no, no. I didn't want you to. We just hadn't talked."

He grins at me, more relaxed as well. "Oh, Kitten. I'm just here to watch you play."

Ooooh, okay. Guess Jon and I are totally on the same page about tonight. I press against him, kissing him deeply, letting my tongue tease his while I run my hands up his chest.

I take Jon's hand and grin at him. "Are we ready for this?"

Jon squeezes my hand as we walk towards the mansion together. "Yep! This should be interesting."

CHAPTER 4

At some point, the night became a blur. Jon and I wandered the halls for several hours, visiting different rooms and watching all sorts of kinky shit go down. This party was more hands-on than I expected, and multiple people toyed with me. Most notably, I licked a domme's pussy while her dom fucked me from behind. That was a new experience, and I'm still reeling from the aftereffects from that when we approach the next room.

A small group of people are standing outside the door watching something, and I duck under a few arms so I can get a better look. Everyone is staring at a man who is probably in his 50s strapped naked to a St. Andrew's Cross with a ball gag in his mouth. Wonder what's going on here?

A young woman calls from behind the crowd, "Please let me through," and the small sea of people part to let her in. When a person in the back comments that someone is coming to take over, the young woman states that it's her and she's in charge now. I'm impressed. She's younger than me and commanding the room full of people.

I watch the woman grab the guy's cock, working it in her hand, and I get a nice sexual zing from the show. I'm still mentally buzzing from all of my encounters tonight.

When the woman announces, "We have a nice stiff cock here. Would any of you like to use it?" I step forward, almost without realizing it.

Oh fuck, what am I doing? I glance back at Jon to make sure he's okay with this. He looks shocked but he doesn't tell me to stop. I assume his surprise is that I volunteered so quickly, and I surprised myself with that one as well. I turn and stroke his face, kiss him, and then walk over to the domme.

The domme asks me, "What's your name?"

I tell her and she instructs me to turn around and look at the guy so he can see me. He's pretty handsome, and I've always had a thing for older guys. I can't resist leaning in and giving him a peck on the cheek.

As I kiss him, the domme pulls up the back of my dress. Hey, what's this now? I'm not wearing panties, and I don't like the thought of being exposed.

"Would you like to fuck our toy?" the domme asks me, and I'm distracted away from her pulling up my dress.

I look at the guy on the cross and wrap my hand around his cock, squeezing him as he pulsates. *Oh, yeah, I want to fuck him.*

"Yes, please." I try to tone down my eagerness, but I really want his guy's cock inside of me.

I almost shiver when she whispers in my ear, "Do you want to feel that lovely, thick cock in your pussy?"

"Oooh, yes," I groan out. *Fuck, yes, I want this.* My entire night has been one sexual high after another and I'm beyond caring that the room is full of people.

When the domme slaps me on the ass, I yelp. *Jesus, this woman is good.* I could use some lessons from her on how to handle Jon.

I'm stunned when the domme says, "Actually, I think I want him to fuck your ass."

Oooh, fuck. I've never done anal yet. Do I want to do it in front of all these people? I glance over at Jon, and he's shifting from one foot to the other, but nods his head, giving me permission. A rush of excitement hits me. I expected him to say no, but since he agreed, my entire body is now on board with the plan.

The domme announces she needs to take my butt plug out, and I groan when she removes it. Fuuuck. My head is already spinning and his cock isn't even in my ass yet.

She hands me a bottle of lube and tells me to make sure he's nice and lubed up. I squirt some on my hand and work it into his shaft. His cock twitches in my hand and I swear it gets larger. Uh, is this thing even going to fit? I've only had a few fingers up there at once and a butt plug, nowhere near the size of a cock.

When I believe he's lubed up enough, I set the bottle on a side table and look at the domme. I'm a bundle of nerves and afraid this is going to hurt. Maybe this is a bad plan?

The woman turns me and guides me back towards the guy on the cross.

"Miranda, I want you to guide him in. Reach back." I do what she says, still uncertain about the potential pain, but when the tip of his cock presses against my asshole, I almost groan from the pleasure. Oh god, I want to do this.

The domme continues, "That's it. Can you feel him pressed against you?"

Mmm, yeah I can. I nod and my eyelids flutter. Shit, this feels amazing.

The domme moves forward and kisses me hard. Our tongues flick against each other and we both moan. Well this is fucking awesome. I've got this guy's cock just barely in my ass, and a sexy woman kissing me. Can this night get any better?

I press down on his cock slowly as she continues to kiss me. The pleasure gets too intense the deeper he gets, and I moan so loud, I break off the kiss. It hurts a little, but the pressure of him inside me also feels amazing.

When she says, "Miranda, you set the pace. He is only here to provide you with a cock," I breathe out a "Yes," and half close my eyes as I slowly move up and down his shaft. With each downward stroke, I can take a little more of him in me.

Jesus—fuck. I want to close my eyes and let ecstasy overwhelm me, but instead, I reach out and grasp onto the domme's hand. I need something to focus me and the warmth of her palm does the trick.

The guy underneath me jerks and starts pumping his hips, trying to fuck my ass as much as he can. His movements cause me to rock against him faster.

"Oh, god," I moan out, closing my eyes as the pleasure swiftly builds to a peak. I didn't realize having a cock in my ass would be this great. I should have done this ages ago.

I'm about to bliss out, so I open my eyes and look at the domme. We stare at each other for a moment before she asks, "May I?"

I don't know exactly what she's asking, but she can do whatever the fuck she wants with me. I'm chasing my orgasm and I'm close. When I say, "Yes," she reaches between my legs, her fingers stroking my clit, and we lock eyes.

Working the guy's cock in and out of my ass while this woman rubs my clit is too much for me to take. I barely have time to register I'm about to climax when the strength of my orgasm hits me like a tsunami.

I cry out, "Oh, my god," as my entire body quivers. Waves of pleasure wash over me and I fall forward against the domme. I'm moaning and shuddering for what feels like forever until Jon's arms are around me. I hold on to him as tiny aftershocks course through me. Holy mother of Christ.

"Are you okay?" he asks.

I smile at him weakly before I answer. I don't have any energy for anything else. "Oh Jon, that was so fucking good."

He pulls me towards the door, but I stop him so I can grab the butt plug. I don't know why, but I don't want to leave it.

CHAPTER 5

I'm flushed and breathless as Jon and I stumble out into the hallway. He shelters me in his arms, as if he's protecting me, as we head towards our assigned room. Holy shit, I just did full anal! After months of experimenting with one of my boss's fingers in my ass and Jon occasionally fingering me at home, I can't believe I finally did it.

I want to run a victory lap down the hallway, except no one's running anywhere in these shoes. My feet ache after wearing four-inch spiked heels for hours. The wide straps around my ankles and the two tiny padlock decorations are hella sexy, and I plan to wear these shoes again someday when the opportunity presents itself.

I'm still buzzing from my orgasm and my stomach flutters as I think about how I let an unknown guy be the first cock in my ass. My inner slut relishes the knowledge that I'll relive this night in my head for months—so damn hot. I expected to be sore, but I only feel a void where there was once weight and fullness, which could be from wearing the butt plug all night. I peek down at the red-jeweled plug in my hand and smirk. Guess I got half my question answered from earlier when Nick inserted the butt plug in my ass—he gave me a red one. I briefly wonder what color Liz has, but I don't feel like talking about her right now, so I don't ask Jon. The butt plug will be my souvenir from this wild night.

All I want to do right now is climb into bed, snuggle with Jon, and demand a foot rub. I think he had a good time tonight, and he was such a good boy while watching me sink my ass down on the dude strapped to the St. Andrew's Cross. I was hesitant at first and might have said no, but Jon's nod of agreement prompted me to continue. It'll be a delightful surprise when I tell my boss he can now fuck me in the ass all he wants. It wasn't scary at all and felt fucking amazing.

I'm not feeling particularly domme right now, especially after my experience just a few minutes ago in the other room with the young girl controlling me. But Jon has been a good boy and he hasn't come yet, so I should reward him. I think it's time to do a more formal D/s relationship with Jon, and I'll talk to him about it when we get home. He's enjoyed the light domming I've done in the past, and we've both had fun.

Earlier, Master X took us on a private tour of his downstairs playroom, and when Jon tested out the leather crop on his leg, a strong need washed over me to use it on him and make him cry out. We're definitely buying a leather crop immediately, assuming Jon is down for it—and I think he will be.

My brain is a swirl of thoughts about Jon, me being a switch, and what this will look like for our marriage, when we stumble into the bedroom. Jon shuts the door and I notice a padded bench across the room before we both flop down on the bed, looking at the ceiling. I sit up briefly to unbuckle my shoes and the buttplug accidentally slips out of my hands and drops to the floor. Eh, I can find it later. My shoes shortly join it on the floor and I lie back again.

I can't relax too long before I give Jon his treat because I'm going to zonk out immediately once I crash from this sexual high. Every hole of mine got stuffed tonight, so maybe I'll let Jon decide what he wants. That would be a suitable reward for my obedient boy.

A giggle slips out as I think about our night. Jon spent half the night looking bewildered, and the other half intrigued by everything we saw.

Master X sure knows how to put on a party. If I ever invited to another one, I'll accept the invitation immediately.

"Miranda, why are you giggling?"

What's this? Jon's voice has a flat tone, and something seems off.

God, I hope he's not getting cranky because he's tired. It has been a long night though, so I suppose I can't fault him. Maybe he's grumpy because he hasn't come yet, but I can fix that easily.

I try to keep my answer light and playful. "Oh, I was remembering how cute you were tonight, and laughed. I think you were adorable and funny."

Jon still sounds unamused. "I suppose you also found it funny when I watched you getting railed from behind while eating that domme's pussy?"

Uh... what's going on here? A rush of heat heads straight to my pussy and a gush of wetness leaks out when I think about how hard I came from the domme commanding me to lick her while her dom nailed me from behind. So... fucking... hot... I totally plan on masturbating often while thinking of that experience. That one is going in my "spank bank," so to speak. I may not be happy with my boss, Nick, right now, but he always has interesting friends.

I try to focus on Jon again. Getting all hot and bothered over the domme and dom from earlier won't make him any happier. Jon and I had a threesome with a woman for his birthday, and a few weeks later, I had an entire night alone with a different woman. So what's his problem? He's seen me fuck plenty of other guys before—he watched me have an entire conference room gangbang with my bosses.

My voice is meek when I answer. "You didn't enjoy watching?"

"You didn't ASK!" Jon explodes with the last word.

Oh, fuck. He's angry? And when in the hell do I have to ask for permission? Wasn't the entire night free for me to do what I want while he enjoys the show? I'm confused, and I don't like his tone one bit. He doesn't know it, but he just lost his shot at coming tonight. I don't want to fight and I'm still hoping to get some snuggles once we talk this through, though I'm sure a foot rub is now out of the question.

I roll onto my side so I'm fully facing him, and attempt to sound slightly contrite. "Jon, I thought you agreed to this?"

Jon snorts harshly as he turns on his side to face me as well. "No, Miranda. I didn't agree to watching you ass-fuck some random guy."

Whaaat? Hold the phone. I think Jon and I had a miscommunication at some point.

"Uh… Jon?"

"How do you think that made me feel, Miranda?"

Jon's brown eyes are cold and hard, and my stomach drops. The room spins and I can't respond. I close my eyes in hopes everything will stop whirling.

"Miranda, answer me!"

My brain freezes. I've never seen Jon like this. He and I always sit down and work out our differences, and it usually involves laughing and poking fun at each other, but never this steely anger emanating from him.

The bed shifts and my eyes pop open when Jon shoves me on my back, grabs my wrists, and pins them above my head. *Ooooh, fuck—what's this?* I'm immediately wet and I strain briefly, but the more I struggle, the more arousing it is.

My heartbeat thuds in my head, and I'm breathless when I speak his name. "Jon?"

He laughs bitterly. "Oh, now you can finally talk? I had to get rough with you to get your attention?"

Jon switches to using one hand to pin my wrists and slips the other one up into my short latex dress. His fingers skim my inner thighs and I spread my legs for him. Whatever is going on, this side of my husband is hot. Who knew angry Jon would get physical with me?

When he presses a finger into my sopping wet pussy, I gasp.

"I shouldn't be surprised at how wet you are. After all, I married a slut."

I go completely still when he calls me a slut and the sense of vertigo intensifies. Jon has never called me anything like slut before. He tried it once and giggled.

He finger fucks me slowly. "Miranda, look at me."

A familiar buzz in my brain kicks in and the edges of the room become fuzzy. I look at Jon and blink, trying to focus. The lines on his face are blunt and unforgiving, and the coldness in his eyes shocks me. I squirm and the need to be fucked punches me in the gut.

When he knows he has my attention, he continues. "Tell me. Are you a slut?"

Oh, god am I ever. I stop breathing for a moment when the deep realization hits me that I'm not just a slut—I'm HIS slut.

I didn't want to be a hotwife at first and he's the one who convinced me to try it. And yes, I have a blast with it, but all this time I've been his slut, doing his bidding. I come home and tell him everything I do, and then he fucks me however he wants.

In all these months, there were only two times where I chose what we did: his birthday threesome, and the time I came home and rode him during my domme power trip, after I fingered Chloe in the bathroom for her birthday.

My limbs go heavy and my ears ring. He's been controlling me all this time?

My breath whooshes out. "Yes, Jon. But I'm not just a slut. I'm YOUR slut."

He gives me an amused grin and says, "Good girl," in a soothing tone.

I get tingly and warm from his words. This new Jon has me so confused and spinning in a good way. When did he learn how to do all this?

He picks up speed with his hand and adds in brushing his thumb back and forth on my clit.

I moan out, "Oh my god," and arch against his hand. The abundance of sex on display turned me on as soon as we walked into the mansion, and I'm extra sensitive from all the various sexual encounters tonight. Any slight stimulation could make me come at this point.

I'm racing towards an orgasm when Jon removes his hands and climbs between my legs. Ugh, fuck. Even though I know I'm about to get something better than his hand, I'm still desperate and wish he had continued until I got there.

I sink into a warm and fuzzy place where time has no meaning, and I dreamily watch Jon unbutton his pants and pull them down. His cock is hard and throbbing, and I almost giggle because it looks as angry as he was a few minutes ago.

Jon takes hold of my chin and squeezes my cheeks together gently, moving my head back and forth slightly.

"Huh, what?" *What the hell is he doing?*

"Miranda, focus."

Oh, oops. I actually do giggle this time.

"Miranda, focus on me. I need you to understand what I'm going to say."

Shit, FINE. I blink a few times and take some deep breaths. The room details become crisp again.

"Okay, I'm listening." I'll do whatever it takes to get his cock inside me, even if it requires listening to a lecture.

Jon fits the tip of my shaft against my aching hole, but doesn't press in. The studs from his harness reflect softly in the dim lighting and I want to caress his bare chest and lick his nipples, but I'm too far gone to try and slow us down. I need him inside me... NOW.

"Ooh, Jon, please fuck me." I can't hold back, even though he told me to focus and I squirm against him.

"Miranda, I will not say it again. Listen to me now or I'll jack off over your face and you won't get anything more tonight."

The resolve in his tone leaves me no doubt he'd do it. Imagining a waterfall of his cum falling on my face is hot, but I need to be fucked.

I purr at him, "I'm sorry, I'm listening," and attempt to sound sexy.

Jon says, "Good girl," as he thrusts inside me, sinking to my core.

"Ooooh fuck!" I wasn't expecting it since he told me to listen to him and the pleasure is intense.

"We've got some new rules, Miranda."

Jon hammers my pussy as he talks, and he's not being gentle. Spikes of delight ping me with every thrust. *What? What is he saying? New rules?*

"From now on, you will ask me before you fuck anyone else unless it's one of your bosses."

Ooooh, what? I can't think and the spinning in my head increases again.

"I realized tonight you didn't know you were my slut, and that I CON-TROL who you fuck."

I moan out, "Oh my god." Holy fuck, did a body snatcher take my husband?

He's harsh as he continues to talk while plowing into me. "While you were fucking around all night, I watched in agony as you came multiple times. Did you think about me even once?"

Uh... did I? Probably not during any of it.

Knowing that there is only one path to me coming, I try to sound remorseful. "I'm sorry. I didn't think."

Jon whacks against me sharply twice. "No, slut. You didn't."

It's so insanely hot when he calls me a slut. My goofy, loveable husband has somehow morphed into the dominant man of my dreams, and part of me wonders if I'm passed out asleep. Every plunge of his cock tells me otherwise. No way a dream is this intense.

Jon pauses and pulls fully out of me, causing me to cry out in distress.

"Oh god, don't stop, Jon!"

He grins at me. "Oh Kitten, I'm not stopping until we both come and you know who owns you."

OH MY GOD. A tremor of pleasure runs through my body out to all my extremities when he says he owns me. Jon ever so slowly presses back into me.

"One final rule."

He fucks me slowly for a few strokes before continuing. I'd agree to anything at this point.

"From this point on, no one fucks your ass except me."

I don't know how to reply, but I don't have time because he pulls out fully again and immediately rams all the way back to my core and starts jackhammering into my pussy. My body tenses and I'm getting close to coming.

Jon pants out, "Do you understand, slut?" He punctuates his sentence with a swift knock against me, and the pleasure almost takes me over the edge.

"Your ass is mine." Another hard bump and my thigh muscles tremble. I moan out and writhe underneath him.

"Do." Whack. "You." Whack. "Understand?"

He bucks against me roughly one last time and I explode, screaming out "Yes!" as waves of ecstasy wash over me. My entire body quivers and I thrash against him while he jerks and peaks. A rush of emotion hits me and I'm seeing stars as Jon spurts all the cum he's been saving up for hours.

He convulses from the strength of his orgasm and my pussy milks his cock while tiny aftershocks spread through me. He doesn't soften like usual, and he continues to fuck me for several strokes while I moan. I'm so sensitive it borders on pain, but he finally pulls out and collapses on the bed next to me.

I blank out and I don't know how much time passes before Jon pulls me against him to snuggle. Giving a soft murmur of protest, I almost tell him to let me take my dress off first because I'm sweaty and desperate to remove it. I don't want to think about putting it back on to wear home, but I'm left with little other choice. I give in and relax against him; he's sweaty too, so it doesn't really matter.

Jon kisses my forehead. "Kitten, are you okay?"

I didn't realize until he called me Kitten that a part of me was worried he didn't love me anymore. He's never been that angry before and that might have meant he was giving up on us. An unexpected release of tension brings tears to my eyes.

When I try to speak, my voice is shaky and brittle as I try to hold back the flood. "I'm fine."

I sniff as he pulls me even tighter against me, speaking softly. "Oh, Kitten. I love you so much."

When I start shaking, I can't hold back the tears any longer, and I wail at Jon.

"I thought you hated me now." I sniffle after every couple of words and want to bury my face in his chest.

Jon pulls away long enough to get a box of tissues from the nightstand, hands it to me, and snuggles back in. I blow my nose loudly as he continues.

"Oh, Miranda, my Kitten, I still love you. I didn't know I'd care until I saw you with the other guys. Otherwise, I wouldn't have agreed to let you play tonight."

I hiccup as I try to calm down and Jon rubs my arms soothingly. Then I wasn't unreasonable, and we had an agreement that I could play.

"Jon, did you mean everything you said?"

I get a tiny thrill remembering him saying he owns me, so I hope he doesn't back out now.

"Yes, I meant it. I don't want you doing that with anyone else."

I peep out a small, "oh," and pause for a moment. "And you own me?"

Jon laughs his goofy normal laugh, and it eases the last of my anxiety. "Oh, Kitten, I own you. You're mine and I'm never letting go."

He leans over and kisses me deeply and adds, "This okay with you?"

I sigh against his mouth as he kisses me again, and I'm breathless when he breaks it off.

"Sounds good to me, but you'll have to say it often so I don't forget." My light tone and cheeky smile tell him I'm not likely to forget it.

Jon grins back at me. "Yes, we wouldn't want that, now, would we? You might need punishment if you do."

Oh fuck, Jon really is taking the dom thing to heart. My pussy tries to sputter to life and I tell her to calm down. I'm mentally drained and physically exhausted. I'm going to crash really hard soon, so I glance around the room looking for a drink. Jon figures out what I want, and scrambles up again to bring me a bottle of water that was thoughtfully provided in the room. He unscrews the cap and hands it to me. I sit up, take a long swig and chug half the bottle, and then lean back, enjoying the warm glow from the hard fucking.

After I relax for a few minutes, the dress bugs me more and I need to get it off. I scoot off the bed and Jon helps me out of the dress, and then I return the favor by unbuckling his harness while he pulls off his leather pants. He sets all our clothes on a chair across the room, close to the padded bench I noticed earlier, and for the first time I look around, curious to see what other wonders we missed out on.

A side table against the far wall holds a variety of small torture devices, and I smile as I see a leather crop. Well, damn, we could have had fun with that. I yawn noisily and know it's too late now.

"Jon, let's go to bed. We can talk more in the morning."

Jon kisses my forehead and then each cheek. "That sounds good to me. But first, do YOU still love ME?"

I detect a hint of vulnerability when he asks, and my heart melts. I'm sincere when I tell him, "Jon, I've never loved you more than I do right now."

It really is the truth. The night didn't turn out anything like I originally hoped, but it's so much better. Somehow I was married to a switch and didn't know it—though a small part of my brain reminds me of being on my knees in the kitchen before his birthday threesome and how hot and domineering he was...okay, maybe I thought it was possible. But this party brought out more than I knew was in him, and I can't hate on that.

I've come down from my high and I'm going to fall asleep as soon as my head hits the pillow, but he needs to know something. I yawn loudly while asking, "Love, you may own me, but you know I own you too. Right?"

"Oh, Kitten. There was never any doubt." Jon relaxes and smiles at me while we turn off the lights and climb under the covers. His reply pleases me but I'm barely able to mumble a goodnight before I'm zonked out.

CHAPTER 6

I wake up a few hours later on my back. The rising sun illuminates the room and I can see everything. Jon is on his stomach next to me with his face smashed into his pillow and a hand stretched out, cupping my breast. He's gently tweaking my nipple in his sleep.

I'm about to punch him awake and tell him to cut it out when he teases it a little rougher and I gasp from the pleasure. My pussy is already wet, but my mind hasn't totally caught up. When I give him the side-eye, I can see his one visible eye open and half of a shit-eating grin. *Oh, so this is how he wants to play the game, is it?*

I roll on my side and snuggle close to him while he does the same. We kiss briefly before I push him on his back and climb on top to straddle him. He's nice and passive while he's groggy, though his cock is wide awake. I reach between us and guide him into my slick pussy, moaning as I press down fully. I pause for a moment, and then rock my hips gently to tease him—barely moving.

I didn't want to be awake yet, so I'm going to make him pay for waking me up this early. Maybe I'll take my time and edge him a bit, turn my switchy man into MY slut this time and make him beg for it. I'm flushed with a nice pleasant tingle radiating from my core as I grind against him for a moment and then stop before starting up again. When Jon groans, a flash of satisfaction hits my brain. I've got him right where I want him.

My satisfaction lasts all of ten seconds because Jon grips my waist and tosses me over so he's on top.

"Hey, what are you doing!" I try to use a stern domme voice, but it comes out more breathy and not at all commanding.

"What... this?" Jon is all casual as he plows into my pussy.

I moan and arch against him, finding it hard to remember what my objection was about.

"Kitten, you forgot something."

Hmmm, what's this? I don't respond and just push against him again.

Jon speeds up, fucking me so hard my head spins and he growls at me. "You forgot I can do whatever I want. I own you."

Ooooh... I splinter around him and realize I was wrong earlier. I could love my husband more.

Once we're done with our morning delight, we sneak downstairs, giggling like naughty children and beaming at everyone we pass. There are a lot more people awake than I expected, but it's possible no one slept. Jon and I snuggle on a couch in the sitting room, feeding each other berries and bites of a croissant while we wait for the Uber I ordered.

I let the house staff know a car was coming for us so there won't be any confusion when the driver is at the gate. I don't know if Nick is still here with Liz, and I don't want to talk with him until work on Monday, so getting our own ride home seemed best. Liz made it clear that my dalliance with Nick was over, and that's fine with me.

Jon yawns. "Kitten, let's nap when we get home, but later we need to talk about how all this is going to work."

I lean over, kiss him gently, and just smile. He doesn't know it yet, but that talk is going to include a discussion about how often I get to domme him. We also need to define limits, safe words, and work on open communication so we never get to the point we did last night where one of us explodes in anger—no matter how much it thrilled me. I can now easily see us being rougher in the bedroom as well. My slutty pussy gives a slight twinge. Okay, yes, and I need to order that damn leather crop.

I sink and relax into the couch, resting my head on the back and closing my eyes. Jon slips his hand in mine, and leans back to join me. I sigh with contentment while my limbs feel lighter and I have an overall feeling of weightlessness.

This party has changed my life and probably the course of our marriage. I reflect back to less than two weeks ago when I was sitting at the kitchen table with the invitation in my hand, debating whether to go. Thank God I listened to my inner voice that told me I'd have fun. The fates have handed me a gift, and I'm going to make sure I appreciate it.

The End

BIRTHDAY IN PARADISE

Hotwife Let Loose

Lacey Cross

Chapter 1

I'm startled awake by the loud ding of an incoming text message, and it takes me a moment to understand where the noise is coming from. Picking up my phone, I realize it's not even 9 a.m. I was out way too late last night, and I grouse about inconsiderate people as I check the message.

The text is from my best friend, Dina, and she demands—in all caps—that I call her as soon as I can so she can fill me in on the details of what happened with a hottie she met last night. Dina decided she's ready to settle down and wanted to test the waters at a club and begged me to go with her. I'm not sure the club is the right place to find lasting relationships, but I went to be supportive. I'm regretting it now.

Dina ditched me fairly early to spend the rest of the night with the sexy guy. I hung out, danced with various people, and drank too much. Since I didn't want to risk my car being towed by leaving it in the city parking lot overnight, I called my husband, Jon. He had a friend pick him up and take him to the club to drive me home. I haven't been out drinking like this since my younger, wilder days, so Jon teased me a little, good-naturedly, and reminded me neither of us are as young as we used to be.

I'm hungover but curious what Dina wants to tell me, so I stay snuggled in bed and call her. When she says hello, I'm still cranky because I wanted to sleep longer and grumble about her use of all caps in her text message. I yawn into her ear and ask, "So, was he fabulous in bed? Did he make you breakfast?"

Dina giggles. "No breakfast, and he wasn't fabulous in bed...he was fabulous in the car."

That wakes me slightly, and I demand she tells me everything. She explains they left the club together and ended up fucking in her car because they were too turned on to drive to her place. I almost laugh at the thought of trying to have sex in her tiny car, but my pussy gives a slight twinge at the idea of riding Jon in our compact sedan. *Maybe it would work?*

I ask Dina if she's going to see him again, and when she doesn't answer immediately, I talk to myself to fill the silence. "God, car sex sounds really fun. I wonder if Jon wants to go on a drive today."

I'm distracted and imagining several scenarios with Jon when the floodgates open up and Dina tells me everything that happened, and how Mr. Hot Stuff wants to dom her ass now, but she's not sure what she wants to do. She's conflicted, so I promise to send her some BDSM websites for research. I'm about to get out of bed to go to my computer with her still on the phone when Jon yells from the hall.

"Miranda, I'm running to the store."

I jolt straight up, wincing from the pain in my head from the abrupt position change. *Ugh, does he have to be so loud?* I swear at myself again for drinking last night.

Despite the hangover, my pussy likes the idea of taking Jon for a "ride," but I didn't realize he had anywhere to go today.

Since I don't want to miss out on my opportunity, I tell Dina in a rush, "Oooh, sorry, I need to run. Jon just told me he's heading to the store, and I want to see if he'll let me come along and play with his stick shift, if you know what I mean. I'll send you some stuff when I get home."

She replies, "Go have fun. I'll be here all day...."

I laugh at her. "Do an internet search while I'm gone. Enjoy falling down the rabbit hole!"

I scramble out of bed and stumble into the kitchen, blinking at the harsh lights, but my heart quickens when I see Jon at the counter. I was afraid he'd already left. Being hungover isn't conducive to sexy-time fun, but maybe the flow of endorphins will help my head. I'm also hoping he'll postpone the trip to at least let me shower. He's writing something down, and I walk up behind him and fondle his ass through his jeans.

"Whatcha doing, babe?"

He slips the paper in his jeans pocket without answering and turns to encircle my waist with his arms. His lack of response is curious, but before I can question him again, he kisses me so thoroughly, I forget my own name for a moment. My bare toes curl on the linoleum and I moan against him when he breaks off the kiss. What was it that I came in here for again?

"Kitten, do you need anything from the store? I won't be gone long."

Ooooh, yeah... the DRIVE.

I purr at him in my sexiest voice and rub the front of his jeans, pleased to find he's already hard. "Want some company? I've got an idea I want to try out that involves you inside of me."

I leer and wiggle my eyebrows at him, but he laughs and steps out of reach of my hand.

"You're adorable, but not today. Hold that thought for another time. I've got to run past Steve's place and drop off some tools he's borrowing to build his deck, and he's waiting for me."

Oh, bleh. I don't really want to see Steve today, so it's good Jon turned me down. I've felt a little awkward around Steve ever since Jon bet me I couldn't get him to fuck me and I proved him wrong. Supposedly I'm getting a tropical vacation for my 30th birthday out of that, but my birthday is still six months away so I haven't started planning the trip yet. I should probably get on that soon, and Jon better not have forgotten he's taking me. Not that it was a hardship to fuck Steve, but I rarely crush on my husband's friends that way. The memory of how I was bent over the side of the couch while Steve plowed into me is hot. But the problem is that I'd do it again in a heartbeat, and Jon isn't likely to go for that.

Things have changed between Jon and me. Over a year ago, Jon wanted me to be a hotwife, and I started sleeping with my bosses. It revitalized our marriage, but it also led us on a BDSM journey. Recently our relationship has shifted to a more formal dom-sub relationship after a wild BDSM party we attended. Before the party, he'd given me carte blanche to fuck my bosses, and I was basically telling him what I was doing before it happened, but not asking permission.

Now I'm not as free to fuck other people, and if I want to play with someone other than him, I have to ask for permission. I like it better this way. Something about the control turns me on like crazy, and thinking he might say "No" is so fucking hot. Jon's spontaneous side makes me unsure how he's going to react to an idea. When I tried to get him to go on this drive with me, he was just as likely to bend me over the kitchen table, fuck me, and tell me he doesn't need to be in a car if he wants me. I used to think his goofy, fun-loving side would make a bad dom, but I was definitely wrong. He's learned how to give me the control I crave and still be funny at the same time.

Jon interrupts my reminiscing. "So you don't want anything?"

"Oh, no. I'm good."

My pussy twinges and protests that she isn't good, but there's no point in complaining since Steve is waiting for the tools. I suppose I'll be a good friend and find some websites for Dina while he's gone.

Jon kisses my nose. "Okay, Kitten. I'll see you in a bit...and go brush your teeth."

He smirks at me, and I stick my tongue out at him. It wasn't MY idea for him to kiss me senseless before I brushed my teeth; that's all on him.

I set the thought aside, unconcerned. That's the benefit of being married for years. A little morning breath never killed anyone. When I get into the bathroom and see myself in the mirror, I laugh loudly. I look as if I've been ridden hard and put away wet after my night at the club. My long, wavy brown hair is a rat's nest, and I can tell it's going to take an extra-long time to work out the snarls.

After I shower and eat breakfast, Jon still isn't home. I send Dina a couple of decent websites that have good information and tell her to call me if she has questions. She's supposed to do research and see if she wants to let this new guy dom her, but knowing her, she's probably already at his house getting fucked on every flat surface available.

I yawn, and the fog from the hangover has me considering whether I want coffee or if I should take a nap instead. It seems like too much work to make coffee, and the bed calls to me. I snuggle in and quickly fall asleep.

CHAPTER 2

I'm woken up by...something. I'm disoriented and feel like I'm still dreaming. Sniffing the air, I realize it's the scent of chocolate. What the fuck? It's mouth-watering, and I climb out of bed, following my nose to the kitchen. A cooled, freshly baked chocolate birthday cake sits on the countertop. And there is no mistaking that's what it is, as it has numbered candles in the middle of it—a three and a zero.

I blink, confused. My 30th birthday is six months away. *What is going on?*

"Happy early birthday, Kitten," Jon says as he walks up behind me and kisses my neck.

"I...." I'm at a loss for words. The oven mitts on the counter tell me he baked this himself. "How...."

"You've been asleep for a long time," he says, turning me around so I'm facing him. "I kept thinking you'd wake up, but you must have needed the sleep."

This all still feels surreal, and I can't seem to shake the grogginess.

"Why are we celebrating my birthday early?"

Jon smiles coyly at me. "Because we're not waiting until your birthday to take the vacation I promised you. I booked us five nights at a resort in the Bahamas, and we leave in a week."

WHAT? I stare at him with wide eyes. I must still be dreaming.

"I arranged time off for you at work. Your bosses all know. It's all booked and planned, so what do you say? Want to go to a resort next week?"

I almost laugh that he's asking me after he's booked the trip, but this is seriously one of the most romantic things he's done in our entire marriage. I really thought he had forgotten about the bet and about taking me on vacation.

"Of course I want to go. Thank you," I say, beaming up at him. "Thank you so fucking much!" I throw my arms around him, hugging him tightly. He kisses my cheek and squeezes me.

"I love you, Miranda," he says softly.

"I love you, too," I respond, kissing him enthusiastically, twining my tongue with his until my head is fuzzy with lust.

He's always been good at little gestures, letting me know how much he loves me, but he's never done anything this big.

"We need to light the candles," he tells me as I pull away. He opens a kitchen drawer to get a matchbox. Watching his fingers as he takes out a match and strikes it is sexy. It's probably a weird thing to find arousing, but almost everything he does is tantalizing. A splash of wetness hits my panties, and I plan to rub my pussy against the hardness in his jeans the first chance I get. My neediness consumes me, and I need his cock so bad, I almost can't think straight.

He lights both candles before waving out the match.

"Make a wish," he says, nodding towards the cake.

"Aren't you gonna sing for me?" I tease as I approach the cake on the counter. He rolls his eyes, but I can tell he's amused.

"Make a wish and blow them out," he orders, and the hint of steel in his voice perks my pussy up. Oh yeah, she wants him to get all demanding.

I give him a cheeky "Yes, Sir" and close my eyes. I wish for a long, happy marriage. It's incredibly corny, I know, but it can't hurt to wish for something like that.

I open my eyes and blow right as the candles start melting onto the cake. Now comes the most important part: tasting it.

"Let's have some cake. Um, I don't know how it tastes," he says, and I can tell that he's nervous. "I've never made a cake with this many layers before."

"I'm sure it will be good." I try to soothe him as he gets out a knife to cut it.

I can tell that since he made the cake, he wants to serve it, so I allow him to cut it and place it on little plates. As I watch, I salivate, becoming impatient. I love chocolate cake to the point where we had to have two wedding cakes: one that was traditional, and one that was pure, chocolatey decadence.

When he finally hands it to me, I quickly fork some of it into my mouth. Its several layers of chocolate icing are rich and smooth. I moan out loud; it's better than any cake I've tasted recently. Or maybe it's because I know he made it. Whatever the reason, it's absolute heavenly, euphoric, perfection.

"This is fucking perfect," I moan around the fork as I take another bite.

"Is it really that good, or are you faking it?" he asks teasingly, but I can tell that he's genuinely worried about what I think.

I wink at him. "When have I ever faked anything with you?"

He gives me a dirty smirk. "We aren't talking about food anymore, are we?"

"You tell me," I say, a mischievous lilt in my voice. I put some more cake in my mouth, but before I swallow it, he surprises me by kissing me. His tongue invades my mouth, tasting the chocolate and practically fucking my mouth. He reaches one hand down to slide under my yoga pants and panties, and goes straight for my clit. I'm already soaking wet, and his finger makes tiny circles around the sensitive bundle of nerves, and I moan.

"You were right about the cake," he tells me, "but when did you get wet for me?"

"When you were using the matches." I pant, "Oh, fuck," as he plunges two fingers inside me.

"Well Kitten, what do you want today?" he asks, as he nibbles on my neck.

"W-What do you mean?" I groan, my head clouded with arousal.

"Tell me what you want me to do to you," he says. "Anything at all. And I'll do it."

All the BDSM research this morning for Dina turned me on, and then the cake and surprise trip made me want him even more. Thinking about how this trip came to be and how Steve was pounding into me from behind, I blurt out, "I want you to bend me over the couch and fuck me hard."

He grabs my hand and hauls me to the living room. I barely have time to gasp as he bends me over the armrest on the couch and rips my yoga pants and panties down to my knees. He doesn't remove them fully, and I hear the zipper of his jeans a moment before he slams his cock straight to my core.

"Oooooh, fuck!" I cry out as intense pleasure floods through me. I know I asked for this, but I'm not sure I expected him to do it.

Jon hammers away behind me while the room spins, and I gasp and moan with every stroke. He's not always rough, but the times he is, my entire body thrills at the change in him. My normally sweet husband turns savage, and if it includes reclaiming me after I fuck another guy, even better. I joke and call it "beast mode," and it's not far off from the truth. Sometimes he goes primal and has to have me, and it's glorious.

He groans as he fucks me. "Is this what you want, Miranda?"

"Yes. God, yes, fuck me harder!"

Even though I can't get great leverage, my feet are on the floor, so I'm able to push back against him, meeting his every thrust. Since my pussy has been at a low simmer since this morning, I'm spiraling towards my orgasm faster than expected. I'm chanting, "Oh, my god," and a sharp smack on my ass makes me squeal in delight.

"Miranda, you better come before I do," he warns in a harsh tone.

My brain blips out at the thought of not coming. I'd be a desperate wet puddle, and the fear of him stopping and not letting me come is what tips me over the edge.

I cry out a long "Ohhhh my god" as an enormous wave of ecstasy smashes into me. I buck against him as he continues to pound into me, and the zings of pleasure reach my fingertips and toes.

He comes with a roar, and I can feel his hot cum painting my cave walls. We recently decided to start a family, so knowing anytime we have sex, I could get pregnant, makes everything more erotic. I used to love the feel of cum dripping out of me, but now I like to lie there, messy, while it stays inside me as long as possible.

Jon gives my ass one final smack before pulling out, and I whimper at the sting. He moves to sit on the couch in front of me and pulls me into his lap. I try to protest, wanting to tell him to let me be so none of his cum slides out, but the desire to cuddle with him is too strong to complain.

Giving a contented sigh, I lean against him and put my head on his shoulder. He picks up one of my hands and twines his fingers with mine, and I stare down at our joined fingers. He gets more sun than I do, so he has a nice golden tone, while I'm fairly pale. I wonder if I have time to get in for a fake tan before our trip.

I whisper softly to him, "Thank you for the trip, Jon."

He kisses my forehead, "You're welcome, Kitten."

Later that night, Jon forwards me an email with all the details of our travel plans. We're going to a resort in the Bahamas called Temptation in Paradise.

I've never been to the Bahamas, but as long as they have a beach and good food, what more could I ask for? Jon is in the garage doing...whatever he does in there, while I get on the computer to do research for the trip. I find the resort's website, and I'm immediately giddy at the beautiful pictures. Oh yeah, this place has my beach and multiple dining options. I'm going to relax all week, read a few books, and fuck Jon's brains out whenever I get the urge.

I'm scanning the website, glad that it's an adult-only resort—not because I don't enjoy kids, but I have always wanted to go to one, and since we're trying to get pregnant, now might be the only time to try. Suddenly, I realize the timing of this trip is perfect. My new cycle just started, so there is no way I'm pregnant at the moment. I can party all I want without consequences. Hell, yeah! Now I'm super glad we didn't wait for my 30th birthday. I don't even know if Jon considered all of this, but the trip is going to be perfect.

I'm curious if I can find any reviews about the resort on the internet that aren't on the official website. I never trust reviews that a company boasts about on their main page. It's not as if they're going to highlight the negative reviews. A quick search finds up a surprising amount of chatter about the resort...on poly websites.

My eyes widen as I read through comments about hookups and group sex. I go back to the tab on my browser for the official website again and look at it more closely. It's a lifestyle resort where I can indulge in my most secret, hedonistic desires. Uh...did Jon know he's taking me to a sex resort? I don't even know if that's what it would be called, but it seems like people go with the intent to hook up.

I get out of my chair and hunt Jon down. He's in the garage digging through a storage box and pulling out old hats of his and trying them on. He has a fedora set aside, and I hold in a laugh. If he thinks he's taking a fedora to a sex resort and planning to wear it, he's going to find his hat "falling off" into the pool the first time he walks past it.

My stomach muscles quiver with nervous energy, and I lean against the doorway of the garage, pretending to be casual. "Hey, hun?"

He looks up from his box with a bright orange sun visor in his hand. "Oh, hi."

"Jon, did you know you were taking me to a sex resort?"

He squints his eyes at me, confused. "What's a sex resort?"

My husband is crazy about research. Did he only see the pretty pictures and decide that was good enough for him? I don't answer him and ask a different question. "Why did you choose this resort?"

He grins at me and pops the fedora on his head. "Oh, Chuck at work took his wife there a couple of months ago, and he told me it was a trip of a lifetime."

"Did he tell you what they did at the resort?"

Jon takes switches off the fedora and puts the ghastly orange visor on. "No, but I'm sure it was resorty things."

The term "resorty things," along with the orange visor, has the corners of my mouth turning up, and I'm about ready to burst into laughter. Clearly good ol' Chuck left out a few key details.

I'm uncertain whether I want to tell him about the resort, so I change the topic. "I'm hungry and going to start dinner. Spaghetti sounds good to me tonight."

Something in the box distracts him, and he's reaching into it when I turn to go to the kitchen. I'm a few feet from the doorway when he asks loudly, "Hey, what's a sex resort?"

I giggle, but don't stop to answer.

Chapter 3

The week flies by, and before I know it, we're standing in the resort's lobby. I'm pleased that it's as gorgeous in real life as it was in the website's pictures. The marble floors gleam and the couches in the reception area look plush and comfortable. Jon checks us in while I peer around, hoping to see some sexy shenanigans. I still don't trust that this place really is a sex resort, and until I see it with my own eyes, there's no way in hell I'll believe that people come here for casual encounters.

To my chagrin, after last weekend Jon wouldn't drop his questions about what I was talking about when I asked if he knew it was a sex resort, so I finally broke down and told him what type of vacation he'd booked. He was shocked and delighted...too much so, but it led to a productive talk about expectations on the trip. He assured me that being on vacation will change nothing and he has no intention of fucking anyone else.

I was relieved to hear he didn't want to play but also knew I was going to have to ask him if I'm allowed to fuck someone, and he might say no. Half the fun of asking is thinking he might tell me no, and I love it when he gets all possessive and wants me just to himself. Before we got to the resort, I told myself that I wasn't interested in screwing around, but as soon as we step into the lobby, my body zings alive and I rub my thighs together in anticipation. Yeah, my slutty pussy is all on board for some vacation fun.

When a handsome surfer type of guy walks past in only swim shorts and sandals, my eyes follow him across the lobby and I lick my lips. I'm glad I didn't tell Jon I didn't want to fuck anyone else in a show of solidarity since I'm not sure what I want anymore. I'm more intrigued at the thought of having a stranger's cock pounding my pussy with every passing moment.

Jon gets my attention. "You ready, Miranda?"

My damp panties say I'm more than ready, but I know he isn't talking about sex. I grip the handle of my suitcase. "Yeah, let's go."

I follow Jon out of the lobby into the sunshine, and the salty warm breeze washes over us as we head towards our cabana. Jon leads me down a path, and I admire the vivid colors of the tropical plants we pass. The air holds a floral hint, and that mixed with the scent of the ocean relaxes me. I've been so keyed up the last week, planning and rushing around to get everything done before the trip, I expected it to take more than a few minutes at the resort to drain the tension. Now all I want to do is change into one of the five new bikinis I bought and find the nearest pool.

The cabana they put us in is adorable. Each cabana is a separate building painted in bright colors, and ours is a pretty pastel blue. The area ours is located borders the "clothing optional" side of the resort, and I wonder if that means I'll be able to gaze out the window and see naked people all day long. This thought doesn't sound horrible. We can move a table by the window and I can entice Jon to bend me over it while we fuck and enjoy the view.

The inside is spacious, with a king-sized bed dominating the center of the room. Tucked into a corner is a couch and a couple of plush chairs, and an archway leads to a tiny nook with a dining table and four chairs. There is a big window by the table, but it only overlooks some tall trees and shrubs. Each cabana has a privacy screen of trees around it, which is a nice touch but it doesn't let me people-watch easily.

I explore the nook while Jon scopes out the bathroom and the other living spaces. I'm delighted to find a mini fridge against the wall with cold bottles of water, and a counter above it with a coffee maker and a selection of coffee. *Fuck yeah, no cranky Miranda in the morning.*

Jon calls from the other room. "Hey, Miranda, come look at this."

I peek my head out from the nook, and he's standing in front of opened double doors leading out to a deck overlooking the ocean. When Jon told me he booked us a room with an ocean view, I didn't think much of it since I figured I'd see a lot of the ocean on the trip, but being here in person is indescribable compared to pictures on a website. The sparkling, iridescent, turquoise water is going to be the perfect backdrop for my morning coffee. I'll bring my cup out here and soak in the glory.

Jon didn't talk about finances for the trip, and I purposely didn't check our bank account or credit card this week because I didn't want to see the charges. I know we can afford it, but there's a big difference between affording it and wanting to pay for it. Normally I wouldn't spend the extra for a pretty view in a room I wouldn't be in that often, at least not during the day, but the gorgeous ocean makes me glad he did.

I turn and give him a big smack on the lips. "Thank you for this!"

He laughs and leans in for a deeper kiss than I intended. Lust zings through my core as his firm lips coax my mouth open. His tongue teases mine, and my pussy heats up even more. Right when I'm considering maneuvering us towards the bed, he breaks off the kiss.

"Let's go get some food. I'm hungry."

I pout at him for a moment, but the rumble in my tummy from the mention of food makes me decide it's a good idea. I tell him I want to change first, and I put on my new black string bikini and a red cotton summer dress. Jon changes into swimming trunks and a clean t-shirt, and assuming he's interested in trying out the pool or ocean, I grab a small beach bag to hold sunscreen, a towel, and a map of the resort. Only one towel will fit, so if we go to the ocean he's going to have to share with me.

When we step out of our cabana Jon whispers, wickedly, "Since we're so close to the clothing optional side, do you want to check it out first?"

My pussy gives a nice pulse of pleasure at the thought while my stomach growls and protests at the delay. It's like the physical version of a devil and an angel.

The devil wins. "Sure, but only for a minute. I'm hungry."

We walk down the path and out to the sandy beach. The beach and sparkling ocean is magnificent, and a naked couple strolls past us with a cheerful hello. The woman is a busty redhead, and the man is easily in his 50s. He's got that hot dad thing going on that I so dearly love. I turn my head slightly so I can discreetly eyeball them as they pass, and I notice Jon doing the same. I'm not surprised since the woman is redheaded. Oooh, I bet after seeing a bunch of naked people today I'm going to get fucked good tonight.

My eyes drift around the room, and I notice a cute guy sitting at a table diagonally from us. He's reading a paperback book while he eats. One hand holds the book, and whenever he flips a page, his fingers hold my attention. I imagine them between my legs, caressing my clit. My pussy throbs and I shift in my chair, pressing down against the seat in the hopes it will ease the ache.

The guy catches me watching him, and he flashes me a smile. A tingle runs down my spine, and I can feel myself flush. I want to squirm more in my seat but don't want to alert Jon to the fact I'm getting hot and bothered by another guest. *Wait, or maybe I do…would it unleash the beast?*

Jon is so engrossed with the map it would take a pretty big disturbance for him to notice what I was doing. I use the freedom to study the guy reading. He's dark haired and is easily a 10 in my book. I can see muscles underneath his T-shirt, which means he's very well defined… and those arms…*mmmm, those arms.* If I could fuck that guy, I would in a heartbeat.

More wetness leaks from my pussy, and I realize it's stupid to deny myself at a resort whose purpose is exploring your desires. I should probably get at least a small sample of the experience, otherwise I might regret it my entire life, and I don't want to waste the opportunity.

Yep, I'm going to go for it if the right opportunity comes along. Having settled that, I debate whether to tell Jon my decision now or wait and see if I meet a guest I want to fuck. My mind wanders back to the sexy book-reading guy, but I need a more organic meeting with someone. I'm not going to walk over to his table, sit down, and be all, "do me." I decide to let fate work its magic before I talk to Jon. If the sex gods want me to fuck someone on this trip, they will put someone in my path.

Jon lays the map on the table with a sigh. "There are too many things to do here. I can't decide."

I giggle at him. "Well, I want to swim after lunch."

He murmurs, "That's fine with me," and we eat our lunch in companionable silence.

We dawdle over lunch, and I notice his eyes are following every woman who wanders by. I almost want to joke with him and snap my fingers in front of his face and tell him to focus on me, but decide to let him have his fun. He's only whetting his appetite for me later.

After lunch, we mutually debate on which pool we want to try out. The resort has one that is clothing optional and one that requires bathing suits. We decide to not do the clothing-optional pool since we're not ready for that. The water is the perfect temperature, and we swim together for a while, laughing and chasing each other around in the water. He wants to go for a walk around the resort, so we dry off and take a stroll.

The scenery is beautiful, and I wish I could identify the vibrant flowers, but since I can't grow them at home it probably doesn't matter. I'm surprised to hear birds chirping and had assumed they would stay away from a resort, but they add a nice chorus to the relaxing ambiance. With Jon's warm hand in mine, I can't imagine any place I'd rather be than here on vacation with him.

Halfway through our walk, I realize I'm exhausted from traveling and swimming. The rest of the evening is a blur. We visit a hibachi grill for dinner, but towards the end of the meal, the combination of an alcoholic beverage and tasty food in my belly makes me start to nod off. Jon has to practically carry me back to the cabana, and as he tucks me into bed, I briefly mourn the lack of first-night vacation sex, but I'm fast asleep within minutes.

CHAPTER 4

I'm woken up in the morning by a gentle tweak of my nipples and a warm mouth engulfing one. I keep my eyes closed, pretending I'm still asleep.

Arching my back and moaning, I purposely say the wrong name. "Oooh, Matthew, that feels so good."

A gentle slap on my breast makes me gasp, and my eyes fly open. "Hey!" I protest, all pretense of sleep gone.

Jon grins at me. "I had to wake you from your dream of another man."

I blink innocently. "Did you? Matthew was just about to show me how thick his cock was and promised to fuck me from behind."

My comment gets the desired effect. I quickly find myself on all fours, looking through the open balcony doors while Jon fucks me thoroughly, making me forget my fictional Matthew. Once we both come, we snuggle together, enjoying the warm morning breeze wafting through the room. Morning sex is better than whatever would have happened last night with how tired I was, and now we've started our day on a positive note.

I'm staring dreamily outside when I start to wonder. "Jon, have you been awake, or did we sleep with the doors open?"

He kisses my shoulder. "I've been awake and was going to make you coffee to wake you up, but your nipple called to me like a siren."

I snort. *Yeah I bet it did.* He was never one to hold back when he wanted sex, but I appreciate that quality and I also like how he doesn't take offense if I'm tired and say no. He and I have a suitable arrangement where he takes care of himself with little fuss if I'm not in the mood. But we've had a healthy sex life ever since I became a hotwife, so lack of sex hasn't been a problem in over a year.

The morning workout has me limber and feeling sexy. "Hey Jon, let's try out the nude beach today."

"You sure, Kitten?"

A small hint of anxiety in my stomach tells me I'm not totally sure, but I put on a brave face. "Yep, let's do it."

Before hitting the beach, we get breakfast at a place called the Quickie Café, just muffins and coffee. The food at the resort is fabulous, but I'm too impatient to spend much time enjoying it. The beach is fairly empty when we get there, and we both strip as soon as we enter the clothing-optional area. I brought a beach bag to hold our belongings, and we stash it close to the path next to a pile of other people's bags. We stroll along the coast, hand in hand, and the sense of freedom from wearing no clothing is exhilarating. This is the first time I've gone nude in public, and knowing I'm on display for everyone has my pussy buzzing.

We pass a few couples and everyone says hello, but it's nice and casual, with no uncomfortable vibes. I notice a couple of men and women checking me out, but no one is overtly obnoxious about it. I'm doing the same to them, so I can't blame anyone for taking a peek at my exposed body. Since this is a nudist beach, I almost expected no one to care, but since it's part of a poly resort, I think the atmosphere is different. People are interested in having sex, so we're all enjoying the eye candy.

Far ahead, strolling towards us, I spot the hot guy from lunch yesterday and my skin immediately tingles. The surprise of running into him again makes me pause. When Jon keeps walking, the yank of his hand has me almost tripping over my own feet.

Jon helps steady me. "Kitten, you okay?"

He skims my body with a concerned eye, which quickly turns speculative. I'm sure he can tell I'm practically vibrating.

"What's got you so hot?" he jokes, and I dip my head toward the approaching man.

Jon murmurs, "Oh, really?" and studies the guy more closely.

"Kitten, look at me."

I glance up into Jon's eyes.

"If you want to play with the guy, you have my permission."

Love for my husband washes over me, despite me knowing that this isn't altruistic of him. He gets off on it as much as I do, but I still appreciate that he enjoys this lifestyle.

Jon rubs my ass while leaning close to my ear and whispers, "I'm going to go relax in a lounge chair while you work your magic."

I open my mouth to protest, but he's gone so fast that I'm left standing like an idiot with a gaping maw. The sexy guy is almost upon me and close enough that if I wanted to, I could check out his package. I struggle to keep my eyes from drifting downwards. *How in the hell am I going to get him to stop and talk to me?*

Suddenly, it's as if the last year didn't happen and I'm the awkward administrative assistant at work, trying to get my boss to fuck me. I've grown more confident in my sexuality in the last year, but this situation is so new I'm back to my old self and tongue tied.

The hot guy doesn't pause but grins, and I can tell he recognizes me. He says a brief hello, and as he walks past me, I panic. *Fuck, I can't let him leave.*

"Hey," I call out.

When he turns around to look at me, all thought drains from my head. *Shit, what was I going to say?*

We stand there for a few moments until he finally speaks again. "Did you need something?"

I blurt out the only thing I can think of in a rush of words. "Did you enjoy your book?"

I can tell he wasn't expecting the question, and he pauses for two heart-beats and smiles at me again. "It was good, kept me entertained."

Trying to keep my eyes on his face so he doesn't see me taking a gander at his cock, I shuffle my feet and realize I am going to have to say goodbye and try again with another guy I find attractive. I can't do sexy on a nude beach at the drop of a hat.

He reaches out his hand. "I'm Cooper."

Ooooh, maybe he's going to save me. I relax a little and shake his hand. "I'm Miranda."

He's boyishly charming, and my pussy hums her approval.

He scans around, as if looking for someone. "The guy you were with, he's your husband, I take it?"

I wonder for a second why he assumes we're married and that Jon's not a boyfriend, and then realize that although I'm naked, I still have a wedding ring on.

"Yes, that's my husband, Jon."

Cooper exudes confidence, but not in a cocky way. I can tell he converses easily with people, and that he knows he's fit and attractive. Probably the latter helps with the former.

"Are you and your husband both enjoying the...amenities of the resort?"

The way he pauses before 'amenities' makes me think he's not talking about the sandy beaches.

I try to act casual. "Oh, we're interested in sampling all that the resort has to offer."

My reply obviously pleases him. He arches an eyebrow at me. "Anything I can help you explore?"

Oooh, yeah, there is…like how your cock would feel thrusting into my pussy, but I can't say that.

Suddenly, I know exactly what to suggest. "That depends, Cooper. Does your room have any alcohol? I could use a drink tonight, but I'd like a more private setting than the bar."

He picks up my hand and kisses the back of it, and his breath tickles. "Miranda, for you, I'll make sure I have something delicious."

I giggle at how stupid we probably sound, but my pussy doesn't care. She's raring to go and unhappy that I don't get his cock right now.

"Does 8 work for you?" I ask in my best sultry tone.

"That sounds perfect to me."

Surprising myself, I step towards him and slide my hand around his neck, applying slight pressure as I tip my face up. He takes the hint and brushes his lips over mine. The brief contact thrills me, and I want to rub against him. But we're in public, so there's no way I'm doing that. Plus, Jon has only ever seen me touching someone else a couple of times, and we didn't discuss me doing anything in front of him. I'd rather wait until I'm alone with Cooper tonight.

Cooper tells me his cabana number and explains the general area of the resort while I repeat his number in my head so I don't forget it. Now that he's agreed to drinks—and most likely other stuff—tonight, I'm excited to get back to Jon and see if this gets me some afternoon delight. I wouldn't mind coming a second time now and then again later with Cooper. Three orgasms in one day while on vacation isn't greedy.

I caress Cooper's cheek and purr at him. "I'll see you tonight."

His eyes light up, and he replies with, "I'm looking forward to it."

I walk away, heading towards Jon, and give my hips an exaggerated swing in case Cooper's still watching.

As I get closer to Jon, I can tell he's curious how it went, so I move my hand in front of my stomach and flash him a thumbs up sign so Cooper can't see. His wide grin tells me he's totally fine with the plan.

CHAPTER 5

Jon and I spend part of the afternoon at the clothing-required pool and the other part exploring an adult toy shop and the bar off the main lobby called Lustful Libations. We eat at the buffet for dinner, but I only have soup and buttered rolls because I don't want to get sick before meeting up with Cooper. I'm full of nervous energy, so I have a margarita with dinner. Jon laughs at my choice and says we could get margaritas at home, but I want to take the edge off and stop overthinking what's going to happen with Cooper.

By the time we get back to our cabana and I'm changing into a dark blue cotton sundress, I'm nicely buzzed and giggly. Jon lies on the bed, watching me get dressed, and strokes himself.

I can't help but razz him. "If you keep doing that, you won't be any good to me when I get back tonight."

Grinning, he says, "Oh, I'll be ready again, don't worry," ending his assertion with a wink.

I laugh at how stupid and adorable he is, but I know he'll be all over me as soon as I walk in the door. I'm about to slip on a pair of sexy black panties when Jon stops me.

"Kitten, no panties tonight."

I flush at his command, say, "Yes, Sir," and toss the panties at him. I'm disappointed when he catches them midair and they don't hit him in the face.

Before I leave, I bend over the bed to give Jon a deep kiss, and he reaches up my dress to fondle my already-wet pussy. *Shit, that's hot.* I don't think he's ever warmed me up before I left on a date. I spread my legs and sway against his hand.

He pats my pussy and talks in the general direction of my crotch. "You be good tonight, and I'll take care of you later."

I'm uncertain if he was talking to me or my slutty pussy, but it makes me giggle. I blow him a kiss on my way out the door.

When I knock on the door of Cooper's cabana, he opens it quickly and a zing of pleasure runs through me. He must have been waiting by the door.

He holds it open for me. "Come in, Miranda."

He's barefoot and wearing gray basketball shorts and no shirt. His defined chest muscles make me itch to touch him, and my pussy clenches in excitement. *God, I need him inside me.*

He closes the door behind me and walks past me a few steps but pauses. I've been looking forward to fucking Cooper all day, but I realize I never considered how it would happen. Jon kept my attention on himself today, and I didn't have time to stew about tonight. I'm guessing it was intentional on his part, and I'm glad he distracted me.

I clasp my hands in front of myself and twist them. Cooper and I speak at the same time. He asks, "Do you want some wine?" right when I blurt out, "I'm not wearing any panties."

Oh fuck, did I just say that? I mentally curse the margarita at dinner for giving me a loose tongue, and I can tell a blush is staining my cheeks.

Cooper smiles at me. "That's good info. Do you want some wine first?"

Knowing I shouldn't drink more, I shake my head and softly reply, "No thanks."

He takes a step closer to me, picks up both my hands and pries them apart gently so he can tug me towards him. I melt against his bare chest and tip my head up so he can kiss me. He bends down and brushes his mouth against mine before kissing me deeply and applying pressure to coax my lips open. I glide my hands over every part of his exposed chest. He's warm and solid and I resist the urge to kneel and remove his cock from his shorts and taste him.

I'm not sure how we went from zero to sixty so fast, but my pussy hums her approval. I kick off my sandals and press against him, grinding my lower half against his growing hardness.

He moves both of his hands down my sides and up under my short sundress to grip my bare ass, causing a nice zing of pleasure. He plunders my mouth, and I murmur, "Thank you for inviting me over," when he pauses for air.

"I'm glad your husband is okay with you being here."

His words make me think of Jon, and a wave of love for my husband washes over me. I also appreciate how Cooper is talking freely about me being married and not trying to pretend we're cheating.

He kisses the column of my neck, and I moan and try to rub against him harder. I ache with how much I want him, and he's basically a stranger. I haven't had sex with someone the same day I met them since…I try to think back, but my head is spinning. I think it was close to a year ago with my boss's college friend Alec. Everyone else I've fucked, I at least got to know them a little better before jumping into bed with them.

"I'm glad you invited yourself over." He kisses along the top of my sundress and continues. "I wasn't sure you'd want to do this, or—."

I put a finger to his mouth, pressing firmly with to get him to stop what he was about to say. I whisper, "Cooper. I want to fuck you."

He relaxes and chuckles. "Good, because I haven't been able to stop thinking about you and imagining how that first slow thrust inside your pussy is going to feel."

Oooh, I like the sound of that. I don't have time to respond, because he suddenly nudges me backwards until I'm against the closed door. I arch my spine, trying to get closer to him while he kisses me hungrily, wishing he was sliding inside me right now. Slipping my arms around his neck, I squeak out in surprise when he clutches my ass with both hands and boosts me up. I wrap my legs around him, and he uses the door as leverage to keep me in place while he shoves the hem of my dress up and presses his hardness straight against my naked pussy. The ridge of his cock grinding against me through the fabric of his shorts sends ripples of intense pleasure straight to my clit and makes me groan.

He's breathing heavily when he says, "You're so fucking sexy."

All I can do is moan as he kisses my neck more and gropes my ass. It's crazy how he seems to know exactly how I like to be dominated.

"Please...fuck me," I sigh, desperate and needy for more.

Without taking his lips off of my neck, he carries me over to the bed and drops me on it.

My body tingles with desire, and I watch him remove his shorts. I don't wait for him to tell me to strip before I lift my ass off the fabric of my dress so I can yank it off over my head.

I can tell he's as eager as I am, and I gaze lustfully at his fit muscles for a few seconds before stating, "Fuck me, don't make me wait."

"Gladly," he grins as he catches my waist and hauls me towards him. He nudges my knees apart and climbs on the mattress between them. I love the roughness as he forces me to do what he wants. Pressing his cock against my waiting pussy, he rubs the head against me, spreading my slick lips with it, teasing me. I moan, trying to buck my hips to get him to push in.

I can't believe I walked into his cabana less than 10 minutes ago and he's already about to fuck me. I'm loving how slutty this is, but I'm confused when he covers his body with mine without shoving his cock inside of me. He reaches an arm past me, opens the drawer of the nightstand, and gets out a condom.

Ooooh, fuck. I almost forgot a condom, and I'm not sure if I'm happy or sad that he remembered. I don't want to get pregnant unless it's Jon's baby, but a part of me thrills at the thought of walking to my cabana with Cooper's cum dripping down my inner thigh.

He quickly puts the condom on and kisses me while he probes the tip against my entrance again but doesn't press in. Grinning, he says, "You're so wet and ready. You want my cock, don't you?"

I moan out desperately, "Yes, give it to me," and wiggle against him, trying to tempt him to plunge into me.

He chuckles as he guides his cock with his hand so it's at the perfect angle, pressing slowly inside.

"Fuuuuuck," I groan, and he pants, "God, you're so tight and wet." My brain goes fuzzy, and I'm overwhelmed by the delicious stretch of my cave walls around him.

He fucks me leisurely, clearly enjoying every second as my pussy grips his cock. Spikes of pleasure shoot from my core, and I want him to fuck me senseless, but he's taking his time, as if he's trying to make this last as long as possible.

His shaft massages a pleasure point along my cave wall with every thrust, and tendrils of bliss ripple over me. Even though he continues to plow into me slowly and I'm craving roughness, I can already sense my first orgasm building deep inside me.

"Ooooh, god. Right like that," I cry out, and I'm rewarded with him speeding up until he's pounding against me.

I'm chanting, "Yes," and spiraling higher with each whack against my pussy.

When he pants out, "Come for me," it's so close to how Jon sounds when he commands me that my orgasm hits, making my entire body shake. He slows down his fucking as waves of pleasure wash over me.

He leans down for a kiss, pushing his cock deep inside me, and whispers, "Holy fuck, you're amazing. Do you think you have another one in you?"

When he says that, I realize he didn't come. My brain is short circuited from my orgasm, and I can only nod and say, "Please?"

He smiles. "I want to fuck you harder. Is that okay?"

Oh hell yeah it is. I nod again, "Do it."

He slips his cock out of me, backs off the bed and grasps my hips, dragging me all the way to the edge this time. When he takes hold of my ankles and brings them up by his head, my pussy buzzes in delight.

He doesn't wait and slams his cock straight to my core, pounding me hard and fast. I moan loudly, enjoying every thrust.

"Do you like this?"

I cry out, "Yes," as he hammers into my pussy.

I realize my hands are on my tits, playing with my nipples, and I don't know how long they've been there, but each tweak shoots a bolt of ecstasy straight to my pussy.

I hear myself chanting, "Please make me come." I'm close to tipping over the edge again as he bangs into me.

When he gives a few sharp whacks, I can't handle it, and I shake violently when the second orgasm hits. My pussy pulsates around his cock, and I groan and buck wildly against him. He comes with a roar, and despite him wearing a condom, I imagine I can feel his cum spurting inside me. The slutty knowledge that I would have fucked him without a condom just so I could have his cum dripping out of me spirals me higher, and I shudder and quake around him.

My brain is a pile of mush when he removes his cock from my sopping wet hole and lowers my feet to the ground. I'm not sure I've ever been so thoroughly fucked so soon after meeting someone. He hauls me up onto the bed, removes the condom, and puts it in a trashcan by the nightstand before he snuggles against me. It's odd to be lying with him when I barely know him, and yet comforting at the same time.

I'm not sure how long I've been here, but thinking of Jon waiting for me in the cabana makes me eager to get back to him and tell him how hot it was to walk in the door and be immediately taken. I don't want to seem rude to Cooper though, so I don't say I have to go. He's a fabulous lover, and he deserves some post-coital snuggles after making me come twice. He plays with my hand and strokes each finger between his as we relax.

He leans in and kisses me softly before saying, "I need some water. Do you want any?"

I murmur, "No thanks," and he gets up, picks up his shorts, and heads to what I assume is the mini fridge in the nook of his cabana.

As soon as he's out of my line of sight, I realize I am thirsty, so I haul myself off the bed, pluck my sundress from the floor, and slip it over my head before following him. He's leaning against the counter, sipping a bottle of water, and when he sees me, he opens the fridge and hands me one.

He put his shorts back on, and I squint at a clock on the wall, amazed that it's only been an hour. Hot damn...he got me in the door, fucked me thoroughly, and gave me two orgasms during that time. I take a few sips of my water, fidgeting and uncertain how to leave. I don't want to be the 'fuck and run' type.

He must have been able to tell what I was thinking because he casually says, "I don't mind if you want to get back to your husband."

I scrutinize him to gauge whether he's sincere, and his face is open and friendly, so I assume he is. "You sure? I feel like I used you."

That makes him grin. "I don't mind being used like that." His eyes sparkle when he adds, "I'm here for several weeks. You can use me like that any day."

My pussy perks up at the thought of fucking him again. Shit, would Jon let me? I'm noncommittal and tease, "I'll take that under advisement."

I slip my sandals back on and he walks me to the door and opens it for me. "Miranda, let me take you home."

His offer is kind, but I want to be alone with my thoughts. "No, that's okay. Thank you, though."

"You sure? It's no trouble."

Kissing him deeply one last time, I flick my tongue against his before breaking it off. "I'm good. Enjoy the rest of your night."

He says, "You too," and stands in the doorway, watching me until I turn a corner and the privacy trees obscure his view.

I'm relaxed and want to skip back to my cabana. What a fabulous night so far. My pussy hums in pleasure, and the closer I get to Jon, the needier she becomes. Oh yeah, she's not dumb. She knows what's waiting for her.

CHAPTER 6

When I walk in the door, Jon is on the bed with his shorts down far enough to free his cock. He's stroking himself and glances up, startled.

"You're done already?"

I close the door, kick off my sandals with a "Yep" and rip my sundress off over my head.

Jon's eyes narrow with a predatory gleam. "Well, this is a delightful surprise."

When he climbs off the bed and stalks toward me, I shiver and take a few steps backward, darting my eyes around the room to see if there is somewhere to run.

Jon's voice deepens, "Going somewhere?" and my pussy clenches in glee. *Oh fuck yeah, it's beast mode.*

I enjoy playing cat and mouse with him when he's like this, so I make a quick dash out the double doors onto the deck. He grabs me from behind before I'm two feet out the door and grinds his erection against my ass. He never put his cock back into his shorts, and he keeps one hand around my waist while he adjusts his shaft so he's rubbing against my pussy but not pushing in.

He's half amused, yet still sounds harsh. "What did you think was going to happen out here, Kitten?"

I figured he was going to carry me back into the bedroom caveman style and fuck me silly, but I don't say that and try to sound sweet and innocent. "Um, we were going to sit in the lounge chairs and enjoy the warm night air?"

He pushes me forward, and I stumble slightly until I'm pressed against the wooden railing of the deck. It's dark, but there are couples out on the beach enjoying moonlit strolls. With the light spilling out the doors of the cabana, anyone who gazes in our direction would clearly see me naked.

I'm about to protest the public nudity when Jon steps back, pulling me with him and then applying pressure to my shoulders until I bow down, leaning my upper half on the railing.

"Oooh, fuck," I breathe out, realizing what he's doing a few seconds before he nudges my legs open and slams his cock inside of me.

I cry out and slap a hand over my mouth to stifle any further unintentional sounds as he pounds against my pussy. I close my eyes so I can't see if anyone spots us. Just thinking someone could thrills me, but I want to avoid knowing for sure.

My pussy is still sensitive from fucking Cooper, and each vigorous plunge from Jon is a fantastic blend of pleasure and pain. I'm quickly spiraling towards my fourth orgasm of the day.

Jon leans over me and whispers harshly, "Tell me exactly how he fucked you."

Oh god, I love it when he makes me tell him the slutty things I did without him.

I pant out, "He pushed me against the door as soon as I got there."

Jon slows down his strokes. "Oh?"

Ooooh, fuck. Somehow it's more difficult to think when he's taking his time.

"Yes—yes...and he picked me up and carried me to bed."

Jon's only response is a "Mmmhmm," so I continue.

"He fucked me on the bed." I gasp out when Jon does a rough stroke. "And I came all over his cock...for my first orgasm."

Jon stills for two heartbeats before pounding into me fast again. I moan out, "Oh, my god," and my pussy quivers from the intense pleasure.

"Don't stop, Kitten," he pants out. "You were about to tell me about your second orgasm."

*Fuck, I can't think straigh*t. I search my brain to remember what happened. "Then he put my feet on his shoulders and fucked me until I came again."

I hear Jon murmur, "Nice," under his breath, and he whacks against me so hard I almost see stars. I hold onto the railing while he plows into me.

"Was that all?"

"Fuck... yes, that was it. Then I came home to you."

Jon slaps my ass, and I gasp from the sting. "Do you know why, Kitten?"

I don't understand what he's asking me. I can't think while he's fucking me this roughly, and I peep out a small, "What?"

Jon gathers my hair in a hand and tugs on it, forcing me to lift my head. His voice is low, and I almost don't hear him over the sound of the ocean.

"Kitten, why did you come home to me?"

Ooooh, fuck. I know what he wants. My heart races while my entire body lights up. I can tell I'm going to come.

My body tightens, and I moan out, "Because I'm yours."

A forceful thrust tips me over the edge, and I cry, "Oh, my god," loudly while fireworks explode behind my eyelids and waves of ecstasy ripple from my well-fucked pussy all the way to my finger and toes.

Jon comes with a groan, and this time I don't have to imagine the load of hot cum coating my inner walls. A blast of heat runs through me as he shudders. When he slows down his strokes, I get the guts to open my eyes, sighing in relief when I don't see anyone watching us.

When he pulls out, my poor aching pussy complains, and I know I'm going to be a little sore tomorrow, but I don't care. Jon helps me stand up, and we walk hand in hand to the bed so we can lie down and snuggle.

He spoons me, and my heart sings when I get to be the small spoon. I love feeling his warmth against my back. He slides an arm around my waist and draws me close to him.

"Did you have fun tonight, Miranda?"

I giggle and think of how many orgasms I had today. "Yes, Jon. It was a great day."

He murmurs, "Good," and kisses my shoulder.

Thinking of Cooper, I'm reminded of how the night ended with him. I give a loud yawn. "Cooper said he's open to fucking me again, if I want."

Jon licks my shoulder and blows on the skin, making me shiver. "Do you want to?"

His voice doesn't indicate how he feels about the idea, so I reply. "Nah," while my pussy twinges in protest and wants me to say, "Hell, yes."

Jon kisses close to my ear and whispers, "I love you."

I turn my head and kiss him softly. "I love you too, Jon. Thank you for tonight."

I'm tired and know I'm going to fall asleep soon. So far this vacation is pretty dang spectacular.

Chapter 7

The next day, after my 4 orgasms yesterday, I'm strutting around like a sexual goddess and wanting to embrace everything the resort offers. Jon overheard someone talking about paddle boats and suggested we try it. I look at him like he's insane but let him drag me down to the shore, where we get fitted for life jackets and climb into a paddleboat. As we cruise along, we stick to the same area with several other couples in boats, and I swear we pass one with a woman giving a blowjob to a guy. We don't get close enough to be certain, but what else would she be doing bent over his lap?

I catch Jon's eye, and he glances down at his junk, which makes me inspect him as well. The hard outline of his cock is visible through his shorts, but he doesn't demand it, so I don't offer. I'm still not sure I'm up for public sex. This resort really is a no-shame vacation, and we've already encountered many couples in various stages of undress playing together, some clearly fucking, and I get a delightful zing whenever I spot people being naughty in public. But enjoying seeing it and doing it myself are completely different.

Our time in the water is fun but exhausting, and I get a better leg workout than I've had in a long time. After we return the paddle boat, we walk along the coast, appreciating the fresh air and gorgeous ocean. This is already day three of our trip, and there are so many things we haven't explored yet, but I'm enjoying the slower pace. We're not trying to do everything, and I'm able to relax. This might be one trip where I won't need a second vacation afterward just so I can sleep for two days before returning to work. And I certainly won't complain about all the sex we're having.

As we leave the beach, I'm thinking about how hot the sex with Cooper was and wishing I had jumped Jon's bones this morning. I should drag him behind some bushes and have my way with him—it's not like other people aren't doing it. I could probably find a good hiding spot, and if I was on top, no one would see much if they wandered by.

He doesn't give me a chance to suggest it though, because he turns to me with sparkling eyes. "Kitten, let's try out the nude pool."

My inner goddess is down for a little kinkiness today, so I smile at him and say, "Sure."

The pool is enormous, and even though there are several naked couples playing in the water, it still seems empty. No one pays us much attention as we select lounge chairs and lay our stuff down. I am wearing a red and white striped bikini today, along with shorts and a T-shirt. This bikini is smoking hot on me, so I'm wistful as I remove it, but maybe I'm sexier without clothes. I'm not paying attention to Jon as I strip and put everything in our beach bag.

Once I'm naked, I realize he's still clothed. "Hey, what are you doing?"

This was his idea. Why am I the only one naked?

He grins at me. "I want to watch you swim."

A sexual tingle runs through my body and my pussy reminds me she wants to be fucked. I was hoping to fondle him underwater and drive him wild, but if he doesn't want to play, that's his prerogative.

I give him a cheeky, "Okay, enjoy the show," and wiggle my ass as I sashay to the pool and descend the steps into the water.

I'm not really sure how much he's going to see if I'm swimming, so after I dip my head underwater, I float on my back with my eyes closed.

My nipples pucker as I imagine his smoldering gaze on me, and my pussy throbs from the awareness that I'm on display for everyone. This is so fucking hot, and I'm more turned on than I expected.

I relax, and I'm not sure how long I float, but when I open my eyes, Jon is at the edge of the pool, motioning to me. I'm a strong swimmer from years of swim team in high school, and it only takes a few strokes before I'm in front of him. He's looking over at the other end of the pool.

"Kitten, isn't that your guy getting undressed?"

My guy? I peer across the water, and Cooper is taking off his clothes. He's obviously getting ready to go for a swim. My pussy clenches at the sight of his firm, muscular ass when he bends over to remove his shorts. *Mmmm, oh yeah, that's my guy.*

I'm slightly breathless from how turned on I am. "Yes, that's Cooper."

Jon contemplates Cooper for a moment, and when Cooper dives into the deep end of the pool, Jon turns back to me.

"Kitten?" His voice has a hardness that makes my pussy throb. She knows that tone, and he's about to command me to do something.

I can't help my response, and say, "Yes, Sir?" automatically.

"You're going to go talk to Cooper and fuck him in the pool where I can see you, but make him stop before he comes."

Um, what?

I sputter, "But someone else might see," as a spear of desire shoots straight to my pussy. I want to rub against something hard...but can I do that with Cooper...in public?

Jon simply says, "I know."

Oooh, fuck. An inferno of need in my belly makes me want to do it, but I'm also scared. I've never had sex in public.

"Are you going to do it, Kitten?"

Am I? Cooper is swimming in my direction, and I make a split-second decision. "Yes, Sir."

Jon smiles at me. "Good girl." I get a punch of pleasure from him saying that as he walks back to his lounge chair.

I turn my attention towards Cooper, and I can tell he spotted me because he swims up to me.

He hangs on to the edge, and he's close enough that our shoulders almost touch. "Hey."

"Hi," I smile at him and then go silent. I don't really know how I'm going to go from "Hello" to "Fuck me in the pool."

Cooper continues on when I don't. "I was hoping I'd see you again before you left. I wanted to thank you again for last night."

Oooh, he was hoping to see me again. His comment gives me courage, and I move my hands from the edge of the pool and slide my arms around his neck. He has to keep holding onto the side so he doesn't dip underwater with the added pressure of my weight. When he doesn't pull away from me, I wrap my legs around him and kiss him softly.

"I enjoyed last night too," I purr at him, and his cock stirs against me.

I'm not sure if he was hard before I climbed on board, but I reach down between us and stroke him in the water. He sucks in his breath, and I'm tempted to adjust my position so he can slip inside me, but we're too close to the edge where Jon is seated. He won't be able to appreciate the view unless we move.

I whisper in Cooper's ear. "Hold on to me and swim over to the opposite side of the pool."

Cooper doesn't question anything, and his powerful muscles bunch underneath my hands as he moves to the other edge. Now Jon has a better view, even though he won't be able to see all the underwater action. Cooper seems like a wonderfully obedient man, so I stroke him some more, but this time I move the tip of his cock against the entrance of my cave.

I ask him in a flirty tone, "Are you okay with this?"

He glances in Jon's direction before turning back to me. "Yeah. More than okay."

I'm so damn horny, and I want him to fuck me hard, but I also want us to be as inconspicuous as possible. A quick scan of the area tells me everyone is busy with their own shenanigans and not paying attention to us.

I kiss him again, and say, "We don't have a condom, so fuck me and stop right before you come."

He groans, and I tighten my legs around him, making his cock press into my pussy. As soon as he's inside, he takes control and turns so my back is against the cement. I let go of his neck, spread my arms out to the side, and grip the edge. Letting myself float a little, he holds onto my hips and fucks me.

I close my eyes as the pleasure swirls in my core. Cooper's ragged breath tells me he's enjoying this, and his cock without a condom is amazing. I really wish he could come inside me. I never knew how much I craved being filled with cum until I started fucking all my bosses. Going about my day at work with their stickiness dripping out of me after they blew their load deep inside me was so fucking hot. Then after work, Jon would come home and fill me up again.

Fuuuck, I want Cooper to come. I open my eyes and glance over Cooper's shoulder. Jon is stroking himself while he watches us. Shit, that's even hotter. I moan and arch my back, and suddenly Cooper pulls out.

I mewl in frustration and Cooper kisses me softy. "I'm sorry. I had to stop or I was going to come."

Shit, I was soooo close to my orgasm. "It's okay," I pant. "I'll be fine."

Jon can tell we've stopped, so he beckons me over to him while Cooper grins sheepishly at me. "Damn lack of condoms in a pool."

I giggle, relieved he's not angry. "I need to go. My husband wants me."

Cooper barks out a loud laugh. "That doesn't surprise me."

I eye him. "Are you okay?"

He kisses me again. "Yes, Miranda. I'm a big boy, and you just gave me a nice thrill."

I smile and say goodbye to him and swim to Jon who is now waiting for me by the pool stairs with our beach bag and towels. As I ascend the stairs, Jon takes my hand and I glance over my shoulder. Cooper is studying us and I wave goodbye to him and blow him a kiss. He smiles broadly in response.

Jon helps me out of the water and kisses me so fiercely, my pussy becomes extra wet. I'm guessing this kiss is for Cooper's viewing pleasure.

He plucks my sandals from the beach bag and once I slide them on, he says, "Let's get back to the room," and sets off at a brisk pace.

I have to skip to keep up. "Uh, can I put my clothes on?"

"Nope."

I shiver, despite the warm air. *I'm soooo about to get fucked hard.*

We pass several couples on the path and I can sense a blush creep up all over my body. It's not against the resort's rules for me to be naked since we are right at the edge of the clothing optional area. Parading around in my birthday suit thrills me more than I expected, despite being embarrassed. Every time someone looks at me, my pussy gets even more wet. My brain might not be totally sure about this, but my slutty beaver is loving it.

As soon as we're inside the door, Jon pushes me to the bed, turns me around, and bends me over. I rest on my elbows and wiggle my ass at him. *Mmm, yes, this is just how I like it.* I hear a brief rustle of clothes and then he's fucking me hard and wild.

"Ooooh, god," I groan out and I clutch at the bedding and reposition my feet for more stability.

After having Cooper's cock in me and being turned on all morning, it doesn't take me long to reach the peak. While I'm moaning and reeling from the waves of rapture, Jon comes with a growl and hammers into me until he's unloaded the last drop of his cum.

I collapse on the bed, face down, while Jon lays next me and rubs my back. I'm relaxed after being thoroughly fucked, and enjoying his cum leaking out of me. At least I get the pleasure of Jon's cum inside of me.

"Miranda?"

"Hmmm?"

"I feel bad for Cooper."

I giggle and lift my head to peek at Jon. "I think he was fine."

Jon plays with my hair for a moment before speaking again. "Do you want to fuck him again?"

I thought I was satisfied, but my pussy hums to life again. She's VERY interested in where this conversation is going.

Not playing coy, I reply, "Yes, I'd like to, but only if you're okay with it."

My answer is truthful. I have no desire to be a hotwife with an unwilling husband. I get more enjoyment from coming home to Jon and seeing how crazed and turned on he is than I do from sleeping with other guys. What we're doing is ten times hotter because of his reaction.

"I want you to invite him over here tomorrow so I can watch."

Ooooh, fuck. What's this? He's never been in the room when it's just me and another guy before, and has only watched a few times total. He saw me fuck all my bosses in the conference room at work when they video conferenced him in, but he'd been at home. We also attended that intense, but messed up, BDSM party, and he saw me play with other guests, but it wasn't an intimate setting.

Excitement churns in my gut, and if he wants to do it, it would be erotic with him there. But I need to double check. "Are you sure, Jon?"

He trails his fingers down my spine, tickling me, causing me to giggle and squirm. "Yes, I'm sure. Seeing you fuck him in the pool made me think of this."

"Okay, I'll go to his cabana tomorrow and invite him over."

Jon kisses me deeply, and I'm eager to see what tomorrow brings.

CHAPTER 8

I wake up the next morning refreshed and ready for adventure. Jon and I stayed in our room most of the previous evening, and by the time I fell asleep, I counted 5 orgasms for the day, a record for any trip we've taken after our honeymoon. I assumed I wouldn't be interested in sex right when I woke up, but my pussy is throbbing and needy. I need to find Cooper before he makes other plans tonight since our vacation is almost over, so I don't want to risk spending hours fucking Jon this morning.

I'm also hungry, so I throw on green khaki shorts with multiple pockets and a white T-shirt. The shorts are my favorite because they hug my ass and end a few inches past my butt, so they make my legs look long and sexy. I get a nice confidence boost whenever I wear this outfit. We decide to try The Bahaman for breakfast, which is casual dining but fancier than the buffet. We're seated at a four-person table with two chairs per side, and Jon sits across from me.

As soon as we settle in, Cooper walks into the restaurant and my pussy pulses when I see him.

I'm immediately breathless. "Jon...Cooper is here."

"Oh, yeah?" He enthusiastically glances around, looking for him. "Invite him to sit with us."

I'm about to stand up, but Cooper must have spotted us because he's strolling over to our table. I assume he's going to greet me, but he turns to Jon instead and holds out his hand.

"Hey, I wanted to introduce myself if I saw you guys again. I'm Cooper."

Jon shakes his hand, looking pleased, and greets him. I mentally admire how thoughtful Cooper is. Jon invites him to join us for breakfast and within moments, Cooper is sitting in the chair next to me. Normally if Jon and I are eating with a third person, he and I would sit on the same side, so it's odd with Cooper next to me instead. I snake my hand across the table to twine my fingers with Jon's, craving the connection since I can't lean against him.

We make small talk with Cooper, but all I can think of is inviting him to our place tonight. I order French toast with a side of mixed tropical fruit that I can't identify. The meal is delicious, but I'm too distracted to give it the proper attention it deserves. Cooper mentions he's having an extended stay at the resort, and I'm curious how someone can afford that, but there's no way I'd ask him.

I'm almost done with my food when my phone vibrates in the pocket of my shorts. Assuming it's Dina, I almost don't check, knowing I'll call her later. But the guys are discussing a sci-fi book I never heard of, so I take a peek at my phone. The message is from Jon.

Kitten, rub Cooper's cock through his shorts under the table.

I glare sharply at Jon, but he's purposely ignoring me. When did he have time to send this text? I debate what I'm going to do for a moment, and then decide 'fuck it' and put my hand on Cooper's knee.

Cooper jumps and stutters before continuing the conversation with Jon about a Comic Con convention he attended last year. I creep my hand up his inner thigh, rubbing circles, and his leg muscles twitch. I study Jon, and when his face flushes pink and he shifts in his chair, I can tell he's getting turned on by imagining what I'm doing.

Cooper's cock is hard, and I wonder if it was like that before I touched his knee. I stroke him slowly, using enough pressure to give him a thrill through the fabric. After a couple of minutes, he can't hold a conversation, and his eyelids flutter from the pleasure.

He clears his throat and asks, "Uh, what's going on here?"

I give Jon a questioning look, and with lust-glazed eyes, he nods at my silent question. Jon's reaction gives me the confidence I need.

"Cooper," I purr at him. "Jon wants to watch us fuck. Do you want to come to our room tonight?"

Cooper lets out a sigh and shivers against my hand. "Yes."

I didn't expect such a simple reply, and it makes me want to call him a good boy. Jon would not take kindly to that, since he's my only good boy, so I rein in the impulse.

Once Cooper agrees, I remove my hand and grin at both guys. "Okay, guess it's settled," and I take a big bite of the last of my French toast. The guys laugh with me and switch topics to an upcoming TV show they're both excited about.

When breakfast is over, and we get up to leave, we arrange with Cooper for him to come to our cabana at 7 p.m. and give him our room number. He kisses me on the cheek and says, "Looking forward to it," and heads off with a jaunty wave.

When he's gone, Jon turns to me. "So Kitten, what do you want to do today?"

There are so many things we haven't explored yet, but I'm curious about the spa and wonder if they have any openings for a massage. It would have been smart to pre-book one.

"Want to come with me to the spa?"

He debates for a second. "Nah, you go have fun. I need a nap for tonight." He gives me a meaningful look. "Someone kept me up late."

Remembering last night creates a warmth in my belly, and I kiss him. "Maybe that someone deserves a spanking when she gets home for being a bad girl and keeping you up past your bedtime."

He chuckles, "Oh, she does," and swats my ass.

I giggle as we part ways.

The spa had an opening in 30 minutes, and I sign up for a 90-minute massage. Fuck, this is going to be terrific. I wait in the lobby and read magazines until my appointment time. I wasn't wrong, and when I'm done with the massage, I'm amazingly relaxed and ready for a nap as well.

I enjoy the short walk back to our cabana. It's another beautiful, warm day, and I love the smell of the flowers at the resort. It's going to be difficult to return home to everyday life after this since being here refreshes my soul.

When I'm almost back to our room, I pass a group of people, and one woman is wearing adorable gray kitten ears with little puffs of pink fur on the inside of the ears. *Oooh, shit...*why didn't I think of bringing my cat ears?

I was going to pout at Jon about missing out on some kitten fun, but he's asleep when I get into our room. I remove my clothes and crawl into bed beside him. He's snoring gently and doesn't wake up. I easily fall asleep listening to his breathing.

The rest of the day speeds by, and Jon and I are both full of nervous energy. We're laughing and cracking jokes but avoid talking about tonight. We go to the Au Natural Grill on the nude beach and have a light dinner of seasoned chicken skewers and vegetables, and we're back at our cabana by 6:30 p.m., waiting for Cooper.

I want to pace around the room but force myself to sit on the bed. Jon requested I wear only a bathrobe, and I rub my thighs together in anticipation. Knowing Jon is going to be watching has my stomach fluttering, and I'm hypersensitive to the slightest touch. I'm so dang wet already, and it hasn't even started.

Jon positions a chair across the room for himself. While we wait, Jon absentmindedly strokes his cock a few times, and I'm curious if he's going to whip it out while Cooper is here or if he's going to wait and fuck me once we're alone. Whatever he does is fine with me.

When Cooper knocks on the door, nerves jump in my belly. I glance at Jon sitting in his chair. "We ready for this?"

He replies, "Yep," and I get up and open the door.

Cooper walks in, gives the room a quick scan, and zeros in on Jon. "Hello."

I close the door behind Cooper, and Jon and I say, "Hi," in tandem. Jon being in the room makes me uncertain how to start the sexy stuff with Cooper. Normally I get slutty in my cute awkward way and the guy takes over.

Jon must have sensed my hesitation because he states, "I want you two to both forget I'm here."

Cooper replies, "Works for me," but I want to snort and say, "Not likely." Plus the point is to NOT forget since his presence is making this more arousing for me.

I'm about to say I want to think about him being there, but before I have time to speak, Cooper turns to me and pulls me in for a deep kiss. We start out slowly, but the kiss quickly turns heated and our tongues swirl together while I moan. Cooper plucks at the sash of my robe to open it and nudges it off my shoulders. My pussy is wet and needy, and I desperately want his cock inside me. Jon might want us to ignore him, but I want him to see me fuck Cooper instead of only hearing about it afterwards.

Cooper moves his hands to cup my breasts and play with my nipples, sending zings of joy to my nether region and making me more wet. "Miranda, I've been thinking about you all day."

Oooh, that's hot. I get a carnal thrill from knowing someone other than my husband was daydreaming about me. He continues to kiss me, and his hands at my breasts makes my pussy ache while spikes of joy ping through my core.

One of Cooper's hands glides down my stomach and slips between my legs. A finger probes between my folds and massages my already swollen clit. I gasp from the ripples of bliss. "Miranda, did you think of me after we fucked?"

Oh, shit. I can't help but peek at Jon. He's grinning and stroking himself through his shorts, and my wanton side comes out after seeing he's Okay with everything.

I keep my voice low and sultry. "Yes, I did, and I was hoping to fuck you again."

Cooper murmurs, "So was I," against my mouth and nudges me backwards until my legs hit the edge of the bed.

"How do you want to be fucked tonight?" he questions, and a dribble of wetness leaks from my pussy at his words.

The dirty talk is twice as hot with Jon in the room. I hesitate for a second, and Jon's lust roughened voice calls out.

"Fuck her like you did last time, with her feet by your head. I want to see it."

Ooooh, shit. He didn't say he was going to interact with us.

Cooper replies, "As you wish," and pushes me onto the bed.

I prop myself up on my elbows and enjoy the show as Cooper removes all his clothes. His body is firm and sexy, and I want to touch him everywhere. I swear I can see his cock pulsing, and I lick my lips, imagining him sliding inside me.

Before he drops his shorts to the floor, he fishes out a condom from the pocket and puts it on. I'm glad he remembered to bring one, since we don't have any.

Cooper hooks his hands under my knees and pulls me towards the end of the bed, while I gasp from the sudden movement.

"I think we were like this, weren't we?" he asks as he puts my ankles on his shoulders and rubs the tip of his cock along my wet slit. *Fuuuck*, the zing through my pussy makes me desperate.

I moan out, "Yessss," as he pushes into me, and pleasure radiates from my core.

I want him to plow into me, but his deliberately slow strokes are making my head spin.

"Miranda, did I fuck you hard and fast, or was it slow?"

Oooh, does he not remember he drove me wild with how slow he was? "Hard," I gasp out. "It was violent and rough."

That makes him laugh as he continues his leisurely thrusting. "No, that doesn't sound like me at all."

I whisper, "Please?" and he ignores me.

I check on Jon, and I'm surprised to see his cock out of his shorts already. Guess that answers my original question about what he planned to do tonight.

Cooper distracts me from watching Jon. "Miranda, play with your nipples and show your husband what a filthy little slut you were for me."

Jesus Christ, this is so fabulously dirty. I bring my hands up to my tits and tug my nipples, sending pings of pleasure straight to my clit. I turn my head to look at Jon again, and he's stroking himself faster.

I'm crazed and want to come, and about willing to beg. "Oh, god, Cooper. Fuck me harder. Please?"

Cooper gives a few powerful thrusts. "You mean like this?"

I moan, "Yes," and he slows down again.

"I don't know if you want it enough. Does she look like she wants it, Jon?"

Oh wow, he really is getting Jon involved. Movement from Jon's direction has me turning my head, and he's walking to the bed with his cock out. My breath catches. What is Jon coming over here for, to get a better look?

Jon sits down next to me, and the bed dips slightly. I'm shocked but so fucking turned on by this turn of events. Jon reaches his hand between me and Cooper and brushes his fingers against my clit while Cooper continues to plow into me slowly.

"Oooooh, fuck," I cry out and almost come, but Jon eases the pressure of his fingers.

Jon announces, "Oh yes, my slut is ready for it."

When Jon calls me his slut, I give in to the experience and close my eyes. They can do whatever they want to me, and I'm going to love it. With Cooper standing up and fucking me, Jon has room to lean over and attach his mouth to my nipple. He sucks on it while his fingers rub circles around my clit, and I'm lost in a sea of bliss. Cooper speeds up his thrusts, and my body and mind can't handle all the pleasure. I edge closer and closer to my climax.

Jon continues his ministrations on my nipple but removes his fingers from between my legs briefly to pick up my hand and lay it on his cock. When I take the hint and stroke him, he returns his fingers to my clit. The tip of his cock is wet with pre-cum, and I know exactly how he wants to be stroked. He's pulsing against my hand so I can tell he's close to coming, and knowing that makes me moan and spiral higher. I mewl and thrash about as Cooper bulldozes into me, and I'm going to tip over the edge at any moment.

Jon stops sucking on my nipple. "Kitten, look at me."

"Wha...?" I open my eyes, and he's gazing at me with love.

"Miranda, I want you to come for me."

As soon as he tells me to come, my orgasm rips through me. I scream out, "Oh, my god," bucking my hips wildly, forcing Jon's fingers harder against my clit and Cooper's cock deeper inside me. Jon groans as he blows his load, his cum coating my hand. I continue to stroke him, milking every drop from him as I calm down.

Jon removes his hand from between my legs and plays with my nipples, causing tiny aftershocks of pleasure to radiate through me.

Cooper locks eyes with me, and I realize he hasn't climaxed yet, even after watching Jon and me come. His eyes glaze over, and a sheen of sweat on his chest glistens in the soft lighting while he whacks against me repeatedly.

Smiling at him, I wiggle my hips as best I can. "Cooper, it's your turn to come."

My words make him groan and explode as he pounds against me savagely. Jon kisses me, and our tongues entwine as Cooper shudders with his release.

Time slows down, and I drift in a haze of sexual satisfaction as Cooper pulls out and discards his condom. He and Jon haul me up on the bed so I'm more comfortable, and Jon snuggles in beside me while Cooper puts on his shorts and sits at the end of the bed. I'm too content to talk, and barely listen to Jon and Cooper's conversation. My head is reeling from Jon playing with us, and I don't know what this means for the future. Did he plan to do that, or was it spontaneous?

Cooper gets off the bed, disappears into the nook, and returns with bottled water. Jon forces me to half sit up to take a few sips, and the water revives me. This experience really made this trip unforgettable.

I smile at both men. "Thank you, guys. This was so fucking amazing."

Cooper doesn't sit down again, but beams at me in return. "I had a great time as well. I'm going to head out and leave you to your evening. It was nice meeting you both. We had fun this week."

I almost giggle at how polite he is after fucking me. He's such a sweet guy, and I hope he finds happiness in life. I know I'm never going to forget him. I sit up fully to say goodbye, and he leans over to kiss me tenderly.

"I mean it Miranda. I'm glad I met you."

I give him a soft smile. "I'm glad I met you, too."

Jon walks him to the door, and I flop back onto the bed, staring at the ceiling and trying to process everything. Is Jon going to want to watch more often now, or every time? I desperately want to call Dina and tell her everything that happened tonight, but I need to wait until I get home so I can talk to her while Jon isn't around.

Jon removes his clothes and climbs into bed, facing me, and cuddles close. We're both silent for a few minutes, lost in thought.

The question is weighing on me, so I finally ask him what's been on my mind. "Did you really like that?"

He kisses my forehead. "Kitten, that was unbelievable. Watching you orgasm with another guy inside of you..." He trails off.

I don't press him to explain his feelings. I know my husband, and he'll talk more about it when he's ready.

He traces one of my nipples with his finger and it tickles, but I hold in my giggle and ask, "Do you think you'll want to watch again?"

He's hesitant. "Probably. Would that be okay?"

I cup his chin, turning him so I can kiss him soundly. "You silly goof, of course it is. I loved having you here."

He sighs and I can tell he's pleased. We snuggle together, listening to the ocean through the open window. We're going home soon, and I don't want to fuck anyone else but Jon for the rest of the trip. This was a wonderful experience with Cooper, but it's time to focus again on the one man in this world who loves me unconditionally.

I twine my fingers with his and fiddle with his wedding ring. If someone had told me on our wedding day that someday we'd be lying here after another guy fucked me, I don't think I would have believed them. The Miranda of today is so much wiser and more worldly than my innocent bridal self. I thought Jon was going to be the last man I ever fucked, and here we are almost ten years later, sharing this together. Our sexual journey was kinkier than I ever expected, and this trip just adds to it.

Jon kisses me tenderly. "Kitten, stop thinking so much. Just enjoy it."

I giggle at him, sigh, and roll over to readjust myself so he's spooning me. He's totally right, and he knows me so well.

"Hey, Jon?"

He kisses my neck, close to my ear. "Yes, Kitten?"

"I think we should buy a souvenir for Chuck to thank him for recommending this resort."

Jon laughs. "Sure, we can get him a shot glass from the gift shop, though branded lube might be more appropriate."

I smack his arm playfully. "We aren't getting him lube."

Jon growls softly into my ear. "No, we aren't, because we'd end up using it all." I feel his hardness poking against my ass, and he pushes me onto my stomach, covering me with his body. Oooh, fuck yeah. Seems the night is still young. I groan as he slides his cock into my pussy.

The best thing about Jon is his desire to try everything. He fucks me for hours in a variety of positions, and I lose count of my orgasms after six. Luckily, we brought lube from home because all my holes were stuffed before he was done with me.

The sun is coming up when we're finally exhausted and sexually drained. We're on the floor, a sweaty mess, and tangled up in the sheets. I can barely keep my eyes open, so when Jon reaches his hand between my legs and I think he's trying to start something up again, I yawn loudly.

"Sir, you better not be getting any ideas. This kitten needs sleep."

Jon presses a finger inside me, creating a tiny thrill, and laughs, "Nope, just checking what's mine." When he removes his hand, he slaps my ass.

I whimper, but he didn't spank me painfully, so it's only a tiny protest.

"Jon, did I ever tell you how much I fucking love you?"

He brushes aside the strands of hair stuck to my sweaty face. "Yep, Kitten, almost every day."

I smile at him. "Best... trip... ever."

He chuckles, gets off the floor, and helps me up onto the bed. "You think so?"

We adjust the comforter over us. As soon as my head hits the pillow, I can tell I'm going to be asleep within minutes. I mumble, "You should bring me here every year."

Jon replies, "I might have to do that." I fall asleep, dreaming of throwing a party with a parade of 20 guys taking their turns fucking me. And of course, Jon is there, watching.

The end

Hot for Her Husband

Hotwife Let Loose

Lacey Cross

PREFACE

These three shorts were originally written and posted on a blogging platform, and aren't available there anymore. The stories are all with hotwife Miranda, and they are sexy little erotic shorts with her husband. She'll think about her hotwife adventures with other men while her husband thrills her. The subtitle for each chapter says where it falls in her journey.

Enjoy!

Lacey

CHAPTER 1

AFTER BREAKING IN THE JUNIOR PARTNER, MY HUSBAND TAKES HIS PLEASURE WITH ME

My favorite day of the week is Saturday because Jon is usually in bed with me when I wake up. After a long week, it's wonderful to savor our time together. Regardless of what we do when we wake up, whether it be sex, cuddling or something else, it's nice to have that time to bond with him.

When I wake up on this particular Saturday morning, I find Jon lying beside me, facing me as he stares at me.

"Good morning, Kitten," he says with a twinkle in his eye and a smile on his face. I immediately suspect he's up to something. I know that look.

Some people might find it creepy to wake up with their spouse watching them, but Jon isn't the only one who does this; sometimes, when I wake up in the morning before him, I look over at him and study him because he's so fucking sexy, and I love him so damn much. He's told me he stares at me for the same reason.

"Morning, my love," I tell him as I sit up and stretch. I slept naked last night and my nipples harden in the cool air. My pussy hums and I'm already wet. I wonder if he's going to pounce on me for some morning fun.

Him watching me this morning intensifies my need to get his cock inside me.

"You hungry?" he asks me.

My pussy aches and I'm hungry... but not for food.

I shake my head. "Not at the moment."

He chuckles. "Okay, we'll eat breakfast later, but we're still going to go to the kitchen."

What's this?

"Why?" I ask, only to watch a devious smile spread across his face.

"Oh, you'll see," he tells me as he reaches over to play with my nipple. "I have plans for you." With the tone of his voice and his hand on my breast, I think I know what those "plans" are. I'm down with this thought, but right now I wish he'd move his hand between my legs and rub my clit.

Instead, Jon removes his hand from my nipple, and I want to complain, but keep quiet. If he's got plans, I don't want to derail them. He's an inventive lover and I usually have fun with whatever he dreams up.

"Miranda, go to the kitchen, sit on the counter, and wait for me."

Ooooh, what's this? He's not usually dominant with me, and a splash of wetness leaks from my pussy. The few times he's gotten demanding and told me what to do, I loved it and I wish he'd do it more often.

Hoping to encourage the behavior, I giggle out, "Yes, Sir," and watch his eyes light up with that word.

I get out of bed, leaving him there, and go out to the kitchen, naked. We stayed up late while experimenting with tying me to the bedposts. One of my bosses at work recently tied me up, and we've been trying it at home ever since. I rub my thighs together in anticipation of what is about to happen, and from remembering how hot it was last night to be at Jon's mercy.

Quickly, I sit on the countertop and await his arrival. What in the hell does he have planned for me? Oooh, it might be food related. Maybe I'm *HIS* breakfast. I reach my hand between my legs and stroke my clit for a moment. I like the idea of him coming into the kitchen and licking me.

The last time he sent me here by myself, he brought out some M&Ms from the pantry and tucked them between my pussy lips before fishing them out with his tongue and eating them. It's possible today will be like that. I'm fine with whatever he wants to do as long as it gets me an orgasm.

My food hypothesis is proven wrong, however, when he enters the kitchen, naked and hard... with his red toy lightsaber in his hand.

"What... the fuck?" I murmur.

What is this? Last week I had to seduce one of my bosses at work, and he was... hesitant, so I took his green toy lightsaber off the shelf in his office and shoved it up my twat. That got me bent over his desk, so it was all worth it.

I told Jon about it afterwards, and that got me another hard fucking while similarly bent over the desk in our home office. But I thought that was the end of it. I mean, it's possible he wants to do some Star Wars roleplay? I'll be the Leia to his Han Solo. We've been getting more creative with our sexual play lately, and I could get into some roleplay with him. Oooh, I'll totally do the buns on the sides of my head.

"Do you know what I'm going to do with this?" he asks, disturbing my fantasy.

I shake my head, 'no,' not wanting to give him any ideas if he didn't already have them.

"Guess," he orders.

"Um, you're gonna spank me with it?" I ask hopefully. He never spanks me hard, to my disappointment, but the toy might sting more.

He shakes his head. "No," and turns it on, causing it to light up with a bright red glow. "Guess again."

Oh shit, he's totally going to do it. My pussy clenches at the thought of recreating the scene with my boss. When I did it at the office, it was me holding the toy and fucking myself with it, but somehow I don't think Jon's going to hand it over.

"You're gonna fuck me with it," I state matter-of-factly.

He gives me a firm glance. "Yes. And call me Sir," he orders.

"Yes, Sir." I get a nice zing at how commanding he's being and instantly want to please him.

He grabs a paper towel from a roll on the counter and wipes the toy down. "I cleaned this earlier," he tells me as he steps close to me and pushes my knees apart. "I'll be gentle, I promise."

This is so fucking erotic. I breathe out, "Yes, Sir," and wish he wouldn't be gentle. But just the fact that he's standing there about to shove a toy up me is more than I ever expected from him.

He reaches his free hand forward, sliding his fingers past my folds, rubbing my clit. I sigh as tiny pings of pleasure run through me. Oooh, god, this is exactly what I needed. He rubs little circles around my bundle of nerves and I close my eyes, letting my head fall back and thrusting my hips towards his hand.

He speeds up, and the pleasure intensifies until continuous waves of bliss threaten to tip me over the edge, but when he slows down, I bite my lip and a tortured moan slips out.

He keeps teasing me, slowing down when I almost orgasm, only to speed up again. I grip the counter for leverage and thrash against his hand, desperate for more. When he removes his hand completely, I open my eyes and watch as he sucks my juice off his fingers, one by one. God, he's so sexy.

He smirks at me. "You taste divine. Perhaps I'll get a better taste later tonight." The thought of his mouth on my clit makes me want to beg.

"But for now," he says, holding up the lightsaber, "let's concentrate on stretching that tight little slutty pussy."

I love it when he calls my pussy "slutty," since that's how I think of it myself. I like to blame my cunt for a lot of the crazy things I do or think. She's a slut, and she loves being one.

"Okay, Sir," I agree.

"Good. Now open your mouth," he orders.

I do what he says, and he nuzzles the tip of the lightsaber in my mouth. It's slightly warm from the light inside the tube, but not hot enough to burn anything. He fucks my mouth with it slowly, before picking up speed. Wetness leaks from my pussy as I imagine him sliding it inside me.

He pulls out and orders in a low voice, "Spread your legs."

"Yes, Sir," I say as I follow his command.

When he slides the tip of the lightsaber into my pussy, I'm struck by how filthy this is. I'm sitting in my kitchen, letting my husband fuck me with a toy all because I did this with my boss last week. I have a fabulous life.

It feels so fucking good. As he speeds up, plunging it into me faster and faster, I moan out, "Oh, god" with every thrust, until it stops being words and becomes a long string of moans.

He knows how much I can take, and the longer he pumps it inside me, the more difficult it is to think. I lift my hips with each thrust, wanting it harder and faster. I'm a wet mess and I'm going to come all over it soon if he doesn't stop.

As I spin higher, my pussy clenches around the toy and I groan, "I'm going to come."

"Ask for it."

Oh shit. He's never done this before. "Please?"

"Please, what?" he asks harshly.

God, whatever has gotten into Jon today is amazing. This side needs to come out more.

"Please, Sir, may I come?"

"No," he states, while a devilish smirk plays on his lips.

Fuuuuuck. I try again, and peep out my cutest, "Please, Sir?"

"No," he tells me again, and I moan in both desire and frustration.

"Patience, Kitten. You can come soon enough."

I know I won't be able to hold back much longer. Each thrust shoots pleasure through my core.

He slows his strokes, stalling my orgasm for a little bit. I sigh in relief, yet slightly irritated. I want to complain, but with the mood he's in, that'll get me nowhere good.

"Do you like this, Kitten?"

I nod, and he stops the movement of the lightsaber. "No. I want to hear you say it."

I cry out and jerk my hips, trying to fuck myself. The way he's teasing me is so hot, and I'm beyond caring what happens as long as I can come. I'll be the sluttiest Miranda ever if he gets me what I want right now. I look him in the eyes and pant, "I like it when you fuck my slutty pussy with the lightsaber, Sir."

He grins at me and starts fucking me with it again. I give a high-pitched "Oooh, god," at how amazing it feels.

I close my eyes and welcome the approaching bliss as my body tightens. Shit, he still didn't say I can come.

"Please, Sir, may I come?" I ask, hopefully.

His tone is playful. "Should I let you?"

"Yes, Sir!" I groan while I writhe to avoid coming. "Yes, Sir! Please, Sir!"

"No," he states as he pulls the toy out.

UGH! My climax melts away once more, and I'm suddenly so irked I want to scream.

Jon leans in and kisses me deeply. "I want you to come while I'm inside of you."

Oooh, that is exactly what I needed to hear. He sets the lightsaber on the counter next to me and stands between my legs. I wrap my arms around his neck and spread my legs as wide as I can while he holds onto my waist with his hands and sinks into me. I arch my back as his shaft stretches my pussy. *Mmmm, yes*. He's thicker than the tip of the lightsaber and after teasing me so long with the toy, it's fantastic to have his cock inside me.

"That feels good, doesn't it?" he murmurs.

"Yes, Sir," I moan as he strokes steadily for a moment, before picking up speed.

"You're so fucking perfect," he growls, and I get a zing of lust from knowing I'm driving him crazy.

My fingernails dig into his shoulder blades and a part of me knows that it's hurting him, but he doesn't complain. He continues to fuck me, and I creep closer to my orgasm with each thrust.

"Your slutty pussy loves my cock, doesn't it?" Jon asks me in a low voice.

"Yes, Sir!' I cry in response. "Yes, it does, Sir!"

"More than those other guys?" he questions.

"Yes, Sir! Yes—oh, fuck," I moan. It's dirty when he makes me tell him how much more I love his cock than my bosses'. The lawyers at work give me pleasure, but my love for Jon makes the delight more intense.

My orgasm is fast approaching, and I need permission. "Please, Sir, may I come?"

"No," he says, a teasing lilt to his voice as he continues to fuck me at a moderate pace.

"Please, Jon—I mean Sir, I can't hold it!" I cry.

Jon isn't harsh, so I'm not really afraid of what will happen if I come without permission. I just have this overwhelming desire to please him and I need to hear him tell me to come.

"You can hold it, and you will," he tells me and gives a hard thrust deep inside.

Shit! "No, I can't! You know I can't!" I whine in aggravation.

"What do you call me, Kitten?" he demands, halting his strokes.

"Sir," I breathe, realizing that I called him Jon. "Sorry, Sir."

He's really leaning into the domination act and knowing he's doing it to please me makes it even more arousing.

He fucks me again, and I'm so close to coming that any little thing is going to send me over the edge.

I groan and cry, "I can't hold it—I can't, please, please, please!"

"You've been a naughty kitten," he tells me with a sharp whack against my pussy that almost sends me over the edge. "Not addressing me properly. Maybe I shouldn't let you."

Ooooh, fuck. My head spins and I almost come right then at the thought of him telling me no, but babble, "I'm sorry, I'm sorry, I'm sorry, Sir."

He sighs, "Very well," and moves a hand between us, pressing against my clit. My entire body is tight, and my thigh muscles quiver as the pleasure threatens to overwhelm me.

He brushes his finger in tiny circles against my clit, and says, "Come for me, Miranda."

I cry out as euphoria spreads through me like wildfire, the ecstasy momentarily blinding me as waves of rapture wash over me.

"Ooooh, fuck." I dig my nails even further into the skin on his upper back as I ride my climax.

His fingers get more aggressive against my clit and my orgasm spirals into a second one. I come all over his cock again, bucking and shuddering.

While I'm overtaken by the pleasure of two orgasms, Jon comes with a growl, spurting his hot, sticky cum deep inside. As he slows his thrusts, my pussy clenches around him, milking his shaft as tiny aftershocks of delight ripple through me.

Eventually he stops moving and we stay like that, panting and breathless as he goes soft inside of me. I rest my head on his shoulder, enjoying being close to him, and he wraps his arms around me.

He leans into me for a moment, but eventually pulls out with a grin. "That was perfect."

"You're perfect," I tell him, and his smile widens.

Even though he was edging and tormenting me, I loved every second of our play. I hope this dominant side of him comes out more often now.

Jon picks up the toy, switches the light off and moves to the sink to clean it. Seeing the toy in his hands makes me chuckle, and he looks up.

"What?" he asks.

I giggle more before speaking. "I've had a green and a red one inside me. Do they come in any other color?"

"Blue," he states simply, and my pussy clenches at the thought of being fucked with a blue lightsaber next time.

The End

Chapter 2

Caught Having Sex on a Pool Table Was More Thrilling Than I Imagined

Jon has always been good at turning me on, no matter what the circumstance. Sometimes, just looking in his direction is enough to make my panties wet. This, however, is not one of those circumstances. This time, he's actively fucking with me.

"Are you gonna tease me all the way to the party?" I ask him as he caresses my thigh. He's driving tonight and I'm supposed to be the navigator, but his fingers are distracting me.

I'm wearing a short black dress, making it easy for him to reach wherever he wants to touch. It's a week before Christmas and we're heading to a party one of his friends is throwing. I've been dreading this party for days now because I know the guy hosting it was at my little holiday get-together not too long ago.

My party was not a normal party. It was a wish fulfillment Jon did for me because I wanted a train of guys at my ass. Jon invited 20 friends over and as I was fucked for hours in the middle of the rec room, I was... not quiet.

I squirm in my seat and bring myself back to my more immediate problem. Jon seems to want me to be a wet puddle tonight.

"Oh, yes, Miranda. I plan on messing with you all night." Jon sounds amused and way too pleased with himself.

Honestly, the perfect evening for me would be if we just stayed home and fucked, but since that's not happening, I need more. I want him to rub my clit or finger me. I shift in the seat and spread my knees apart, trying to tempt him to do more than just caress my thigh. My clit swells at the thought and I almost whimper as he brushes his fingers higher, but not quite reaching the promised land.

"Impatient?" he asks me.

"Yes," I groan out and move my hips, pushing them forward to try and force his hand higher. Before we left the house, Jon made me take off my panties, which makes this even more arousing.

He laughs at my antics. "Be patient, Kitten. I'll deal with you when we get home."

Shivers run down my spine when he says he'll "deal with me," knowing it's a good promise, but I don't know if I can wait that long. My pussy is on fire and if he doesn't stop touching me, it's going to get worse. We've had a busy week and only had sex twice. My body is craving a release in some way, preferably from his cock, but at this point I'm not picky; I'd take his fingers, mouth, or a combination of anything.

When we pull up to the party he removes his hand from my leg, and I'm disappointed. I really wanted him to finger me in the car, dammit!

"Come on," he says as he climbs out. I do the same, feeling the moisture from my pussy drip down my thighs as I walk.

My expression must have given something away because he pauses. "You okay?"

"Yeah, just... wet."

I don't mean to sound enticing. I'm just being honest. But the glint in Jon's eye has me imagining him pinning me up against the car and fucking me right there. Mmm, Jon in beast mode is hot. Maybe I can get him there tonight.

"Are you trying to tempt me, Kitten?" he asks.

Quickly, I glance down at his hardness outlined against his jeans. I quirk an eyebrow at his erection and when I look him in the eyes, there's no mistaking the challenge.

"Nooo, I wouldn't do that. Would I?"

"Hmm," he murmurs to himself as we approach the front door. "I think I need to check how wet you are. Lean against the wall," he commands.

Wait, what? He must be joking. I don't move, so he pushes me against the wall himself.

"What the hell, Jon. What if someone opens the door?"

He gives me a devilish grin. "I guess we better be quick with this, huh?"

A brief jolt of electricity zips from my core at the thought of being caught. Oh, shit. That is sort of hot.

He wastes no time reaching one hand under my dress and fondling my pussy, soaking his fingers with my juices.

"Oh, fuck, Jon," I hiss as his fingers caress my clit, rubbing circles.

He doesn't stop, and instead, he presses his fingers into me, pumping them in and out, fucking me quickly. My heart rate speeds up and tendrils of delight radiate from my core. "Oh, my god," I moan as I edge towards an orgasm.

Just as I am about to climax... he stops and removes his hand completely.

"What the fuck?" I'm dazed, and half annoyed with him, yet so aroused. The emotions war inside me and his shit-eating grin isn't helping matters.

"I told you to be patient, Kitten."

He sucks my juices off his fingers and uses the opposite hand to ring the doorbell. Before I have the chance to say anything, the door opens and we're beckoned into the party by one of his friends.

We mingle for a bit, and every time we run into a friend that was at our holiday party and heard me begging to be fucked, a wave of humiliation hits me and I get uncomfortably more turned on. This party can't end fast enough. I need to get home and get my pussy stuffed by my stud of a husband, but he seems to be in no rush to leave. Jon is more of a party person than I am, and it's usually difficult to get him to leave early. Obviously I wasn't alluring enough in the car.

Eventually we end up squished together on the sofa, eating appetizers off paper plates. I can't help but watch Jon's nimble fingers and imagine him shoving them into whatever hole of mine he wants. My body is on fire, and I need him. Goddammit. I'm so horny I want him to take me to the bathroom and pleasure me to the point of tears. Would he do it if I ask?

He rests the empty plate on his lap, and now that he's done eating, I take my chance. I put one hand on his shoulder and lean over close to his ear.

"I want you to fuck me right now," I whisper, and his shoulder tenses beneath my touch.

He says nothing at first, but I hear a groan under his breath. When he swiftly gets to his feet and grabs my hand, I almost cheer. He excuses himself to his friends, taking me along with him farther into the house.

"Trying to get me hard in front of everyone?" he asks, his voice rough.

"Um, maybe?" I say in my cutest voice possible. "I just want you to fuck me."

"Oh, I got that loud and clear."

Uh oh, is he angry?

"So you want me to fuck you?" he restates my intentions harshly, and I quickly nod.

"You're sure about that?" he asks, stopping in a hallway, facing me. I see the lust in his eyes and a thrill shoots through me. Hell yes, I think I've unleashed the beast.

I nod again, silently affirming his question.

He grabs me with one hand and swiftly pulls me into the closest room. As the light flickers on, I see a large pool table in the center, but the room smells musty, as if it's unlived in.

"Nobody uses this room much," he says, confirming my suspicion.

Gripping me, he lifts me so that I'm sitting on the edge of the pool table. The table is firm beneath my ass, though not the most comfortable.

He unzips his jeans and frees his cock, clasping it firmly with one hand while I gaze at the thickness. A drop of pre-cum glints in the low lighting and I lick my lips. Fuuuuck, I want him to stuff that in me immediately.

He pushes me back by the shoulder, spreads my legs open, and slides up my little black dress, exposing my pussy to his view. Rubbing his cock against my wet folds, he teases me, tapping the head against my clit and making me gasp. My head spins from how fast we went from zero to sixty, but I'm about ready to beg when he finally sinks his cock into me.

"Oh, my god" I cry out, my hips jerking forwards to meet his.

"Shhh!" he insists, using one hand to cover my mouth. I continue to gasp into his hand, unable to keep completely silent.

I realize the door to the hallway is wide open, and I stare out the door at a painting on the opposite wall while he fucks me relentlessly.

"Oh, god," I cry out weakly, his hand still over my mouth. His fingers dig into my flesh as he thrusts in and out, sending waves of ecstasy rippling through me. My entire body responds: my nipples harden and goosebumps cover my skin.

Every slap against my pussy makes a wet sound, and I reach a hand down between my legs to rub my clit while he pummels into me. Every touch, every part of me, is hypersensitive and attuned to him. My breathing is heavy as the thrill builds, drawing me closer and closer to climax.

And then, something unexpected happens.

Over Jon's shoulder, someone appears in the doorway. A tall, skinny man, who I briefly recall seeing at the party, but I don't remember his name.

Ooooh, shit. The titillation I get from knowing we're being watched keeps me quiet about him there. My inner slut loves that he caught us. There is something so dirty about being fucked in front of someone else.

I lock eyes with the man right as I climax. Crying out Jon's name, I'm louder than normal, wanting to put on a show for the guy.

Jon comes with a roar, and I feel him spurt deep inside me, painting my cave walls with his hot, sticky cum. I'm shaking and quivering in his arms as we both pant and sigh from the release.

The man stands there, watching us in shock for a few moments, before dashing down the hallway. I keep quiet, deciding it's better Jon doesn't know the guy was there.

Jon's cock softens inside of me, and as he pulls out, his cum leaks out of my pussy and onto the floor. He looks at it as he adjusts his clothes.

"It's all right," he promises, reaching into his pocket and retrieving a tissue before bending to wipe it up partially with his fingers and using the tissue to get the rest. When he stands up, he brings his cum-coated fingers to my lips. I immediately lick them clean before he demands it.

"Good girl," he murmurs and kisses me softly, tasting himself.

"I love you so damn much, Miranda," he whispers against my lips. Even though he tells me it all the time, I don't think I'll ever tire of hearing those words.

"I love you, too."

We finish straightening our clothing and head back to the party. No one has a clue what we were up to, other than the man who saw us. When I notice the guy standing near the Christmas tree, inspecting it, he and I make eye contact across the room. He gives me a slight nod and smile before looking at the tree again.

A zing of sexual delight zips through my core. I didn't expect the thrill of being caught to be so arousing.

Fuck, I think my inner slut wants to experience it again.

The End

CHAPTER 3

A FIESTY KITTEN GETS THE HARD BIRTHDAY SPANKING SHE DESERVES

My 31st birthday starts off shitty. I accidentally sleep through my alarm and have to rush around in a panic to get ready. Fuuuuck. I can't be late again this week. A new lawyer recently joined the firm and he's got a stick up his ass. The big boss told me we had to cool it with the office shenanigans, so nothing fun happens at work anymore—no spankings, no being tied up, not even being bent over the desks. Now I'm hella bored all day while I daydream about how I used to fuck my sexy older bosses.

My husband is still asleep when I leave for work, so I expect a happy birthday text when he wakes up. I get nothing from him until after lunch, and then it's a stupid GIF of a dancing eggplant. If he thinks I'm fucking him tonight after getting no happy birthday message, he's going to have one feisty kitten on his hands.

I get home earlier than he does, so I'll have plenty of time to work out my aggression before I see him. I'll go out to the garage and beat on the punching bag he recently installed. Exercising on my birthday isn't my idea of fun, but being exhausted from the workout is a better plan than being irritated all night. Last year's birthday was better. My husband had been out of town, but at least he had an excuse for not being home to celebrate it with me.

I'm grumbling to myself when I walk in the front door. I can't believe he fucking forgot my birthday. As I drop my keys on a side table something on the couch catches my eye. It's silver and sparkly. Huh, what the heck? I kick off my high heels, flex my toes in relief, and as I step closer, I figure out what it is.

It's a tiara.

A silver, sparkly tiara with fake jewels. It's gorgeous and not something you'd pick up at the party store down the street, so he must have pre-planned this. A lightness enters my chest and I laugh loudly. Fuck, it's just like Jon to leave me a tiara to wear on my birthday. That asshole probably knew I was getting cranky all day when he didn't wish me a happy birthday.

A note is on the couch next to the tiara.

When I get home, I want you wearing only the tiara and kneeling in front of the couch.

All my angst from the day immediately drains away, and my pussy buzzes. Well fuck yeah, this is more like it. My wonderful hubby has embraced his kinky side in the last couple of years, so who knows what nasty fuckery he's got planned. I'm sure it's going to thrill me, and filthy thoughts of being bent over the couch consume me. My nipples harden while my pulse quickens. Fuck, now I have to wait for him to get home, and instead of being irritable, I'm going to get more and more turned on.

Taking the tiara with me, I head to the bedroom and strip. Jon won't be home for a while, but he's ensured I won't be doing anything but thinking about what he'll do to me when he gets home. I don't put any clothes back on. I want to walk around nude and get more worked up while I wait.

He better plan to fuck me since it's my birthday. He's been exploring his dom side, but I doubt he'd just use me and leave me a wet mess on my birthday… except he knows how much I like that.

Fuck, what if he plans on making this a several-day event where he edges me until I have a massive orgasm after two days? Lust burns in my brain and all I can think about is being on my knees for him while he demands that I rub my clit until I'm mewling in desperation, and then not letting me come. Wait, the note didn't say I couldn't touch myself while I waited. Hrmm, but what if I do and that makes him decide to punish me and then he really does edge me?

My brain whirls with indecision, and my pussy clenches as wetness coats my inner thigh. My slutty pussy hasn't gotten the memo that she needs to chill out right now. I don't want to risk whatever Jon has planned for a few moments of bliss with my fingers.

I rest the tiara on my head and examine myself in the bedroom mirror. My wavy brown hair is in a long braid down my back and the tiara contrasts against it. It's sparkly, and feminine, and I adore it. Damn, I should wear a tiara every birthday. Next year, I can pull this out and tell Jon he's going to worship me all day.

I try to keep myself busy around the house to occupy my time, because I don't want to fold to my desire to sit on the couch, spread my legs, and massage my clit as I wait for him. I'd rather he be the one to touch me, to please me, to make me come.

When I hear the garage door, I scamper to the living room and position myself on my knees in front of the couch, facing the entry. The telltale beep of the car alarm alerts me right before he opens the door to the house. He can't see the living room from where he is, and his shoes clunk to the floor as he removes them. After that, I don't hear his footsteps approach, but the keys jingling gives him away right before he comes into view. My nipples pebble painfully as I shiver with goosebumps. Giving me the tiara and making me wait was an effective way to drive me crazy with desire. My heart races when our eyes meet. His blaze with lust that only feeds the raging fire that burns within me. He smiles, but when it doesn't reach his eyes, it tells me he's feeling very dominant.

My pussy pulses in response when he speaks. "Look at my good kitten waiting for me."

Licking my lips, I can only stare at him. I'll be the best kitten ever tonight if it gets me a wonderful birthday fuck.

"Kitten, kneel on the couch facing away from me."

I quickly obey him. Not being able to see what he's doing heightens my senses. His clothes rustle, and I can tell he's removing most, if not all, of them. He steps up behind me and the warmth on my back soothes me until he puts one hand around my throat, squeezing gently. He always does this to make sure I know he's in control, and the splash of wetness against my thighs tells me that my slutty pussy understands.

"Good girl."

He moves his hand from my throat and cups my ass, squeezing it harshly, and I gasp, not expecting him to be this rough. My pussy quivers for me when he massages my butt cheek. He applies pressure on my shoulder and I lower my head towards the back of the couch, presenting my ass to him.

"Did my kitten think she wasn't getting a birthday spanking?"

I try to answer, but a sharp smack on the ass makes me draw out my, "I don't knooooow," as I moan from the pain.

Another strike lands harder than the first, making me whimper, and he continues, pounding my bottom with the flat part of his hand. Each blow builds the heat in my core, and I'm groaning from the painful pleasure.

I lose track of how many times he spanks me, but he eventually slows his pace so that his palm glides across my cheeks instead of slapping them. My brain is fuzzy and I relax after the initial shock passes. His fingers slide along the crease between my ass and thigh, seeking my wet pussy. His finger is gentle when it slips into my opening, fucking me slowly. I close my eyes in bliss. Mmm, yes... this makes the birthday spanking all worth it.

The light touches turn more demanding as Jon increases the intensity. Fuck! His teasing is driving me crazy. When he removes his hand from my pussy and runs a fingertip over my puckered asshole, I groan, but he doesn't press in before sliding his digits back into my cunt. He finger fucks me faster until my hips buck forward, begging for release.

"Oh god, Jon. Fuck me... please?"

He chuckles in response, removes his finger from my pussy and runs his finger up and down my slit to torment me.

"Is this what you want?"

Shit, why won't he just give it to me on my birthday?

"Mmm, yes, but your cock."

My eyes pop open when he positions the tip of his cock against my wet pussy. Ohhh, yeah. It's happening! I grip the back of the couch, and he slams into me, pushing me forward. I squeal in delight as he starts fucking me with long, hard strokes.

My head spins and I want to prolong the fun, but I know I can't. The tightness of my inner walls constricts as the tension mounts, making me grind against him, trying to reach my climax. Pleasure radiates through my entire body, and he grasps my hips with both hands and pulls me back against him with every thrust.

I groan loudly as he continues his punishing pace. His balls slap against my clit with every downward stroke and I'm crying, "Oh my god," repeatedly, as I race towards my bliss. His cock throbs inside of me and I'm afraid he's going to come before me.

"Please," I beg. "Please make me come."

My words make him slow down. "It's my kitten's birthday and she deserves to come."

I moan, "Uh huh," as he circles his hands to my front, cups my breasts, and pulls at my nipples. Fuck! I clench around his cock and rotate my hips, trying to force myself to come.

"Rub your clit," he commands, and I slip my hand between my legs, seeking the swollen bud.

When he grabs my hips again, and slams his cock straight to my core, I cry out in delight.

He whacks against me and pants, "Rub harder."

I caress my clit faster and my hips rotate from the mounting pleasure. My body tenses as he drives into me over and over. He doesn't allow me any respite and my head tips back as I chant for him to fuck me.

"Come for me," he demands and my pussy convulses.

"Ohhh, god!" My orgasm hits as waves of rapture crash into me. I'm breathless as he pounds into my pussy, seeking his own release. I'm breathless when he finally groans and bathes my cave walls with ropes of his sticky cum. We rock together as we come down from our high, and he eventually slows down and pulls out.

I lie my head on the back of the couch as he sits next to me and pulls me into his lap. We're a sweaty mess and in need of a shower, but I cuddle close, enjoying the moment.

He adjusts my tiara and chuckles. "Did you enjoy your birthday spanking?"

I sigh in contentment and only murmur, "Mmm hmm," as my eyes drift closed.

He kisses my forehead. "I love you, kitten."

I peek up at him. "Hey, I'm a princess today. Not a kitten."

His eyes crinkle up and I can tell he wants to laugh. "I love you, princess."

"Mmm, better. I love you too."

We snuggle for a few more minutes before he asks, "What would my princess like for dinner?"

Oh well, now... a myriad of possibilities pop into my head. "Let's order teriyaki and then you can have me for dessert. You aren't done servicing me tonight."

His response of, "Whatever my princess wants for her birthday," warms my heart.

This birthday is pretty damn fabulous, after all.

The End

The FreeUse Office Toy

Hotwife Let Loose

Lacey Cross

Chapter 1

Work is going to be wonderful this week, I can feel it.

The office is going to be mostly empty.

Three of the lawyers are out of town, attending a conference together. The receptionist, Cindy, is off on a bingo cruise, and the paralegal is working from home for a couple of weeks. They switched the phones over to an answering service, so I don't even have to listen to them ringing all day. I'm going to rock out to music and do absolutely nothing.

To start the week off right, I'm running late on purpose since no one is around who cares. The office is dark and still. I glance at my cellphone to confirm what I already know—yep, I'm ten minutes late. I sashay past Cindy's desk and stick my tongue out at her empty chair.

Suck it Cindy. You're not here to raise your eyebrows in disapproval. It's just me and Mr. King all week.

I'm not sure why he didn't go to the conference, but it doesn't matter since he won't be bugging me, that's for dang sure. I don't think he even likes me; we mostly ignore each other.

He's got a stick up his ass anyway, and he messed up my job satisfaction when he joined the firm, so I dislike him on principle. The big boss, Mr. Jacobs, told me we couldn't continue our work shenanigans because of Mr.

King. No one fucks me at work anymore. Me and my slutty pussy are both unhappy with this development.

If only Mr. King was a little less attractive. He's in his mid-40s and hits all the right notes. He's fit, with yummy broad shoulders. His brown hair has a little salt and pepper starting at his temples, and those piercing blue eyes made my stomach drop the first time I met him.

Oh, and let's not forget his hands...

Mmm, yeah, those massive hands make me wonder what they would feel like rubbing all over my body. He's like candy in a candy shop that I'm not allowed to eat. Or, worse yet, the candy shop is actually closed and I can only peer through the window with longing and reminisce about the good ole days when I could gorge myself on all the candy I wanted.

He's all business, dammit. Yeah, work sucks. Now it's just a normal job again, and when I'm late, no one spanks me for it.

I put my lunch in the breakroom fridge and settle in at my desk. I daydream about the past and Mr. Jacobs noticing I was 10 minutes late. He'd call me into his office to 'discuss' my tardiness. My pussy hums to life and I can tell I'm going to be horny all day.

This is really all my husband's fault.

They promoted my wonderful husband at work and it requires more travel. Jon's on a work trip right now and he won't return for another week. We usually have some fun over video chat when he's traveling, but it's been nine whole days since I've had a real cock in me. It makes the lack of work-time sexiness more noticeable. Previously, I'd just fuck the guys at work if Jon wasn't available. Now, it's just me and my sad panda pussy having to make do with my fingers and toys.

Heh.

Maybe tomorrow I'll bring a toy to work with me and have a little fun whenever the mood strikes.

I slip my earbuds in and lean back in my chair. Since I don't get fucked at work anymore, I'm back to wearing my favorite black pencil skirts and a garter belt with thigh highs. The garter belt is my sexy little secret at work, and I'm glad I took the time to wear it today. I slip my heels off and put my feet up on the desk, crossing my ankles. I wiggle my toes, enjoying the freedom.

Hell yeah, this is the life.

I have little work to do today and could probably put it all off until tomorrow. The lawyers need to go to conferences and leave the office mostly empty more often. This is a fun way to spend my Monday.

I'm rocking out to some embarrassingly catchy music (that I refuse to admit to anyone that I enjoy) when I notice my instant messenger on my computer flashing.

Oops.

We're a small business and we use IMs to communicate. There's only one person this could be, and my fun Monday comes crashing down around me. Oh God, what does he want? I hope it hasn't been flashing for too long.

> **Please come to my office.**

I study the message for a moment. I'm not sure I have to go because he asked. Is he even my boss? No one outright said, "Hey, meet your new boss." Not that I'll be a bitch to him, but I'm too comfortable to move without a good reason.

I lean forward, grab the keyboard, and type to him.

> **What can I help you with? I'm in the middle of something.**

> **Get your feet off your desk and come to my office. Now.**

I jerk my head back and my heart rate speeds up. What the fuck? I drop my feet to the floor and peer down the hallway suspiciously. How did he know they were on the desk? Is he spying on me? Some kind of creeper? Now my fear is turning to anger. What right has he to be watching me?

Yeah, he and I need to have a little chat.

CHAPTER 2

Setting the keyboard back on the desk, I slip my feet into my heels and stalk towards his back corner office. I'm getting more incensed with every step.

It's not Mr. King's fault, but his office holds too many uncomfortable memories for me. I never enjoy visiting him there. He took over the back corner after Mr. Knight, one of the firm's partners, left. Mr. King replaced the furniture and redecorated it with light colors, and it looks nothing like it used to, but just walking the back hallway makes me think of times past...

Which makes me even crankier by the time I knock on his door.

His sharp, "Come in," doesn't put me in any better mood. I'm flushed when I open the door and prepared to do battle.

I only get a foot into the office before I halt. He's in front of his desk and leaning his sexy butt against the surface. Not that I ever looked at it before, I swear. I'm just guessing it's sexy.

His arms are crossed, and there is one chair in front of him. The second one, the one usually in front of his desk, is pushed against the wall. I immediately feel like I've been naughty and I'm about to get chastised. My pussy hums to life and my nipples harden while I imagine him bending me over his knee.

Well, this just got more uncomfortable.

I cross my arms to match his and raise an eyebrow at him. "What did you need me for? Or did you bring me here to tell me you were spying on me?"

The corner of his mouth twitches, as if he's trying to not grin. He studies me for a few heartbeats before he replies.

"Lets get one thing straight. I wasn't spying on you. You were listening to your music so loud you didn't notice me walk past."

His voice is firmer than I've ever heard it, which doesn't help the situation between my legs. My slutty pussy thinks Daddy King is going to spank her.

I force myself not to fidget.

"And second, I called you back here to make you an offer. Now, I'm not sure."

My pussy perks up and tingles at offer.

Jesus, my body is like Pavlov's dog, trained to think everything is sexual at work. This dude isn't bringing me back here to fuck me. My pussy needs to chill out, but it's tough. It reminds me too much of the past, when Mr. Jacobs would bring me to his office and offer me sexual favors.

A small voice in the back of my head chants, "Please be sexy times."

His eyes sweep over me from top to bottom and his gaze lingers on my breasts and hips. I flush even more and my pussy clenches. Ohhh, wait. I think it *is* sexual.

A rush of desire runs through me. I shift my weight to my other foot and straighten my posture, pushing my breasts out a little. When he's done checking me over, his eyes meet mine again. Why am I getting turned on? I don't even like this guy.

Since he didn't continue, I try to prompt him, but use my sexiest voice. "An offer?"

I mean, I don't have to like him to fuck him, right?

This would make work enjoyable again. I do this guy, then Mr. Jacobs can bend me over his desk whenever he wants. It's a total win/win situation.

His eyes hold a wicked glint, and he smiles. "Yes. I heard rumors about things that went on here before I joined the firm. If there is any truth to those, I was going to make you an offer."

My breath catches and my nipples harden even more. Someone's been spilling the beans about how much of a slut I am. My pussy throbs. Fuck, that's hot.

I can have some fun with this.

Smiling coyly, I slink towards the chair in front of him, swaying my hips. I gracefully sink into the seat and slowly cross my legs, letting the edge of my tight skirt ride up. I've upped my game. I'm not the naïve woman who started fucking my bosses over a year ago.

His gaze intensifies as he leans closer to me. I'm breathing heavily, and trying to play it cool. His voice drops to a husky whisper that sends shivers through me. "Are the rumors true, Miranda?"

Oh no, he's not getting me to admit anything without knowing what he's talking about.

"Maybe," I say seductively. "It depends on what you heard. I can only imagine what it could be."

I've never seen Mr. King like this before. He's always so serious and businesslike, but now? His lips twitch again as he considers me, but he doesn't speak.

Taking a deep breath, I lower my eyes to my lap, trying to look shy. "I have to be discreet."

I peek up at him and he nods. "Fair enough. I think we all appreciate discretion in situations like this."

Mmm. When you fuck me over all the surfaces in the office, you don't want me blabbing it around?

It's time to move the conversation along, since he obviously knows I'm a slut. I raise my eyes to his and keep my tone flirty. "I'm very good at keeping my mouth closed...or opening it. When requested."

He grins, his eyes crinkling at the corners, and my pussy tingles with need.

Shit, he's got a sexy smile. I swallow a little lump in my throat at the thought of him smiling at me while he takes my panties off and slides his cock inside me. Is it wrong I'm turned on by that image?

Mr. King stands and walks around to the back of his desk. He opens a drawer, pulls out a small black box, brings it to me, and holds it out.

Hmm, what's this?

I reach up to take it, but he doesn't let go.

"If you're as naughty as I think, open this at your desk and message me your response."

Oh, wow. I nod, unable to speak. My hands shake a bit when he releases the box to me. What does he have in store for me?

"Go look at it. Message me before lunch."

My cheeks heat as he watches me rise from the chair. "I'll let you know."

His eyes follow me as I leave. I try not to stumble until the door is firmly closed behind me and he can't see me.

I stand in the hallway, gathering my wits. What just happened? I thought he didn't like me.

I look down at the box. Pandora's got nothing on me. I need to find out what's in there, so I speed walk down the hall as fast as I can in a tight skirt and heels.

When I get to my desk, I set the box down and plop into the chair. I take a deep breath before opening it. Inside, I find a bullet vibrator, the kind that connects to a phone via an app. It's new and never used before. An envelope with instructions is also included, along with a note from Mr. King.

My offer is an afternoon of fun. If you want it, message me your agreement. Put the vibrator in after lunch. - Mr. King

Oh god, I want this.

I blush furiously, my heart fluttering. A thrill of anticipation runs through me and my panties grow wet. If Jon is okay with it, I'm going to take Mr. King up on his offer.

I type out a quick text message to Jon.

> Yeah, so you know how I said my boss hates me? Come to find out, he doesn't. He wants to play with me this afternoon. How do you feel about that?

It doesn't take long to get a response. The first thing he sends me is a GIF of a dancing eggplant. Yep, that's my goofy husband for you. He follows it up with a message.

> If it feels right to you, go for it. I expect all the details later over video chat. With you naked.

Of course he'd use this as an excuse to get me naked on video. He tries every night when we talk, and it works half of the time. Last night he told me he'd be able to listen better if my shirt was off.

News flash: He didn't.

I send him a kissy fish GIF and focus on the instructions. It's fairly easy to download the app and pair the vibrator with my phone. Mr. King included his username with the instructions and told me to give him controlling access once I set it up.

I spend a few minutes playing with the app and changing the vibration settings while holding the bullet in my hand. Within moments, I'm flushed as I imagine the different pulses against my clit. Okay, yeah, I need to put this away until lunchtime.

I squirm in my chair, trying to ease the ache between my legs and I message Mr. King.

> Yes, I accept your offer.

He replies almost immediately.

Mr. King

> Excellent. After lunch, prepare to be my freeuse office toy.

Wait, what?

Lust burns in my brain as I imagine what he could do to me as a freeuse office toy. He can't know I'm mostly submissive in the bedroom, since my bratty switch comes out regularly at work. The idea of being a freeuse toy pings the subby side of my brain. Once I'm in that mindset I'll do anything he asks.

I'm too distracted to get any work done. I spend my time before lunch daydreaming about wearing kitten ears and staying under his desk, lapping up all the cream I can.

Lunchtime can't come fast enough.

CHAPTER 3

When lunchtime finally rolls around, I'm too excited and force myself to eat. I need my energy for this afternoon, but who wants to think about food when they can imagine being fucked all over the office? Not this girl.

I'm in a daze by the time I get back to my desk and confused by the stack of files that appeared on my desktop since I left for lunch. There's a note on top and my heart races in anticipation as I read it.

Put the vibrator in and connect the app. Then I need you to copy all those files for me. I hope you're prepared to work this afternoon. - Mr. King

I eye the stack of files. Um, he better not mean *actual* work. If he thinks he's going to dictate a bunch of letters and expect me to type them up to get his cock inside me, he'll find out I'm a terrible employee.

Wait, who am I kidding?

I did exactly that to get Mr. Jacobs' cock inside me before. I snort as I remember dictating a letter while Mr. Jacobs fucked me. Mmm, yeah...fine, I can be a good office toy.

Because of my poor choice of the pencil skirt, I have to go to the restroom to get the vibe in place. My guardian angel should have warned me to wear a loose skirt today. I'll make it work, but something short and flowing would have been easier.

Once I'm in the restroom, I unzip my skirt and let it pool on the floor. I step one high-heeled foot out and spread my legs. Turning the bullet on the lowest setting, I slide my hand down the front of my panties and press half of the toy's length into my pussy. I've played with this type of toy enough to know the tricks. There's a perfect way to position it, so when I sit down it can almost touch my clit and still be partially inside me as well. That gives me the maximum fun and edges me until I'm crazy with need.

I'm both nervous and unbelievably aroused by what I'm doing. This is such an abrupt turnaround from how I thought my day was going to go. I pull my skirt back up and straighten my clothes before going back to my desk. The light buzz in my panties is a pleasurable tingle. It's a little distracting, but not bad.

I grab the stack of files and take them to the supply room where the copier is located. As I scan the files, every few minutes I have to stop as pleasure surges through my body. Little moans escape occasionally, and I imagine what it would be like to be doing this with an office full of people. What if someone heard me or I lost control? The possibility of being caught makes everything so much more exciting.

I can't help but fantasize about Mr. King's huge hands all over me, his skilled mouth, his cock teasing me, then thrusting into me. His control over me as I do everything he commands. The more I think about it, the more aroused I become and the vibrations in my pussy get more intense.

When the vibrator buzzes with a new pattern, I know he's controlling it. My heart races and my breathing becomes ragged. Suddenly, I'm very aware of how wet I am and I'm so close to orgasm...

Just as I'm about to tip over the edge, I hear Mr. King's voice in my head.

"Not yet, my freeuse toy. I'm not done with you."

He never said I couldn't come, but I don't want the afternoon to end before I get his cock inside me. I pull myself back from the edge. Ugh, that was close.

Shit, okay, concentrate Miranda.

My head is fuzzy as I copy the files. His control of the vibrator is making it almost impossible. I'm leaning against the copy machine and moaning when he startles me by pressing against me from behind. I was so involved in trying not to orgasm I didn't hear him approach. My heart pounds and my body hums with anticipation.

His breath is warm on my neck. "Keep copying."

Uh...really?

Fuck.

I open the top of the copy machine and switch the paper. I'm adjusting it to the guidelines on the glass while he unzips my skirt and pulls it down.

He fingers the lace top of my thigh highs. "Mmm, nice."

He uses his knee to nudge my legs apart. I shift my position to help him, pretending I had to move my leg as I reached for another file.

His fingers run over my panty-clad ass, and then down to my pussy. He pulls aside the edge of my panties so he can reach the vibrator.

Ohhh, fuck. I bite back a moan as he moves it from my pussy and presses it fully against my clit. The room spins and I grip the edge of the copy machine. The tip of his cock probes the entrance of my wet hole. Shit, he must have had his cock out when he came in here.

This is so amazingly filthy. I've never had sex out in the open in the office like this before. I'm rarely alone with the lawyers unless I'm in their office. Plus, him leaving my panties on makes it seem even dirtier, like he's using me and I won't come.

His cock is thick and long. I'm so turned on, my juices are flowing freely. He pushes the tip of his cock inside me and I whimper in response. He doesn't move for several moments, as if he's enjoying my warm wetness and the vibrations of the toy.

This is torture for me as I keep moving files to copy. I'm positive I'm making a jumble of everything. I'm not even sure I'm putting the right papers in the right folder. When I can think again, I'm going to have to go back through these.

Finally, he pushes himself further in. It feels amazing, and my hips instinctively rock in response. He eases deeper until the entire length of his cock is buried inside me, then pauses. I moan softly as I try to get my bearings and focus on the files in front of me. I feel the vibrator buzzing away, keeping my pussy on fire.

Suddenly, he shoves my shoulder down onto the copy machine and starts hammering into my pussy. I cry out from the sudden position change and my legs quiver. Pleasure ripples from my head to my toes. It's impossible to focus on anything other than his cock slamming into me and the constant vibration of the toy.

My eyelids flutter as I near the edge of orgasm, suddenly noticing my own muffled cries. I bite my lip as I'm bombarded with pleasure and I can't hold back any longer. I cry out as I'm consumed with a blissful and tumultuous orgasm that rocks my body, sending waves of rapture crashing through me.

I'm stunned when Mr. King wraps my hair around his fist and pulls my head back. He leans forward and bites my earlobe gently, sending a shockwave of surprise through me and a gush of wetness from my pussy. I whimper and moan as he keeps fucking me. It's been so long since one of my bosses controlled me like this at work. This is amazing. I'm helpless under his assault, and it's driving me wild as he fucks me through the waves of my orgasm.

Suddenly, he pulls out.

I'm gasping and can't catch my breath. I hear him zipping up his trousers, like he's putting away his cock. He slaps my ass and I yelp. I'm dizzy, like I've been spinning around in circles for several minutes. When I straighten up, my legs are wobbly. I can barely coordinate them and keep my balance.

His voice is gruff. "Get back to work."

I hear him walk away, whistling, and I stand there in shock for a few seconds.

Holy fuck. I don't think he came. In fact, I'm sure of it.

I'm in a daze as I pull my skirt up and straighten my clothes.

I gather the files and take them back to my desk. They get unceremoniously dropped in a pile as I slump into my chair. Only then do I realize the vibrator isn't buzzing anymore.

Oh, thank God. Maybe now I can calm down.

Chapter 4

I'm not sure how much time passes before I notice my instant messenger is flashing again.

"I'd rather be on his cock," I grumble as I go to the breakroom. We have a single serve coffee maker, so it only takes me a few minutes to make his cup. I'm halfway to his office when the vibrator starts again. I gasp and hold steady. Jesus Christ, I could have spilled hot coffee all over my hand.

I don't bother knocking. I'm ready to give him a piece of my mind.

Except...he's sitting in the chair in front of his desk and his cock is out. He's stroking himself slowly, and I'm mesmerized. I watch his hand travel up and down his length.

"Set the coffee down," he commands, and I set it on the desk.

His laptop is open and facing us, and I see a video paused on his screen. Was he watching porn?

His voice sounds normal when he speaks, as if it's the most natural thing in the world for his cock to be out and him stroking it in front of me.

"It's come to my attention you didn't watch the recent required safety training videos, so you're going to do so now."

Uh...

"Get on your knees."

Fuck, this is so damn hot.

He spreads his legs. I take it as a sign he wants me between them, so I kneel in front of him and look up, trying to avoid staring at his cock. He studies me, still stroking with one hand, and reaches over to turn the video on with the other.

A stupid safety training video comes on, the type I usually try to sleep through. He pushes my head down to his cock, and knowing he wants me to suck on it, I open my mouth.

He gathers all of my hair to one side of my head, leaving my neck bare on one side. I'm confused at why, but I'm too busy with his cock to really care. I run my tongue around his shaft, licking it and sucking it, taking him deep into my mouth. He tastes slightly salty and sweet, just how I like my men.

"Miranda, watch the video. You have a test to take afterwards."

Da fug? These training videos always have a test at the end to make sure you really watched, but suddenly it's clear he moved my hair to the side so I could see the video without it blocking my view.

He picks up his cellphone from the desk and fiddles with it. The vibrations of the toy in my pussy ramp up and my head spins while I suck on him and try to watch the video.

Jesus Christ.

I bob my head up and down his cock as I hungrily swallow every inch of him. Each swirl of my tongue around his shaft sends a thrill through my body, even though I'm pleasuring him. Every time the bullet between my legs shifts patterns, I moan louder and suck him deeper. I'm barely aware of the video playing in the background while I devour him.

Mr. King moans now and then, letting me know he's enjoying my service. I'm so close to coming, and I can feel him trying to hold back his own release, too. Twice, maybe three times, he holds my head still, as if he's trying to avoid coming. I sit there panting and trying to calm myself until he allows me to suck on him again.

The vibrations between my legs electrify me, making me gasp. With each pulse, my pussy muscles tighten and coil. I clench my thighs together and try to muffle my moans. I'm clinging to the edge, desperate for release, and I'm not sure how much more of this I can take.

He increases the vibration again. My eyes roll back as I feel my orgasm building and I struggle to remain in control. Oh God, I'm going to come! And then...

Moments before I orgasm, he stops me sucking on him.

I throw my head back and cry out. An all-encompassing surge of pleasure crashes through me. My pussy tightens as my orgasm intensifies, every spasm spiraling me higher until I'm screaming in euphoria. I rock my hips in time with the waves of pleasure, wishing I was riding his cock as rapture skyrockets me to a higher plane of pure bliss.

He turns off the toy right as the video ends, and I float down from my high. He puts his still-hard cock back into his trousers, takes a sip of his coffee, and leans back in his chair. His expression is smug and satisfied, and I can feel my face flush from my wanton behavior.

"Now go back to your desk and take the test. If you pass it, I'll give you a reward."

I blink at him.

There is no way in hell I'm going to pass. He stretches out his hand to help me to my feet, and I stagger up. Jesus, I'm going to need recovery time.

I can't help teasing him. "What happens if I don't pass?"

His eyes glint wickedly. "You don't want to find out."

Hmph.

When I turn to go, he smacks my ass. I squeak as desire shoots through me. Fuck, it's been way too long since someone has spanked me at work. I twitch my ass in his direction as I leave his office without looking back.

When I get back to my desk, I slump in my chair. Holy fuck, I just got off while watching a training video. Now every year, whenever I have to watch one of these stupid videos, I'm going to think about this.

I guess there could be worse things in the world.

I check my emails, and Mr. King sent me a link to the video and the test. Shit, I better get this done. I have a suspicion the reward is his cock inside me again, and I don't want to miss out on that.

I hunker down and concentrate as best I can with a buzzed pussy. The test takes longer than it should. I have to re-watch part of the training video. I'm not surprised since I was a little busy at the end there.

When I take the test, I get enough points to get a passing grade. Not bad, considering even on a good day, I usually barely pass. I spend too much time daydreaming while watching these videos. At least the quizzes at the end are simple, so it doesn't require too much concentration. Time to let the boss know!

Miranda

I passed the test.

Mr. Knight

Good. Come to my office in 15 minutes. Leave the vibrator at your desk. I have more work for you.

Oooh, more work. I have to fight the urge to reply with, "Yes, sir."

Miranda

Okay. See you then.

I'm too horny to actually work. After I remove the vibrator, I spent the rest of the time texting back and forth with Jon. I'm purposely vague to mess with him, and keep sending him fireworks emojis whenever he asks me how it's going or tries to pry for details.

When the time is up, I tell him I'll talk to him later and slip my phone into my purse. I love fucking with him when he's on a work trip. The few days after he returns home are always fun while he works his pent-up aggressions out on me.

Mmm, yeah. We're going to have a good time when he gets home.

Chapter 5

The walk to the office reminds me, again, of Mr. Knight. God, that all went wrong, but it was so much fun at the beginning. Mr. King might do a better job of working me up than Mr. Knight ever did. This vibrator and fucking me multiple times is more intense than anything I've done in the office during a workday.

Wait.

I almost trip and grab the wall to steady myself, and then laugh delightedly.

Oh my God, the Knight was replaced by the King.

I'm not so sure how much I like Mr. King yet, but I'm definitely warming up to him...or some parts of me are. He might be the superior boss, after all.

I'm still giggling as I open the door. He cleared his desk of everything except the landline phone. Oooh, I know where I'm getting fucked. Now, whenever I come in here, I'll think of the dirty things we've done on the desk. I'm okay with this.

I smile at him, and his eyes are dark with desire. He licks his lips before he speaks. "I want you to take off all your clothes." I start to shimmy out of my skirt before he raises a hand. "Slowly, then lay on my desk."

Oh, heck yeah. I can give him a good striptease. He's going to be putty in my hands by the time I'm done with him.

I give him a smile full of promise and a flirty, "As you wish," before I strip.

The first things to go are my shoes. I step out of my high heels, enjoying the way my arches feel. I flex my toes into the carpet and massage my feet. I unzip the side of my skirt and let it fall to the floor before I make a show of unbuttoning my shirt and tossing it aside.

My fingers fumble with the clasp of my bra as I spin around before I remove it, coyly hiding my exposed breasts. Since I'm wearing a garter belt and stockings, I use the chair to prop my foot up while slowly unrolling the silk down my legs one at a time. My inner voice is screaming at me to hurry the fuck up, while a secret part of me is enjoying this slow-burning game.

With each item I slip off, I can feel his eyes roam my body. I wiggle my ass at him as I take off my panties and garter belt. When I turn around to face him and let him see me fully naked, I take a deep breath before meeting his gaze.

Mr. King's eyes are blazing with desire and I can see his cock straining against his trousers. I'm being a tease, but can't help it. As I lay down with my back on his desk, the wood is cold against my skin, but it's not uncomfortable. I spread my legs, and he gets a good look at my pussy, before I cross my arms behind my head and give him a saucy smile.

"What do you plan to do with me, boss?"

He doesn't answer and starts undressing by removing his shoes. Yummy. Now I'm the one who gets the striptease.

He moves as slowly as I did, taking off his tie, shirt, and trousers. I can't help the jolt of anticipation when he's down to his boxer briefs. When he removes them, I smile at the sight of his cock. I was sucking on it earlier, but I still appreciate a sexy, naked man. Mr. King is definitely sexy. His cock is hard and ready.

Mmm, that is going to feel so good inside me.

When he walks around the desk by my head, I'm confused. Um, that's not where my pussy is. He takes the receiver off the landline phone and hands it to me. I stare at him like he's grown two heads. What the hell is up with this?

"I need you to call the maintenance company and ask them to come check out a problem with the air ducts. One of them doesn't seem to blow air and it might need cleaning."

He presses some numbers on the phone and the automated recording for the maintenance company comes through the receiver. Oh fuck. I hold it up to my ear and listen to them telling me I'm on hold for the next available representative as Mr. King walks to the end of the desk by my feet.

He hooks his hands under my thighs and pulls me down the desk until my ass is at the edge. My breath catches and a flush of heat spreads across my body. He lifts my feet and puts them on his shoulder. Shit, I want him and I want him now. I'm tempted to toss the phone to the side, but chances are he'd retrieve it and make me wait longer for his cock.

His hand glides over my wet and eager pussy, sending zings of pleasure through me. I whimper as he presses in and brushes his fingers against my clit. I stifle my moans. Oh no, no, no...how am I going to be on the phone while he's doing this?

He replaces his fingers with his cock, rubbing the head against my clit and coating his shaft with my juices. My head spins as the hold music continues to play. This is so fucked up.

Right when someone answers, Mr. King thrusts inside me and I press my lips together to hold in my cry of pleasure. Wait, what did they say?

The guy on the phone has to repeat himself. "What can I help you with today?"

Oh shit, um...

I try to keep my voice cheerful. "Yes, hello? I'm calling regarding a problem with one of the air ducts in my office. It doesn't seem to be blowing air..."

Mr. King keeps plowing into me, and I'm not sure what the person on the phone is saying exactly. Each hard whack of his cock is hitting a spot inside me that forces tiny peeps from me, and my hips buck.

The guy tells me someone can't come out today. I know I sound out of breath when I try to talk. "Yes, that's right. Yes, I understand it can't be fixed today, but could somebody come look at it?"

Mr. King is hitting the magical spot as he slides in and out of me. The pleasure is building and I can feel my orgasm approaching. The longer I'm on the phone, the more intense it gets. I slap my hand over my mouth to hide my moans and cries of pleasure.

The operator keeps asking me to repeat what I'm saying. I try to sound calm as I echo my request, but inside my head? I'm screaming. I finally get them to agree to send someone out tomorrow. When they disconnect the call, I can't reach the base and let the receiver drop.

I'm panting, and each thrust sends spikes of bliss through me. With my feet on his shoulders, I can't do anything but grip the edges of the desk and hold on while he jackhammers into me.

"Now, my little freeuse office toy, play with your tits while I fuck you until you scream."

His order sends a thrill through me. My mind spirals out of control as I reach up to my nipples, teasing and tugging them. Mr. King slams into me over and over, his grunts mingling with my moans of pleasure. His hands grasp my hips as he drives deep, and I'm so lost in bliss I can't control my body. I'm quivering and crying out as I edge closer to my orgasm.

Mr. King's pace speeds up, and the harder he fucks me, the faster I lose control. I'm moaning and gasping as I beg. "Oh yes! Fuck me! Oh please, I'm so close!"

My words spur him on as he fucks me relentlessly, and I'm shaking with every thrust. He's driving me to new heights of ecstasy.

Right when I am about to tip over the edge, he pulls out. I mewl out in distress. "Nooo."

He growls, "Don't worry. I'm not done with you," as he lowers my legs.

He helps me stand. My legs tremble as he turns me around to face the desk. This is good. He doesn't have to apply much pressure to get me to bend over. I grip the edges of the desk, comforted by the familiar pose as I wait for him to either spank me or fuck me. A hard smack on my ass makes my pussy throb and my toes curl. My ass clenches involuntarily from the sting.

Spanking it is.

He smacks my ass again and again, and each time, it's a bit more painful than before. Oh my God, this is what I've been missing. I need to be spanked whenever I misbehave. A warm fuzziness steals over me. I'm reveling in my submission when he twists my hair in his fist and pulls my head up. I gasp in surprise when he plunges his cock into me.

He groans, "You're mine now, slut. You'll do whatever I want."

I can barely form words as he pounds into me, but gasp, "Y-yes, sir."

It's true. I'll do anything he wants today.

He continues to say filthy things. "I'm going to cum inside you. Are you going to let me?"

I don't even have to think about it before answering, "God, yes. Please, give it to me."

My answer pleases him and he pants, "I'm going to fill you up, and you're going to be a mess when I'm done with you. But you'll love it, won't you, because you're just a filthy little slut who enjoys being used?"

"Fuuuck," I moan loudly. He already had me close to orgasm and the dirty talk keeps pinging my brain with shocks of delight.

He groans and I feel his cock spasm. "You better come now, my freeuse fucktoy. I'm about to, and then it's over."

Shit, he can't come first! I move a hand between my legs to rub myself. I frantically brush my fingers against my swollen clit and close my eyes. Hot waves build in my core and travel to my fingers and toes. A wave of euphoria envelopes me and my pussy clenches around his cock as I explode. I scream as I come, and a tidal wave of pleasure sweeps over me. I'm coming so hard it feels like I'm about to pass out from the sweet bliss as I shudder and buck against him.

I'm still riding the tsunami of pleasure when Mr. King climaxes with a roar. He fills me up, every thrust pushing his cum deeper as he empties himself into me. His grunts become louder and more desperate as his hands drive me forward, pushing me around like a rag doll with no resistance. I'm taken by a blissful numbness. All I can do is lay there and accept whatever he does.

I'm not sure how long he fucks me. I'm floating in a haze of rapture. At some point, he finally pulls out. He collapses into a chair with a groan. I stay where I am, too drained of energy to move. We're both silent for a few minutes, lost in our thoughts.

Wow, I can't believe what we did. If someone told me this morning I was going to fuck my boss, I wouldn't have believed them.

Once he's recovered, he gets up and pulls some moist towelettes from his desk. I watch him through my sexual daze. That's a little suspicious. He happens to have the same industrial-sized container in his desk that the other lawyers always kept around for cleanup after fucking me? It's not like they were left over from past fun times, because he replaced the desk. Though, maybe he uses them for spilled coffee.

It doesn't really matter, so I don't mention it.

As he gets dressed, I slowly stand up. My legs are still shaking. That was...beyond words. I can feel his cum dripping down my inner thigh, and I hold in a giggle. I'm a mess and his desk isn't much cleaner. Good. He can use the wipes to clean up his desk.

He picks up my clothes and helps me dress. We're both silent, but he's treating me tenderly as he holds onto each piece of clothing for me.

When we're both presentable, Mr. King leans in and presses a gentle kiss to my lips. "You were an amazing freeuse office toy," he whispers.

I can't hold back my giggle this time. That's the last thing I expected to hear today.

I give him a saucy grin. "Thanks, I had fun too."

The workday is almost over, so I give a dramatic sigh. "I guess I better go get some work done. My hard-ass boss might fire me if I slack off too much."

That makes him laugh loudly. "I think your boss might forgive you, just for today."

I give him a little wave and a, "Maybe," as I leave his office. As I close his door, I realize I've been thinking of him as a boss. I guess he can be. It's dirtier to assume he is, since fucking my boss seems naughtier than fucking another employee.

As I pack up to leave for the day, I have an intense feeling of gratitude for this twisted, yet pleasurable, experience.

God, I hope it continues.

When I'm in the car, I text Jon. It's game on with my dear husband.

> I'll be naked when we talk tonight, but you better have your cock out and stroking it when I call you. If you're a good boy, I'll tell you all about my amazing day and let you come.

I snort, drop my phone into my purse, and turn on the car. I'd bet a million bucks by the time I get home he'll have blown up my texts with promises to be the bestest boy in the entire world.

Yeah, he won't want to miss this story. I'm going to have some fun playing with him tonight.

The End

THE FREEUSE OFFICE TOY BONUS

THRILLING HER HUSBAND WITH TALES OF FUCKING HER BOSS

I'm naked and my body is burning with anticipation as I lie on my bed, waiting for the agreed-upon time for a video chat with my husband, Jon. Although I'm ten minutes early, I'm trying to restrain myself from contacting him. Shit, I need to be patient.

Jon is on a work trip and he gave me permission to be a freeuse toy for my boss, as long as I share all the juicy details with him. When we made plans for tonight's video chat, I warned him to have his cock out and stroking it when I call. I want my good boy to be nice and worked up, so I need to wait the full ten minutes.

I discovered through trial and error that my laptop is the best way to have some naughty fun while video chatting in bed. When I recline on my side with my head propped up on my hand, my other hand is free to explore my body or follow instructions from Jon. He's usually in charge of ordering me to touch myself, and I'm his good girl who follows his commands.

But tonight, he's mine.

I'm ready and the laptop is open, so I allow myself to drift into a pleasant daydream about the experience with my boss earlier today. My long brown hair falls against my bare breast, lightly tickling my sensitive skin. My nipples harden as I imagine my boss sucking on them. Work today was so fucking hot. Who knew that Mr. King was so kinky?

Mmm…. Today was easily one of my top ten favorite days at work. Jon will love the story when I tell him about it. I imagine his hands trembling as he strokes himself, desperate for all the details of what happened with Mr. King. I may even tell him…if he's lucky.

My heart hammers as I close my eyes and slide a hand between my legs. Jon's face fills my mind as I imagine him touching himself right now and waiting to talk to me. Having a husband who likes to share me is so fucking amazing. Since I got home, I've been a wet, needy mess, and a rush of pleasure surges through me as I brush my fingers against my clit.

As the minutes tick away, my fantasies become more detailed and vivid. I relive the moments with my boss and rapture swirls in my core as I quicken the motion against my clit. My breath fasters as visions flood my head of being bent over the desk or spread out across it on my back— the delicious feeling of being my boss's playtoy that he can use however he pleases.

I'm so lost in my fantasy that reality slips away…until my laptop's ringing jolts me with a start.

Yay, it's time!

I quickly remove my hand from between my legs, and I'm practically vibrating with lust when I open the video chat. Jon is true to his word; his cock is out, and he's stroking himself slowly. Ohh, such a good boy. A gentle pulse of pleasure ripples through me. I wish I were there, and it was my hand caressing his shaft and teasing him.

He lounges in his chair, laptop placed on a table beside him. I can see him from his knees to his face, and there's a twinkle of excitement in his eyes and a broad smile across his face. It's clear he's been thinking about the story I'm going to tell him.

My voice is laced with desire as I greet him. "Mmm, hi. Just as I wanted you."

He murmurs, "Yes, mistress," and a thrill of power runs through me.

Positioning my laptop far enough back to show me from the waist up, I brush my fingers suggestively over a nipple. Teasingly, I ask him, "Do you think you deserve to hear about my slutty day?"

He groans, "God, yes," and his hand movements speed up.

My body tingles, and I slide my hand between my legs again, caressing my clit. I don't need to tell him what happened if I don't want to. His glazed eyes tell me he's got an illicit fantasy of what he imagined transpired. But the actual story is too good—I have to share it.

My mind races as I imagine myself on top of Jon, grinding against him as I describe my day. "I had that vibrating toy inside me while I was making copies and Mr. King bent me over the copier."

I savor the memory, recounting all the details. Every word makes Jon stroke faster. His eyelids flutter shut as he moans. "Did you come?"

I slip two fingers into my wetness and fuck myself while picturing Mr. King's hard cock. I only give Jon a mischievous "Maybe."

"Fuuuuck," he moans, and I can tell he's loving my teasing him.

I consider telling Jon to stop stroking, just to torture him, but I want to see him come all over his chest. When he's this worked up, sometimes his cum spurts further than I expect.

I wet my lips with my tongue and keep talking. "You would've been so turned on if you'd been there. He had me completely naked on top of his desk. He pulled me to the edge and then put my feet on his shoulders."

Jon's leg muscles twitch as he moans, "Yes. God, yes."

Passion overflows from him, driving me wild with desire. My hips buck uncontrollably, forcing my fingers into my pussy deeper and edging me closer to a mind-numbing climax. My toes curl and my thigh muscles tremble. All I can focus on is the burning sensation inside me as I creep towards the brink of euphoria.

"He made me come so hard," I moan, remembering Mr. King's thick cock thrusting into me while he commanded and instructed me to do exactly as he pleased.

"Oh god, Mistress. Can I come? Please?"

Jon's begging is my favorite part when we play. I consider if I should draw out the pleasure by saying no, but the bliss spiraling in my core tells me I'm about to come. I want him to come with me.

"Answer something first. Do you want me to fuck Mr. King again?"

Jon looks enraptured, but he's still able to speak. "Yes...fuck, yes. Every day."

Well, now. A jolt of surprised delight hits me with his answer, threatening to push me over the edge. I hadn't expected him to say 'every day.' I'll verify he really means it later, but just imagining my boss using me every day this week is the breaking point.

I cry out, "Come for me," as I explode. My body trembles with exhilaration as I shatter into a million pieces.

Jon tugs on his cock, groaning loudly. I keep my eyes on him as I ride the waves of ecstasy. His eyes close and his muscles twitch. Three spurts of cum hit his chest as his body spasms with his release.

Once he comes, my mind drifts as I finger fuck myself through my orgasm. Every nerve ending is ignited and a wild rapture envelops me. The high I'm on is euphoric.

I slowly come down from it, savoring every moment as the ecstasy fades away. A contented sigh from Jon is enough to put me in a bubble of happiness. His dreamy expression tells me everything I need to know. He loved hearing what I did with Mr. King, which is exactly why our hotwife arrangement works for us.

"So..." Jon's voice rumbles through my peaceful haze. "Are you going to keep being your boss's toy this week?"

My need to control him faded with my orgasm, and I smile softly. "I don't know. Do you want me to?"

He leans in, and I'm met with an up-close view of his toned chest. After he leans back, he's holding a few tissues, which he uses to clean the cum off of him. Damn, I wish I was there so I could have licked it off.

He grins at me after he's done. "Only if you tell me all about it."

My pulse quickens at the thought of being my boss's freeuse office toy all week. A fire inside me blazes, creating an intense and urgent craving that I can barely contain. Oh, yeah, I want it.

I blow him a seductive kiss and purr, "I promise to tell you every single sordid detail."

Jon and I chat for a bit longer until he needs to turn in for the night. After I close the laptop, I flop onto my back and stare into space while my thoughts run wild.

It'll be just me and Mr. King in the office all week. Will he want to fuck me again?

Oh God, I hope so. The thought of getting spanked even harder than earlier today makes my pulse quicken.

Tomorrow can't come soon enough.

The End

Freeuse Gaming Night

Hotwife Let Loose

Lacey Cross

CHAPTER 1

I set the bowl of chips on the dresser so I can look in the mirror, and eagerly adjust my kitten ears. Adrenaline surges through me as I position the black headband just right and trail my fingers over my black collar with a silver open heart at its base. My brown hair is in a ponytail to keep it from getting messy. Apart from the ears and collar, the only other thing I'm wearing is a pair of black fishnet stay-up stockings.

Desire pulses in my core and I can feel the slickness between my thighs. I'm not sure where I'm getting my courage today, but I'm ready to be the ultimate slut. Hopefully, this will be a fabulous surprise for my husband, Jon.

Smiling to myself, I pick up the bowl and head to Jon's gaming room. As I get closer, I can hear laughter from the men. For the last few months, four of my husband's friends come over every Sunday to play a roleplaying game. My husband is the only married guy out of the bunch, and last week when I brought them refreshments, I heard them joking about how hot I am and how lucky he is to have me. Hearing them talk about me like a hot piece of ass gave me an unexpected sexual jolt, and I spent way too much time thinking about fucking all of them afterwards.

They don't know they're about to get lucky, too.

Jon never told them, but he shares me sometimes and gets off on knowing I've fucked other guys. He's even watched occasionally. A few nights ago, I jokingly suggested to him that I should offer myself to his friends on Sunday. His response was enthusiastic and the next thing I knew, I was getting railed over the side of the couch as he thrust into me vigorously. He demanded I tell him how hot it made me to think about fucking his friends. I came harder than I have in recent memory. At the end, he told me if I ever wanted to do it, I had his blessing.

My husband doesn't know that today is the day.

I pause at the door to the game room, and a low and pleasant hum of desire warms my blood. My hand trembles with eagerness when I knock to give them warning I'm about to enter. They're laughing at something, but when the door swings open, all laughter stops. Five pairs of eyes bore into me, but Jon is the only one I care about. I search him out at the head of the table and the appreciative gleam in his eyes tells me what I'm doing is more than okay with him. We'll see how fast I can turn the appreciation into lust.

I add an extra sway to my hips as I cross the room. "Figured you guys could use some snacks," I purr as I place the bowl of chips at the center of the table. Being bent over is my favorite position, so I lean over at the waist to make them think about fucking me like this. When Greg, the guy closest to me, tips back to examine my ass, the filthiness of what I'm doing makes my nipples tighten into stiff peaks. At least Greg is interested.

I grab one chip from the bowl, and when I straighten up, I eye Greg and try to be as suggestive as possible. "So, who wants me to feed them?"

There's a moment of silence, and my stomach tenses from worry. Oh shit, did I read the room wrong? Then Max, one of my husband's closest friends, speaks up, his gaze burning into me. "I do."

Yes! That's all the invitation I need. I feel my pussy buzz in response, already wet for what's coming. Taking a deep breath, I slink around the table, pausing briefly by my husband. I move in close to his ear and whisper,

"You'll get dessert later." His eyes darken with desire, and I give him an impish smile as I stand back up. I'm a dirty girl and I know how to get what I want. A satisfied and happy husband lets his kitten play.

I keep moving and stand next to Max. He tries to take the chip from my hand, but before he can, I hold it up in the air so he can't reach it. I'm close enough that if he turns his head, he could suck on my nipples.

Even though I'm wearing my collar to show my husband owns me, I feel sexy and powerful. "Open your mouth."

He complies and I lower the chip to his mouth, then pull it away, making him bite at nothing. His eyes never leave mine and the second time I bring the chip down, I let him eat it. Max smells of the outdoors, a combination of musk and earth, with the faintest hint of woodsy cologne. I love how he smells, and I can feel the electricity gathering between us. I give him a naughty grin, and just before I'm about to back away, I gently rub my leg against his. Excitement thrums through my veins. This is awesome. Jon's friends are under my spell. Today is going to be wild.

There's just enough space between Max and the guy next to him for me to bend over the table. The surface is covered with dice and miniature figures, and I sweep them out of my way as I press my breasts to the cool wood. One person makes a tiny squeak in protest, but I'm not sure who it was. When no one outright complains, I smile inwardly. That's right, you know this is a once-in-a-lifetime opportunity to get a piece of me. Who knows if I'll ever want to do this again.

Wait, why is no one touching me yet? Do I need to give them a golden invitation? I'm about to joke about me being laid out for them, but a hand brushes against the skin of my ass. Oooh, that's more like it. I can tell it's Max's hand, and I prop myself up on my elbows and smile at him over my shoulder. "Do you want to do more than touch?"

His eyes flit to my husband, and Jon states, "Do whatever you want, guys. She's offering, so take it. You might not get another chance."

See, even my husband knows this is a special occasion. My stomach flips from longing as I realize I'm about to get multiple cocks inside me—or at least I hope so. If someone doesn't fuck me soon, I'm going to make them all roll a d20 and hope for a high number. Anyone who rolls low doesn't even get to watch.

Max rises and positions himself behind me, his hands roaming over my body. All right, now we're getting somewhere. My breathing almost stops as he grabs my hips and pulls me against his hardness. His hands travel to my breasts and I lift slightly so he can slide underneath them, rolling and pinching my nipples and making me moan.

Knowing all the guys are watching is arousing, and I grind back against Max's cock through his jeans. Jesus, he needs to take his cock out and fuck me before I go insane. My husband's words to his friends about enjoying my offer still ring in my ears, and I throw my head back and sigh in pleasure as Max tugs on my nipples again.

He's pressed so close to my dripping pussy that there's going to be a wet spot on his jeans. I like the idea of branding him with my juices—a calling card of sorts. When Max trails a hand down my ass and slips two fingers inside my pussy, I moan and arch my back as he thrusts them in deep. God, I'm so wet and ready for more.

Max removes his hands just long enough to unbuckle his belt and unzip his jeans. A neediness pulls deep at my core at the sound of his clothes rustling. I peek at my hubby to make sure he's all right, and his hand's under the table. I can tell by the movement of his arm that he's stroking himself. Are other people rubbing too? I look around and all the men have their hands under the table. Well, fuck, that's hot.

Lust sizzles my brain and turns it into a buzzing mess of static as Max's cock slides along the length of my wet slit. He doesn't thrust in and I groan as he teases me. Wait, when did I lose control of the situation?

Max's voice is husky. "Is this okay?"

I assume he's talking to me. It's sweet that he's asking since my husband already gave him permission—especially since I'm the one who bent over the table willingly. It's not like I'm under a Compulsion spell. I want this. I glance at him so he can see I'm sincere. "Yes, now please fuck me."

He growls and then thrusts inside me without warning. I cry out, "Ooooh, fuck!" as his hands dig into my hips, holding on tightly as he plunges his cock in and out, faster and harder. Oh no, wait...he's going so fast he might blow his load before I come.

But this is why I wanted to do this. I was craving the feeling of being a fucktoy for men to use, and offering myself up to my husband's friends was an easy way to scratch the itch. There was never any guarantee I'd come tonight. I wanted to do this and be out of control.

My pulse quickens with forbidden longing as a sense of acceptance washes over me. I close my eyes and feel myself sinking into a submissive state, becoming a toy for them to use. Even if I don't come, my wonderful husband will take care of me later. The temporary desperation will be worth it since I love being treated like I'm only there for men's pleasure.

When Max slaps my ass, I cry out, and it brings me back into the moment. I'm moaning nonsense as he pounds into me. The breathing of the men around the table becomes labored as they're obviously getting a kick out of the show. Mmm, they aren't the only ones having fun—this is awesome and dirty.

Delight swirls in my core as Max hits a sweet spot deep inside me repeatedly. My head is turned towards my husband and I crack my eyes open to peek at him. The lust is clearly written all over his face. Oh, thank god. He's enjoying this. Seeing his expression is all I need to fully embrace the moment, and heat streaks through me as I moan loudly.

Max holds down one of my shoulders, pinning me to the table, as he jackhammers into my pussy. Oh fuck. Every inch of my body is alive with a frantic energy as I shift my hips to meet his thrusts. The table rattles and several of the figurines fall over. I really should have made them roll for initiative to see who got to fuck me first. The thought makes me laugh, but it quickly turns to a gasp when Max's strokes become wild.

I have nothing to hold on to, and Max is like a beast. I moan "oh god" continuously as I spiral higher and higher towards an orgasm. Max is a champ and he's lasting long enough, I'm going to come. Who knew he was such a rock star? I should have asked to fuck him months ago.

A second before delight overtakes me, my heated gaze locks onto my husband. Desire flares in his eyes and the roguish smile pulling up the corners of his mouth adds a layer of happiness to what I'm doing. Convulsive waves roll over me, and I let go.

I cry out as I explode around Max's cock. A bone-tingling orgasm consumes me as liquid fire streams through my body, and I shudder around his cock.

Knowing I came tips him over the edge. He pounds home and groans loudly as his body jerks, every muscle tight as he pours himself into me. It might just be my imagination, but it feels like ropes and ropes of sticky cum paint my insides as his cock pulsates and he unloads into me.

The joy skyrockets me to a higher plane. Everything becomes fuzzy around the edges, and I almost giggle from euphoria. I want every guy to take a turn with me until I'm glazed with cum. Hopefully, Max is just the beginning.

When my body stops trembling, Max pulls out and sits down. The room goes silent, as if everyone is stunned at what they just saw.

Even though I can barely think clearly, my eyes meet my husband's again. His voice is quiet but clear in the silence.

"I love you, Miranda."

I grin at Jon. His love gives me strength and I find my voice.

"Okay boys, who's next?"

CHAPTER 2

The room is so still that my query of "who's next" bounces off the walls.

I hear someone clearing their throat from the far end of the table and turn my attention towards him. Oh, it's Marty. I don't know him that well, but he's always been kind to me. He appears to be nervous and I want to reassure him this is just a game. Everyone will have fun if I have anything to say about it.

After seeing me willingly accepting anyone who wanted to shove their cock in me and Max giving me an enthusiastic pounding, you'd think he wouldn't be so shy. Hell, I really thought once the round started, they'd be lining up for their turn. For a group of gamers, they sure lack perception. I'm here—naked and bent over the table—someone needs to fuck me.

Hoping to give Marty courage, I keep my voice soothing. "Don't worry, I won't bite."

Or at least I won't bite tonight.

Marty pushes his glasses up his nose and clears his throat. "Can I go next?"

I want to giggle that he's asking, but I hold it in. He has this awkward-cute thing going on, and I don't know why, but it's totally doing it for me. My pussy hums at the thought of what I could do to this guy. I want to see if I can unleash the beast inside of him. That's me, Miranda: The Corruptor of Innocents.

Uncurling from the table, I set my sights on Marty and sashay towards him. With my kitten ears on, I feel like I'm stalking my prey. He's flushed and practically shaking—yeah, he's charmed me. I could be mean and make him do a persuasion check before he gets to fuck me, but let's be honest, he'd probably get a negative modifier.

I coo at him as I walk closer. "Oh yeah, it's your turn."

His cheeks redden even more, and his eyes are locked on my breasts as they bounce with each step. Being naked in front of others isn't an issue—I've done it enough—but this is a group of my husband's closest friends. I only fuck people he knows on special occasions, and being this exposed to guys that I'll see every week is filthy and erotic.

When I reach Marty, he looks so nervous I'm afraid he might hyperventilate. He needs someone to cast Calm Emotions on him. I give him a soft smile. "I want this just as much as you do."

I trail my fingertip down his cheek, and he shudders as I sweep across his jawline. Emboldened by his reaction, I give him a small push so his chair rolls backwards. Keeping my voice light but firm, I command, "Now, get your cock out so you can fuck me."

"Wait." My husband's voice makes me freeze, and I turn to him. Uh oh, he better not want me to stop.

Jon winks at me before announcing to the guys, "My sexy wife enjoys being used. Consider her your freeuse fucktoy for the next hour. Play with her all you want. The rougher you are, the harder she'll come."

Everyone pauses and takes in Jon's words. Oh, holy fuck–he's giving them freeuse of me. My brain fizzles and my thoughts won't line up. Scarlet heat warms my cheeks, and momentary shame washes over me until I push it aside. Jon just voiced my innermost desires, and I've never been more in love with him. He knows me so damn well.

My heart rate speeds up as I watch the men digest that I'm now their toy to use for an hour. I'm ready for them to fuck me, and if I'm lucky, it will be enough to satiate my wicked inner kitten.

The sound of Marty's zipper brings my attention to what he's doing. He pulls out a gargantuan beast of a cock, and my mouth drops open. Um… okay, I wasn't expecting *that*. It's thick and long, and I lose focus a little as I imagine him sliding inside me. What's this guy nervous about? If he knows how to wield that thing, he'll have women panting at his feet. I'll call him a Beast Master.

As I gawk at the monster, I swear it gets thicker. Fuck, I'm the one who's about to be panting if I don't get that monstrosity inside me. He grips the base, and I lick my lips.

He still looks hesitant when he clears his throat before speaking. "If you're a freeuse slut, come ride my cock."

Animal hunger takes over as I face away from him and lower myself onto his cock. Sinking down, I hold in a gasp from the intense pleasure as his thickness stretches me. Jesus Christ, how does he walk with this hanging between his legs? I try to keep my breath steady as I work my way down his shaft until he's all the way in. Every inch of him massages my cave walls, sending tendrils of bliss through me. Holy fuck. Thank god this guy is the second one to take a stab at me. I needed Max's cum to lube me up for this.

Marty kisses my shoulder, and I shiver. He whispers in my ear, "Are you okay?"

"Mmm-hmmm," I murmur as the room blurs. It's difficult to actually think, but I haven't passed out from rapture… yet. I don't bother to tell him that he's not supposed to ask if the freeuse slut is okay. I'm not sure I could even form the words if I tried.

A crunch from the end of the table draws my attention. One guy has a handful of chips. What the hell? The chip-eating dude's name is Ian, and when he gives me a goofy grin and pops another chip into his mouth, my laughter turns into a groan as Marty flexes his hips and presses further inside me. Oh yeah, this is going to be good.

As I glance around the table, I realize my mistake at sitting with my back to Marty. All the guys are staring at me with lust. My nipples pucker into sharp diamonds and I suddenly feel feverish. I look at my husband last, and Jon's pupils are wide with desire. He knows my facial expressions when I fuck someone with a massive cock, so he can tell Marty's got some impressive equipment that I just planted myself on.

When Marty grasps my hips and rocks me against him, I close my eyes and welcome the delight. I assumed I'd have to lead us, but he's gotten a taste of power and it's gone to his head. He takes charge and I love it.

My hands claw at the edge of the tabletop as he lifts me up, forcing me to ride him. It's not nearly as rough as Max's pounding had been, but it still has its own delicious flavor. Every time I slam down onto his cock, sparks shoot through me.

I chant, "Fuck me... fuck me..." and since my eyes are shut, I don't realize that someone moved close to us until I feel a hand on my tit.

My eyes fly open and I see that it's Ian. He kneels next to us and nuzzles my breast, savagely licking and sucking on my nipple. I moan as he caresses the other breast, gently at first, and then rougher. I want to lose myself in the moment, so I close my eyes again and slip a hand between my legs to rub my clit. My fingertips brush against Marty's length as he slides in and out of me. Shit, this is fucking amazing.

Ian continues to tease my nipple with his tongue. When he bites down gently on the sensitive peak, I whimper and rub my clit faster. The pleasure builds and I can tell this will be another powerful orgasm.

I steal a look at Jon, wanting to see his reaction. His hand is under the table again. Mmm, nice. I love that he's touching himself.

Writhing in Marty's lap, I moan louder and link my gaze with Jon's as I imagine the view from his perspective. He's watching me take a massive cock from his friend, while another friend is sucking on my nipple. The fact that Jon loves me living my best slutty life is why our marriage works as well as it does. And fuck if I don't enjoy every minute.

Ian puts his hand between my legs and takes over on the clit action while Marty bounces me faster on his cock. A surge of heat rushes through my core. I'm going to come any second. My toes curl and I moan loudly as I'm consumed with pleasure.

My brain blanks out as the rapture overtakes me. The entire room disappears, and I scream when my climax hits. Bliss ripples from my fingers to my toes, and I barely notice Marty's cock pulsating and unloading into my pussy. I keep pounding down on him, trying to savor every moment.

When I come down from my high, Ian moves away from me. I collapse forward, resting my forehead on the table. If I tried to talk right now, it would probably come out as gibberish.

The sound of Ian's whispered, "Holy shit..." makes me turn my head towards him. His face is flushed, and he's licking my juices off his fingers. My pussy spasms around Marty's softening cock and Ian grins around the finger in his mouth. All his concentration is on me.

I know who is planning to use this object next.

CHAPTER 3

I quirk my lips at Ian and arch an eyebrow, curious to see where his confidence will take him. Marty slips out of me, and I'm ready to be used again. I want one of them to take control and really turn me into their freeuse slut.

Ian stands and motions towards the floor. "Get down on your hands and knees like a dirty whore so I can fuck you from behind."

Oooh, bingo. Ian has hidden depths.

Heat flares in my pussy again, and I waste no time assuming the position he demanded. While I get into place, Ian drops his pants to the floor. His cock springs out, and my mouth waters. Ian has a slender but long dick, and I can't wait to have him inside me.

Someone scoots his chair next to me, and I peer over to find Jon gazing down at me with pride and love. I smile at him and then realize I can see under the table and all the guys have their cocks out. Damn, this is so hot.

Ian kneels behind me, grasping my hips. I wiggle my ass at him, begging for him to slide into my pussy, but he takes his sweet time and caresses my butt cheeks. Fuck, he might be paying me back for making him nervous before.

When he finally pokes my soaking wet pussy, I inhale deeply as he enters me. This is different from the deep thrusts of Marty, and I moan as Ian hits new pleasure spots inside me.

Jon reaches down and strokes my hair, calming me as Ian slides deeper inside. I peek up at him, loving that my husband is comforting me while I get fucked by someone else. Oh, there will definitely be dessert for him later.

Greg saunters over, his cock sticking out of his unzipped jeans. He doesn't take them all the way off, and I shiver from arousal as he kneels in front of me. He squeezes his cock and pushes his velvety hardness against my mouth. I part my lips and he presses it against my tongue. I can taste the salty, earthly flavor of his desire. Mmm, this is heaven. Two cocks in me at once is one of my favorite things, and Ian starts a slow, teasing rhythm that's guaranteed to drive me crazy.

I lap at Greg's cock, pretending he's the tastiest treat in the world. If I'm lucky, he'll give me some cream. He moans and bucks his hips, sliding his cock to the back of my throat. I relax as much as I can to take him all the way in. Knowing Jon is getting off on watching me with his friends makes everything so much hotter. I twirl my tongue around Greg, and he holds onto the sides of my face, dragging my head up and down his shaft.

Ian speeds up, and my body tingles in delight. I moan around Greg's cock and suck on him, wanting to bring him to the edge. Since Jon only gave us an hour—which seems oddly specific, but maybe he's in game master mode—I want Greg and Ian to come fast so someone else can join the fun.

Greg wraps my ponytail around his fist and holds me still while he thrusts in and out of my mouth. Mmm, he enjoys being in control. I hollow out my cheeks to increase the suction, trying to give him all the pleasure he can stand. His cock swells and throbs against my tongue a second before he groans and blows his load. Salty liquid spurts against the back of my tongue.

Fuck, yes, this is hot. I lick him clean, wishing I could purr in contentment. He gave this kitten what she was craving.

As Greg withdraws, Ian's thrusts become more aggressive, and I almost lose focus as he hits that delightful point deep inside me. Oh god, he found it fast. Pleasure spirals through me, and when he smacks my ass, I whimper and almost come.

I'm momentarily distracted as another cock finds its way into my mouth. Mmm, there will never be a shortage of dicks to please.

I force myself to focus and look up to see Max kneeling in front of me. How the fuck did he get hard again so fast? It's like a Regeneration spell.

Max wraps his fingers around my ponytail, guiding me on and off his cock. A warm, musky scent fills the air, a tantalizing mix of masculine sweat and arousal. Ian matches his speed, and I roll my tongue around Max, reveling in the sensation of being ping-ponged between two cocks.

Someone else kneels next to Max and the next time Max's cock pops out of my mouth, I turn my head to suck on the other guy's cock. It's Marty again. Holy hell, the guys are coming back for seconds already? Wait...is Marty's cock even going to fit in my mouth? It's thick and long, and I try to relax my jaw as he nudges against my lips.

Marty doesn't force his way in, and I'm grateful as I adjust to his size. Ian speeds up, and Max moves a hand underneath me to rub my clit as Marty's cock slides to the back of my throat. Holy fuck, they're going to overwhelm me with desire.

Max presses down on my clit, and I gasp as Ian hits that magical spot again. I'm overcome, and my eyes tear up as I near the edge of ecstasy. When Max grazes my clit roughly, the tension inside me explodes. I scream as a white-hot climax shatters all my senses. The cock stuffed down my throat muffles the sound.

Wave after wave of pleasure consumes me, and my brain turns to mush as I shudder and my pussy clamps around Ian's cock. With each pulse, Ian pounds into me and I dig my fingernails into the carpet, holding on for dear life.

Ian cries out with his orgasm, and his cock jerks inside me, filling me with warmth. Marty pulls out of my mouth without coming, and Ian collapses against my back, pinning me down to the ground. I try to catch my breath as stars twinkle behind my eyelids. Once all the guys are done using me, I still want to take care of Jon, so I can't pass out from bliss. He deserves everything he wants tonight.

Ian rolls off me, his breathing still ragged from his orgasm. As the room comes back into focus, I look at my husband. Jon's eyes twinkle as he mouths, "Love you."

"Thank you, guys," I murmur, before blowing Jon a kiss and a wink, hoping he realizes how fucking great this was for me.

Max's voice is husky as he stands over me. "Oh, Miranda, we aren't done with you yet."

Oh, yay. Bring on more cock!

I almost giggle. Okay, yeah, so I'm loopy from all the orgasms. Shifting onto my back, I spread my legs as an invitation to whoever wants to use me. If I have my way, I'm going to fuck every guy at least twice before Jon gets his dessert. This is the best Sunday game day ever.

CHAPTER 4

The guys murmur together for a moment and I squint up at them. Um, hello...wet pussy down here waiting to be used. What're they doing?

When the clatter of dice hit the table, my eyes widen. Are they rolling for something? Am I the something?

Jon speaks up. "Okay, Miranda, everyone rolled above a 12, so you're going to service them again in order." Jon motions around the circle. "Ian, Marty, Max, and Greg."

What the hell, is he just making up rules as he goes? Why above a 12? Shit, what do I care—I'll service them all happily. The thought of being used again is exhilarating, and I arch an eyebrow as the guys shift into position: one man in front of me, and the other three surround me. Well now, this just got interesting.

Ian is the first to kneel by my head, and I greet him with a smile and open my mouth wide to accept his cock. Marty lines up to use my pussy, and Max and Greg each kneel to take a nipple and pinch them until they're stiff and aching. Ian slides his shaft into my mouth, and I moan around Ian's cock as elation floods my senses.

When Marty pushes into my pussy, my noises turn into a groan of pleasure as he stretches me with that massive cock. With Max and Greg tugging at my nipples, I'm already halfway to another orgasm, but when Ian pulls out of my mouth, I speak up.

"Mmm, fuck me like I'm a dirty whore."

Jon's voice rings out in his game master voice. "Freeuse sluts don't get a choice."

Marty moans, and the other guys tweak my nipples. All the sensations spellbind me deliciously. When the combination of pleasure and pain mix, it makes everything brighter, more alive.

Ian holds on to the edge of the table so he can get leverage to fuck my throat. Ohhhh, shit. This is wild. My brain fogs as Marty pounds into me. Max and Greg twist my nipples and bring me to the brink of exploding.

Ian sinks deep into my throat, and I almost gag. When he holds still, I know I need to relax to take him down my throat and not choke, so I take a deep breath through my nose and try to swallow around his cock. Ian groans and plunges in and out, hard and fast. Jesus, I love this.

Marty continues slamming into my pussy, and the sheer thrill of it all is too much. I spiral towards another orgasm. As my body trembles and my back arches, the guys cry out and all come at once: Ian shoots down my throat, Marty blows a massive load in my pussy, Max's warm ropes hit my tits, and Greg glazes my stomach.

When Marty pulls out of me, I'm so overwhelmed I can't think clearly. Someone flips me over onto my hands and knees again, but my legs are so shaky I fall flat to the ground. Holy fuck, that was a lot of pleasure at once.

Max's voice is gruff. "Miranda, we're not done."

Um...what? They all just came again. Are they all chugging Potions of Vitality?

As I crack my eyes open, I realize he's rubbing his cock to harden it again. Oh yeah, he's planning to use me some more. Mmm, this is awesome, but I hope he's fine if I just lie here for this one. I couldn't move if I tried.

Max spreads my legs and grazes his cock against my pussy. *Just like that, perfect.* He covers my body with his, and I'm slick with so much cum that he slides in easily. Max's cock isn't as big as Marty's—let's be honest here, whose is?—but he's thick, and every inch of him massages my cave walls. Holy shit, this is going to be fantastic.

Jon kneels beside my head. Uh, is he going to fuck my mouth in front of his friends? I mean, bring it on, but this seems unlike him. When his warm hand presses against my head and he strokes my hair soothingly, I know something else is up.

Jon leans down and whispers in my ear. "Do you trust me?"

Do I trust him? Of course I do. Jon is my rock and my best friend. There's nothing I wouldn't do for him.

When I murmur, "Yes," Jon runs a fingertip down the bridge of my nose and then applies pressure against my lips. I open my mouth willingly, and Jon's finger slips into my mouth. I curl my tongue around him and make a big deal of sucking on his finger to entice him to put his cock down my throat. God, I wish he really would make me suck on his cock in front of his friends. I want him to claim me and prove that I'm all his. They might use me, but it's with his permission, and he's all that matters to me.

As Max fucks me, every thrust makes me peep out little sighs and moans. Jon removes his finger from my mouth, and at some point, the pleasure becomes one long orgasm. Ecstasy washes over me, and everything takes on a dreamy quality.

I giggle from the rush when Max blows his load deep inside me. He groans as he spasms and jerks, unloading more cum to mix with all the other guys'.

When Max pulls out, Jon speaks up, his voice loud and clear. "Game over, everyone. Miranda's had enough."

Ohhhh, that's sweet. I want to tell Jon I love him, but I'm too loopy to talk.

As the guys tuck themselves away and start tidying up the table, Jon picks me up and carries me to the couch. As he lays me down, I try to get handsy with him and he bats me away from the hardness under his jeans.

"Kitten, behave."

I pout at him. *Fine, I'll be a good kitten...for now.*

Jon walks his friends out the door, and their chorus of "Thank you" warms me. When Jon comes back, he has a bottle of water and a banana. He watches over me, making sure I drink and eat. After I finish the banana, I murmur, "Love you," to him again.

Jon kisses my forehead. "I love you, too."

I expect him to fuck me now, but he leads me to the master bathroom and starts the water to fill the tub and adds in my favorite vanilla-scented bubble bath. He strips off my fishnet stockings and removes my kitten ears before helping me into the tub. As the warm water envelops me, I rest against the edge and sigh with contentment. This is perfect. Jon washes me with a loofah and massages my shoulders while I hum with happiness. Being used and taken care of is the best.

After the bath, Jon wraps me in a warm cotton robe and guides me to our bedroom. He changes into his pajamas while I collapse on the bed, ready to drift off to sleep.

Jon keeps me awake by propping me up with pillows. "Drink some more water."

When I roll my eyes at him, he arches an eyebrow and gives me a warning tone. "Kitten."

Fine, fine. I'll behave. But when is he going to fuck me?

I take a few more sips, and when I set the water bottle on the dresser, Jon lies down next to me and pulls me into his arms. Mmm, best husband ever.

As he strokes my hair, I whisper, "Thank you."

Jon chuckles. "For what?"

I give him a coy smile and a quick kiss. "Oh, I don't know...maybe for letting four of your friends fuck me until I practically pass out from pleasure? And then you bring me upstairs and help me take a bath...without fucking me like I know you desperately want to."

I slide my hands down to his hard cock and rub him through his flannel pajama pants to prove my point. Jon pushes me onto my back and opens my robe before kissing his way down my neck and breasts. I moan when he lingers on each nipple. Fuuuck, this is what I was waiting for.

As his lips trail lower, he pulls off his pajama pants. When his tongue brushes against my clit, I hunger for more than he's giving me, and he holds my hips down so I can't knock against him—he's such a tease.

Jon continues to lick and suck on me, and my entire body thrums with need. When his tongue finds my entrance, he traces around the edge, and then slips inside me. Mmm, Jesus, even though I took a bath, this seems dirty, tasting me after his friends filled me up. But it's so damn hot.

Jon murmurs against me. "Kitten, you taste so fucking good."

Ohhh, now that's even hotter. As he flicks his tongue faster against my clit, I buck my hips against him, eager to come again. Jon holds on tighter, controlling me as he brings me to the brink. When he nibbles on my clit gently, I scream as I come undone. Delight pulses through me, and I shiver as he keeps licking me while I ride the wave of bliss.

When my body settles down, Jon climbs onto the bed and nudges my legs apart. He's finally going to fuck me!

"Did my Kitten enjoy all the cream she got tonight?"

"Mmm, you know I did." I love it when he talks dirty to me.

"That's because you're my slutty freeuse wife who wants all her holes filled."

Even though I didn't actually get all my holes used, he knows I love it when he talks this way to me. I moan and arch against him, trying to get him to fuck me. "Yes...god yes, I'm such a slut who loves being covered in cum and used."

When he plunges into me, I gasp as he fills me. I love how every guy's cock is different, but Jon feels natural inside me. We fit together perfectly.

Jon pins my hands to the bed above my head and fucks me slow and deep. This is so different from what happened with the other guys, and I tilt my hips up so his cock rubs against my G-spot. Ohhhh, fuck. As my core warms again, I wrap my legs around him and moan.

Jon speeds up and kisses me deeply. When I taste my juices on his tongue, it turns me on even more and I get close to the edge again. Holy fuck, how is that possible after today? I try to grind against him faster and he releases my hands so he can grasp my hips and hold me still.

"You're mine."

I love it when Jon gets all possessive after I fuck other guys. "Yes, yours," I moan.

He pounds into me harder. Delight ripples through me, and when his eyes lock onto mine, the love I see on his face makes me fall apart.

I cry out as another orgasm rips through me like wildfire. Mindless ecstasy floods me as I thrash and moan. Jon doesn't let up. Every time I think the rush is over, he hits a new spot inside me that adds to the euphoria. I shudder, pinned underneath him as my body is wracked with joy.

"Fuck, kitten, I'm going to come."

Jon fucks me faster, knocking the bedframe against the wall as he chases his own release. His cock jerks and he blows his load deep into my pussy. I moan as his warmth fills me. He fucks his cum back up into me, unloading everything he's got while I float in a haze of pleasure.

As our bodies settle, he collapses next to me, out of breath. "Holy shit, Miranda, that was crazy."

Oh, I totally agree. Today was so wild, and I'm glad he enjoyed it too. "Mmm hmm, I loved it."

Jon pulls me close, kissing my forehead. "Just remember, no matter how many cocks fill your holes, I'm the only one who gets to keep you."

His scent is reassuring as I snuggle against him. "I wouldn't have it any other way."

This is the life: tons of cocks filling me up, love, and cuddles with my wonderful husband. I can't believe he let me fuck his friends, but damn, this was the best game day ever. I'm going to make this happen again, even if it's just once a year. Hell, maybe next time I'll make Jon write it into the game, and if they win the campaign, they get to choose which hole.

If they lose...well, I'll just tell them they really don't want to lose and keep the punishment a surprise.

The End

Freeuse Gaming Night Bonus

A Freeuse Toy for My Husband and His Friend

Two weeks after Jon's gaming buddies fucked me senseless, he's demanding his own freeuse night. I'm hardly about to say no.

As soon as we've finished eating dinner, Jon pushes me to my knees on the cold linoleum in the kitchen. "Take my cock out, Kitten."

An ache between my legs makes me shiver from desire as I reach for his fly. This is going to be hot as fuck. When I have him exposed, I lick my lips in preparation. His cock is already hard and pulsing against my palm as I grip the base.

I'm his freeuse fucktoy, and he didn't tell me to use my mouth, but he's not trying to stop me either. I give one long lick from his balls to the tip of his shaft. The texture of the skin is smooth, making it easy for my tongue to explore and savor every inch. I've sucked on his cock so much, the taste of his pre-cum is familiar, yet never fails to turn me on even more. He shudders as he takes control and applies pressure to my head, urging me to take him in my mouth. I wrap my lips around him as I bob my head up and down, swirling my tongue.

Whenever I agree to be a freeuse slut, my fantasies involve tons of orgasms for me—but that's not always what happens. We'll see what Jon wants tonight. He's in charge and I love giving up control.

He fucks my mouth slowly, and each thrust makes my brain fuzzy until all I can think of is giving him pleasure. The ache between my legs grows more and more intense, and I shift on my knees to relieve it. I have a sneaking suspicion he isn't planning on letting me come tonight. Ugh, I hate the idea and love it at the same time.

He's still thrusting in and out of my mouth leisurely when the doorbell rings. Uh...are we expecting anyone?

Before I can get up, Jon grasps my ponytail and pushes his cock further in my throat. I moan as I swallow him down, relaxing as much as I can. Yeah, who cares who's at the door? I just want him to keep using me like this all night.

The doorbell rings again. Shit. He pulls out and saliva runs down my chin. "Go get the door, Kitten."

My brain isn't connecting with his words and I glance up at him, confused. He tilts my chin up. "Be a good slut and see who's at the door. Whoever it is will take advantage of your freeuse mouth or pussy. Do you want that?"

Ooooh, who is here? I don't answer him because I have to see who it is first. I rush to the door and open it wide. Standing on the front porch is my husband's friend, Steve. He relocated to another state last year, so it's been a long time since we've seen him. I fucked him once with Jon's blessing and won a bet that got me a trip to a poly resort—those were fun times.

I squeal in happiness and launch myself at him. He smells like peppermint and I want to gobble him all up. Oh yeah, I'll be his freeuse slut too.

Steve grabs my ass and pulls me to him, laughing. "Hey, Miranda, it's been a while."

I'm not interested in small talk. "Shut up and fuck my mouth."

I hope he knew he was coming over to use me—what a greeting if not. Mmm, maybe I'll get to come tonight after all. My pussy tingles, and I can feel my panties growing more wet as I plaster my body against his.

His eyes light up at my offer. "God, yes," he mutters, and we tumble into the house. He closes the front door, and I sink to my knees as Jon walks out of the kitchen. Jon's cock is back in his pants—boo! The men greet each other, laughing like this is totally normal. They need to shut up and use me soon.

Jon pulls my shirt off. "Kitten, open your mouth for our guest."

I'm not wearing a bra and my nipples pebble in the cool air as my entire body buzzes with lust. I open my mouth wide, eager to do as I'm told. Steve stares down at me for a moment and unzips his jeans. His cock is out in a second and he doesn't waste any time thrusting it between my lips.

I moan around him as he pushes all the way to the back of my throat. Steve's cock tastes slightly sweet, with a hint of an unfamiliar muskiness that reminds me I'm not sucking on my husband.

Jon and Steve talk about Steve's trip like I'm not even present with a cock in my mouth. "So, how was the drive?"

Steve's voice is breathy as he answers and continues fucking my face. "It wasn't too bad. I'm not used to the traffic around here anymore."

I swirl my tongue around the head of his cock while he pumps into my mouth. Each thrust sends sparks through my body, and I hum with delight. Jon moves closer, pulling on my ponytail so my neck bends back. My moans draw a hiss from Steve as Jon pulls me off his cock. I don't care what they talk about or do—I love this.

I look up at Jon, and he gives me a wink. "Make sure our guest is pleased."

He releases my hair and the boys continue their conversation as I suck on Steve's cock again. Jon slides a hand around me. My skin sizzles as he caresses and kneads my breast, pinching my nipple, then smacking my tit. The stinging sensation radiates down to my pussy. Damn, I hope they will take mercy on me and fuck me soon.

When the conversation switches to the weather, I whimper as I bob up and down on Steve's cock. He withdraws from my mouth, surprising me. Hey, that was my lollipop! I know how to be a good slut and make sure they both enjoy my services. Trying to get them to fuck me, I purr at them, "I can be a good fucktoy for you both."

Jon pets my hair. "That's nice, but I just want to chat with my friend. Be a good slut and keep sucking him for the next hour. Then if I feel like it, I'll make you serve me again. Is that clear?"

I'm assuming he's not really going to make me suck on him for an hour, but there's just enough doubt in my mind to embrace the fantasy. My pussy is soaking wet and I'm so turned on at being reduced to nothing but a toy that I have to take a deep breath to stop myself from begging for more.

"Yes, Sir," I reply, and wrap my lips back around Steve's cock.

Steve sighs and thrusts his cock deeper down my throat. I want him to fuck me hard, but I have no control over that—he's in charge, not me.

I don't know how long the guys talk, but my mind drifts and all I think about is how badly I want a cock inside my pussy. I'm quivering with lust the longer he face fucks me. The taste of Steve's salty pre-cum and his unique musk turn me on even more. I'm a filthy slut who's willing to be used however they want, and the fact they want to chat instead of fucking me switches my brain off. I'm just a mindless hole.

When they decide to sit down in the living room, Steve pulls out of my mouth long enough to sit in the armchair. "Come here, Miranda, suck my cock again."

I stay on my knees and crawl towards him. When I get close, he pushes my head down to his cock. He slips into my mouth and down my throat. How has this guy not come yet?

As I suck him deep, Jon turns the TV on. What the hell? Steve holds onto my ponytail, rocking me back and forth on his cock. He murmurs something about a football game that I ignore. I suck faster, trying to make him lose interest in the TV. It doesn't work, but he spills pre-cum into my mouth.

The game playing in the background and the rhythmic motion of my head lull me into a trance. I could do this all night. When I sense Jon behind me and his hand caresses my ass through my yoga pants, I moan around Steve's cock. Oh god, please let him fuck me.

As if reading my mind, he slips his hands under the waistband of my yoga pants and peels them, and my panties, down to my knees. His fingertips are rough as he traces my skin and fondles my ass cheeks. I moan, and Steve tightens his fist around my ponytail, forcing me to bob on his cock faster. It's fucking delicious having two men play with me. I swear I could come from just this.

Jon slides his fingers between my legs and caresses my pussy. I mewl around the cock in my mouth. *Fuuuuck, yes, please, use me.* I wiggle my ass at him and he teases my slit before sliding one finger inside. Oh shit, I'm not going to last long at this rate. He fucks me with his finger before adding a second, and I suck on Steve harder as euphoria rolls through me. My clit aches and I squeeze around Jon's fingers, silently begging for him to push me over the edge.

When Jon slaps my ass, I almost come. Holy hell, this is intense. I close my eyes, giving all my concentration to the cock in my mouth and Jon's fingers. I rock against Jon's hand and moan as Steve drives his cock deep into my mouth. When Jon pulls his fingers out of me and spanks my pussy, I almost explode. My head spins as they both touch and caress my body. It's almost too much pleasure. My thoughts narrow to a single point as my core winds tight and I try not to orgasm. Jon usually demands that I ask for permission to come. I don't want to be punished for coming, but my mouth is too busy to ask if I can.

Jon groans and lodges the tip of his cock against my pussy. *Mmm, yes!* When he slams into me, I buck my hips and squeal. They jostle me between them like a rag doll, fucking my mouth and pussy as I groan from pure euphoria. The pressure builds, and I wonder if Jon will allow me to come. Maybe if I'm a good fucktoy, he'll let me.

Steve groans as he grips my head tightly, thrusting into my mouth with long strokes. How's he still going—and how are all of Jon's friends fucking champs?

Jon starts hammering into me, and every thrust hits a pleasurable spot inside me that threatens to make me lose my control. I moan in bliss and relish being their toy to use. Every slap against my ass and pussy sends ripples of delight through me.

The sound of their labored breaths and moans drive me wild. Fuck, if they keep this up, I'm going to lose it. I clench around Jon as I try to contain the pleasure. When Jon smacks my ass again, I yelp around Steve's cock in my mouth before finally giving into the rapture.

I scream and my body trembles with wave after wave of pure ecstasy. Sucking and bobbing faster on Steve, hoping to make him come deep inside my mouth.

They both continue thrusting into me, sending shivers down my spine as I writhe under them. Jon comes first, and feeling him filling me up, pushes me over the edge once more. My throat clamps tightly around Steve and he growls loudly as hot cum floods my throat. I lick Steve's cock until every drop is gone.

Jon pulls out and the room spins. Collapsing onto the floor, I stare at the ceiling, floating in a warm paradise. That was fucking incredible.

Jon pulls my yoga pants and panties back up, and I giggle. Oh yeah, I'm a slut. He turns off the TV before scooping me up in his arms. I love how he always takes care of me. He cradles me, carrying me to the couch and holding me close when he sits down. "You all right?"

I beam at him. "Never better. You?"

Jon chuckles and exchanges a glance with Steve. "Fucking fantastic. Good seeing you, man."

We all relax for a moment, basking in the peaceful afterglow. When Steve stirs, he smiles at me. "That was insane. I've got to go, but thank you for the incredible evening, Miranda. I hope you'll let me visit again before I head back home."

Jon's voice rumbles through his chest. "Text me when you've got time this week. My freeuse kitten might need more cream."

I giggle and snuggle closer to Jon as Steve heads out. When we're alone, Jon kisses my temple. I can tell he's happy, and it warms my heart.

I adore being his slutty freeuse kitten, and I love that he's willing to share me.

The End

THE FREEUSE PLAYTHING

Freely Used for Christmas series.

LACEY CROSS

CHAPTER 1

It's 8:05, and I'm sitting in my car in the parking lot of the lawyer's office I've worked at for years. I'm already late, so another few minutes won't matter. I should have just called in sick. My mood is particularly low today.

It's a dreary morning, and the rain is an annoying mist that I know is going to coat me as soon as I step out of my car. I picked up a latte from the local coffee stand this morning, and I blame the coffee for my mood. My usual cafe shut down last week, and the new place is serving swill.

Sighing, I give up. As I get out of the car, I swear the mist makes me damp instantly. Yep, called it.

I need to just go in to work and forget about my boring life. I'm thirty-four years old, and if I'm not careful, I might blink and be forty-five, still working at the same firm. Fuck, what am I doing?

Jon and I decided a year ago that we didn't want kids yet, and we went through the process to freeze some of my eggs. We're not sure if we're ever going to want kids, but now we have some options down the road if we need them. I always assumed I'd take a few years off if we had a kid, but is this going to be my life now if we don't? Working here forever?

Grabbing my purse and lunch sack, I scurry across the parking lot and into the building. The receptionist, Cindy, has an uncharacteristically huge smile on her face, and I don't want to deal with her happiness this morning.

I force a tight smile and greet her with a cheery, "Good morning," as I continue down the hallway. I wish I could say I felt as chipper as my tone, but I'm an emotional mess this morning, and I don't like how grumpy I am. Is it time to move on?

I've been considering finding a new job, and maybe my mood means it's time to pull the trigger. There's just one problem. I make a lot of money here, and it would be near impossible to find a job that pays as well. Come to find out, if you fuck all your bosses, they make sure you're happy with your salary. That was never my intention when I started fucking them six years ago, but it's been a nice perk.

The sexy stuff ended a couple of years ago, which might be part of my job dissatisfaction. A new lawyer, Mr. King, joined the firm, and I had an amazing week of being his freeuse office toy.

Then, a week later, they opened up a position for an office manager, and they hired a woman named Bonny who ended up being a stickler for rules. I don't know what Bonny heard, but her first meeting with me included information about not fraternizing with people in the office. The new policies put an end to all the fun times at work. Somehow, I doubt Cindy got the same talk.

I just need a change of scenery—maybe a trip. It's the beginning of December, so it's not the optimal time to book a vacation, but perhaps after the new year, Jon will take a weekend getaway with me. Some vacation sex should boost my spirits.

Just as I settle into my chair and slide my purse into my desk drawer, Cindy saunters over to me, wearing a mischievous grin. "Have you heard the news?" she asks.

I like Cindy—I really do—but I'm not in the mood for games this morning, so I turn on my computer and give her my serious tone. "No, tell me."

Cindy's eyes light up with excitement. "When I arrived at work today, everyone was in a meeting in the conference room with Bonny."

She's got my attention now, and I tip my head, interested. "Really? Do you know what it was about?"

"Yes and no," she replies, still smiling. "But when the meeting was over, Bonny packed up her desk and left."

My mind races with possibilities. "Is she gone for good?"

Cindy nods triumphantly. "Yep, she was fired."

Cindy and I may not see eye to eye all the time, but our shared disdain for Bonny's changes has bound us together in animosity. Cindy didn't like how she couldn't leave early whenever she wanted anymore, and I was annoyed by not being able to fuck the lawyers. Not quite the same thing, but this new development won't break either of our hearts.

My desk phone rings, and as I answer, Cindy gives me a little wave and departs. I spend the next few minutes dealing with questions from another law firm about a bounced email. When I finish, I'm still in a daze, contemplating the implications of Bonny's sudden departure.

I take a sip of my coffee, now oblivious to its unpleasant taste. I could fuck my bosses again if we all wanted to, but do I? And more importantly, would Jon let me?

It's been over a year since I've slept with someone else. Jon and I never said we were finished with me being a hotwife, but once easy access to my bosses' cocks was gone, I was content to snuggle up with Jon at home instead of hunting for other men to fuck. It's not that Jon isn't satisfying me, but lately our love life has been growing stale again. He's not in the mood as often anymore, and I blame stress from his job. He's only five years older than me, but I know stress can dampen a man's libido.

Jon might be okay with less sex, but lately I've been running to grab a sex toy whenever I'm alone in the house. A girl's got needs, and mine seem to be increasing right when his are decreasing. Whose bright idea was it to mismatch women's and men's sex drives? Fucking human biology.

I spend my morning fantasizing about the good old days when I'd sashay into work late and receive a spanking as punishment. What if I could have that again?

My pussy is already soaked when lunchtime rolls around. I settle in at a table in the breakroom, clutching a bottle of water and a container of leftover pasta. But before I dig in, I send Jon a text.

Miranda

> So...can I fuck my bosses again?

I follow it up with a puppy GIF with pleading eyes to sweeten the deal. I'm not expecting him to turn me down, but if he even hesitates, I won't do it. We're in this together, or I'm out. He texts back immediately.

Jon

> What about Bonny?

That wasn't the response I hoped for. I wanted him to be thrilled and then ask about the specifics.

Miranda

> She was fired today, and I don't know why. This is all my idea. No one asked that I fuck them. I wanted to talk to you first.

Shit, I should have waited until I got home to have this conversation with him. I take a sip of water, intending to suggest we discuss it later, when a message with an image attached pops up. It's a picture of my husband's slacks, focused at his crotch. Rusty—the nickname my husband gave his cock—is evidently hard beneath his pants.

Jon

> Rusty approves of you fucking your bosses, and you know he makes the decisions around here.

My sudden laughter makes me spit water over my pasta. *Damn, Miranda, smooth move there*. I grab a paper towel and reply.

> Well, my pussy says she wants to be filled up by someone besides her owner. Are you in agreement with Rusty?

His reply makes my body hum and my heart rate speed up.

> Go to town. Have fun, Kitten, and fill up on some fresh cream. You can tell me all about it while I fuck you later. Text me when you have some news.

Look at that, just talking about fucking my bosses again has Jon ready to go to pound town. Bonny should have left months ago.

> Thank you, my love!

It's time to find Mr. Jacobs and offer myself to him. He's the big boss; it's only right he gets first dibs.

Chapter 2

I want to surprise Mr. Jacobs, so I don't ask to speak with him first before showing up at his office door. Straightening the hem of my pencil skirt, I adjust the front of my pink blouse and try to calm the butterflies in my stomach. I'm glad I chose this outfit today, since I'm also wearing sexy lace underwear and a garter belt with black stockings to make myself feel good. If Mr. Jacobs gets to see them, I'll consider my mood brightened.

He calls out, "Come in."

I straighten my shoulders and sway my hips as I enter. I'm flushed and hope my face isn't as pink as my blouse. It's been way too long since he's bent me over his desk, and just seeing him behind it makes my nipples harden.

I'm not the same naïve woman who once sat before him and negotiated how fucking all the lawyers here would work. Now I'm a woman who knows how to get what she wants. And this slut wants Daddy Jacobs's cock inside her as soon as possible.

Mr. Jacobs is in his late 50s, and his hair is more salt than pepper these days. He wears it well. I've definitely got a kink for men in charge. His usual poker face shows his surprise when, instead of sitting in a chair, I walk behind his desk and perch on the edge next to him. My flirtatious smile blossoms slowly as I cross my legs, letting my skirt ride up. The edge of my stockings shows, and I notice his gaze flick down towards my legs before returning to look me in the eye.

Oh yeah, I know what Mr. Jacobs likes. We're playing my game now.

His voice is stern. "I was about to call you in here. We need to talk."

I lean forward, knowing it puts my cleavage on display, and walk my fingers up the front of his white button-down shirt. I fiddle with the top button, pretending that I'm going to open it. He's not wearing a full suit, but he still gets my pussy buzzing. He doesn't need to wear a jacket and tie to make me want to fuck him.

"Do we?" I pout. "I can think of better things to do with our time now that Bonny's gone."

Mr. Jacobs's face darkens. Oops, did I push him too far and he's going to scold me? Mmm, wait, I like what he does when I misbehave. This is going to all work out just fine.

Mr. Jacobs doesn't disappoint. In a deep, commanding voice, he orders me, "Up and over, slut."

Liquid pools in my center, and I quiver with excitement as I roll off the edge and turn around so I can bend over his desk. I lift my hips and press my ass toward him as he stands. He expertly unzips my skirt, and I sigh in delight as it drops to my feet. I'm getting whiplash from how quickly my sucky day has turned into the best workday in months.

He plays with the edge of my stockings and glides his fingers up my garter belt until he reaches my ass. His voice is rough as he says, "Nice."

I step one high-heeled shoe out of my skirt and spread my legs for added stability. He leaves my panties on, and I brace myself with my hands flat on the desk right before he smacks my ass cheek. I hiss with pain as his palm connects, and he leaves a stinging spot on my bottom. The hiss transforms into a moan as he caresses the silky fabric over my throbbing flesh, soothing the ache.

"Is this what you want?"

My thoughts are foggy with desire, and I moan, "Yes...no."

He chuckles softly at my obvious uncertainty. "You need to learn a lesson."

Lesson? The only thing I need to learn is how his cock feels sliding inside me again.

He rubs the wet patch of silk across my pussy, causing a delightful tingle to course through me. I thrust my hips back, seeking his fingers. I'm already addicted to the feeling of him between my legs again, and I haven't even had his cock yet. He should have fired Bonny the moment he realized it meant he couldn't fuck me anymore.

When he presses his fingers down harder, I whimper and sway my hips, grinding against his hand.

"I think I'm learning my lesson really well," I purr at him. "I'm a quick study."

He laughs darkly. "Class hasn't even begun."

What is he talking about? I look over my shoulder at him the moment he spanks me again...hard. I yelp in shock and reach forward to grip the edge of his desk to prepare for more spanking.

He rains down slap after slap on my tender cheeks, and I'm lost in the painful pleasure as the world becomes hazy. I'm fast approaching the point where I'd do anything to please him.

My moans echo through the room, and when he strokes my pussy again, I'm frantic to come. I can feel the pleasure building in my core. Just a little more...

When I'm seconds away, he moves his hand and steps back so he can sit in his chair. I groan from displeasure. What's he doing? He needs to fuck me. Wait, I can ride him just as easily. I stand up and face him, resting my tender ass on the desk. I'm radiating with desire, and all I can think about is getting his cock inside me.

"Like I said, we need to talk."

His voice is surprisingly calm for a man who's sporting a massive hard-on through his slacks and a slight sheen of sweat on his forehead. Someone is worked up, and it's not just me.

"Mmm…less talk, more action," I coo and make another move towards the buttons on his shirt.

He clasps my wrists together and holds them firmly. "I'll tell you what's happening."

Why is he being difficult? I'll beg if I need to. I give him my most seductive smile. "You could tell me while you fuck me…I'm fantastic at taking *dick*-tation."

When his cock twitches and his jaw flexes, I know I've almost got him.

Before I can celebrate my win, he regains control and leans back in his chair, his eyes intense. "I wanted to bring you in here for an offer."

Oooh, an offer? "Okay. I'm listening."

When I relax and he can tell I won't pounce on him, he releases my wrists. Hopefully, this is an offer for his cock, or he'll have a cranky employee on his hands.

He pulls a business card from his desk drawer and hands it to me, and I study it, not comprehending what I'm looking at. It's a thick, black card with shimmering silver lettering. All the card says is "Plaything Resort," along with a phone number and email address.

"What is this?"

He smirks indulgently, and my pussy quivers with frustration.

"That's your Christmas gift from all the lawyers in the office, if you want it."

Can't he just be my Santa and I'll polish his North Pole?

"Okay, but what is it?"

"It's a weekend at a private sex resort where you can be a freeuse plaything for all the men there. Jon can go with you if he wants."

Wow. I look at the card again and a thrill runs through my veins like electricity from surprise and delight. Wait… I hesitate a moment, and I'm about to tell him that Jon wouldn't want to be used by a bunch of men for a weekend, but he seems to read my expression.

The corners of his mouth twitch. "Jon can watch. I know he likes that."

Mmm, yeah, my dear husband gets off on watching me be a massive whore. The thought of multiple guys at a freeuse resort using me makes my core heat, but I don't want to appear too eager.

"This is an interesting gift..."

Mr. Jacobs gives a self-satisfied smile. "Talk it over with Jon. If you still want to be fucked at work after you go, we can talk."

I want to argue that visiting the resort won't change my desire to be fucked by all our lawyers, but I keep quiet. I can play this game.

I slip the card into my bra and bend over to retrieve my skirt from the floor. "Okay, but I hope you realize what you're missing out on right now."

He caresses my ass after I stand up, and his voice is husky. "Believe me, Miranda. I know. But take a few weeks and think about whether you really want to start this up again."

His eyes seem to twinkle. "We might not be so easy on you this time now that we know what you're willing to do as a freeuse office toy."

Ooooh, fuck. Mr. King spilled the beans on all the filthy things I did for him back when I was his toy for the week before they hired Bonny. If I ever get to fuck him again, I'm going to give him a hard time about that, but I can't be too angry since it sounds like I'm going to get some thrills because of it.

"Yes, sir," I reply as I zip up my skirt. "I'll find out what Jon thinks about the resort."

I can feel Mr. Jacobs's gaze on me as I exit his office. As soon as I shut the door behind me, my body quakes with desire. Fuckity, fuck. I need a cock inside me, and now I have to work all afternoon while I'm turned on.

I take the business card out of my bra and study it. Hmm, if the resort is as lavish as this card is, this could be an exciting weekend. I'll have to see what Jon wants to do.

CHAPTER 3

Jon was all for a trip to the resort. We planned with Chris, the owner of the resort, to visit the weekend before Christmas. They had a cancellation, and I jumped at the chance. My pussy immediately got wet thinking of all the men I'm going to fuck. I even bought a new black bikini to wear in their hot tub and heated pool.

Chris talked to us about the resort and asked for our safewords. We also filled out forms about our sexual likes and dislikes. Jon will be at my side to watch over me, but it's nice to know the resort takes our safety and pleasure seriously.

After that, all I had to do was wait for the trip. The days crawled past and I got more and more turned on. Once Mr. Jacobs found out I was going to the resort, the lawyers at work started teasing me and brushing their fingers along my hand when I'd bring them paperwork. Those jerks knew exactly what they were doing.

I was getting a second dose of lust from home as well. Once I told Jon about the resort trip, we were fucking nonstop, every evening after work. He bent me over every surface in the house and made me beg, but then abruptly three days ago he stopped touching me and told me I'm not allowed to come until we're at the resort—the sadistic bastard. But that's why I love him.

It's fine. The day of the trip is finally here, and this hotwife is going to be stuffed full of cock soon. The resort is a few hours from our house, and I spend a large portion of the drive rubbing Jon through his jeans while he's behind the wheel. I'm trying to get him to pull the car over and fuck me before we get to the resort. It doesn't work. My man has learned restraint as he's aged, and he loves sexually tormenting me.

An hour into the drive, I bring up something we need to discuss before we get there and I'm trying to fit three cocks in my mouth. "Hon, you know what's going to happen this weekend, right?"

He blows me a kiss while still paying attention to the road. "Yes, my wife is finally getting her dirtiest gangbang fantasy fulfilled while I watch and count how many orgasms she has."

Whoa, he's going to keep track? That's hot.

I giggle. "Well, yes, that—but also, this is probably a once-in-a-lifetime opportunity. I'm going to embrace it and go wild."

Jon reaches over and squeezes my hand. "I wouldn't have it any other way, Kitten."

My heart flutters in my chest as a feeling of warmth steals over me. Yeah, I love my man.

I let my mind wander during the rest of the ride, and I suppress a giggle as I remember the Christmas party Jon threw for me a couple of years ago. This could be my chance for a do-over. I had a fantasy of having a train of twenty men on my ass, but I was afraid to actually go through with it. I've only had a few encounters with groups of men, the most notable being the conference room party with the four lawyers and then a crazy night when my husband's gaming buddies were over and I offered myself to them.

For the previous Christmas party, Jon set up this elaborate plan to make me believe that all of his friends were fucking me, when in reality, it was just him. He got me nice and subby by tying me up and making me wait. By the time the party started, I was in subspace and ready to believe anything he said. It was an amazing experience to realize at the end that Jon had orchestrated everything for me, but ever since then, I've been thinking about how I want the real thing. I want all the men's cum inside me. It may not be twenty guys this weekend, but I'm prepared to embrace a real gangbang.

As we pull up to the wrought-iron gates of the Plaything Resort, Jon rolls down the window and punches in the code the owner gave us into the keypad. The gates creak open, and he smiles at me.

"Kitten, you ready for this?"

I've been ready for this weekend from the moment Jon said he'd love to see me being a submissive slut for a bunch of men.

"Absolutely. I was made for this resort."

He places a warm hand on my leg and smiles. "You are. That's why I married you."

Oh God, as if. He didn't know how big of a slut I was until after we'd been married eight years—hell, I didn't even know—but the fact that he loves my dirty side is what's made our marriage so amazing all these years. Jon fucking me all over the house in response to the resort offer proves that maybe I need to keep fucking other men. I enjoy my possessive husband when he seems to be on a mission to prove that only he knows exactly how to please me.

I peek out the windows as he drives slowly down a long driveway to a gorgeous white house. There are tons of Christmas lights on the trees and bushes, but they're not currently turned on. I bet this place will look magical once it gets dark. I'm practically bouncing in my seat from a mixture of excitement and being horny. Jon chuckles at my enthusiasm as he parks the car next to an elaborate fountain in the middle of a circular driveway.

Before we get out, I lean across the console to kiss him and murmur, "Thank you for loving me, you big hornball, and thank you for allowing me to keep being your slut."

He takes advantage of my closeness and pulls me in for a deep kiss. As our tongues twine together, my core trembles with desire. Mmm, do I really need to fuck twenty guys when I have Jon for a husband? I rub his cock through his jeans again and moan as it pulses against my palm. Well, except he enjoys sharing me, and I've had more sex in the last two weeks than I've had in months. It's clear that my slutty ways benefit our marriage.

Our intimate moment is cut short when someone taps on the driver's side window. We pull apart, and I giggle when Jon groans. When I turn my attention to the man standing outside the car door, my body lights up with desire. Oooh, he's hot.

This guy is older, and he's wearing tight jeans and a snug T-shirt that showcases his muscular physique. He's in great shape for his age, and my mind conjures up images of him joining in on my gangbang fantasy.

Jon opens the door, and the guy introduces himself. "Welcome to the Plaything Resort. I'm Chris."

Oh shit, he's the owner. Bleh, he probably doesn't fuck the guests. What a waste. But hey, at least I'll get some delicious eye candy to enjoy while we check in.

I grab my purse and climb out of the car while Jon gets our luggage out of the trunk. I straighten my flowing red dress and try not to shiver because of the cold.

Chris approaches me, and his eyes twinkle. "I'm thrilled you both could make it during the holiday season. We go all out for Christmas."

I flirt a little as we follow him towards the house. "A bunch of orgasms is the best Christmas present."

Chris holds the door open for us and winks at me as I pass. "There are plenty of men here who would love to give you a gift."

Yeah, I'm willing to take all their "gifts" of cum. I wonder how many men I'm going to fuck this weekend. It better be more than five, since that's my current record. I want this weekend to be one that I'll remember forever.

As we follow Chris inside, he leads us to a cozy reception area where he hands me some papers. "I just need to see your ID and have you sign a few forms."

I take out my ID and hand it to him. Once he returns it, I sign the documents before letting Jon handle the rest of the check-in process. While Chris goes over the resort's amenities with Jon, I wander off to the magnificent Christmas tree in the corner with colorful ornaments and twinkling lights. There's also a little ceramic Christmas village set and wreaths and garland decorating the walls. It's charming, and I can't wait to explore the rest of the resort.

Chris calls out to me. "Miranda?"

I glance over my shoulder. "Hmm?"

"All the men know your safeword. There's no shame in using it if you need a break."

"Thank you."

I focus on the tree again and smile to myself. He doesn't know me. Super Slut Miranda this out this weekend, and I left Demure Miranda at home. I'm likely to take the twenty men all in a row and then ask for more. I doubt I'll use my safeword.

Two sexy, muscular, bare-chested guys walk in wearing shorts and sandals. Wait, bare-chested? It's not snowing, but it's chilly outside, so they must be freezing. I guess they could have been in the pool or hot tub, but they aren't wet, so I don't think that's the reason.

One guy picks up our luggage and carries it out of the lobby while the other man approaches me. My body instantly tingles as I grow more aroused. I'm in such a sexual haze at this point that I'd welcome this guy taking me right here, but I'm sure that isn't how it works.

Actually, how does this work?

The rule at the resort is that I can't ask the guys to fuck me, which is a bummer. With how wet and needy I am, I'd be going around and begging everyone to use me. I want to be a glorious mess by the time this is all said and done, and I'll enjoy every minute. I've given them free access to me while we're here unless I use my safeword, but it all depends on whether they want to fuck me. Oh shit, they better want to fuck me. How much would that suck?

I glance down at the guy's shorts and I can tell he's hard. Guess I don't have to worry about him not being interested, unless that isn't for me. The guy is in his prime and he's ripped. My fingers itch to trace the lines of his muscles on his abs.

When the man steps close to me, my eyes widen and my breath catches. Um, we haven't even finished checking in yet. He walks me backwards until I'm against the nearest wall. A delicious shudder shoots through my body as he takes my hands and pins them by the wrists above my head. He's massive, and he only needs to use one hand to keep me immobilized. I squirm, loving the sensation of being restrained and unable to escape.

My head swims with desire, and I don't know how to behave properly here. I don't want to screw it up and make him walk away, so I just watch him with hungry eyes and wait for him to do whatever he wants.

He explores my curves with his free hand, squeezing my breast roughly and making me moan. His gaze follows his hand as he checks me out. "Sexy," he says appreciatively. "Glad I won you."

Uh, he won me? I want to ask him what the hell he's talking about, but his fingers roam under the hem of my dress and I get distracted when he caresses my inner thigh. As his fingers inch closer and closer to my pussy, I can feel my panties growing more wet. Holy fuck, I need him to touch me.

When his fingers trace the edge of my panties, I press towards his hand, hoping he'll go for more. That earns me a sexy laugh, and he leans down to whisper in my ear, "I'm Tyler."

I smell a delicious cinnamon scent and want to lick his chest to see if he tastes as good as he smells.

"I'm Miranda," I say breathlessly. "Pleased to meet you."

I'm so turned on that my brain isn't working right. I'm barely able to stop myself from asking him to finger me.

His eyes crinkled with a smile. "You're not Miranda this weekend. This weekend you're our fucktoy plaything, and we'll call you whatever we want."

My face flushes, and I think about the questionnaire I answered before coming here. I said I enjoyed dirty talk and being called filthy names. I also stated I'm submissive, and I enjoy being tied up and spanked. The "our fucktoy" remark makes my core melt, and I can feel myself dropping into a submissive state. I'm dripping wet now, and my knees tremble. I've got a feeling that's the exact response he was aiming for.

When his fingers ease the lace of my panties aside, I have to remind myself to breathe as he explores my pussy. My stomach quivers when he nuzzles his mouth against my neck. His fingers spread my slick juices up to my clit, then circle it in agonizingly slow motions. I buck my hips in pleasure, wishing he was fingerfucking me—or better yet, had his cock inside me.

"Such a good slut," he whispers in my ear. "So turned on."

I moan softly as his fingers dip lower and plunge into my pussy. I whimper and shift my legs, spreading them further apart to give him easier access.

"Oh god," I gasp as he massages a pleasure point inside me and sends a zing of bliss through my core.

A small, amused chuckle rumbles from Tyler and he sounds proud of himself. I start to lose my grip on reality as the orgasm builds. I'm just a fucktoy this weekend, and I'll do whatever he wants.

I rock against his hand, seeking my release. Right when I'm on the edge of an orgasm, he slips his fingers out, and I whimper. No, he can't stop!

I'm dazed, and it's difficult to see straight while my body vibrates with need. When he brings his wet fingers to my lips, I immediately open them. I'll do anything he asks of me now that I've been teased by his magic fingers.

"Taste yourself," he orders as he slides his fingers in my mouth. "And clean them."

I swirl my tongue around his index and middle finger while he rocks them back and forth in my mouth like he's fingering a pussy. I taste myself as I enthusiastically bob my head as I clean him up. Mmm, I wish I could beg him to shove his dick down my throat instead. I've never been shy about my love of sucking cock, but I think that's too close to asking him to fuck me.

Tyler releases my wrists and pulls his fingers out of my mouth. When he steps back, I'm disappointed. Shit, I don't think he's going to fuck me yet.

He cups my chin, tipping my head up and forcing me to look him in the eye. "I'm done with you for now. Go to your cottage and know that at some point tonight, I'm going to take what I won."

There's that talk about winning me again. I'm about to ask him about it, but he slaps my breast hard and all thoughts drain from my head as I gasp from surprise and pleasure. Smacking my breasts was another thing I told them I liked. How closely will they follow my list?

With a knowing smirk, he walks away towards the rear of the house. My eyes follow him as he exits and I take deep breaths, trying to calm my racing heart and clear my head. That was...hot. I already have so many questions. Why didn't he fuck me? Am I a prize of sorts? If so, did he win my pussy for the night, or is it for the entire weekend?

Jon and Chris are both leaning against the counter, looking amused. Jon has a gleam in his eye and my face grows hot as I feel a little embarrassed about being such a thirsty slut before we've even made it out of the lobby. I said I was going to go wild, but I expected to unpack first.

Jon comes over and hugs me. "Come, my slutty wife, let's go to the cottage."

I laugh and give Chris a wave while he calls out, "Have a good time!"

CHAPTER 4

As I unpack my bags in the cozy, one-room cottage decorated for Christmas, I'm all aflutter from excitement. There's a small tree decorated in silver and red with multicolored lights, and it doesn't take long for me to get a feel for the space. There's a kitchenette with a dining area and the main room with a king-sized bed. The bathroom is the most impressive feature, designed for indulgence with a massive tub that can fit multiple people, as well as a separate spacious shower. I'm so getting Jon in that shower before the trip is over.

Jon's lounging on the bed, and it only takes a moment of indecision before I pounce on him and straddle him.

"Hey, whoa," he laughs and wraps his fingers around my hips. "What do you think you're doing?"

I fit my pussy against the hardness in his jeans and grind against him before giving him my sexiest smile. "Enjoying my vacation?"

I phrase it like a question, but we both know what I'm after. I want his cock.

Jon 'tsks' as if I'm misbehaving and thrusts his hips up to press his cock harder against my pussy. I moan as he controls my movements, making me rock against him faster. Jesus, if he keeps this up, I'm going to come.

When he bucks his hips and his cock rubs against my clit, my vision tunnels with pleasure. Just a little more pressure, and I'll climax. This is exactly what I was craving during the car ride down. Just a little more...

Jon abruptly pushes me off him, and I tumble onto the bed beside him with a pout. "Hey, I was almost there!"

He laughs. "Let's go check out the hot tub. I can fuck you whenever I want at home. This is my chance to see other guys use you."

I narrow my eyes at him and I want to protest that he can't just fuck me whenever he wants, but if I'm being honest with myself, he probably could. All he has to do is call me a good girl and tell me to kneel, and I turn into a needy, cock-hungry slut. Sometimes he teases me and makes me work for it by begging for his cock. Other times, he enjoys using me as if I'm his sex toy.

Occasionally, he lets me be in control, but that's not happening this weekend.

With a dramatic sigh to make it appear as though I'm not overly enthused with the idea, I get up and grab the black bikini from the dresser. I love that he wants me to get railed by other men instead of fucking me himself, but I don't want to be too eager. It's a fine line between panting over other guys' cocks while still making my husband know he's the love of my life. Not that I'm really fooling him. He knows exactly how turned on I am by the thought of a gangbang.

Jon finishes changing faster than I do, and as I bend over to put on the bottom bikini piece, he swats my ass as he walks by. I yelp from pleasure as he brings me my slip-on sandals.

"Don't take too long, my kinky Kitten."

I stick my tongue out at him as I slide the sandals on. There's no way in hell I'm walking to the hot tub in just my bikini, so I wrap a terry cloth bathrobe around me. Once I twist my long brown hair up in a messy topknot, I'm ready.

He's rummaging through our suitcase, and I can't help teasing him. "Geez, slowpoke! Let's go!"

When he turns around, one fist is closed, like he's got something in it. Uh-oh, what's he up to? I eye his hands suspiciously and he puts the thing in his hand into the pocket of his shorts.

Jon shrugs and closes the lid of the suitcase. "Ready"

Raising my eyebrow, I decide to let him have his secret for now. I'm sure I'll love whatever it is.

Since it's the end of fall, it's already getting dark, and as we step outside, I notice that someone has turned on the Christmas lights. The entire property glows like a fairytale wonderland, with colored lights on bushes, trees, and fences. I'm delighted and skip ahead of Jon, wanting to find the hot tub as soon as possible.

Jon and I walk through the light display, following a stone pathway to the center of the resort. As we get closer to the pool, the scent of chlorine gets stronger. They only allow one group of guests here at a time. That means if we encounter anyone, they are part of the resort crew and can use me. I'm trembling with lust at the thought, and as soon as the hot tub comes into view, my stomach drops when I see it's empty. Damn it, there's no one to fuck me.

I pause next to a patio table and remove my robe and sandals. Jon approaches me and rests his hands on my hips. I'm staring at the hot tub, feeling disappointed, when Jon gently nudges his erection against my ass, distracting me. Mmm, okay, so there might not be other people here, but I've got my husband to play with.

I place my hands on the patio table and bend over, grinding against him. What if he fucks me, and someone comes to watch? The idea is dirty, and I hope it happens. He takes a step back and uses his fingers to rub the fabric of my bikini bottoms against my pussy. I moan softly and my pulse speeds up, heating my blood.

We've been married long enough that I know how to get what I want. I wiggle my ass and look at him over my shoulder. "Sir, will you please fuck me?"

"Later," he replies, and then adds with a sly grin, "slut."

I sigh. Jesus Christ, someone needs to fuck me. He pulls me up and turns me around before lifting me and setting my ass on the metal table. I don't know what he's got planned, but I lean back, propping myself up on my elbows, and swing my legs while I bat my eyelashes at him.

"So what now, Daddy?"

He laughs at me calling him 'Daddy,' since it's not something I usually do, and he pushes my bikini top up, exposing my nipples to the cool air.

"Now, you're going to be a good girl while I do whatever I want to you."

My nipples harden from the cold, and he slaps one of my tits playfully. I giggle with surprise, and then moan from pleasure when he leans over me and sucks on the breast he just slapped. He tweaks the other nipple, and I run a hand through his hair while I close my eyes and enjoy the pulling sensation deep in my core. I can feel the wetness between my thighs increasing, and I might go insane if I don't orgasm soon.

His hand leaves my breast for a moment, and my eyes fly open when I feel something hard and cold touch my nipple. Jon stops sucking on my breast, and he's holding nipple clamps.

Oh, holy fuck.

"My Kitten needs some extra pleasure tonight," he murmurs while he opens the clamp and clips it onto my nipple.

I cry out from the sting, and he quickly puts the second one on. I rest back on my elbows again, and he stands between my legs and rubs my pussy through my bikini while the initial pain from the clamps dies down. Now it's just making me needier, though I know the real pain will come when he takes them off.

Just as my body tightens with need, the sound of masculine voices grabs my attention. I look down the path to where it leads to the main building and my heart races when I see a group of guys, which includes Tyler, coming towards us.

Three guys jump into the pool, and I shiver as I imagine how cold it will be when they get out. Tyler and two guys walk in our direction, and I whimper in need. I'm splayed out on the table with my tits out and nipple clamps on—not exactly how I thought I'd meet a group of guys for the first time. When Jon steps away, it's worse, and I fight the urge to cover myself. I feel like a sideshow attraction, but when my pussy gets wetter, I know I enjoy being the center of attention—especially since I look like a complete slut waiting to be used.

Jon sits in a chair close by as if he's settling in to watch a show. Yeah, I'm so about to get fucked, and I welcome it. When the men get close enough, I swing my legs again and try to pretend like nothing is out of the ordinary. I'm sure it's an everyday occurrence to have a woman in a bikini in the cold with her nipple-clamped tits hanging out.

Tyler smirks. "Looks like the slut is ready for us."

As they surround me, their collective gaze travels over my body, lingering on my breasts before moving down to my bikini-covered pussy. If there was enough lighting, they'd be able to see a damp patch on my bikini. I hope they're enjoying the view.

Tyler steps between my legs and trails his fingers over my pussy. I moan and wish the bikini fabric wasn't between us. Tyler pulls down his swim trunks, and I'm curious enough about what he's packing to lean up a little to get a good look. His cock is thick with an upward curve. Oh god, I want that in me.

When he slides my bikini bottom down part way, I lie back on the cold surface and lift my knees towards my chest to help him remove them. He grabs my ankles and looks at my feet, admiring the red polish on my toes.

"She's got pretty feet," one guy points out, and my slutty pussy clenches as if she just got complimented.

Oh god, I'm their freeuse toy to use. They don't even have to fuck my pussy if they don't want. My expression must have changed, because Tyler laughs and starts massaging my feet.

"Looks like the toy just figured out that we can do whatever we want to her."

One guy steps close and tugs on a nipple clamp, and I arch my back and cry out from bliss. No, no, no, they've got to fuck my pussy, right? What guy would have a wet pussy to use and choose to fuck something else instead?

One who wanted to prove his domination, that's who—because that's what I said got me turned on the most...being controlled.

The edges of my vision dim, and I shiver as a feeling of acceptance comes over me. If they don't want to fuck my pussy, I'll still enjoy every minute of being used. I came here wanting to be treated like a sex doll, and now everything I wrote down that I like might be used against me. They know I get off on being edged, despite hating it. They have all the tiny details of sex acts I prefer. Hell, they probably read that I enjoy having my feet rubbed since I put it down.

Tyler keeps my legs together and rests my feet over one of his shoulders. When he fits the head of his cock against my pussy, I almost laugh from joy.

He slams into me, straight to my core, and I writhe from ecstasy while he moans. "Lucky for this slut, I want her pussy."

As he thrusts into me, my whole body shudders as he massages the most sensitive spots deep inside me. It feels amazing, and I reach my arms above my head to hold on to the edge of the table and brace myself to let him pound into me harder.

One man plays with the nipple clamps while the other stands by my head and says, "Open that gorgeous mouth. It needs something in it."

I turn my head to obey, and he slides his cock between my lips. He's not as thick as Tyler, and I'm grateful for that while I'm in this position. His pre-cum is salty on my tongue, and I lick and suck for all I'm worth as the two men fuck me. I drift on a cloud of euphoria as every nerve ending in my body comes alive with the sensations of being taken. I love every moment of this, and I want more.

When the guy fucking my mouth suddenly pulls out, he sprays ropes of cum on my mouth and cheek. I moan in appreciation and lick my lips, savoring the flavor. Shit, he came before I did.

As soon as he's finished, the other guy takes his place, and I eagerly take him in my mouth. I close my eyes and just enjoy being holes for them to use. The new guy in my mouth has a slightly bitter taste, but it's not bad. I've swallowed my fair share of cum, enough to know that every guy tastes different.

Tyler continues to fuck me vigorously, and when he starts in with the dirty talk, my mind whirls.

"Fuck, I love the way your pussy milks my cock."

Mmmm, me too. I hum with appreciation.

"So good," he moans, and picks up his pace, fucking me so hard that the patio table shakes and creaks.

As he rides me, he growls, "I'm going to fill this pussy with so much cum, you're going to be dripping for days."

Shit, I wish that were true. Tension coils low in my belly as I feel my orgasm build. Why was I afraid of a gangbang? This is fucking fabulous.

Just as I'm on the brink of ecstasy, the guy in my mouth blows his load deep into my throat. He moans and shivers as multiple spurts fill my mouth, and I happily lick my lips when he pulls out.

"Such a cum dumpster whore," Tyler grunts as he keeps fucking me.

That's what I am. Just a vessel for their cum. I moan at the thought, and when Tyler whacks against me extra hard, I fall apart and scream as my orgasm hits me like a truck. All I see is twinkling lights as my body throbs from rapture.

"One," Jon calls out, and I giggle. I love that man.

Once I recover, I'm dimly aware of Tyler continuing to fuck me, but I'm too blissed out to pay attention to how his strokes change or what he's saying. It's not until a few minutes pass that my awareness snaps back into place when he stiffens.

Tyler groans as he thrusts balls deep, holding still. I whimper in approval, knowing he's pumping me full of his cum. Finally, he relaxes with a contented sigh and holds onto my legs, his breathing harsh.

"Alright boys," he declares. "I know I won control of the slut when I beat you at cards earlier, but I'm feeling generous. Line up and have at her."

My jaw drops in amazement. He really did win me.

The guys all laugh, and one of them grabs my arm. "She's facing the wrong way."

I blink with surprise as Tyler moves aside and two guys with wet hands pull me off the table. They evidently came out of the water. They turn me around and I see all six men gathered close by before they shove my head to the table. When the nipple clamps drag along the tabletop, I flinch from the pleasurable pain. Oh shit, I'm fucked.

One man stands behind me and runs his fingers along the curve of my butt. "Such a gorgeous ass. I wish I could fuck it."

Jon laughs. "Sorry guys, that hole is mine."

I recall a few years ago, at a BDSM event, when Jon's dominant side emerged, and in a possessive rage he said no one but him was allowed to fuck my ass ever again. No one has.

"Oh well," the guy says amiably. "I can fill her pussy with cum just as easily."

He holds onto my hips and thrusts into me so hard, I'm pushed against the table and the nipple clamps send a zing of pleasure straight to my clit.

"Fuck! Shit!" I cry out as he pounds into me.

He seizes my elbows, drawing them backwards, and he uses them like reins so I'm unable to stop my breasts from rubbing against the table as he fucks me. The bliss builds in layers, and I scream when I come once more, and it's so intense my eyes tear up.

The guy in my pussy only lasts two more thrusts before he groans and fills me.

"Two," Jon's voice rings out, and I have the insane urge to sob. I'm not sure how many orgasms like this I can handle.

Another man replaces him, and the sound of flesh slapping together echoes through the night as he fucks me. I barely recover from the previous climax when I'm coming again. This one is a full-body orgasm, and I convulse as lightning runs from the top of my head to my toes. I can feel my pussy fluttering and gripping onto the cock inside me, and my vision swims while the guy pounding my pussy finishes inside me.

I hear someone say, "Three," and I close my eyes, submitting to the moment. Everything hurts, but in a wonderfully exquisite way. I need these men to fuck me forever, and when the cock inside me slips out, I hear someone begging for more.

It's me.

I'm the one pleading for them to keep going as they swap positions and another man takes me. There are no words this time, just a cock thrusting into my pussy in a rapid-fire assault. In what feels like less than a minute, he's filling my pussy with cum and I shake as another orgasm crashes through me. I don't hear Jon call out the number. This time it's too much. There's so much pleasure running through my body, it feels like I'm a live wire as I tremble and moan. I sob incoherently as I plead for more while simultaneously begging for the torture to be done.

Someone turns me over and lays me on my back on the table again. I close my eyes, limp from joy as more men use me. I don't even know how many cocks are inside me, and at some point, someone shoves their dick in my mouth. It barely registers when he blows his load. He's got so much cum that it runs down my face when he pulls out.

I can feel the tension growing in my core again as someone fucks my pussy, and this time I can tell it's going to be a massive orgasm. I'm chanting out, "Oh god," as I hurtle towards ecstasy.

When someone removes a nipple clamp suddenly, I scream as the blood rushes to my nipple. I clench around the cock in my pussy, and the guy swears.

"Jesus, take the other off her," the guy fucking me demands, and I realize it's Tyler.

He hammers into me, and when the other nipple clamp comes off, the mixed pain and pleasure are too much. I explode and a surge of euphoria rips through my body so powerfully, all I can do is moan incoherently as it rolls on and on until the world around me dims.

I don't blank out, but I reach a point where it's just one continuous wave of rapture. Tyler finishes inside me, and when I hear a bunch of moaning but no one is fucking me, I try to focus and realize there's a circle jerk happening over me while each guy strokes himself.

I barely know what I'm doing as I open my mouth and stick out my tongue, hoping that someone can aim true. As cum shoots over my body, a spurt lands on my tongue, and I swallow it happily. I don't know how many loads hit me, but I can tell I'm going to be a sticky mess.

As I float in a sea of happiness, I hear murmuring, and then I feel weightless and realize Jon is carrying me back to the cottage. The air is chilly, and I'm naked, so I must have lost my bikini top at some point. Wrapping my arms around his neck, I rest my head on his shoulder and enjoy being taken care of.

I feel adrift as he carries me to the bathroom in our cottage, but I come back to earth when he sets me on my feet and hands me a bottle of water and a piece of string cheese.

"Drink and eat, Kitten. Then we'll get you cleaned up."

I devour the string cheese, not realizing how hungry I truly am until it touches my mouth. Jon removes his clothes while I'm eating and drinking, and he enters the shower with me when I'm finished. The warm spray rains down on me as Jon's soapy hands wash away the other guys' cum. Shivers run through me every time his fingers brush against my sensitive nipples.

After the shower, I'm relaxed but still flying high from the endorphins. I can tell Jon is very turned on by the way he's touching me everywhere and the sparkle in his eyes. As he dries me, I wrap my hand around his cock, enjoying the smooth softness of his skin on the steel rod underneath.

"Kitten, don't do that. You need rest."

I can hear the ache in his voice, and I tighten my grip on his cock and lift my gaze to his. "No, I need you."

That's all I need to say. He swoops down and kisses me passionately, sliding his tongue into my mouth like he owns me—which he does. He makes a soft moaning sound, and I squeak when he picks me up and carries me into the bedroom, his lips never leaving mine as we kiss with a fervor and desire that's all ours.

When Jon tosses me onto the bed, he's on top of me in seconds, pinning me down. I adore it when he manhandles me. I can be a dirty slut with other men, but only he gets all of me—body and soul.

Right now he's so horny, he doesn't want to make love to me. I eagerly spread my thighs wide as he slides inside me. He pounds me into the mattress, trying to prove he's better than all the other men. I love it when he fucks me like this. We surge together, and I'm surprised when I come quickly. My inner muscles clamp around him as pleasure rips through me.

"Ohhh, god," I cry out as the waves of bliss peak multiple times.

Jon grasps my hips and pulls me against him as he comes. As he fills me with his warm seed, he thrusts slowly, growling until he finishes. This man is all mine, and he knows it. I'll let him have me any time he wants, any which way he likes, and I love that he lets other men fuck me.

When he's finished unloading, he pulls out, and we cuddle together. As he holds me and strokes my hair, I'm surrounded by feelings of love and comfort. This is the man who loves me unconditionally, who gets aroused by the idea of men using me, and who wants me to come home afterward so he can have his cock in me and I can sleep contentedly with him by my side.

We kiss softly and whisper words of love, but I soon fall asleep in his arms.

Chapter 5

The next morning, I'm woken up by male voices in the kitchenette. Jon and Tyler are setting the table with covered dishes. I presume Tyler must have brought us room service. My stomach rumbles, and I can tell I'm going to enjoy breakfast.

I quickly dash to the bathroom to freshen up. Since we left my robe by the pool, I feel oddly vulnerable walking out naked in front of Tyler in the light of day. I'm digging around in the dresser for my nightgown when Tyler presses up against my ass and cups my breasts. They're still sore from the nipple clamps last night, and I moan as he pulls on them. Fuuuuck, that feels good. My pussy hums alive and I'm barely surprised when I find myself face-first against the closest wall with his cock sliding inside me from behind.

Movement from the doorway reveals Jon, who leans on the doorframe and watches us with an expression of amusement. He's casually stroking his cock through his jeans as he observes us, and he gives me a slow smile as I bounce against the wall, taking everything that Tyler gives me.

There's nothing subtle about this fuck, and Tyler pounds into me rapidly. I whimper in pleasure when he massages my clit. Oh god, I'm about to come. My head spins from the quick turnaround, from waking up to now being railed against a wall, but I embrace it.

As my inner walls tense up, he slows his fingers. I groan in frustration. Noooo! I'm so close.

"Beg for it," comes a voice that's not Tyler's. Jon is taking over, forcing me to accept his dominance.

"Please," I plead, squirming against Tyler, trying to get the stimulation back. "Sir, please let me come!"

Tyler resumes his circular motions on my clit, and I let out a throaty moan as it just fuels the fire building inside me. This is so dirty, with both men controlling my pleasure.

As I tremble from the oncoming climax, I wish it was Jon slamming into me. It's his touch I crave the most as the rest of the world fades away.

"Come for me," Jon demands, and Tyler increases the speed of his fingers on my clit.

My orgasm explodes, and my pussy flutters as a gush of wetness runs down my legs.

"Ohhhh, fuck," I cry out and press back against Tyler as every muscle in my body trembles.

Waves of pleasure pulse through me, radiating outward to the tips of my fingers and toes. This is amazing, yet I want something else, too.

I vaguely register Tyler roaring with release as he shivers and then goes still, but I'm focusing on Jon walking towards us, his cock glistening with his pre-cum. When Tyler pulls out of me, I immediately face Jon, kneel on the floor and part my lips as he feeds me his cock.

Sucking on my husband in front of Tyler is my way of demonstrating who owns me, but the truth is, I'm just a filthy whore who will do whatever I'm told right now. I'm in my element, and I'm living my best slut life.

As Jon rocks his hips, moving his cock in and out of my mouth, I think about the rest of the weekend. This isn't something I'm likely to experience again and I'm going to let this resort fulfill my deepest, darkest desires.

As I take my husband deeper into my throat, I glance up at him through my lashes, my expression filled with lust and neediness. I need more orgasms, but first, he needs to come for me.

Jon's movements grow more erratic as his breathing becomes shallower. He's fucking my mouth like it's my pussy. I tingle from enjoyment as he comes in my mouth. His hot, thick cum hits my tongue and I swallow it all. I'm a slut who knows how to please her man.

When Jon pulls out, I quickly swallow everything I can and then grin at him. My, "Good morning, my love," has a sing-song quality, and I can barely contain my laughter. Shit, what a way to start the morning.

Tyler touches my shoulder, and I turn around to face him. "Have a good breakfast." He winks at me.

He says goodbye to Jon before he leaves.

Jon helps me stand and pulls me in for a hug and a deep kiss. I sway a little and laugh. "I'm going to go clean up again."

He slaps my ass when I turn towards the bathroom. "Make it quick. The food is getting cold."

"Yes, Sir!"

I twitch my ass at him as I disappear into the bathroom.

I rub my belly through my nightgown after we finish breakfast. "Oh God, I can't eat another bite. What's on the agenda for today?"

He smiles mysteriously. "You'll see."

Hah, the jerk. I blow him a kiss. "Yes, Sir."

Jon cleans off the table and tells me to meet him outside in 10 minutes and to dress casually, so I decide on jeans and a tank top under a warm hoodie. If we're doing something outdoorsy, I want to be comfortable.

Plus, this way, if we run into a guy who wants to fuck me, he's going to have to work for it.

I wrap my hair with a tie to make a ponytail as I step outside. Jon examines my outfit, but remains silent. I fidget with the strings on my hoodie, wondering if it's appropriate for whatever he's got planned.

He takes my hand and leads me along the stone pathway around the center building of the resort. I feel confused, but willing to go with the flow as he guides me to a smaller building. When he opens the door, I see it's a recreation room... full of sexy, muscular men wearing nothing but Santa hats.

What sort of fucked up scenario is this? I try to count the men but get distracted by all the exposed cocks once I hit 10. My pussy hums and my nipples harden, and I almost laugh. Yeah, it doesn't matter what's going on. I'm a thousand percent down with whatever raunchy thing he has planned.

The men watch us as we enter. Some are playing pool, and some are at a card table with cards in their hands. I suddenly feel like I'm in a porno with a corny name, like "Here 'Comes' Santa Claus".

Jon holds my hand and pulls me over to a couch, but we don't sit down. He takes a cushion off of it and sets it on the floor.

"Kneel," he commands, and I obey without hesitation.

I look up at Jon with big eyes, waiting for more instructions. He picks up some rope off a side table that was hidden by the arm of the couch. When he ties my wrists behind my back, my vision goes fuzzy around the edges as I sink into submission. He knows exactly how to get me into subspace when he wants it, and I can tell I'm heading in that direction quickly.

"So, Kitten, here's what's going to happen."

Oooh, I get info! I perk up, and wiggle my ass in happiness and settle in, waiting for the explanation.

"A few years ago, I planned a holiday party for you..."

I nod eagerly, and he continues. "Today is for me, not you. This is my party."

I furrow my brow in confusion. Uh... what?

He leans in and presses his lips against mine before whispering into my ear, "I want to see how many Santas you'll blow before you say your safeword."

Ohhhhh. A shiver runs through me as Jon straightens up. Why is this so hot? He signals to the guys and they line up in front of me. As I open my mouth and a guy sticks his cock in, I give Jon the side-eye as he settles into a nearby loveseat.

This might be the most messed up thing Jon has ever asked me to do. I love it.

Well, if he wants to watch me blow some Santas, let's see if this slut can outlast the men. I focus on the dick in my mouth and try to bring him to climax as quickly as possible. That should send the message that this slut means business. I'm not saying I won't use my safeword, but I want to blow an impressive amount before I give in.

I want to see Jon's reaction. When my eyes dart over to him, he smirks like he can read my mind and knows I'm determined to swallow as many loads of cum as possible. I smile around the shaft in my mouth, giving it a little bit of suction and tongue action that makes the man grunt and thrust his hips.

Yep, that's the ticket. Come for me. I love how filthy this is. I'm just a cum dumpster slut.

The guy in my mouth groans as he spurts down my throat. As soon as he's done, another takes his place. I scoot forward while the new guy takes over my mouth. It's my train of twenty cocks, except instead of fucking my pussy, they're just fucking my face.

The current cock is nicely formed, and I lavish attention on it, sucking him deep and holding him there until I need to breathe. It doesn't take long for him to come, and after I swallow him down, another takes his spot.

I heat up quickly, and now I know why Jon was eyeing my outfit. He knew I was going to get warm. With my arms bound behind my back, there's nothing I can do but bob on every cock presented to me. The helpless feeling turns me on even more. My heart races with excitement as I get sloppier on this guy, and drool runs down my chin onto my hoodie.

After he comes, he pulls out, and the guy behind him laughs as he steps forward and tips my head back.

"Nice, slut."

It's Tyler. Hasn't he had his fill of me yet? When he slides his cock between my lips, I giggle. Guess not. When I taste myself on him, I shiver in pleasure. Okay, that's extra dirty. He didn't even shower after fucking me earlier.

As Tyler thrusts into my throat, he places a hand on the back of my head and twists his fingers around my ponytail, keeping me still so he can go deep. I've been conditioned to enjoy being used by now, and I moan while my pussy quivers.

Tyler's cock pops out of my mouth as he straightens up. He hasn't come yet, but someone else stands next to him and shoves his cock towards me. Well hell, okay, let's do this. I eagerly suck on him for a few minutes before he withdraws, and Tyler's cock returns to take his place.

I alternate between the two, anticipating the moment I get to swallow all their cum. It's interesting how different each man tastes and smells. It's more noticeable when you've got a string of cocks in a row, and I love the texture difference of each cock. Everyone is unique and I want to worship them all.

While Tyler slides in and out of my throat, I start to sweat. The front of my hoodie is soaked from all the saliva I keep losing. Am I supposed to tire of sucking cocks? I feel like I'm in my element, and the longer I stay on my knees, the more fun I'm having. I've never made so many men climax in such a short span of time.

Jon might think this blowjob party is for him, but I think he underesti-mated how big of a slut I am.

Tyler's thrusts speed up, and within moments I'm swallowing his load of cum. He pulls out and the other guy quickly shoves his cock into my mouth and explodes. Cum joins the saliva on my hoodie because I can't swallow it down fast enough.

I barely pay attention to who I'm blowing, and I'm lost in a sea of cocks. My eyes widen when I see the next one. It's thicker than any I've sucked so far, and I'm not sure I'll be able to fit it in my mouth. He enters me gently, allowing me to adjust, and I appreciate his consideration. If any cock was going to make me use my safeword, it would be this one.

He fucks my mouth slowly, and the rhythmic movement lulls me, and the world takes on a dreamlike quality. I no longer feel my body; I'm just a mouth for these men.

When he comes, it feels like it's never ending and streams of cum run down my chin. When he pulls out, I stick out my cum-coated tongue and wait for the next guy.

I lose track of how many men I've blown, but when it's Tyler in my mouth again, I wonder if I'm on a second round with everyone. Time loses all meaning, and I'm covered in cum and floating in my happy place as the men use me.

It could be hours or minutes when Jon calls out, "Okay, she's done."

Oooh, he called it. Does this mean I won? And what's my prize? There's no answer to the questions, and my mouth feels oddly empty as they all leave.

Once we're alone, Jon frees my hands and rubs my shoulders as I roll them. Everything feels good. He lifts me and sits with me on the loveseat, holding me in his lap.

"You're a beautiful mess."

He kisses my forehead, and I nestle into his chest, smelling his spicy aftershave that I adore. This is where I belong.

As I relax, my pussy throbs, reminding me I didn't get fucked. I wiggle against Jon, enjoying the feeling of his hardness. I bet I could dry hump him and come.

He groans. "Kitten, behave."

Does he even know me? I wiggle around some more and he kisses me softly before asking, "How are you?"

I know why he's checking. He needs to make sure I'm okay before he snaps and fucks me.

"I'm really, REALLY, good."

When I rock against his hardness, he laughs. "Yeah, you're good."

He lifts me off his lap, and when I stand up, I unzip my jeans and reach for his cock. He stops me and pulls his own pants down to free Rusty. I expect him to bend me over the couch, but he pushes me toward the pool table.

"Remember the last time I fucked you on a pool table?"

His voice is husky, and as he bends me over the side, I recall the day he fucked me at a friend's holiday party. Some guy walked past the doorway and saw us.

Jon pulls my jeans and panties down just far enough to fuck me. "Yes," I moan as he slides his cock inside me.

There's a slight soreness from being used so much, but that just makes it hotter. I wanted to leave this weekend the ultimate slut, and I'm getting my wish.

As he fucks me, I rub my clit. Between my slick fingers and his cock, I'm quickly soaring. When my orgasm hits, the intense pleasure makes me tremble as I buck my hips and push back against him as he fucks me through my climax.

Once I can tell he's about to come, I rock against him, urging him to finish faster. I'm desperate for him to fill me up—to prove that even though I'm a total slut, he still wants me.

He groans and I can feel his warm cum shooting deep inside me and joining all the other cum. When he pulls out, we both hastily pull up our pants before collapsing on the chair with me in his lap once more. He holds me close as he catches his breath, and I giggle.

"How many times did I come yesterday?" I ask as I close my eyes.

He snorts. "I lost track."

Yeah, I'm not surprised he doesn't know. It was a lot.

"Hey, what did I win for taking all those cocks?"

His laugh rumbles through his chest. "A lifetime of happiness with me."

I don't think there's anything I want more, but I playfully protest and swat his chest. "Bastard, that's not a win. That's just everyday life."

This might be the best vacation ever. We laugh together as I curl up against him and rub my cheek on his shoulder.

I peek up at him. "My love?"

"Yes, Kitten?"

His eyes glitter and I already see the answer in them before I ask my question.

"Do you still love me?"

As he gives me a huge smile, my heart beats faster, and my insides melt as he speaks the words I love to hear so much.

"Forever."

I twine my fingers with his and whisper, "Always," back at him.

We sit on the couch, holding each other as if we're in our own little bubble. I don't know if I want to fuck other guys today, and I know it doesn't matter whether I do, because everything I want is sitting here with me in my arms.

This is perfect. This is real, and this is everything.

The End

FreeUse Office Slut

Shared at the Office

Lacey Cross

CHAPTER 1

My loose black skirt swings around my knees as I stroll into work five minutes early. I can't remember the last time I was on time, let alone early, on a Monday. I was too excited to dawdle at home today, and I even skipped coffee.

Butterflies swirl in my stomach as I give Cindy a big smile. "Good morning. Isn't it a gorgeous day?"

Cindy looks at me like I've grown horns. "It's freezing outside...and it's a Monday...and we have to work for three more days before Christmas."

I laugh. "Exactly. Only three more days, and then we're off work until the New Year. It's a fabulous day."

Cindy raises her eyebrows, and I can tell she still thinks I'm crazy for being happy this early in the morning, but she doesn't say anything else as I head to my desk.

What Cindy doesn't know is that today is fabulous because there's a chance I'll get Mr. Jacobs' cock inside me. It's been almost two years since I fucked my bosses, and that's about to change. Slut Miranda is back in the building.

I drop my purse and lunch on my desk and perch on the edge of my chair as I log into my computer. I only plan on being at my desk long enough to message Mr. Jacobs and tell him I need to talk to him right now.

My hands tremble as I log into my work systems. The only reason I've got a shot at fucking Mr. Jacobs today is because they recently fired the office manager, Bonny, who's been cockblocking me since she started here. The last lawyer I fucked at work was Mr. King. I had a wonderful few days of being his freeuse toy, and then they hired Bonny. It was all over after that.

Now that Bonny is gone, everything's changed again. A couple of weeks ago, the lawyers gifted me with a weekend at a freeuse resort. Mr. Jacobs told me to think about whether I wanted to start back up with fucking them at work and to let him know after my trip. I got home from the resort last night, and I'm ready to lie on his desk and tell him to do me—okay, so let's be real here: I guess it's more like bend over his desk and beg to be spanked, but same difference, right?

When I finally get logged in, I send a quick instant message to Mr. Jacobs.

Miranda

> Sir, I'd like to request a meeting with you ASAP.

That should be enough to get him interested. I can tell he's online, but he doesn't answer immediately. Shit, I'm going to have to be patient.

I spend about ten minutes pretending to go through my email inbox, but my body is tingling with anticipation and I'm barely reading anything. When the messenger flashes that he's responded, my heart leaps into my throat.

Mr. Jacobs

> I'm free in 10 minutes.

Miranda

> Eager to begin, sir. I'll be there.

There's no way he could misinterpret what I'm wanting to 'meet' about. I don't normally tell him I'm eager for anything.

I lean back and daydream about walking into his office and immediately dropping my panties to the floor. That would get the message across. I wonder what he would do?

Giggling at myself, I glance at my computer, and the flash of my messenger app catches my eye.

> Meet us in the conference room instead of my office.

Uh...*meet us*?

> Yes, sir.

My brain blips out, and I stare at my monitor, not seeing any of the words on the screen, while I consider his last message. What's going on in the conference room? I'm not sure I'm ready for what would happen if I walked in and dropped my panties for all four lawyers. Mmm, or am I? My slutty pussy buzzes as if she's trying to convince me otherwise.

Shit, fine, okay, Kinky Miranda wants it, even if Regular Miranda has some reservations. But it's not going to happen. My husband, Jon, said he's fine with me fucking my bosses, but a gangbang would need some discussion in advance, so there's no point in stewing over it.

A meeting with all of them is a good idea. I need to set some ground rules with them that include no ass stuff—especially for Mr. Parks. My heart races at the thought of Mr. Parks and his nimble fingers, which he's stuck in my ass before, and I flush with heat all the way to the tips of my toes as my pussy thrums in excitement. Jon has made it very clear that only he gets to fuck my ass, but I might need to find out if fingers are okay.

Shaking my head, I stand up and straighten my skirt. Enough fantasizing. I have a job to do, and if I don't have a cock in me by the end of the day, I'm going to be one unhappy Miranda.

I take the back hallways to the conference room to avoid Cindy. If she saw me, she'd pry and wonder why I had a meeting with all the lawyers.

She'd get cranky when I couldn't tell her anything. While I love the idea of my secret sex life starting up again with the bosses, it's not something to broadcast to my co-workers.

As I enter the large room, my mouth goes dry at the sight of all four men sitting on one side of the long wooden conference table. My gangbang over the weekend is forefront in my mind as I imagine what they would do to me right now if I begged them all to fuck me.

When they see me, they stop talking, but none of them rise to greet me. Their eyes linger on my curves, and I can feel my nipples harden as a slideshow of possible positions goes through my mind. Which one would fuck me from behind while I was blowing another? I'm a horny slut, and it wouldn't take much to get me to start begging.

Since I don't know exactly why I'm here, I decide to play it cool. I give a brief nod towards Mr. Jacobs. "Thank you for taking the time to speak with me."

Out of the corner of my eye, I see a slight smirk from Mr. Parks, and that expression alone makes me want to drop to my knees and crawl towards them. Just the possibility of fucking them again has turned me into a nympho—though it's probably the result of my wild weekend at the resort. I'm primed and ready for more sex.

As soon as we lock eyes, Mr. Jacobs responds. "Sit, Miranda."

He points to the chair across the table from where they're all sitting. Oooh, are they going to interrogate me? I can handle this.

When I sit down, Mr. Jacobs nods at me. "How was your little vacation?"

Little vacation? Hah! How do I respond to that? Should I tell him about how there was nothing little about all the massive cocks I had inside me? Probably not.

I settle on something vague. "It was very relaxing. Thank you all for the gift."

It's unsettling to be the center of attention when I'm uncertain exactly why I'm here. I scan the faces of the lawyers and pause when I reach Mr. King. His eyes bore into me, making me breathless, and I resist the urge to grind against my chair. I wish they would just rip my clothes off and take turns with me already, but it appears they didn't ask me here to fuck me...again, not that I would let them, but it still would have been nice if they had tried.

Goddamn, I'm a thirsty slut today. Jon is going to laugh his ass off when I tell him how horny I am. This is what happens when I'm offered the keys to the castle again. I might go crazy for a few days, but I'm sure my slutty side will calm down again.

I smile at the lawyers, acting like I'm unfazed, but I clench my hands together in my lap and tap my feet restlessly. They need to get to the point so we can discuss how and when they're going to fill my holes.

Instead, they remain silent as Mr. King places a tablet on the table in front of me and turns it on. Uh, what's going on?

A video starts playing on the tablet, and my eyes widen. Oh God, it's security footage of me sitting on this very conference table and fingering myself. I'm alone in the room, and the video has to be close to a year old. Can the earth swallow me up now? I'm flushed with embarrassment and lower my eyes as the recording plays out. I didn't expect a dose of humiliation to go along with this meeting.

No one says a word, and I can't stop myself from squirming under their gaze. My clit throbs with dark pleasure and it's difficult to focus on anything else. It's super fucked up how turned on I am right now.

After what seems like an eternity, Mr. Jacobs speaks. "We have at least four other videos like that of you around the office. What do you have to say for yourself?"

Do I apologize and offer to suck their cocks? I'm not sure what I should say, and I have no explanation for my actions...sometimes I get turned on at work, and I didn't know the cameras were on.

When I don't reply, Mr. Jacobs keeps talking in that firm, sexy voice of his that makes my stomach muscles quiver. "Why would a woman act like such a slut at work?"

I know he's not trying to slut shame me, and this is all part of whatever game he's playing. I look at him through my eyelashes while feigning innocence. "Well, maybe I was turned on?"

Or maybe I work with four sexy lawyers who were off limits and sometimes my fantasies got away from me. So yeah, it wasn't the smartest plan, but what're they going to do, fire me? We all know that's not happening.

A wicked grin crosses Mr. Jacobs' face, and I squirm as he speaks. "You're probably wondering why you're in the hot seat today."

I nod, my heart racing, and I can hardly focus on what he's saying. All I'm aware of is his mouth and tongue doing filthy things to me in my imagination. I need to get fucked so badly that my brain can't think properly.

"After firing Bonny, we had a long conversation, and we're not sure it's appropriate for us to engage in sexual behavior with any of our employees."

My mind freezes for a moment, and I suck in my breath. What?! Are these bastards messing with me? There's no way I've been cockteased by getting sent off to a weekend filled with nonstop fucking just to come back to find out they're being 'proper' about work.

He pauses, and I let out my breath. It doesn't register at first that I need to respond, so I continue to sit silently in my chair.

Finally, Mr. Jacobs asks, "Do you understand what this means, Miranda?"

It means they're going to have a mutiny on their hands soon. I almost snort at the idea of me going on strike due to lack of cock at work, but when I notice Mr. Daniels has a soft smile, it makes me relax. Oh god, they're just messing with me. I love and hate them when they tease me like this. It's time to flip the conversation in the direction I want it to go.

Blinking flirtatiously at Mr. Jacobs, I tilt my head and give him my best sultry tone of voice. "I think it means that I've been a bad girl who needs punished."

I can see that I'm getting to him. The corners of his lips twitch, and his tone is gruff. "And?"

I lick my lips while keeping my voice breathless. "Maybe I'm supposed to seduce all of you into fucking me again?"

Their gazes focus on me, and the attention makes my pulse beat rapidly. I feel like prey being hunted by four powerful beasts, and even though I should play hard to get, my pussy buzzes in delight. It takes every ounce of self-control to stop myself from laying all my cards out on the table and begging them to fuck me.

Mr. Jacobs chuckles as if he just thought of something. "No, you don't have to seduce us, but you do deserve punishment."

Mmm, now we're talking.

But before I can say anything, Mr. Jacobs continues. "Cindy is going on vacation after the holiday, and while she's gone, we want you to be our freeuse office slut. Can you handle that?"

My body tingles at how his voice becomes rougher as he's offering me my fantasy. There's no point in pretending I don't want this anymore.

I nod eagerly. "Yes."

He speaks firmly and makes the expectations clear. "For one week, you'll be available to us during normal work hours for whatever use we want. Your sole purpose will be to please us. You'll have a safeword that you can use at any point, and your continued employment here doesn't hinge upon you agreeing to any of this."

Is he saying that for the benefit of the cameras? I'm fairly certain I've made it obvious I'm down to fuck them all, and we've been doing this off and on for so many years there's no way I would assume my job depended on me sucking their dicks. I suppose he might want a record of this, though, so I don't push it and just nod in agreement.

Mr. Jacobs motions towards me. "Good girl. Now show us you're willing. Take your panties off and work the rest of the day without them."

An electric shock of lust runs through my body, and I don't hesitate before standing up and running my hands up my skirt to slide my panties off. I have to step out of my heels so I don't trip on them as I pick them up off the floor.

Dangling the scrap of black lace from my fingers, I purr at them. "Are you done with me? I've got work to do."

Mr. Daniels smiles outright, and the corners of Mr. Jacobs' lips twitch again as he says, "Yes, that will be all for now. No one will touch you until we're back from the holiday."

Well, that's a bummer. I can already feel my inner thighs getting damp, and it's going to be a long few days while I imagine what they're going to do to me.

"Of course, sir."

I start walking away, but Mr. King's voice stops me. "Miranda, we need a list of what we can't do to you and your safeword before Christmas."

Oooh right, I have things I have to tell them they can't do. "Yes, sir."

Mr. Daniels didn't speak during the meeting, and he's still smiling at me, so I ball up my panties and throw them at him. "Save those for me for later."

His grin widens as he catches them, and I spin on my heels and strut out of the room, making sure my hips sway as I walk. It feels like every inch of my skin is on fire and tingling with need.

At my desk, I look at the time. It's only 10:47AM. It's going to be a long two weeks until I get one of their cocks in me.

CHAPTER 2

Jon loves that my bosses are making me wait until after New Year's, and once I'm off work for the holidays, we have a wonderful and relaxing Christmas. Part of Jon's gift to me is a collection of new lingerie in a rainbow of colors. When he makes me model them for him, it turns into a wild fuckfest with him trying his hardest to give me more orgasms than I can count over the holidays. The prospect of me fucking my bosses again has revved his engine in a big way. I'm not complaining.

Despite how time seems to crawl, it's finally the Monday to return to work, and I'm freshly shaved everywhere and ready to be the freeuse office slut. I'm wearing a royal blue dress with a flowing skirt for easy access. I skipped panties, but I have on a garter belt with my favorite pair of silky black stockings with a seam down the back.

As I stroll across the parking lot and into work, my too-tall, strappy black heels click on the cement. I know I'm overdressed, but I look and feel sexy. No one but me and the lawyers are going to be in the office—even the paralegal is on vacation—and I shiver from the delicious unknown of how today is going to play out.

When I step through the door, I stop in surprise. Mr. King is sitting on a leather sofa in the waiting area. Huh, okay, I can make this work.

"Good morning," I purr as I stroll over to him.

Mr. King smiles as I get close. "You look beautiful. I'm going to enjoy taking that dress off you."

I flush at his compliment, and the dirty mental image of him removing my dress. I'm ready for him to take it off me this very second. I stand as close as I can to him, and his hand strokes my outer thigh, running along my silk stockings and up my dress. When he reaches the top lace edge of the stocking, he meets the bare flesh of my hip. His hand continues up, and I can see the recognition in his eyes when he realizes I don't have panties on.

"Eager this morning, I see. Naughty girl."

My breathing speeds up, and I'm practically vibrating with need. I daydreamed about one of them fucking me as soon as I walked in the door, but I didn't think it would actually happen. Now I'm not sure of anything.

As he caresses my upper thigh, his fingers mere inches from my pussy, my brain freezes, and I can't speak.

In a soft, but stern voice, Mr. King says, "It looks like someone is ready to be fucked. Sit on my lap with your back against me."

Oh yeah, I can do that. I drop my purse and lunch on the floor and do as he requests. I can feel his hard cock pressing against me through his pants as I settle down onto his lap. He wraps his arm around my stomach, holding me close to him, while his other hand inches my dress up. He caresses my inner thigh, and I spread my legs to give him better access. I moan when he cups my pussy with his big palm and grinds the heel of his hand against my clit.

Jesus, I barely walked in the door, and he's already driving me insane with lust. This is so hot. I love being the office slut, and Jon is going to enjoy this story tonight.

Mr. King's fingers dips between my folds, spreading my slickness around as he runs his fingers through my entrance and back up to my clit, circling and then moving away again. He's going to drive me insane if he keeps doing this.

I whimper as my head drops back on his shoulder and I tilt my hips forward to encourage his fingers to return to my clit. I'm rewarded with him circling my clit again, and I moan softly, encouraging him to continue as pleasure radiates from my core.

Holy fuck, where are the other lawyers? One of them could walk out here and see this. Pleasure ripples through me at the thought, and I almost giggle. Yeah, who am I kidding? I'd love it if one of them was watching.

It won't take me long to come at this rate, and every brush of Mr. King's fingers sends shivers of delight through me. When he slides two thick fingers inside me, I moan with satisfaction. I'd prefer his cock, but his fingers will do. He's rock hard underneath me, and I wiggle against him while he pumps his fingers in and out of my pussy.

Right before I come, he removes his fingers and pulls my dress down.

What the hell?

"You almost came, didn't you?"

I blink, trying to think clearly through the haze of lust. "Uh...Yes."

"I didn't tell you to come yet, my little freeuse slut," he says with a chuckle. "You only come when I tell you to. Understand?"

Fuck. I whimper as a sharp neediness overwhelms me. He better let me come today, or he's going to have one cranky administrative assistant on his hands.

He pushes me off his lap, and I straighten my skirt before picking up my purse and lunch from the floor. I'm uncertain what I should do and stand there awkwardly while my pussy tingles in protest of not being fucked.

"We're alone today. Everyone else is taking an extra day of vacation."

My eyes widen. Just him?

He continues. "I've got some conference call meetings. Get logged into your computer and come to my office in ten minutes. Be prepared to work," he warns as he rises from the couch and strides towards his office without looking at me.

Prepare to work? Does that mean sexy fun or regular work? Fuck, I guess I'll find out when I get to his office.

I head to my desk, horny and irritated. The jury is still out on how well I like him. He hasn't exactly been the friendliest over the last two years. Getting me all worked up to what I assumed was going to be an amazing orgasm and then stopping doesn't endear him to me.

If I had more time, I'd text Jon and whine. He'd enjoy knowing I'm a needy slut who isn't getting what she wants. Instead, I force myself to log into my computer before putting my purse and lunch away.

Nine minutes later, I'm walking towards Mr. King's office with a notepad and my favorite pen, determined to be a good assistant so he'll fuck me as a reward. His office door is open, and when he sees me, he gives me a charming smile. I take it as an invitation and slink into the room, rolling my hips so he can enjoy the view. I fondly remember being fucked over his desk that one glorious freeuse week, and my pussy is eager for a repeat performance.

He watches me with a sparkle of humor in his eye, like he can tell what I'm doing. "Are you ready to work?" he asks.

I really hope he doesn't mean actual work, but I'd gladly work on polishing his cock. I bat my eyelashes at him while setting down the notepad and pen on his desk.

"Ready to work, boss."

Mr. King gestures to one of the guest chairs in front of his desk. As I sit, I smooth the fabric of the dress along my thighs, and the motion causes his eyes to shift downward. He studies me, and I can tell he's thinking.

When his eyes roam back up, they linger on my breasts before focusing on my face again. I arch an eyebrow in response. He knows he wants to fuck me. He needs to just do it already.

After a minute of silence, I can't handle the suspense anymore and ask, "Is there something specific you want from me?"

Like...maybe your cock pounding inside me. Please?

Mr. King grin and rolls his chair back away from the desk. "I want you on your knees and under my desk. But first, take those ridiculous shoes off."

My brain doesn't know which part to respond to first. The idea of being under his desk is hot, but I choose to think about my shoes first.

I narrow my eyes and lift my leg, pointing the toe of my shoe at him. "These shoes aren't ridiculous." I'm careful to enunciate my words, and I sound argumentative. "They make my legs look amazing."

I pull my dress up to the top edge of my stockings as if to show him my legs and prove my point.

Mr. King responds with a heated gaze as he watches my every movement. "Yes, they do."

I give him a saucy pout.

He just sits there, studying me, before adding, "Now take your shoes off so you can service me properly."

My body buzzes at his words, and my skin flushes. Based on our brief time together, he knows I'm a submissive slut who loves being told what to do, but I'm also a bit of a brat. I stay seated and bend down to unbuckle the strap of one of my high heels.

"Slower," he orders in a gruff voice.

A rush of wetness dampens my thighs. God, it turns me on when he's controlling. I whimper as I go slower to please him.

Mr. King smiles. "Keep going, nice and slow, just like that."

All I can think of is dropping to my knees and sucking on him like the cock-hungry little whore he wants me to be.

Once both straps are loose, I lift one of my feet and remove my shoe, setting it down gently on the floor. Mr. King lets out a deep, sexy rumble of approval. For a guy who called my heels ridiculous, he's sure enjoying the show.

I slide off my other shoe, pausing for a moment before letting it fall to the carpet with a thud.

Mr. King leans forward. "Spread your legs. Show me your pussy."

Damn, he has no mercy, does he? I lift my dress and part my legs so he can see how soaked I am. I'm practically trembling as he leans back and studies me with appreciation.

"Now crawl over here and get under my desk. The meeting is about to start, and you're going to suck on me the entire time."

God, why is this so hot? I've had years of practice kneeling for Jon and other men, and I get out of my chair and drop gracefully to the floor. I crawl over to him slowly, making him wait. When I reach him, I only hesitate briefly before crawling under his desk. I'm a grown-ass woman, and it's going to be a tight fit under here. He pushes his chair in, effectively locking me between him and the back of his desk.

He spreads his legs, making room for me between them. "Now take out my cock and suck on it. I've got to get on this call."

Oooh, he's making a mistake. Does he not realize I'm going to do whatever I can to make him moan? He better keep himself on mute.

I nestle between his legs and undo the button for his slacks. I lower his zipper so it's easier to release his stiff shaft and push down his boxers so they're out of my way. God, I want to suck on him.

I try not to show how impatient I am as I take out his magnificent cock and admire its length and girth. I want to worship his cock and learn exactly how he enjoys being touched, but today I've got to do what he wants, and I better behave.

I hear him connecting to the conference call, and after one quick lick to his velvety soft crown, I open wide to swallow him whole. Mmm, his heady musk sends my senses into overdrive, and I moan happily.

I slowly ease him deeper down my throat until he hits the back. Shit, he's too large for me to fit all of him into my mouth comfortably. After a few shallow bobs of my head to coat him with saliva, I try to suck down as much of him as I can.

He greets the people on the call, and I barely pay attention to what they're talking about. I have better things to focus on. With my tongue pressed against the underside of his shaft, I gag on his cock each time the tip slides into my throat.

I get into a pleasant rhythm as the call continues. Nothing makes me feel sluttier than being under my boss's desk while he's in the middle of a conference call. I feel a glow of satisfaction every time I hear quiet grunts or moans from him. I half hope the people on the call can hear him.

When I suck harder, he thrusts up to fuck my throat. Every noise he makes while trying to stay professional makes me giddy, and I take him down again. He speaks for a few minutes while I continue to suck on him. I have no idea how he's able to concentrate.

When he's done talking, he grips the side of my head with his hands and pushes himself as far as he can down my throat before pulling back while I cough and sputter.

Fucking A, Mr. King is one dirty, cocky lawyer. As if on cue, he thrusts again, this time angling himself so that he slides further down my throat. I try not to make any loud noises, but he's making it difficult.

Even though I hate him for making me gag while he's on a call, my body still thrills at the rough treatment. When he rocks his hips again, I look up at him and attempt to give him a death glare through the wood of the desk. Of course he can't see it, but I hope he feels it.

Him using my mouth like this pings a part of my brain that loves and hates being treated like a fucktoy. I could stop it with my safeword, but I don't want to. I want to feel like I'm just a hole to be used, and he's fulfilling that need superbly at the moment.

When he stops thrusting so far down my throat, I relax. Now that he's being gentler, I'm able to close my eyes and bob my head up and down, enjoying my thick lollipop.

My body trembles with desire while I suck on him and listen to him conducting business. I'm not sure how much longer I can keep this up. It turns me on too much to be used like this, and I desperately want to touch myself. God, I really hope he fucks me after the meeting.

Mr. King goes completely silent above me and holds his body taut. I pause with my mouth stuffed full of his dick as my throat works around him. Is the call almost over?

Right as I wonder if I should stop sucking on him, I feel a burst of wet heat hit the back of my throat. Holy fuck, did he really just come down my throat without warning?

I moan and swallow his offering as fast as I can. The thrill of drinking down his cum while he's on his work call has me tingling and warm with delight. I'm such a slut, and it feels incredible.

I swallow and finish licking him clean while he completes the meeting and signs off the call. When I notice him peek under the desk at me, I stop licking and grin up at him.

I expect him to praise me or give some sort of acknowledgment for being a wonderful office slut, but when he rolls his chair back, he motions me to climb out from under the desk. As I struggle to right myself, pushing up from the carpet, he stands, turning his back to me while fixing his clothes.

Without glancing behind him, he tosses out, "Go back to your desk until I want you again," over his shoulder as he exits his office.

What the fuck? That's it? Not even a thanks for letting me use your throat like a fleshlight? He needs to learn how to treat his freeuse office toys better. I grumble to myself as I put my heels back on and walk back to my desk.

And what's worse...how am I supposed to get any work done? I just want his cock in me.

CHAPTER 3

We spend the next couple of hours working, him off doing whatever legal stuff he normally does and me pretending to reply to emails. And by pretending, I mean me leaning back in my chair and listening to music while texting flirty messages to my husband to turn him on. I'm not totally sure Mr. King is going to let me come, so I need to have Jon primed and ready for me as soon as I get home.

When my work instant messenger flashes, I let out a tiny squeal in delight.

Uh…what? My body buzzes, and I can feel my inner thighs get even more slick at the thought. Oooh, this is fucked up and awesome, and such a perfect way to cap off the day! Jon's going to love this. Maybe I should take some pictures in the mirror. He might not believe I'm walking around naked otherwise.

I pull my dress off and then mourn removing my stockings. Dammit, I'm sexy in these. Why can't I keep them on? Wait, would he spank me if I did? I know he's trying to mess with me, but so far, I love everything he's doing. If this level of fuckery continues with the other lawyers this week, I'll have the best job ever again.

I hold back a laugh as I spread my dress out on my chair so I can sit on it. Yeah, it's messed up that I have to sit on my dress, but I'm so damn wet there's no way I'm putting my bare pussy against the chair.

Now, how can I have fun with him? I'm definitely leaving the garter and stockings on in the hopes of that spanking.

Miranda

I'm naked. Do you need any help with work?

Hmm...that sounded pretty innocent, even if it was a lie and I'm not totally naked.

Mr. King

Touch yourself until I tell you to stop.

Miranda

Yes, sir.

It seems Mr. King is still in the mood to fuck me—or fuck with me—after all. I smirk at my computer screen. Two can play this game, sir, so bring it on.

I slide my hand down my stomach and spread my knees, giving my fingers access to my aching pussy. When my fingertips touch my clit, I can feel exactly how slick and soaked I am. I moan softly as I push my fingers inside my pussy and fuck myself. I need to figure out a way to convince him to let me orgasm today before I go crazy with lust.

I spread my legs as wide as possible and lean back in my chair. I close my eyes as I massage my clit with one hand and finger fuck myself with the other. Oh god, this is so hot. I imagine someone walking around the corner and seeing me fingering myself at my desk, and pleasure swirls in my core at the thought. Yeah, I found out I'm a fucking slut who loves being caught having sex after the night someone caught Jon fucking me on a pool table at a Christmas party. I remember how I felt when it happened and moan loudly, pumping my fingers into my pussy harder and faster.

I'm so busy I almost miss Mr. King's next message. Almost, but not quite.

> **Stop touching yourself now.**

Blah, just like him to ruin my fun. I whine to myself as I stop. My head is fuzzy, and I just want to come. He's successfully gotten me to where I would literally do anything he asked. I'd crawl on my hands and knees from my desk down the hall naked if he promised to fuck me.

> **I stopped.**

> **Good. Now I'm sending you a file and I need you to print it out and spiral bind it for me.**

Uh...my head spins, and I try to focus on his words while my pussy flutters.

> **Bring it to me when you're done.**

Shit. Why does he insist on making me work today? This is starting to feel like two years ago when he made me watch the stupid training video and take a test.

> **Yes, sir. Printing and binding it now.**

I take a minute to navigate to the correct page in our printing program, and I let out a groan of frustration when I see there are 96 pages total to print and spiral bind for him. Jesus, Mr. King, can I smack you now?

I give it a good ten minutes before I walk to the printer across the office. It's been a very long time since I've been naked and walking the halls, and this reminds me of the time I had my arms bound behind me and Mr. Knight was leading me to the conference room to fuck all the lawyers.

There's no way to erase all the memories of Mr. Knight, no matter how badly that ended, but at least I've got Mr. King to make new memories with—though the jury is still out on him. I liked him better earlier when I was sitting in his lap and I thought I was going to get fucked first thing in the morning.

My nipples are hard from the cool air, and it takes twice as long to spiral bind the papers as it normally does. I kept getting distracted by daydreaming of Mr. King coming in and fucking me over the counter in the supply room. That seems to be what he enjoys doing—he gives me a work assignment, and then he sneaks in and fucks me. So why isn't he here with his cock inside me yet?

When I'm finished, he still hasn't shown up, and I sigh in disappointment. Damn him. Guess I'll take it to him. When I stroll into his office, I drop the papers on his desk in front of him with a smile.

"All done, sir."

He gives me a stern look, one of disapproval. "I told you to be naked."

Oh, right. I give him my sexiest grin. "Oopsie. I thought you liked the stockings. Aren't they sexy?"

I lift my foot onto the chair in front of his desk and caress my thighs, as if trying to convince him I should keep them on.

With a slight shake of his head, he shoves his chair away from his desk and walks over to me. Before I can say anything, he's got me bent over the front of his desk. Ooooh, score! I wiggle my butt at him and give him a naughty smile over my shoulder. He rubs the soft skin of my ass, and I hum with pleasure. This is one of my favorite parts.

"I shouldn't spank you. You want it."

I don't deny his accusation.

I stick my ass back at him, daring him to take it, but then he slaps me. Hard.

Fuck, I love this part too, but then I whimper when I realize it's going to be a while before he fucks me. As I relax into the spanking, each smack sends a delicious wave of pleasure to my clit. Heat spreads over the tender flesh of my ass, and each spank hits that wonderful pleasure and pain point where I want him to go feral and pound into my pussy. I'll probably orgasm within minutes once he fucks me.

By the time he finishes, I'm a whining, desperate slut in need of a good fucking. I pant with need as pleasure spirals in my core.

"Get back to your desk."

Um...I look over my shoulder and blink at him, trying to focus through the haze of pleasure. Is he seriously not going to fuck me right now?

When he stares down at me, waiting, I huff and lay my head down against the cool surface of the desk. "Okay," I reply with another whimper. "I'll leave once the room stops spinning."

I'm actually fine to walk, but he doesn't know that. I close my eyes and drift for a moment until I hear him sit in one of the chairs behind me. Oooh fuck. I swear I can feel his gaze on my pussy as wetness drips down my inner thigh.

He clears his throat, his voice husky. "Tell me why you enjoy doing this."

I know exactly what he means, and he doesn't need to explain what "this" is.

"It's something Jon can't give me."

Which is true. Jon wouldn't make me crawl under a desk and suck on him while he was on a phone call. He enjoys edging me and teasing me, but there's a line he won't cross. Maybe he respects me too much, so it's not the same. I can't feel truly used when I know Jon loves me.

Mr. King stands up again and slides his fingers between my slick pussy lips to rub circles around my clit. "Can't? Or won't?"

"Oooooh, god. Does it matter?" I moan and push back against his hand, trying to get him to slide a finger inside me.

He pulls his hand back and, before I can complain, slaps my pussy. I cry out as sharp pleasure ripples from my pussy.

"I asked you a question, slut. Can't, or won't?"

He slaps my pussy a few more times, and I pant out, "Can't—he can't. He's a soft dom. He can't give it to me as hard as I need."

I almost feel like a traitor admitting this to Mr. King, but Jon and I have talked about it many times over the years. We found a very satisfying middle ground for both of us. I've never doubted how much he loves me, so it works, but sometimes I crave more, and I'm so fucking lucky that Jon gets off on sharing me so I can get that part of me satisfied elsewhere.

Instead of slapping my pussy again, Mr. King puts his fingers back on my clit and continues to tease me. This time, though, I'm starting to think he's not planning to fuck me at all. The shitty and wonderful thing about that is I'd be okay if he doesn't. I love the angst of not getting fucked when I want it.

"Are you a masochist, Miranda?"

His words take me out of the moment for a bit, and I look up at him in confusion. "What?"

He rubs my clit again, and the pleasure causes me to jerk my hips towards his hand for more as he repeats himself. "Are you a masochist?"

I think for a moment while I continue to enjoy him circling my clit. "No, I'm just a slut who likes to be used."

Mr. King laughs darkly. "Well, I agree with you on that."

As if to prove the point, he thrusts two of his fingers into my pussy, curling them to massage the pleasure point inside me as he begins to roughly pump them in and out. I gasp at how quickly my arousal peaks, and I'm on the verge of an orgasm within seconds. I cry out, trying to stifle the sound by burying my face in my arm as I force myself not to come. Oh fuuuuck. I don't know if I can stop it.

I'm trembling and on the edge as he pulls his fingers out. I hear the rustle of his clothes a moment before he slams his cock into me.

"Ohhh, god!" I cry out and arch my back as he pushes inside me to the hilt and sets a punishing rhythm, fucking me with long, hard strokes.

"Please, let me come, sir. Please?"

It's pure torture not being able to come, but Mr. King makes no sign of giving me relief. I squeeze down on his cock, and tendrils of pleasure shoot to my core, making it worse. I'm afraid my brain is going to melt from pleasure before he lets me come.

When he abruptly pulls out, I tremble with the effort of holding back an orgasm and mewl at the loss of his cock.

I'm panting, lost to the madness of needing to come. I whine pathetically as I plead with him, "Don't stop. Oh god, don't stop."

Mr. King chuckles as if my desperation amuses him before sinking back into my swollen pussy with a single stroke. When his fingers find my clit, rubbing, circling, and massaging, I can't hold back any longer. My orgasm tears through me with the ferocity of an electric charge, causing all my muscles to lock and spasm and making my lungs seize up so that I can't breathe.

Mr. King's continues to pound into me, extending one of the most powerful orgasms I've had in the last week. Shit, this rivals all the orgasms I had at the freeuse resort.

When my body relaxes, he moves his hand from my clit and lifts me up. His cock is still inside me as he sits down on a chair with me in his lap, his chest pressed against my back. He's still clothed, other than having his cock out, and I can feel his warmth through his dress shirt.

"Now stay still so I can use you like a cum dumpster whore."

It takes me a moment to focus on the present, and I don't reply as he moves my hips like I'm a sex doll that he's trying to get off with. His sheer size overwhelms me into submission, and I'm more than happy to be his fucktoy and just sit here, impaled on his glorious cock.

He runs his hands over my curves possessively, squeezing and pinching wherever he wants. I whimper but don't complain because I love how he's treating me. God, he makes me feel like his slut. When his fingers graze my sensitive clit, I suck in a sharp breath as I feel another orgasm building.

While he pinches and squeezes my clit, I throw my head back to rest against his shoulder and whimper. Pleasure ripples up and down my spine, and I do my best to hold still as another orgasm rips through my body. My pussy flutters and squeezes his cock in response to the ecstasy rocketing through me.

This time Mr. King groans with pleasure when he feels me coming on his cock, but he doesn't relent. While my pussy still throbs, he wraps his arm around my waist, keeping me immobile as he thrusts his hips up, pounding my pussy until his strokes become jerky. He comes with a deep groan of satisfaction as I feel his warmth flood my pussy.

We're both silent and still for several minutes, basking in our afterglow before Mr. King helps me up off his lap. He holds me in his arms, making sure I'm steady. When he kisses my forehead, I get the sense that he's not as rough as he'd like me to think.

As if he can read my thoughts, he tells me, "Now get back to work, slut. No clothes until you leave. And make sure you eat and drink something."

I can't stop myself from grinning. "Yes, sir!"

It's only when I settle down at my desk again that I think about how I feel about him. There's a connection between us, even though we haven't spoken much at all since he joined the firm. We have a sexual chemistry that is unlike anything I've ever experienced with any of the other lawyers before. Back when Mr. Knight was here, he was more of a mentor and teaching me about submission, but Mr. King just enjoys using me with no strings attached. He's not trying to be my friend. It's perfect.

I eat a snack and hydrate as I try to answer the same work emails that I've been needing to reply to all day. I can feel his cum leaking out of me onto the dress I'm sitting on. Fuck, that's dirty.

Oh shit, I never took the naked picture for Jon. I open up the camera on my phone, angle it to show him exactly how dirty and used I look, and snap a pic before forwarding it to my husband with a simple message.

> Fucked on my boss's desk with his cum running down my legs. Do you want me to shower when I get home?

Mr. King may be a bastard for playing with my emotions like he did, but I really do enjoy being his dirty office slut, and I can't wait for what the other lawyers are going to do to me tomorrow.

It only takes my husband a few minutes to text back.

> Nope. You need more cum in you before you shower.

Yeah, he knows what I like. I send him a heart emoji and try to buckle down and concentrate on the emails. After a few minutes, I give up and daydream about fucking Jon. When it's time to leave, I slide my dress on, and I'm adjusting it as Mr. King comes by my desk.

"Mr. Jacobs said to tell you to wear your pink shirt tomorrow."

My mouth drops open, and my pussy buzzes at the thought of them discussing me.

I nod. "Yes, sir. Have a good evening."

He says goodnight to me as I gather my purse and lunch sack. I get into my car with a dazed smile on my face and hurry home to get fucked by

Jon. I'm almost as eager to tell him all about Mr. King as I am to feel my husband's cock inside me.

CHAPTER 4

I'm a good girl and don't shower. I'm sitting on the kitchen table when Jon gets home. The only clothes I'm wearing are my garter belt and silk stockings. I've got my feet resting on separate chairs, and I'm spread wide open. I've been playing with myself while I wait for him, and my pussy is swollen and wet.

His eyes glaze over with lust as he sets his lunch and water bottle on the counter.

"So tell me..." His voice is low, and it sends a shiver of pleasure straight to my core. "How much of a filthy slut were you today?"

I swirl my fingers around my clit and moan, "Mmm, so dirty."

This is the game we play, and I enjoy making him work for all the details after I fuck someone else.

Jon starts removing his clothes, and I vibrate with need. As he pulls off his shirt, he asks, "What did Mr. King do?"

I slide my fingers over my pussy as I talk, stroking and circling my clit with delicate movements, and I watch Jon undress the rest of the way. I'm ready to pull him on top of me the moment he's naked.

"I crawled under his desk and sucked on him while he was on a call."

Jon kicks his pants to the side and moves between my legs. His cock is hard and would slide in so easily. I reach forward to rub his shaft slowly. I want him to be as desperate as I am.

"Did he let you come?" he asks in a hoarse whisper.

I circle the tip of his cock with my thumb, spreading the pre-cum like it's lube. I relish the little shudder that I feel rippling through him.

"Eventually," I admit. I grin wickedly. "He made me come when he bent me over his desk."

Jon groans as I guide his cock to my pussy. As soon as the head slides in, Jon takes over. He sinks inside me balls deep, and I grip his shoulders as he fucks me leisurely. Shit, where is my crazy, worked up husband who was supposed to fuck me hard?

My head spins from the slow pace he's setting, and I wrap my legs around his waist and squeeze tightly. Jon grunts but continues to move in and out at an infuriatingly slow rate. What the hell is going on?

After a minute, he leans in close, putting his cheek to mine before whispering in my ear, "How does it feel to have two men decide when to allow you an orgasm?"

A rush of pleasure zings straight into my brain at his words. Shit. I raise an eyebrow at him and tease, "I don't know, I could do this all night. How about you?"

With a wolfish grin, Jon rears back and slams into me hard, bottoming out. "Game on."

A strangled cry leaves me, and I throw my head back in shock and delight. Fuck yes. I thought he was going to make me beg, but this is so much better. When he slams into me again, my eyes roll back as a thrill shoots through me. Yes, oh god, this is exactly what I need.

For several moments, neither of us speaks, and all I can hear is the sound of our moans and the creak of the table. Jon fucks me like a man on a mission, and I cling to him as I meet him thrust for thrust. A tingling sensation starts in my toes, traveling up my legs and settling in my stomach.

It radiates outward, sparking tiny explosions along the way. My body tenses as it climbs higher. Just before I'm thrown over the edge, Jon pauses mid stroke.

Our eyes lock together as I hover there with his cock buried deep in my cunt.

"No!" I whimper as he shifts back, leaving just the tip of his cock inside me. "Jon!" I try to push against him with my heels, but his hands on my knees keep my legs locked apart.

"Patience, kitten."

He winks, and I whimper with frustration. I'm quivering with lust as I reach up and twist one of my nipples. I can't just lie here like this without coming. I'm about half ready to climb off this table and push him on the floor to ride him.

When he notices what I'm doing with my hand, Jon shakes his head. "Naughty, naughty, kitten."

Grasping my hand, he pins it down against the table next to me before leaning down to suck my other nipple into his mouth. I writhe under him, wishing he was pounding me back into the orgasm I was so close to.

When he switches breasts, taking the other one in his mouth, I wiggle, trying to get friction from his abdomen touching my pussy. I love my husband dearly, and he knows exactly how much teasing I can take. And the best thing about him is that he always delivers on the build-up and makes it worth the wait.

"Do you think you deserve to come again today?" Jon whispers in between gentle nibbles to my breast.

I squeal out, "Yes! Now, can you please fuck me? Please?"

I'm so desperate for release that I can barely see straight.

"Knees together," he orders gruffly, pressing them together with his hands. I leave them that way, pulling them close to my torso to tempt him.

He murmurs, "Good girl," as he slides back inside me. My head spins from the praise, and I shudder at the joy of him filling me.

I grab for the edges of the table so I can brace myself as he fucks me wildly, thrusting like a machine. I close my eyes and let the pleasure wash over me. A rush of euphoria roars through me, and I explode all over his cock.

My moans are just one long cry of pleasure as he fucks me through my orgasm. Tilting my head back, I allow myself to experience every raw emotion racing through me. When he comes, he joins me with a growl, burying himself completely and filling me with his cum.

My mind goes blank from pleasure, and when I come back to awareness, Jon is looking down at me with a wide, satisfied smile. "I'm not done with you tonight, slut. But first we're going to shower and eat."

I nod eagerly.

He continues. "And then you're going to tell me every single detail of today while I fuck you again, but this time, you aren't coming."

Oh god, that's mean. I love it.

I lower my legs, and he pulls me up and kisses me deeply. As our tongues twirl, I think about how much of a needy slut I'm going to be at work tomorrow if I don't come again tonight.

Jon might be a soft dom who can't fuck me as rough as I want that often, but he sure knows how to fuck with my mind in the most delicious ways.

This is going to be a fun week.

The End

Freeuse Office Games

Games

A Hotwife Shared

Lacey Cross

CHAPTER 1

I practically float through the office doors, my mind replaying yesterday's events on a loop. My body tingles at the memory of Mr. King using me and driving me crazy. I really hope no one expects me to do actual work today. I'm revved up and ready for more playtime.

The receptionist, Cindy, is on vacation, and the office is quieter than usual. Which is good, considering I'm the designated entertainment for four very sexy lawyers this week. The thought makes me squirm as I settle into my chair, smoothing down my pink button-down shirt.

Jon chose my outfit this morning, keeping in mind Mr. Jacobs' request yesterday that I wear my pink shirt. To go with it, my husband selected a white lace bra and panty set that he said would blow my boss's mind, along with a short black skirt and spiked high heels. Before I left, he kissed me and told me to "Be a good slut for your bosses today." I'm not sure what I did in a past life to deserve Jon in this one, but it must have been something fabulous.

I'm logging into my computer programs when the instant messenger pings. My heart jumps into my throat when I see who it's from.

Come to my office. Now.

Oh god–Mr. Jacobs is the senior partner at my law firm, and I love it when he gets demanding—especially knowing this might lead to something deliciously inappropriate that includes multiple HR violations. My spiked heels make me feel sexy and I put an extra swing into my hips as I make my way into his office. He's sitting behind his desk, devastatingly handsome in a charcoal suit. My mind flashes to previous times where his pristine suit was significantly rumpled when I left his office. It's been way too long since he's spanked me, and I think it's time to change that.

"Leave the door open. You won't be here long." His voice sends shivers down my spine. Dammit. I wanted the door closed.

He hands me a stack of papers. "These need to be completed within the hour. Miss one, and you'll find yourself back in here and bent over my desk."

My pussy clenches at his words. I scan the list on the top page, trying to focus despite the wetness growing between my legs. What the heck? I'm not in the mood to deal with my job today. He needs to rethink this plan.

"What if..." I pause, and give a sassy smile. "What if I want to be over your desk?"

"Let me be clear," he rumbles with authority, "your chance for an orgasm today depends entirely on your job performance. Understand?"

My pulse quickens. Oooh, stern Daddy Jacobs is out. Challenge accepted.

Lowering my lashes, I give him my best cutesy and contrite, "Yes, Mr. Jacobs," even though we both know I'm probably not going to do any of this paperwork. I'm sure he doesn't actually expect me to.

I rush back to my desk, but my mind refuses to cooperate. I'm too busy daydreaming about the past and remembering how much I loved being spanked by Mr. Jacobs–the heat that radiated from his palm, the lingering sting, the anticipation as I waited for the next strike. Also...each time I finish one task, the pile seems to multiply. I swear it's breeding.

I'm not even halfway through the pile when the hour is up. My stomach flutters with excitement as I wait for his summons. When my instant messenger flashes, I expect him to ask me about the forms, but he doesn't.

Mr. Jacobs:

Please set up the conference room and get coffee ready for the attendees.

Ugh. This is bullshit. My mind races as I do as I'm told. Where's my spanking for not finishing the forms? I'm the freeuse office slut. I was supposed to have four cocks inside me by now. After Mr. King fucked me all over the office yesterday and made me suck him off under his desk, I expected more today. I think the bastard is teasing me and making me wait for it.

My hands shake as I fill the coffee carafe and arrange the cups. I'm so turned on, I can barely think straight. As I'm finishing up, Mr. Jacobs comes in with a stack of papers and empty manila folders.

He closes the door behind him. "Miranda, you're crawling at a snail's pace today. You should be done by now."

I open my mouth to tell him that maybe if he had spanked me, I would have picked up the pace, but I quickly close it again. Yeah, probably not. I would have just wanted more.

I raise an eyebrow at him while he separates the papers into three piles and sets the empty folders next to them on the table. "Each folder needs one of each form before the meeting starts. You have 10 minutes."

There wasn't a meeting on the calendar, and organizing folders this way definitely isn't how things are done around here. This is a set up if I ever saw one–and I'm okay with that.

He doesn't move away from the table and I have to crowd close to him to reach the forms. Daddy Jacobs is being a bit of a jerk, and with how wet my panties are, my slutty pussy loves it.

I quickly start filling the folders, but him watching over me is making me feel clumsy and I keep accidentally grabbing multiple sheets from the same pile. I'm about to snap at him and ask him if he doesn't have something better to do when he suddenly moves in behind me and unzips my skirt. Ohhh, hello.

My skirt pools at my feet and he rubs his hands over my panties. My pink button-down shirt had been tucked in, but now the ends trail down my stomach and ass. From where he's standing, I bet my legs look amazing in these heels.

When he rubs my pussy, I purposely jut my ass out towards him and his attention makes me inadvertently slow my hand movements.

"How long has it been since I fucked you?" he growls as he continues to run his fingers over the fabric covering my pussy.

"Two years," I breathe out softly. Most of our previous fun times at the office started with a punishment spanking that lead to sex. What he's doing now leaves me uncertain what to expect.

His hand lands on my ass in a sharp spank, and I gasp. Yeah, never mind, there it is.

"That's for being such a tease the last two years when you knew I couldn't fuck you."

Ooooh, god. What the hell? It's not my fault he couldn't fuck me. I'm not the one who hired Bonny, which turned out to be the demise of our office fuckfest. Since he's the senior partner, he would have had a lot of sway in their choice for office manager. Maybe HE should have thought of that when making the final decision. I moan when he spanks me again.

"Keep working," he says gruffly.

Fuck, okay. Must concentrate…Mr. Jacobs' spanks fall in a hypnotic rhythm, making it impossible to think straight. Each one sends jolts of delight through my body. I'm torn between the need to complete the folders and the overwhelming desire to close my eyes and bliss out. I'll just get them done quickly. My hands move on autopilot, shoving papers together.

"Time's running out," he warns as he delivers another painful spank.

When he pulls my panties down to my knees, I bite back a groan and grip the edge of the table. He slides a finger into my pussy and fucks me with it as pleasure swirls in my core. Um, how long have we been in here? Are people about to walk in?

He stops finger fucking me and I hear the sound of his zipper as the teeth slowly part. Every nerve ending sparks alive as the tip of his cock gently probes my pussy. Mmm, now this is more like it.

He grasps my hips firmly, his fingers digging into my flesh. I welcome the slight pain when he slowly sinks into me. Holy fuck, I forgot how much I love his cock after having gone so long without it.

He pauses once he bottoms out and I realize my hands have gone still. Oops, shit. I quickly start stuffing files again as delight ripples through me.

Mr. Jacobs pins my hips against the table with every slow thrust. It's almost impossible to concentrate. Although I'm hindered by my panties, I spread my legs as wide as I can to encourage him to fuck me harder, but he doesn't. Each drag of his cock along the sensitive nerve endings inside me makes my head spin and it doesn't take long for me to feel like I'm losing my mind from pleasure.

"The conference starts any minute now and you're only halfway done. I'm not rewarding your poor work ethic with an orgasm," he taunts me as he slaps my ass.

Ugh. What a jerk. I try to shuffle the pages again. Wait, where was I?

When he moves his hand around to my front and fingers my clit, I roll my hips and let out a small involuntary whimper. Oh fuck. My hands tremble as I haphazardly shove forms into the last few folders. I'm not even paying attention anymore to what I'm putting into each one.

When he sees I'm done with my task, he speeds up his thrusts. I try to hold back my orgasm as the delight builds. The tip of his cock hammers against the magical spot deep inside me, and the pleasure is so intense, I'm going to come at any moment.

A knock at the door shatters my concentration, and I let out an embarrassingly loud groan.

"The clients are here," Mr. Parks calls through the door.

Mr. Jacobs slams into me one last time and groans as he explodes. His warm cum coats my inner walls as he unloads. Ohhhh, no, what? It can't be over.

He jerks against me, unloading ropes of cum before pulling out. I slump down onto the table, squeezing my eyes closed for a moment as I feel his cum leak out of me and drip down my leg. Today really isn't going how I expected. I thought I'd have come at least once by now.

I'm in a daze as I watch him move to a side table and pick up a container of wet wipes I didn't notice before. They aren't usually in here. He was prepared.

As he cleans himself up, he says, casually, "You better make yourself presentable before everyone walks in here."

Fuck, shit. I hastily pull my panties and skirt up, tucking my blouse back in. Mr. Jacobs walks back over to me and whispers in my ear, "I'm not done with you. Go be a good slut and earn your paycheck for the next hour."

He spanks me and I yelp. My legs feel like jelly as I leave. I run into Mr. Parks escorting four other lawyers down the hall. Oh god, is my hair a mess? Heat blooms across my cheeks as I realize my skirt isn't on straight.

Mr. Parks gives me a devilish smile as they pass, and I wish the floor would open up and swallow me, even as a zing of naughty delight turns me on even more. When I reach my desk, I plop down into my seat and feel Mr. Jacobs' cum leaking into my panties. This is messed up in the best of ways.

Instead of tackling my to-do list, I grab my phone from my purse and text my husband.

I'm sure you'll be happy to know I just got fucked and didn't have time to come.

That's not very nice of them.

The winking emoji he adds tells me he doesn't mean what he's saying.

I know it's not. Now I have a pussy full of Mr. Jacobs' cum. How am I supposed to work in these conditions?

His reply makes my body buzz with delight.

Send me a picture of that used pussy.

Well, that's hot. I rush to the bathroom and pull my skirt and panties back down before bending over the sink. It takes a couple of tries with the camera behind me, before I get a picture that shows the perfect angle where he can see my swollen, wet pussy.

I send it to him and his reply comes right as I get back to my desk.

Beautiful. I'm heading into a meeting. Have fun today, Kitten.

I stare at the wall in a daze. What is my life? I'm a mess. I don't know what's planned and what isn't—is it even a real meeting? It's only 10 a.m. and something tells me it's going to be a long day of sexual torture. I'm 100 percent on board with this plan.

CHAPTER 2

I attempt to work for the next hour, but all I can do is think about being fucked again. Will one of the other lawyers fuck me too, or is today only for Mr. Jacobs? He's no spring chicken, so how many times can he come in a day? He might need a break.

The meeting must be over now, because the hallway fills with sound a moment before the whole group passes my desk on the way out, and I blush, focusing on my computer screen to avoid looking at any of them. Shit, I hope the room didn't smell like sex. I wasn't exactly paying attention when I left.

Once the other lawyers are out of earshot, Mr. Jacobs saunters up to my desk, carrying a bundle of files. "Go clean up the conference room. When you're done, copy all these reports before lunch."

He sets them on my desk and I eye the stack. Oh, I've been here befo re…I'll clean and then as I'm making copies, someone is going to come in and fuck me against the copier. Just watch.

As he walks off, he adds over his shoulder. "If you get it done by lunch, I'll spank you. If not…"

Well hell, I'm about to be the fastest copy girl ever.

"Yes, sir," I call out sweetly and hurry to clean.

As soon as I step inside the conference room, I'm met with the faint aroma of musk in the air. It smells like me—did all the lawyers notice? I'm suddenly dying of embarrassment. I'm sure they didn't, and I only do because I know what sex with me smells like...right? Right.

The pile of folders I stuffed is at the end of the table and catches my eye. None of them have been touched. Yeah, Mr. Jacobs gave me a stupid task just so he could fuck me. I bet he never planned to let me come.

I'm grumbling to myself as I give the room a cursory cleaning. I can't spend too long in here since I actually want that spanking—and the potential fucking while I make those copies. I grab the files from my desk and dash to the copier machine. I keep one eye on the doorway while I run the files through the machine. Who is going to come in? Maybe Mr. Parks, since he most likely knows what happened in the conference room. I'm on the edge the entire time, just waiting.

No one shows up.

Before I leave the copier room, I check the wall clock. Twenty minutes to spare. Someone could have fucked me, and I still would have gotten done in time. These guys are wasting their opportunities.

I huff and take the copies back to my desk. Before I can sit down, Mr. Jacobs appears. "Bring those with you."

Excitement surges in my veins as I grab the papers and follow him to his office. He steps aside at the doorway and gestures for me to enter his lair. As I pass him, his hand lightly connects with my ass. There'll probably be more of that shortly. I'm not sure I've ever been this eager for a spanking—but then again, have I ever waited two whole years for someone to spank me?

"Put the copies on my desk and then strip." The raw edge in his tone makes me tremble with desire.

Oooh, here we go. He moves behind his desk as I toss the files onto the surface, scattering them haphazardly. I watch with satisfaction as some of the papers slide out.

"Oops, sorry." I try to sound apologetic as I turn around and show him my backside. I'm just ensuring I get a good spanking.

I unzip my skirt ever so slowly and let it fall to the floor as I start to unbutton my shirt. Mr. Jacobs sighs as if I'm exasperating him and says, "Face me."

I spin around and spread my shirt open so he can see my white lace bra. Teasing him is so much fun, and I love riling him up. It will make him all that much rougher when he finally spanks me good.

"Sexy," he says under his breath, his face warming as his eyes feast on my breasts.

That's when it dawns on me. I keep moaning about how Bonny made it so I couldn't fuck my bosses for two years, but it's the same from his side of the fence. It's been a very long time since we've played these games, and he's probably just as wound up as I am. The knowledge sends a ripple of pleasure through me, and I feel like a powerful, sexual goddess.

As soon as I toss my shirt on the floor, he demands, "Come here and put your elbows on my desk."

Oooh, someone is impatient. He didn't even let me undress all the way. I sway my hips as I brush past him and assume the requested position, placing my elbows and palms against the scattered paperwork. I wiggle my backside at him, feeling the stretch of satin and lace across my butt. He caresses my inner thigh before sliding his hand upwards. I rest my forehead on the backs of my hands as a tingling sensation zips straight to my pussy. It's crazy how he only has to touch me and I'm ready to beg him to fuck me.

He hooks a finger into the edge of my panties and pulls it up between the cheeks of my ass. The fabric bunches together and digs into my pussy. Mmm, fuck. I jiggle my ass again, trying to make the fabric rub my clit, but it doesn't move.

He slides a finger into my pussy. "Tell me about Jon."

Jon? Why is he asking about my husband while his finger is inside me?

Before I can ask him why the heck he's bringing this up, he adds another finger. My brain blanks. Uh…what were we talking about? I push my hips back, forcing his fingers in deeper.

He slaps my ass with his free hand, and I wobble in my heels for a moment as heat rushes through me.

"Answer my question."

The spank clears my head and I remember the topic. "Things are going great with Jon."

I'm still not sure why he's asking, and my brain is quickly short-circuiting. Being spanked earlier got me hot and bothered, and I'm still tender from his little show in the conference room.

"How many other guys have you fucked in the last two years?"

I tense, suddenly apprehensive. Where's he going with this?

"Miranda," he growls.

"I don't know," I respond softly. It's weird discussing this with Mr. Jacobs. "The freeuse resort you sent me to had at least a dozen men."

Shit, did all the guys fuck me at the resort? Even though it was only a few weeks ago, my memory of that weekend is a bit hazy. I was so blissed out, I mostly remember the room full of naked guys in Santa hats as they took turns using my mouth.

I rock my hips up and down, trying to force him to finger fuck me harder.

Instead he pulls his hand away. "Naughty slut," he says a moment before his hand connects with my ass.

A pleasurable pain blossoms across my backside and I moan softly. That was a firm hit, and it drives home the fact that he's in charge. My pulse speeds up as I wait to see if he's going to spank me, finger me, or fuck me.

He presses his hand against my pussy, applying pressure but this time he doesn't slide his fingers inside. "You're hoping I fuck you again, aren't you?"

Um…of course I am. I'm not crazy.

I give a breathy, "Please, I want your cock. I'll be a good girl for the rest of the day."

The devil knows that's a promise I'll break at the next available opportunity. But if it gets me fucked or spanked right this moment, I can pretend I'll be good.

He chuckles. "It's a shame you don't deserve it."

I snap my head up and look back at him. Um, what?

My mind spins in confusion as he says, "But I could be convinced and change my mind. Why do you deserve an orgasm?"

He's not supposed to make me justify my desires. He's supposed to just use me! He spanks me again, and I whimper. "I made the folders, set up the coffee, and cleaned."

"Not enough." Another sharp smack.

Shit, what else did I do? I wrack my brain, trying to think of anything else I've done that might warrant a reward. "I...I made copies. I did everything you asked."

"You're missing the point, Miranda."

A painful spank makes me groan as he continues to swat me, alternating cheeks. Each time he makes contact, my ass flares with heat. Within moments, my pussy is practically dripping. I enjoy Mr. Jacobs being grumpy and making me jump through hoops to get what I want...as long as I get what I want eventually.

After a series of powerful strikes, he asks again, "Tell me. What have you done today that deserves an orgasm?"

The correct answer is probably "nothing," since I apparently haven't done enough, but the overwhelming need to be fucked makes me beg. "I'll do anything you want," I babble. "Please..."

Pain explodes across my backside as his hand makes contact again. Ouch. Fuck. Oww. I rest my head on the surface of his desk and close my eyes. Jon never spanks me like this, and something inside me loosens. A warm fuzziness steals over me and I rise above the pain to where all I can feel is pleasure. My awareness narrows to just the satisfying jolts and the slickness between my thighs

I'm shocked when I climax. One second I'm in a peaceful place, and the next moment I'm flying high as an orgasm rockets through me. I cry out as my entire body spasms. Oooh no.

He stops spanking me. "Did you have permission to come?"

I mean, I didn't not have permission. He never said I couldn't. I don't voice my thought. "I'm sorry, sir. I couldn't stop it."

He massages the sore globes of my bottom for a few moments before moving up to unhook my bra. His warm palms caressing my breasts are wonderful, and I relax as he fondles me. At this moment, he really could do whatever he wanted and I'd love it.

CHAPTER 3

I expect Mr. Jacobs to fuck me now that he's spanked me, but he sits in his chair and gives my butt a gentle pat. "Ready to work again?"

Ugh, work. When I try to stand up, he presses his hand on my back. "Stay there. This position is perfect."

A zip of desire runs through me and I relax. I'm up for whatever involves being bent over his desk.

A knock on the door makes me jump, and Mr. Jacobs calls out, "Come in."

Mr. Parks and Mr. Daniels walk in, and take seats across from us. They smile at me as Mr. Jacobs hands me a legal pad and pen. "Take the minutes for our meeting. You'll type them up after."

What kind of meeting are they having with an almost naked woman in front of them? I wiggle my ass to tease Mr. Jacobs. My panties are still wedged together and driving me crazy.

"The clients are demanding..." Mr. Jacobs starts.

Mr. Parks snorts. "They always are."

I'm going to be demanding if I don't get fucked soon. My handwriting is a mess as I try to force myself to follow their boring conversation about a local conference Mr. Daniels is attending tomorrow. When Mr. Jacobs starts fingering my clit, I bite my lip to hold in a moan. I should have expected this.

Mr. Jacobs keeps talking like nothing's happening while he slides his fingers into my pussy and fucks me with them. I struggle to write, my hand shaking from pleasure. It doesn't help that Mr. Daniels and Mr. Parks are watching me. I can tell they're amused.

A jolt of electricity shoots through me as he speeds up his hand movements. My brain goes fuzzy as I barrel towards another orgasm. I can barely manage to write anything. What were they saying?

I'm distracted by the bulges in Mr. Parks' and Mr. Daniels' pants. My mouth waters, imagining sucking them both. Why aren't they all using me if I'm their freeuse toy this week? Or are they taking turns like they used to?

"Miranda." Mr. Jacobs pulls his fingers out and smacks my butt. "Be a good office slut. Crawl over there and take care of them. Your moans are distracting."

Oops, I didn't realize I was moaning. Is he suggesting what I think? I glance over my shoulder at him, questioningly. He gives a slight nod towards the other lawyers. Fuck yes, he wants me to suck their cocks.

I kick off my heels and sink to my knees. Mr. Parks spreads his legs as I crawl over, a thrill shooting through me at the power I wield. My fingers fumble with his belt buckle because I'm so damn eager to get him into my mouth. When I finally free his cock, I pause to appreciate it. He's rock-hard and ready.

I trace my fingertips along his length, savoring the silky texture. God, I love giving blow jobs. A glistening bead forms at the tip, and my mouth waters. I wrap my lips around him, rolling my tongue over the head. He fills my mouth perfectly, and I relish his every twitch and groan. Knowing I'm the source of his pleasure gives me satisfaction. I take him deeper, my own arousal building with each inch.

"Fuck, that's good," he groans, his fingers tangling in my hair.

I hum around him, the vibration making him buck his hips. His reaction spurs me on, and I hollow my cheeks, sucking harder. The taste of him floods my senses, salty and masculine. I press my thighs together, seeking relief. My panties are still bunched up, but they're firmly lodged in a way that only makes me aware of them and doesn't give me enough pleasure.

"Let's finish our meeting," Mr. Jacobs says casually.

They return to their business discussion while I bob my head. I'm getting wetter by the second.

"Miranda, pay attention. You'll still need to write this down," Mr. Jacobs reminds me, with a hint of amusement.

Yeah, these notes I write up later aren't going to be thorough. I'll just have to make them all come so they're happy and don't care. When Mr. Jacobs mentions me going to the conference with Mr. Daniels tomorrow, I perk up. A field trip! Wait...is Mr. Daniels going to fuck me there?

I keep sucking Mr. Parks while daydreaming about being passed around by a dozen horny lawyers. The fantasy makes me quicken my pace, desperate to taste his cum.

"Fuck, I'm close," Mr. Parks hisses.

I double my efforts, my hand working what my mouth can't reach. His hips flex, and I know he's right there. With a final groan, he explodes, flooding my mouth. I swallow greedily, not wanting to waste a drop.

As his grip on my hair loosens, I give him one last lick and pull back with a smile. "Mmm...tasty."

I'm dying for a cock to fuck me—anyone's cock—but Mr. Daniels is staring at me hungrily. Without being told, I crawl between his legs.

Mr. Jacobs sighs. "Suck him off. Make it quick."

That's not quite what I had in mind, but oh well. Mr. Daniels pulls out his thick cock for me, and I eagerly take him into my mouth, savoring his salty taste and the difference between the two men's cocks. He moans when I take him deep, his tip hitting the back of my throat. I cup his balls as I bob faster, determined to make him come quickly. It doesn't take long before his thigh muscles tense and he blows his load. I clean him up with my tongue before sitting back. That was a job well done, if I do say so myself.

The men look well satisfied—well, not Mr. Jacobs. And where is Mr. King today? Why wasn't he at the meeting? I wait for instructions as Mr. Daniels and Mr. Parks straighten their clothes and leave. I guess the meeting is over.

"Think you can write a coherent report?" Mr. Jacobs asks.

I stay silent. Uhh, doubtful. But I can wing it. He beckons me over and I crawl to him, hoping he'll let me suck his dick next. To my surprise, he pulls out a packet of trail mix from his desk drawer and feeds it to me while I kneel on the floor next to him.

Between bites, I ask, "What's this about the conference, sir?"

My pussy throbs, craving his cock. I need to come so badly. Hopefully once he stops feeding me, he'll fuck me.

"We thought our freeuse toy might like an outing," he says. "Have some fun outside the office."

Uh… "Fun with other lawyers?" If this is some gangbang, I need to talk to Jon.

Mr. Jacobs laughs. "No, just Mr. Daniels. You'll have to be discreet. Think you can manage that?"

"I'll be the most discreet slut ever," I promise.

"We're counting on it." He touches my cheek gently, making my stomach flutter. Then his voice turns stern. "Now go type those notes. Email them to me and be back here in fifteen minutes."

"Yes, sir." The air crackles between us—we both know what's coming when I return.

"Leave your clothes. You'll get them when the report's done."

Oooh, fuck. My heart races as I murmur, "Yes, sir."

He nods, satisfied. "Good. Now get to work."

I walk to my desk, hyperaware I'm only wearing my panties. What if a client shows up? My nipples harden from the thrill of possible exposure.

My pussy is drenched and I eye my office chair. Do men even think of these problems? Just go type these up, he says…how am I supposed to sit on my chair like this?

Fuck. I sneak to the break room and grab a cardigan I brought in last week and forgot on the coat rack, tying it around my waist as a makeshift skirt. Not perfect, but it'll do. I rush back, my heart pounding with nervous excitement. The risk of getting caught sends shivers down my spine.

I sit down, glad for the extra padding against my sore ass, and start typing. I try to remember the meeting details through my sex-fogged brain, but the taste of cum in my mouth and the wetness between my legs cloud my thoughts.

I'm almost done when footsteps approach. Shit. Shit. Shit. My heart leaps as Mr. King walks up.

"Miranda, are the notes ready? Mr. Jacobs told me to ask you for a copy," he says casually, though his gaze lingers on my body.

I swallow hard. "Almost. I can email them to you shortly."

He nods, his eyes dropping to my breasts. "You're making me wish it was my turn with you again."

Ooh, so they ARE taking turns. My body vibrates with delight at the thought.

Once he leaves, I quickly finish and email Mr. Jacobs and Mr. King. I'm sure it's missing details, but it's the best I could do under the circumstances. I rush back to Mr. Jacobs' office, leaving the cardigan behind. That thing needs a good wash now.

I knock softly before entering. He looks up, his expression hardened. "Those notes were unacceptable. You missed half the conversation."

No shit. I clasp my hands, purposely making my breasts squish together. "I'm sorry, sir. I was distracted."

By his fingers in my pussy before I sucked on two cocks.

"Come here."

His expression is unreadable and he stands as I come around to his side. He slides my panties down my legs and I step out of them. When he lifts me onto his desk, I wince as the hard wood presses against my tender backside.

He grins and spreads my knees. Yeah, he knows my ass hurts. He kisses my neck. "Did you think if you looked sexy that I wouldn't notice how bad of a job you did?"

I shiver, my body responding to him. "I'm sorry, sir. I can try again—"

"Try again?" His look turns predatory. "Or maybe I'll just fuck you to remind you who's in charge."

Yep, I like his plan better. He pushes me back onto the desk so that I'm lying down and tugs me to the edge. His fingers probe my pussy, making him growl, "You're so fucking wet."

I squirm, aching for more. "Please fuck me, sir."

He pulls out his cock, stroking it slowly. "You need this?"

"Yes, please." I nod eagerly and wrap my legs around him.

He taps the head against my clit. "Beg for it."

I gyrate my hips and whimper, "Please, sir. Please fuck me. I need your cock inside me. I'll do better next time. Please just fuck me."

He grasps my waist with both hands and thrusts in hard. "Ooooh, god," I cry out and arch my back as he starts fucking me fast and rough. I throw my hands over my head so I can hold on to the desk's edge as he ravages me. The sound of skin slapping fills the room as I get closer to my climax.

"You're such a good little slut. You love being fucked like this, don't you?"

I gasp, "Yes, so good," as the pressure builds with each stroke. I'm ready to explode.

He reaches between my legs to rub my clit. "Show me how much you love being our office slut and come for me."

The combined stimulation is too much. Ecstasy rips through me, and I come so hard I see stars. I convulse around his cock as he fucks me through my orgasm.

He doesn't slow down. "You're going to come once more before I fill you up and send you home to your husband."

The desk creaks as he hammers into me and continues to rub my clit. Another orgasm builds as I think about going home to Jon full of Mr. Jacobs' cum. My husband is going to love hearing about my day.

Mr. Jacobs is relentless, and time loses meaning. I play with my nipples, and chant, "Oh my god," as delight twists in my core. He's hitting the good spot deep inside me repeatedly, and I'm ready to come.

His thrusts become shorter, and I finally snap. I scream as another orgasm tears through me. He pulls out slowly without coming, and I feel a rush of wetness leaking out. I hope he has some of those wet wipes in here.

"Look at you, all fucked and messy," he says, appreciatively. "You want more, don't you? You want me to fuck you like the slut you are?"

"Yes, please."

He grabs my arms and pulls me up from the desk. His eyes are heavy with lust, mirroring the hunger in my own. He lifts me off my feet, and I hook my legs around his waist, crossing my ankles behind his back.

His hands grip my butt, fingers digging into the tender flesh as he holds me up. I can feel his hard cock pressing against my entrance, and I'm desperate for him to fill me again.

"Where should I fuck you next?"

He sounds like he's talking to himself, but I answer anyway. "Everywhere."

He carries me over to the couch that was recently added to his office, laying me down on my back. He slowly takes his clothes off and I watch him, curious to see if he looks different than I remember. He's still fit and trim, and I can tell he still exercises regularly.

Once he's naked, he looks down at me and commands, "Spread your legs for me."

I obey, letting him see how swollen and wet my pussy is. He kneels between my legs and moves his face to my pussy. I can feel his breath on my sensitive flesh, and I shiver with anticipation.

"You're absolutely gorgeous like this," he groans. He leans in and licks a slow path up my pussy, my hips rocking as he teases me.

"God, you're delicious." He dips his tongue inside me, and I reach down to grip his hair as he feasts on me.

He pulls back, holding my gaze. "You want my cock, don't you? You want me to fuck you until you can't think straight?"

I'm so turned on, all I can do is say, "Yes."

In reality, he can do whatever he wants. I'm beyond caring. He could stop right now, and I'd probably just thank him for using me.

He grabs my legs, pushing my knees towards my chest and I can feel myself opening up for him.

He slams into me, his hips pistoning as he fucks me hard and fast. I can feel every inch of him, every ridge and vein as he slides in and out of me.

He leans forward, holding onto my thighs as he uses them for leverage. His thrusts become harder and I continuously moan in pleasure.

"You feel so good." His muscles strain as he pounds into me.

I take back everything I thought earlier about him being the oldest. This guy is a machine. He has me pinned to the couch and at his mercy. It's amazing.

"You're just our little toy, a plaything to use whenever we need a release," he groans, and my body lights up at his words.

I gasp when he hits a pleasurable spot repeatedly, and my head spins. He teased me for hours, but this was worth the wait.

"You like that, don't you?" he asks. "Knowing we're going to use you all the time." The raw need in his husky voice sends another tremor of pleasure along my spine.

"Yes, I'm your fucktoy to use. Want it!"

I'd say anything, do anything, I just need to come again, and I need him to fill me up. I can tell the next orgasm is going to be massive. My body is on fire, every nerve ending alive as the tension coils tighter and tighter.

I'm ready to fall, and I moan, "Feels so good."

His tone is harsh as he hammers into me. "Come for me, you little slut. Come for me NOW."

"Fuck!" I scream, as my body shudders. The pleasure is so intense I see flashes of light behind my eyelids as I ride the waves of rapture. It might have lasted a few seconds, or a minute, I'm so far gone it feels like it's never ending.

With a final, deep thrust, he finds his own release. It seems like he's fucking me forever, unloading ropes and ropes of cum inside me, filling me up.

I'm shivering when he collapses on top of me. We're a tangle of limbs and sweat, our breathing ragged and uneven. I can feel him still inside me, his cock slowly softening as we both come down from the high.

I'm not sure how long we lie there, blissed out. But eventually his lips brush against my ear.

"You're amazing," he whispers.

A warmth spreads through me as he helps me sit up. When he kisses me, I'm not expecting it. It's a gentle kiss, but thorough, and as our tongues twirl together, I realize this is something I'm going to have to tell Jon about. Mr. Jacobs has changed over the last two years. There's an unexpected softness to him, but I think I'm going to enjoy it. He can still spank me and fuck me hard, and I know Jon is fine with my play partners being tender towards me.

Mr. Jacobs breaks off the kiss, and murmurs, "Good girl. Now I'm sending you home early because you need a good night's sleep for the conference tomorrow."

Ooh, yeah, the conference. I'm still tingling from my orgasms and give him a saucy smile. "Yes, sir. Thank you, sir."

He laughs and helps me stand up. "Now clean up and go home."

When he hands me my clothes, my body aches pleasantly as I slowly dress. As I leave his office, I make sure to sway my hips so he gets a nice view...and I want him thinking about spanking me again sometime soon.

CHAPTER 4

I call Jon on my drive home, putting him on speaker.

"Hey, Kitten. How was your day?"

The sound of his voice instantly turns me on again, and my body hums with lust. "Eventful. I've got stories to tell."

He laughs. "I'm sure you do, and I can't wait to hear them. Bad news though, I'm stuck here. I might be late."

My excitement deflates. "Nooo, you need to be home soon."

"I know, I'm sorry. I'll make it up to you later, promise."

I sigh and grumble, "Fine. Guess I'll have to entertain myself. Blame work if I'm too exhausted when you get home."

He teases, "Start without me, but you aren't allowed to finish until I get there."

Shit. Heat pools between my thighs. "Hurry home."

"Will do, Kitten. Love you."

"Love you too," I say, hanging up as I pull into our driveway.

As soon as I'm inside the house, I head for the bedroom, removing my clothes as I go. I don't bother putting anything on. I lie back on the bed, letting my mind wander over the day's events—the spankings, the thrill of fucking Mr. Jacobs again. I slide my hand down to my clit, teasing myself, but it's not enough. I grab my phone and text Jon.

You leaving yet?

He responds instantly.

Yes, fuck work. I'm walking out the door right now. Keep that pussy warm for me.

Oooh, nice. His office is only 15 minutes away. I play with myself, moving my hand slowly so I don't accidentally come.

I hear the garage door open and then Jon is in the room, looking as eager as I feel.

"Hey, Kitten," he says in that husky tone of his that tells me he's half crazed already.

I spread my legs wider and he eyes my pussy as he strips. I bet he's trying to see some of my boss's cum.

Once he's naked, he crawls onto the bed next to me and kisses me deeply. I taste his urgency, his need. I love how much he gets turned on by me fucking other people.

Between kisses, he growls, "Tell me everything."

He slips his hand between my legs, and I arch against him as he rubs my clit. How am I supposed to think, let alone talk, while he's touching me? But this is the game we play, and I'm going to tell him everything because that's what keeps our relationship strong.

As he trails kisses down my neck, across my collarbone, and to my breast, I tell him about my day. "I was bent over the desk, and they had a meeting while Mr. Jacobs fingered me."

"Mmm, nice," he moans and takes a nipple into his mouth. He sucks hard and pleasure shoots straight to my core.

While I tell him about the conference and sucking on the lawyers during the meeting, he continues to tease me, circling my clit, dipping his fingers inside me and making me squirm.

I rock against him. "Jon...please."

His eyes smolder with need. "Please what, Kitten?"

"Fuck me," I beg. "Need you inside me."

He grins and positions himself, fitting his cock against my pussy. He doesn't make me wait, and he presses in slowly—oh god, I wish he would pound into me. I love it when he fucks me slow, and yet I also hate it.

As he thrusts into me at his own pace, his cock hits all the right places. I wrap my legs around him and hold onto his shoulders, pulling him closer. Our moans fill the room. I'm close, so close.

I whimper, "Oh, god. I'm almost there."

He looks at me with a fierce expression. "Thank me for letting you fuck your bosses."

"Thank you," I gasp out, my body trembling with the effort to hold back my orgasm. "Thank you for letting me be their fucktoy."

He speeds up slightly, his thrusts hitting me deeper. "That's right, Kitten. You're my little slut, and I love sharing you."

His words send me spiraling and I mewl out in pleasure.

"Good girl," he murmurs. "Now come for me."

I cry out and let go, writhing as the pleasure explodes through me.

My orgasm triggers his. "Fuck, Miranda," he gasps, his cock pulsing inside me, filling me with cum.

We rock together as he finishes unloading, and when he rolls off me, he pulls me close. I'm a puddle of joy as I lay my head on his chest, listening to his heartbeat slow.

"So, tell me more about tomorrow," he says, his voice rumbling under my ear.

I smile, tracing hearts on his chest. "I'll be going with Mr. Daniels. Mr. Jacobs said we'll need to be discreet."

"I'm sure you can handle that," he chuckles. "I want you to have fun, so be their good little slut."

"I will," I purr, snuggling closer.

He kisses the top of my head. "And call me when you get home tomorrow. I want to hear all about it."

"Always, my love."

As we lie there, basking in the afterglow, a sense of contentment washes over me. This is what I love about our relationship. The openness, the trust, the shared pleasure. I'm truly living my best life as a hotwife. And I'm looking forward to whatever happens at the conference. I'm ready to be a slut again for Mr. Daniels.

The End

Freeuse Office Hours

Shared with the Boss

Lacey Cross

Chapter 1

Mr. Daniels' black sedan idles in my driveway at 7:30 sharp. I've been turned on since the moment I woke up, and I have high hopes for our day out of the office. After yesterday's office shenanigans with Mr. Jacobs, I'm eager to see how the most reserved lawyer at the firm handles having a personal freeuse slut for the day.

He's looking mighty fine this morning. His broad shoulders fill out his light blue dress shirt, which contrasts nicely against his rich brown skin. I pause for a moment to adjust my long brown hair, secured in a single braid, before admiring the view and opening the passenger door.

"Good morning." His deep voice wraps around me as I slide into the seat. His gaze travels down my body, lingering on the flared black skirt and lavender blouse Jon picked out. "You look lovely today."

Heat pools between my legs at his appreciative tone. Mmm, I've always loved his voice, especially when he's turned on. Being the firm's designated entertainment this week is turning out better than I'd hoped. I imagine him bending me over a desk, hiking up this same skirt.

"Thank you, sir." The word 'sir' rolls off my tongue with a delicious little thrill. I've grown to enjoy calling him that, each time sending a subtle shiver down my spine. I cross my legs, inching my skirt up to reveal a glimpse of bare thigh above my stockings. His eyes dart to the exposed skin before snapping back to the road.

The sexual tension thickens the air as we hit the highway. I study his profile, wondering if I'll need to drop hints or flat-out beg him to fuck me today. For a man built like a walking wet dream, he keeps his desires locked down tight, even after Mr. Jacobs arranged this special week where I'm available for all their pleasure.

"Looking forward to the conference?" I ask, probing his mood. This conference agenda isn't exactly thrilling, but being alone with Mr. Daniels away from the office certainly is. The corner of his mouth lifts in a half-smile that makes my core clench.

"It could be fun." His deep voice warms with a hint of playfulness. "That convention center does have a lot of...private spaces."

Oh thank fuck. Maybe I won't have to work too hard to seduce him after all.

A shiver runs through me as his large hand settles on my thigh, his thumb tracing circles on the sensitive skin above my stocking. Each stroke sends sparks straight to my pussy.

"Is that so?" I part my legs slightly, giving him better access. Between keynote speakers and networking events, there'll be breaks where he can use me however he wants.

His fingers creep higher under my skirt. "I think we'll find plenty of opportunities to make the day productive."

My breath hitches as his hand slides further up. It looks like Mr. Daniels might have some delicious plans for me today. I'm starting to think Mr. Jacobs knew exactly what he was doing when he assigned me to accompany our most reserved partner to this conference.

The convention center is attached to a hotel, and he parks in the garage in a secluded corner. Once the car is off, he turns to me. "Ready?"

I grab my oversized purse and flash him my most innocent smile. "Always ready, sir."

The registration desk feels miles away, and as we walk, each brush of his arm against mine sets my skin on fire. He checks us in for the conference, and I barely listen. I'm daydreaming of all the places he could fuck me at the hotel. Where can people find private places in a very public setting when it doesn't include spending the night?

We navigate through the crowd of suits and pencil skirts toward the keynote room. His hand hovers at my lower back, not quite touching but close enough that I feel his heat seeping into my skin.

"Let's sit in the back." He gestures to empty seats.

I nod and slide past him, knowing he's watching every sway of my hips. Our legs brush as we settle in and the lights dim. Some CEO takes the stage and drones about AI and legal tech. Mr. Daniels' "accidental" touches to my knee make it impossible to think. The scent of his cologne envelops me, and all I can think about are those private spaces he mentioned.

"Interesting stuff," he whispers against my ear. His hand inches higher on my thigh, and I bite back a moan.

I shift in my seat, desperate for friction. His fingers tighten on my leg when I cross and uncross my legs, but he keeps watching the speaker like he isn't driving me wild.

I glance around the conference room, making sure the other attendees are absorbed in the presentation. Perfect—no one's looking this way. Time to play dirty.

I adjust my position, letting my skirt ride up higher. His hand freezes, and even though he doesn't move it up any further, the weight of his hand is driving me crazy.

The CEO rambles about algorithms while I conduct my own experiment in breaking Mr. Daniels' control. I spread my leg slowly so his hand grazes my inner thigh. His fingers flex, and I can tell he wants to move them to my pussy.

"Pay attention," he murmurs. "You'll need to brief the partners on this presentation."

"I am, sir. I'm a *very* good multitasker."

To show him what I mean, I slide my hand onto his leg. When his jaw clenches, a thrill ripples through me. Oh yeah, he's getting worked up. My panties are soaked, and we haven't even found those quiet corners yet.

God, I hope he fucks me before lunch.

CHAPTER 2

"Fifteen minutes until the next session," Mr. Daniels says, his voice low as we exit the keynote. His hand finds my back, more assertive than ever. "Follow me."

He guides me through the crowds, down a side corridor, and into the parking garage. Each step amplifies the pulsing beat of my heart.

He pins me against his car, hands planted firmly on either side of my shoulders. "These past couple of years," he murmurs, his dark eyes burning into mine, "I've had a lot of time to think about how I used to fuck you at the office. But we've both changed."

The heat of him and the woodsy scent of his cologne is making it difficult to think. "And how have you changed?" I manage to ask.

"I'm not hesitant anymore." His lips curl into a confident smile as he trails one finger down my neck, following the line of my blouse to the swell of my cleavage. "I like to go for what I want now."

Christ, this new side of him—commanding, sure of himself—practically has me panting. His massive hands slide down to grip my hips, and I arch into his touch.

"Ask me what I want," he demands.

Oooh, I like where this is going. "What exactly do you want, sir?"

"I want to show you how much I appreciate all you taught me. I've been putting it to good use since then."

Wait, what did I teach him? I don't have time to ask before he captures my mouth in a searing kiss that makes my knees weak. His tongue sweeps inside, claiming me thoroughly while his hands roam over my body. When he pulls back, we're both breathing hard.

"Turn around, slut," he orders. "Hands on the car.

I comply instantly, pressing my palms against the cool metal. Mmm, I'll be his slut. I definitely like this new dominant tone.

He kicks my feet apart, then runs his hands up my thighs, pushing my skirt to my waist. I'm trembling, and it's a toss-up on whether it's the cool air in the garage or my need for his cock that's doing it.

His fingers tease the edge of my stockings. "Such a good girl. Wearing these to please me." He slides his hand to my panties and presses against the damp spot. "Already so wet for me."

I whimper as he rubs me through the silk. He's right, and I did wear the stockings for him. Jon picked out my outfit and he liked the idea of me looking respectable to everyone else, but a sex kitten underneath my clothes.

Mr. Daniels increases the pressure of his fingers, and I rock against him, desperate to get something inside me. Since he parked in a secluded corner, we're far from the traffic flow. Almost like this was planned—smart man—but my eyes catch a glint of something dark mounted on a nearby pillar. Is that a security camera? The thought of being recorded, of someone watching this later, gives me a naughty zing.

"Remember what you are?" He hooks his fingers on the waistband of my panties and pauses. "You're our freeuse toy this week. *My* toy right now."

"Yes, sir," I gasp. When he tugs my panties down, I'm dizzy with need. When is the last time I was fucked in a parking lot? It's been a long time.

"You taught me how to take what I want." His fingers trace the seam of my pussy, and I shimmy my hips, trying to entice him to slide his fingers inside me as he continues. "You made me realize how much I enjoy watching you submit."

Holy shit. This is a man on a mission to wreck me.

He removes his hand from my pussy long enough to get his cock out. I feel the thick head of it press against me, and I bite my lip to stifle a moan.

"Such a greedy little slut," he growls. "Letting me fuck you where anyone could see us."

Ohhh, god. He sinks his cock into me, and my head whirls from pleasure. He doesn't take his time with it—not that we have much time— and his thrusts are deep and steady. I keep my hands flat on the car to steady myself as he sets a relentless pace.

"Stay quiet," he warns, one hand on my hip, the other tugging on my long braid. "Unless you want the whole parking garage to hear you."

The danger of being caught makes my heart race faster. Every footstep, every distant voice, amplifies the thrill. But all I can focus on is his cock driving into me.

"That's it," he grunts, pulling my hair tighter, forcing my head back. "Take it like the good little freeuse fucktoy you are."

Jesus, was he taking notes all this time? I love his dirty talk. My orgasm builds quickly, pressure tightening in my core.

"Sir, please," I whimper, not sure if I'm going to have time to come. His thrusts grow harder, deeper, making the car rock, and I have the insane urge to laugh when I hear the beep of his key fob, like he's just turned the car alarm off before we set it off.

He can tell I'm distracted; he whacks against my pussy hard, making me gasp as the pleasure skyrockets through me.

"Come for me," he orders. "Come for me before I blow my load and you have to wait until lunch time. Unless you want to feel my cum dripping out of you while you're desperate and horny."

Oh nooo! The thought of being unfilled is what tips me over the edge. Pleasure crashes over me, and I muffle my scream against my arm.

He follows right after, grinding deep as he fills me. He jerks against me a few times, unloading ropes of sticky cum before he stills. For a moment, we just breathe together, his chest pressed against my back.

"Next session starts in five minutes," he says, his voice returning to its usual professional tone as he helps me straighten up. But there's a new spark in his eyes when I turn to him. "Better fix your hair. You look thoroughly fucked."

My mind is fried, and I can't wait to see what else he has planned.

My legs are still shaking as we slip into our seats for the morning breakout session. He was right, and I can feel his cum leaking into my panties. I squirm, and it earns me a knowing smirk from Mr. Daniels.

"Problem?" he whispers, sitting there cool as a cucumber, like he didn't just fuck me senseless in the parking garage.

I just lift my eyebrow at him and try to focus on the presentation about legal document automation. After a few minutes, his hand finds my thigh under the table. His thumb traces lazy circles on my stockings, each touch sending aftershocks straight to my core. My skin is so sensitive I might come just from him stroking it.

I need to tell Jon about this new, commanding version of Mr. Daniels. Carefully angling my phone away from prying eyes, I type to my husband.

Miranda: Holy shit babe. Mr. Daniels just fucked me against his car in the parking garage. When did he get so dominant?

Jon's reply is almost instant.

Jon: That's my good little slut. Is he taking care of you properly?

Miranda: Fuck yes. Still leaking his cum during this presentation abou t...something. Can't focus.

"Miranda." Mr. Daniels' voice is quiet but firm. "Pay attention."

I bite my lip, hyper-aware of his massive hand still resting on my thigh. Jon's next text makes me stifle a giggle because it matches what Mr. Daniels said.

Jon: Better focus kitten, or he might have to punish you later

The thought of Mr. Daniels punishing me makes my pussy clench. There's no way he would have previously done it, but this new version of him? It's possible. His fingers tighten slightly on my leg, like he knows exactly what I'm thinking about.

The presenter drones on about workflow optimization, but all I can do is think about Mr. Daniels and his wandering hand. Every few minutes, he moves closer to my pussy, testing my ability to maintain my composure.

Fuckity, fuck, fuck, fuck. His middle finger traces the lace of my stockings, and I have to fake a cough to cover my moan.

"Shhh," he murmurs, eyes still fixed on the presenter. "Unless you want everyone to know what a desperate little slut you are?"

Yep, it's official. He's trying to kill me with his teasing.

"Twenty minutes until lunch," Mr. Daniels whispers close to my ear, his fingertips now dancing along my inner thigh. "I already know exactly what I'm going to do to you."

Christ. I press my thighs together, earning a warning squeeze from his hand.

This is going to be the longest conference of my life.

CHAPTER 3

The lunch break can't come fast enough. Once we're free, Mr. Daniels practically drags me away from the networking crowd, his fingers locked around my wrist.

"In here." He opens a supply closet door, checking both ways before pulling me inside. The lock clicks shut, and suddenly, I'm pinned against the wall, his massive body caging me in.

"Sir—" I start, but he silences me with a fierce kiss.

"Shh." His voice is pure grit. "You've been taunting me all morning with those little squirms and sighs."

My pulse quickens, and his hands slide up my thighs, bunching my skirt. The closet is cramped, smelling of paper and cleaning supplies, but who cares? His fingers find my drenched panties. "Still wet from earlier?" he growls against my neck. "You filthy girl."

Damn, if I had known he'd turned into a dirty talker, I would have been even more unhappy when not fucking my bosses at work the last couple of years. I press my back against the wall as he tugs my underwear down.

"Step out of them," he commands, and I slip off my heels so they don't get caught in them as I do what he wants.

"Now, open that pretty mouth."

Uh, what's up with this? I open wide, and he stuffs my panties between my lips. My eyes widen as my own taste fills my mouth. This is fucked up, and I love it.

"There's my good little fucktoy. Now your moans won't get us in trouble." The zipper on his pants sounds loud in the room. "Hands on the wall. Spread your legs."

As I turn around to face the wall, footsteps pass nearby, and my heart races. Anyone could hear us, but that only makes me wetter.

"Look at you," he chuckles darkly, pressing his cock against my entrance. "Getting off on this, aren't you? Such a desperate slut."

"Fuck yes, I am," I murmur around my panties, knowing he can't understand me. I try to push back, earning a sharp slap on my ass.

"Patience." His breathing is ragged. He thrusts hard, making me bite down on the panties to muffle my cries of pleasure.

More footsteps, voices discussing the morning sessions. He doesn't slow down, just fucks me harder.

"That's it," he grunts, one hand gripping my hip while the other slides around to rub my clit. "Take it like the fucktoy you are."

My eyes roll back as he hits that perfect spot. Jon's soooo going to love hearing about this later.

"Touch yourself," he orders, moving both hands to my hips. "Make yourself come on my cock like a good girl."

I reach down, finding my swollen clit. The angle's awkward, but fuck, I'm so close.

"After you come," he pants in my ear, "I want you on your knees. You're going to suck me off with that sexy mouth."

That does it. My orgasm rips through me, and I barely keep quiet with the panties gagging me. He shivers before pulling out and spinning me around. I drop to my knees, and he replaces the panties with his cock. "Suck it, slut."

Holy fuck. I moan, tasting myself mixed with his cum. His fingers wrap around my head, controlling my pace.

"Such a dirty little cocksucker," he growls. "You love this, don't you? Being used in a supply closet while everyone's at lunch?"

I hum my agreement, taking him deeper. His hips start to jerk, and I know he's close.

"Swallow it all." It's a command. I feel him pulse on my tongue, flooding my mouth with his cum. Like the good girl I am, I don't spill a drop.

Once he's done unloading, he helps me up and adjusts my shirt. There's a new softness in his eyes, but his voice stays firm. "Clean yourself up. Next session starts in ten. I have sandwiches for us to eat."

In the restroom I look at my balled-up panties with dismay. Fuck, what is worse? Sitting with no panties, or these? I clean up the best I can and put on my panties. The damp fabric makes me feel like a complete slut. It's filthy—and glorious.

I check my phone before I leave. There are two texts from Jon.

Jon: Having fun kitten?

Jon: Can't wait to hear ALL about it tonight

Oh babe, do I have stories to tell you.

CHAPTER 4

The afternoon speaker drones on, but I'm lost in a haze of desire. My body's still buzzing from our supply closet rendezvous, and Mr. Daniels' hand on my thigh isn't helping.

"Take notes," he murmurs. "This is important."

Important? I try to ignore the throb between my legs, but it's no use.

"After this, tell me three key points about the presentation." Mr. Daniels whispers, squeezing my thigh.

Shit, that voice makes my stomach flip. "Or what, sir?"

His smile is wicked. "Or I'll punish you in that empty meeting room down the hall."

My pussy clenches. Yeah, he's not deterring me. Now I might tank his quiz on purpose.

The presenter clicks onto another slide, but Mr. Daniels' hand inches higher, making me squirm.

"Desperate little slut," he breathes. "Still wet from lunch, aren't you?"

I cross and uncross my legs, seeking friction. "Please, sir..."

"Please what?" His fingers tease my sensitive skin. "Please bend you over the table? Please make you scream where anyone could hear?"

My clit throbs with each scenario. Jesus, he really is good at this—or else I'm just that turned on. Either way, today is going so much better than I imagined.

"Five minutes left," Mr. Daniels says softly. "Better pay attention if you want to pass."

I try to focus, but his hand creeps higher, his touch bolder. By the time the lights come up, I'm breathless.

"Well?" He turns to me, all business except for the heat in his eyes. "Three key points. Go."

"Um..." I scramble for answers, but my brain is mush.

His smile grows as I stumble. "Not good enough." He stands, straightening his jacket. "Come with me. Time for your punishment."

Thank god I'm such a terrible student.

Mr. Daniels leads me down the hall to an empty conference room like he promised. My pulse quickens as he shuts the door behind us, the click of the lock echoing in the silence.

"Bend over the table," he commands, and I practically stumble in my haste to get to the nearest table. I do as I'm told, leaning forward and placing my palms flat on the wooden surface. My skirt rides up, exposing my thigh-high stockings and the lace trim of my panties. When I look over my shoulder at him, the heat in his eyes intensifies, and my stomach flutters in response.

Mr. Daniels steps closer and runs a hand over my ass, squeezing gently before delivering a sharp smack. I gasp, the sting sending a jolt of pleasure through me. "You failed your test," he murmurs, landing another smack on the opposite cheek. "What do you have to say for yourself?"

"I'm sorry, sir," I breathe, my voice catching as he continues to spank me. Each strike sends a wave of heat through my body, my pussy throbbing with need. "I'll do better next time."

"Will you?" His hand slips between my legs to press against my clit through my panties. I squirm, desperate for more friction. "Or will you be a bad girl again?"

"I...I don't know, sir," I admit, my voice trembling. He chuckles, a low, throaty sound that makes my knees weak. His fingers delve deeper, pushing my panties aside and circling my clit before pulling away. I whimper as a shiver runs through me. Fuck, this is intense.

"On your knees," he orders, stepping back.

Does this mean he's not going to fuck me? I slide off the table, sinking to the floor. He unzips his slacks, freeing his cock. It's hard and thick, and I lick my lips, eager to taste him. He grips my hair, guiding me forward. "Show me how sorry you are."

I take him into my mouth, my tongue swirling around the head. He groans, his hips jerking slightly. I suck him deeper, my hands gripping his thighs for support. His skin is warm beneath my touch, the muscles taut with restraint. I can feel the tension building in him.

"Fuck," he groans, his voice strained. "Such a good little cocksucker."

Mmm, I'll suck on him all day if he calls me filthy names. I focus on pleasing him, my neediness building with each bob of my head. His fingers tighten around my head, controlling the rhythm. I can taste the saltiness of his precum, feel the throb of his cock against my tongue. He's close, I can tell.

He thrusts deeper into my mouth. I relax my throat, taking him in as far as I can. His breath hitches, and I can feel the pulsing of his cock as he nears the edge.

"I'm going to come," he groans, his voice ragged.

I double down on my efforts, my tongue working furiously. With a final, deep thrust, he holds me in place, his cock pulsing as he fills my mouth with sticky cum. I swallow every drop, trying to make up for not knowing the answer to his quiz.

He pulls out slowly, his breath coming in heavy gasps. I look up at him and he runs a thumb over my wet bottom lip, a satisfied smile on his face.

"Good girl," he murmurs, helping me to my feet. He tucks himself back into his slacks, adjusting his clothes with calm efficiency.

I'm buzzing with unfulfilled desire, and he kisses me softly. "If you're lucky, I'll fuck you again after the next session."

Oooh, yes, please. "I'll make sure to pay attention this time, sir." Though now that I think of it, I did like that punishment. Maybe I won't pay attention after all.

"You better," he says, giving my ass a final squeeze. "Now, let's get back. We wouldn't want anyone to know how much you enjoy being on your knees for me."

As we walk down the hall, my lips feel puffy and I grow hot every time someone looks at me. Yeah, I'm a slut and I actually do wish everyone knew how much I enjoyed being on my knees.

CHAPTER 5

During our afternoon break, I'm on my feet, ready to follow Mr. Daniels anywhere. He leads us to the front desk where he checks in—and he already has a reservation. When I give him a questioning look, he flashes a wicked smile. "I want to take my time, and I'm going to make you scream."

Damn. My pussy throbs at his words.

The elevator ride is delicious torture, and all I want to do is throw myself against him and beg him to fuck me right there. When the elevator open, I practically sprint down the hall.

He unlocks the door, and we step inside. It's just a standard hotel room, but right now, it feels like a sanctuary.

"Undress," he orders, leaving no room for argument—not that I was planning to put up a fight. I'm about to rip off my clothes but pause. Wait, this is my chance to drive him crazy.

I step out of my heels, and he watches with hunger as I begin a slow, sensual striptease. I unbutton my blouse, one button at a time, allowing it to slip off my shoulders before tossing it to the floor. My skirt drops next, and I'm standing in front of him in just my bra, panties, and stockings.

His eyes are glued to me, taking in every movement. I reach behind my back and unhook my bra, letting it fall. His gaze makes my nipples harden. I slowly roll my stockings down, one leg at a time, using my foot propped up on the bed to slide them off sensually. I finally slip off my panties, kicking them aside.

His eyes roam over me, taking in every curve. "Beautiful," he murmurs, stepping closer. He traces the curve of my waist, the swell of my hips. "And all mine right now."

He takes his time exploring me with his hands, like he's unwrapping a gift he's waited forever to open. His touch sets my skin on fire, and I shiver in pleasure.

I can tell when he's ready to fuck me. The tension shifts, and he commands, "On the bed. On your back."

I lie down, heart pounding as he undresses. His suit and shirt hit the floor, revealing his broad chest and defined abs. Fuck, he's stunning.

He crawls onto the bed, covering my body with his. His mouth finds my neck, kissing and sucking while his hands explore. I gasp as he pinches my nipple, rolling it between his fingers.

"I wish we had time for me to play with you all day," he murmurs against my skin. God, I wish that too. If this is what he'd be doing to me, he'd turn me into a mindless puddle by the end of the day.

His mouth moves lower, capturing one nipple, then the other, sucking hard enough to make me arch. My hands grip his hair as he focuses on my breasts.

"Please, sir," I whimper, not sure what I'm begging for. More teasing? Less? Everything?

He chuckles, a low rumble vibrating through me. "Patience, greedy slut."

His mouth trails lower, kissing down my stomach. I tense as he reaches my hips, anticipation coiling tight.

"Open," he orders, nudging my thighs apart. I comply, spreading wide for him.

"Fucking perfect." His eyes are locked onto my pussy. He leans in, his breath hot against me.

The first lick is slow, deliberate. A tease. I buck my hips, chasing his mouth, but he pins me down with a stern look.

"Stay still," he commands. "Or I'll stop."

Fuck. I force myself to obey, gripping the sheets as he licks me again, slow and torturous.

His tongue finds my clit, circling it lazily. I whimper, the sound turning into a moan as he sucks it into his mouth. He releases it, blowing gently on my wet flesh.

"Oh god," I gasp, hips trying to lift. His hands hold me down, his mouth driving me insane.

He slides two fingers inside me, pumping them in and out while his tongue works my clit. The dual sensation is overwhelming, pleasure building fast and hard.

"Sir, please," I beg, head thrashing. "I need to come."

He hums against my clit, the vibration sending sparks through me. "Not yet," he murmurs. "You'll come when I say you can."

Fuck fuck fuck. I close my eyes and tense up, trying to hold back my orgasm. He adds a third finger, stretching me wide. His mouth returns to my clit, sucking and licking until I'm a writhing, whimpering mess.

"Now," he growls, fingers curling inside me. "Come for me, slut."

My orgasm hits like a tidal wave, pleasure crashing through me. I scream, body convulsing as he wrings every last bit of ecstasy from me. When the pleasure dies down to soft ripples, he crawls back up, his cock poised at my entrance. In one hard thrust, he's inside me, filling me completely.

"Fuck, you feel good," he grunts, hips moving in a steady rhythm. "Like you were made for my cock."

I wrap my legs around him, meeting each thrust with a moan. His body against mine, his cock inside me—it's perfection. I can't believe how lucky I am to have a husband who lets me fuck other guys like this. Jon really is the best husband in the world—especially because I'm going to tell him how good this felt, and it's just going to turn him on even more.

Mr. Daniels captures my mouth in a fierce kiss. I can taste myself on his tongue, and it only makes me hotter.

"Touch yourself," he orders, breaking the kiss. "Make yourself come again."

My hand finds my clit, rubbing in time with his thrusts. Pleasure builds quickly, my body already sensitized from the first orgasm.

"That's it," he pants, eyes locked on mine. "Show me how much you love my cock."

I cry out, my second orgasm hitting just as hard as the first. He follows right after, his cock pulsing inside me as he finds his own release.

We collapse together, bodies slick with sweat. His arms wrap around me, holding me close as we catch our breath.

We lie there for a few minutes, basking in the afterglow, but Mr. Daniels breaks the silence with a stern voice. "You never did answer my question from earlier."

I look up at him, confused. "What question, sir?"

"The three key points from the presentation. I'll give you another chance. Give me three things."

I still can't think of anything, and I don't even try.

He looks amused, but his voice is stern. "You failed again."

A shiver runs through me, remembering the earlier punishment. "Yes, sir."

"On your hands and knees," he commands, his voice leaving no room for argument. "It's time for more punishment."

I scramble to obey, positioning myself on the bed, my heart racing. He gets off the bed and walks around to stand behind me. His hand caresses my ass gently at first, then suddenly, a sharp smack lands on my right cheek. I gasp, more from surprise than pain.

"Count them," he orders, his voice stern.

"One," I manage to say, my voice breathless.

Another smack, this time on my left cheek. "Two," I count, my pussy clenching with each strike.

He alternates between cheeks, each smack sending waves of pleasure and pain through me. I count each one, my voice growing more desperate with every number. By the time I reach ten, my ass is throbbing and I'm dripping wet.

He pauses, his hand resting on my heated flesh. "You took that so well," he murmurs, his voice thick with desire. "Such a good little slut."

I whimper, pushing back against his hand, craving more. He chuckles, a low, dark sound that sends shivers down my spine.

"Stay just like that," he commands, his voice rough with need as he climbs onto the bed behind me. His cock presses against my entrance and I moan when I feel how hard he is again. How the fuck did he recover that fast? I'm one lucky girl.

He applies pressure to my shoulders, shoving them down to the bed so I spread open wider for him. "Do you think you deserve to be fucked, slut?"

"Please, sir," I beg, desperate. "I deserve it. I'll be good, I promise."

"We'll see about that."

In one smooth motion, he buries himself inside me, stretching me impossibly wide. I cry out from the pain mixed with pleasure. He starts to move, his pace relentless, forcing every inch of his huge cock into me. His hips slam into my abused ass, sending a constant stream of white-hot lightening through me.

He fucks me deep and hard, his grunts punctuating each thrust. His fingers dig into my hips, holding me steady as he uses my body for his pleasure. I can tell that he's having fun, that he enjoys being in control, and the thought pushes me over the edge. I moan loudly, pleasure radiating from my fingertips to my toes.

"Yes, just like that." He slams into me harder, faster. "You feel incredible. Your tight little hole, all dripping and needy."

Whoa, my head spins as his words turn filthier. I really do want to be his hole to use. I let myself imagine that he's going to keep me restrained all day and come into the room and fuck me whenever he wants before going back to the conference, leaving me a dripping mess. I wouldn't even care if I didn't come.

He changes the angle, and his cock rubs against the magical spot deep inside me. My arms shake from the intensity, but he keeps pounding me into the mattress, chasing his release. It's glorious, and I don't want him to stop.

His pace becomes erratic, his grunts turning into groans. "Fuck, I'm close," he grits out, his cock swelling even larger. "Where do you want it?" He reaches around and rubs my clit while he keeps fucking me.

"In-inside me," I gasp, knowing that him asking me means he might not give me what I want if he has a sadistic streak in him.

He growls, "Good, because that's exactly where I planned to come."

Oh, thank god. He slams into me even harder, and I scream when a sudden orgasm rips through me. He fucks me through the pleasure before he groans and pumps me full of cum. My entire body quivers from pleasure while I imagine his cum coating my insides until I'm overflowing.

When he's done unloading, we both collapse face first onto the bed. My head is wooly, and I'm drunk on pleasure. Yep, I don't think I can move from this spot. I'm going to become one with the bed.

When I giggle, he rolls on to his side, facing me. I can tell he's looking at me, and I open the eye that isn't smooshed into the comforter so I can see him.

He's smiling. "You okay?" His voice is soft and caring. He's back to the Mr. Daniels I know.

I turn my head so I don't mumble into the mattress. "So much more than okay. That was incredible. You're incredible. Thank you for that."

His laugh is joyous. "You're amazing. Thank you, Miranda. But I think that's the last one I had in me."

I'm not sure I have another in me either. I have to save something for Jon when I get home. Though right now, maybe I'll just starfish and tell him to have at it. I keep that thought to myself and reply with a pout. "Probably for the best since I can't walk."

He laughs loudly as he gets off the bed and then pulls me into a sitting position. I pretend to be a limp noodle until it gets to the point where I have to support myself. "Up and at 'em, lazy bones. We need to get you home. I think we're going to skip the last session of the conference."

Oh, thank Jeebus. I give him a cheeky, "Yes, sir," as I climb off the bed.

I sink into the heated seat of his car as Mr. Daniels steers us out of the parking garage. My panties are shot, my nipples hard against my bra. I thought I was exhausted, but knowing I'll soon see Jon is waking my body up. It's still a couple of hours until he's off work, but I'll be more than ready for him when he gets home.

"Tired?" Mr. Daniels asks.

"Not really. Just processing, I guess." Processing how much he's changed in the last two years. God, I really hope Jon lets me keep fucking my bosses after this week. I need more of Mr. Daniels.

He chuckles. "It was quite a day."

Quite a day? That's an understatement. "I enjoyed it. A lot."

He gives me the side eye and a smirk before focusing back on the road. "Oh, I could tell. You're very...expressive."

I blush as a thrill runs through me. "Well, you weren't exactly quiet yourself, *sir*." I make sure to stress the word 'sir.'

"True enough. You have a way of bringing out the beast in me."

Mmm, and I do like his beast.

When we pull into the driveway of my house, he sighs. "Back to reality at the office tomorrow."

Wait, what? I don't want reality tomorrow. Plus, when do I get a day with Mr. Parks? I make a mental note to myself to make sure to ask Jon about anal with Mr. Parks since I keep forgetting and I know Mr. Parks will want my ass.

"But that doesn't mean this has to end," he continues. "We can find ways to make this work, if you want to and if Jon agrees."

If I want to? Fuck yes, I want to. But I appreciate he's considerate about my husband. "I'll talk things over with Jon and let you know."

Hrm, I wonder how many imaginary blowjob tokens I'll have to pony up to Jon if I want to keep fucking my bosses?

Mr. Daniels turns to me, his eyes soft in the dim light of the car. "Thank you, Miranda. For today, for trusting me, for being you."

I smile, my heart swelling with affection. "You're sweet, and thank you, too."

He leans in, his lips brushing mine in a soft, tender kiss.

"Goodnight, Miranda," he murmurs against my lips.

"Goodnight, sir."

Chapter 6

The front door clicks shut behind me, and I jump, startled to see Jon standing there. "Hey, you're home early!"

There's a fire in his eyes. "I took a half day. I couldn't concentrate."

Before I can even drop my bag, he's on me. He spins me around and pushes me against the wall. Fuck, yes.

"Tell me everything," he demands while his hands roam over my body, rough and possessive.

I gasp as he grinds his hard cock into my ass. "He shoved my panties in my mouth and fucked me in a supply closet."

Jon groans, his fingers digging into my flesh. "And?"

"And then in a hotel room. He made me come so hard I couldn't even stand."

"Fuck, kitten," he murmurs, his hands cupping my breasts and kneading them. "It's so hot when you talk like this."

When he pinches my nipples through my blouse, I moan, "Need you."

That's all the encouragement he needs. He hikes up my skirt and yanks my panties down to my ankles. I step out of them, kicking off my heels at the same time. I spread my legs. I need him inside me. Right now.

"Please, Jon," I whimper, my body aching for him.

"So fucking wet," he groans, running his fingers through my soaked folds. "Is this all for him or is some of this for me?"

"You. Always." It's a struggle to keep my words coherent through my moans.

He slams into me from behind, his thrusts hard and deep, his groans mingling with my cries of pleasure.

"Did he fuck you like this?" he growls, his pace increasing. "Did he pound you against the wall?"

"Yes, in the storage closet," I whimper. "Keep talking to me. Just like that."

"That's 'cause you're my slut who likes fucking other guys and coming home and getting it rough from me. Admit it."

Jesus Christ, why does this turn me on so much? "Yes, god, I do. I love it."

He keeps fucking me, and my head spins as he talks. "You love knowing that when I think about you fucking other guys, it drives me crazy, don't you?"

"God yes, I do!" This is the crazed Jon that I love coming home to.

"Do you think about that when you fuck them? Do you picture me listening to this story, turned on and ready to fuck your brains out as soon as you tell me what they did to you?" As he drives into me furiously, the pressure inside me coils tighter, his dirty talk bringing me closer to the edge.

"Yes!"

He bites the soft skin on my shoulder, and I almost come right there from the sting. A wave of lust makes me cry out, "Fuck me hard and show me who I belong to!"

Jon's response is immediate and intense. He pulls out, and I feel like a rag doll as he spins me around and lifts me until I wrap my legs around him. His face is a blend of dominance and ownership, and it sizzles my brain.

He crushes his lips against mine, his tongue claiming me as his own. He drills into me, and his grunts match my moans of pleasure. This man is perfect. We're both crazed, desperate for release. I hold onto his shoulders, letting him have total control.

My orgasm hits like a tornado, a swirling white-hot ecstasy that burns through me. I cry out as the pleasure skyrockets me to another plane. The feeling of him blowing his load inside me makes the bliss last even longer before it finally dies down to sparks. When I come down, I'm spent, unsure if I can even walk.

He kisses me deeply. The world seems to pause as we lose ourselves in the moment. This right here is one of the best parts. When he breaks off the kiss, he carries me into the living room. He lowers us both onto the couch, settling me comfortably in his lap.

Giggling, I nuzzle his neck. "Now that's what I call being well fucked. That was fantastic. Did you enjoy it?" I poke him in the ribs. I know he did, but I still like to hear him say it.

"I fucking loved it. Just like I love you." He's grinning, and a flush is riding high on his cheeks. His voice softens. "So, how was it really? I mean, beyond the fucking."

I rest my head on his shoulder. "It was...intense. And fun. I like how dominant Mr. Daniels is now."

He kisses the top of my head, his arms tightening around me. "Yeah, my slutty kitten would like that. I'm glad you had fun today."

My heart flutters. "Thank you for supporting me, for encouraging me. For loving me."

"Always, kitten. Always."

Later when we're making dinner together, my phone buzzes. It's a text from Mr. Jacobs.

Mr. Jacobs: Tomorrow we will be celebrating the end of your freeuse week with an office party. All of the bosses will be involved.

Holy shit. My heart pounds as I read the message, my body already responding to the thought of fucking all my bosses together.

"What is it?" Jon asks, curiously.

I look up at him, my eyes wide with excitement. "They want to have an office party tomorrow. With all of them. At once."

Jon's expression darkens. "All of them? Together?"

I nod, his expression making me uncertain if this is a good thing. "Yes. But...we should talk about this first, right?"

He runs a hand through his hair, his expression unreadable. "Definitely. I love sharing you, kitten, but all of them at once...that's different. We need to discuss this before I can agree to something like that. I have rules."

My stomach flutters with a combination of disappointment and understanding. Will he say no?

God, I hope not.

The End

FREEUSE OFFICE PARTY

An Edging and Gangbang Adventure

Lacey Cross

Chapter 1

The car pulls up to the curb in front of the office, and my husband Jon kisses me goodbye. "Have lots of orgasms today, Kitten."

I give him my best cheeky grin. "One can hope."

But honestly, how can I not? It's the last day of freeuse at work before Cindy, the receptionist, comes back from vacation and we have to behave—or at least keep the sexy shenanigans behind closed doors. This week has been fabulous, but fairly intense. It might be good that she's coming back. I don't think much actual work was done this week.

I step out of the car, and smooth down my flared skirt before collecting my purse and lunch. Jon waves to me and I blow him a kiss before he takes off. He doesn't usually take me to work, but Mr. Jacobs offered me a party with all the lawyers today, and Jon is going to come back to watch. We're preplanning for once so we don't have two cars here, and he'll drive me home after the party...assuming the lawyers agree to Jon being there.

The office is eerily still like it's been every morning this week, the usual hum of activity replaced by an almost palpable tension. No one is around the reception area, but the hair on my arms raises as if someone is watching me. I expect one of the lawyers to pop out of their office and fuck me at any second.

I barely have time to set my purse down before my phone's intercom buzzes.

Mr. Jacobs' voice cuts through the silence. "Miranda, my office in five minutes."

I get an immediate jolt of adrenaline. "Yes, sir."

I straighten my blouse again, double-checking that the top two buttons are undone to show a hint of cleavage. Actually—I unbutton another one so that the lace of my pink bra is peeking out. Jon chose this outfit for me, and I know he'd approve.

Since I have five minutes to kill, I turn my computer on and put my lunch in the break room fridge. When I get to Mr. Jacobs' office, the door is open and he's sitting at his desk.

"Close the door." He's using his stern tone that makes me instantly wet.

I do as I'm told, and stand in front of his desk with my hands clasped, waiting for his next move.

"Are you ready for your last day as our freeuse office slut?" He leans back in his chair. His gaze travels over me, and I fight the urge to fidget. "If you please us today—if you're a good girl—we'll all fuck you after work in the conference room."

Hmm, does he REALLY want me to behave? I fight the urge to smile, and tilt my head to the side. "And if I'm not a good girl?"

Mr. Jacobs' lips twitch with amusement. "Then we send you home without an orgasm. Simple as that."

Wait, does this mean I won't come at all today until the party? This was not part of my mental plan. I bite my lip, considering. He's manipulating me, and we both know it. But I'm eager to play along. I want this—I want them. But we need to talk about Jon. Shit, he better be okay with Jon watching.

I undo another button on my blouse and trail my fingers along my collarbone, making sure Mr. Jacobs is watching. "All of that is agreeable, but Jon has a demand."

Mr. Jacobs raises an eyebrow and I know he's waiting for me to elaborate.

"Jon wants to watch." Nerves flutter in my stomach. This is a deal breaker. No Jon, no party. "He wants to be here when you all use me."

Mr. Jacobs' keeps his face neutral. "Watch, hmm?" he muses. "And what makes you think we'll agree to that?"

I shrug. "Because you want to fuck me more than you want to deny Jon the pleasure of watching. And let's be honest, you'll get off on him watching too."

At least I hope so. I don't actually know if Mr. Jacobs has an exhibitionism kink, but we did a conference room fuck-fest years ago with Jon watching over video, and everyone seemed to enjoy that–including Mr. Jacobs.

His lips twitch again, and I know I've hit the mark. He's amused by this—the negotiation, the power play. It's all part of the game.

"You're right, but I'm not going to make it easy for you. If Jon wants to watch, that's fine. But you have to earn it. Understood?"

My heart pounds from excitement. I'm not exactly sure what they'll ask of me, but I always revel in whatever kinky thing my bosses come up with. "Understood, sir."

He stands up and moves behind me. "Then let's start with a reminder of who's in charge."

His hands slide down my sides, fingers brushing lightly against my blouse. Even through the thin fabric, his touch sends tingles of electricity through me.

He turns me to face him. "Take off your blouse."

I comply, and unbutton it, letting it fall to the floor. His eyes dip to the pink lace of my bra, and my nipples instantly harden.

"Beautiful," he says, his gaze lingering appreciatively. With one fingertip, he traces the delicate lace, the featherlight contact raising goosebumps across my skin. A mischievous smile plays at the corner of his mouth.

"I think I'll keep this," he says, scooping up my blouse from where it fell. "You can spend the day just like this. Give everyone at the office something to truly appreciate."

"Yes, sir." I really hope no clients stop by the office today.

"Good. Now get to work. You have a lot to do before 5 p.m." I nod, turning to leave, but he stops me. "And Miranda? Don't disappoint us."

I glance back at him. "Wouldn't dream of it, sir."

There's an extra sway in my hips as I leave his office. Dang it, why didn't he spank me already? I probably should have been bratty to start the day off properly.

As soon as I'm at my desk, I pull out my phone and text Jon.

Miranda:

> Babe, the party is at 5. I have to be a good slut today, or no party.

His response is almost immediate.

Jon:

> Then I guess you better be the best office slut ever. I want to see you take on all the lawyers.

I don't even try to stop my laugh. This is going to be fun, but there's one thing I need to know. My fingers hover over the keypad, hesitating for a moment before I type out the question.

Miranda:

> What if one of them wants to fuck my ass?

I hit send and wait, drumming my fingers nervously on the desk. My pulse quickens as I think about having all my holes filled today. Anal's not an all-access pass kind of thing. After I crossed one of Jon's boundaries a few years ago, Jon and I have a deal. My ass is his territory, and he decides who gets the key.

My phone buzzes, and I glance down.

> I'm willing to share my hole today because it's a special day.

A flush warms me. Jon's willingness to share this part of me today makes me feel even more cherished, in a messed-up way. My fingers fly over the keys.

> I promise to make you proud. Love you so much.

My heart flutters with anticipation and affection. Today is going to be incredible.

CHAPTER 2

The clock on my computer says 8:30 a.m, and the day stretches out before me. I'm uncertain what to expect. Am I going to do real work today? I'd rather not, but I'm alone in my little corner and the office is quiet. If I'm going to work without my blouse on, the least they could do was be around to admire me.

My instant messenger on my computer pings.

Come to my office.

Oooh, thank god. I stand and adjust my skirt, acutely aware of how exposed I am without my blouse. What my bosses haven't found out yet is that I'm wearing matching pink panties, along with a black garter belt and stockings. A seam runs down the back of each leg, adding a touch of elegance. Jon wanted me to be a proper freeuse office toy today, and that included wearing fancy undergarments.

My black high heels sink into the carpet as I make my way to Mr. King's office. I should probably ditch the shoes at some point, but I want a couple of the lawyers to see me wearing them first.

Mr. King's door is slightly ajar, and he's seated at his desk. He doesn't speak until I close the door behind me.

"Lock it."

I want to give him a cheeky, 'yes, sir,' but I keep it in. He's the lawyer I've fucked the most at work recently, and I know his MO now. He has a sadistic streak and he likes to provoke my bratty side.

I lock the door and when I turn back to him, he's standing. I take a moment to admire his broad shoulders—there's just something about a guy in a tailored suit that revs my engine and now that I know what Mr. King can do to me? Oh yeah, me and my slutty pussy are willing to jump through a lot of hoops to get what he offers.

His gaze lingers on my breasts before scanning the rest of me. I can feel the slick, wet heat between my legs, and I ache to be touched.

"You look…" He pauses, his eyes narrowing as he takes me in. "Fuckable."

I fight the urge to rub my thighs together in anticipation. "Thank you, sir."

Having a fabulous orgasm would start the day off nicely.

He smirks, and a longing pulls at my core. "Take off your skirt."

I deftly unzip my skirt, and let it pool at my feet. He's the first one who gets to see the garter belt.

"Turn around," he commands.

I pivot slowly, giving him the full view. When I'm facing him once more, I find his expression unreadable, a practiced blank slate from years of negotiations.

He moves behind me like a predator. His fingers graze my hip before cupping my ass. I moan softly at the contact, and my panties grow damp. Heck, at this rate, I'll have my orgasm before 9 a.m. and still have 3 more lawyers to go.

"You want to come, don't you?"

"Yes, sir."

He chuckles. "Too bad. You're not going to."

Dammit. I frown. "But—"

"No buts," he cuts me off, and the sharpness only makes me want him more. "You're here to please us, remember? And right now, it pleases me to deny you."

Fuuuck. He knows exactly what he's doing. It's infuriating and exhilarating. And by how wet my panties are now, I'm clearly getting off on this.

He gestures to a stack of folders on his desk. "File these for me."

I'm caught off guard by the sudden shift. "File them in the cabinet here?"

"Yes. You're going to work while I use you."

My thoughts whirl as I start sorting them alphabetically. I keep imagining him fucking me as soon as I reach for the bottom drawer, so I'm distracted enough that I keep fumbling the order.

He huffs impatiently and applies firm pressure to my shoulder, making me bend over his desk until my face is squished against the pile of folders. Yeah, okay, this wasn't exactly what I expected, but it'll do.

"You like knowing I can use you whenever and however I want, don't you?" I hear the clink of his belt buckle and the sound of him pulling down the zipper of his slacks.

"Yes, sir," I whisper, while a ping of excitement rushes straight to my pussy.

He nudges my panties to the side, the lace stretching as he exposes me. He positions the tip of his cock against my pussy, and I sigh and close my eyes as he thrusts into me slowly.

His thick cock stretches me wide, every ridge and vein massaging my slick pussy walls. I take him deeper and his hips press firmly against my ass. He doesn't rush—he fucks me slowly, each thrust measured, and I shake with the effort to hold back.

"You feel so fucking good." His voice is strained. "So tight around me."

He picks up the pace. Delight spirals from my pussy, but I know I can't come. Not yet. Not until he says so. It would just be momentary bliss, and then he'd find a new devious way to torture me.

He slams against me, and I yelp in shock and pleasure. The longer he fucks me, the more I stop caring about future punishment.

"Please, sir, I need—"

He cuts me off. "Oh, you need to come? That's unfortunate."

Damn him. My groan of frustration ends in a squeak as he smacks my ass. My eyes fly open. The sting creates a rush of ecstasy and I almost come all over his cock.

"Ooooh, god!" I cry out as he spanks me again, harder this time.

I grasp the side of the desk tighter and fight to hold back my orgasm. I don't want to risk punishment by coming.

"I'm going to use this tight pussy until I've had my fill. And then you're going to thank me. Do you understand?"

"Yes," I mewl out as he hammers into me. My cheek is still plastered against a manila file, and my vision swims from pleasure as I stare at the file cabinet across the room. If the plan was to make me a fucktoy first thing, Mr. King is doing a superb job of it. This is what I crave occasionally that my husband has a difficult time satisfying. I always know that Jon loves me. But Mr. King? Yeah, I'm being used. It's amazing.

"You're going to work like this all day," he growls as he pumps in and out of me. "Aching, desperate, and denied. And if you're a good girl, maybe—just maybe—you'll get to come at the end of the day."

I press my lips together, trying to hold back a whimper. He seizes my forearms, pulling them back and forcing me to rise up from the desk just enough that my nipples rub against the wood through my bra. The additional pleasure is almost my undoing as he fucks me harder.

His cock throbs inside me. He's close—I can tell by the way his breath hitches and his grip on my forearms tightens.

"Fuck, so good." He groans, a guttural sound, right before his cock pulses. He explodes, his hot cum filling me, coating my insides, and making me squirm.

He lets go of my arms to clasp my waist, holding me still while he unloads. I'm almost surprised when I don't come just from the warmth of his seed inside me. My pussy milks every last drop, as if draining his balls is my job.

"Good girl." His breath is ragged as he removes his cock. He slaps my ass and I don't even squeak. I'm too fuzzy-headed. "Now get back to work."

Oh god. I straighten up and look around the room. What am I even doing? I notice my skirt on the floor—oh yeah, I need that. I put it on and fasten it the best I can. I'll fix it later.

"Don't forget the folders," he grouses as he sits down at his desk.

My hands shake as I try to focus on gathering them into a pile. It's impossible. All I can think about is my throbbing clit and his cum dripping out of me.

"Mr. King," I say softly. "Please—"

He cuts me off. "Have you had breakfast?"

I blink in confusion, trying to recall the morning's events. Then I remember that Jon made me oatmeal and fruit before work, insisting I needed the energy for the day ahead.

"Yes," I reply, the memory of Jon's caring gesture warming me.

Mr. King nods and stands up. "Come with me," he says gently, holding on to my arm and leading me to the break room.

The change in his demeanor throws me off, but I follow without question. He grabs a bottle of water from the fridge and hands it to me. "You will drink all of this."

He escorts me back to my desk, his hand on the small of my back. He sits me down, his touch lingering for a moment before he pulls away.

"Drink up," he says, and then he turns and leaves.

I take a sip of the water, the cool liquid soothing my dry throat and perking me up a bit. It really did take me a bit to warm up to Mr. King when he joined the firm, but damn does that man know how to make me a submissive little slut. He ended up being the perfect addition to the firm.

The wetness between my legs and the way my damp panties cling to me are maddening. I'm going to be wrecked by the end of the day. And I can't wait.

Chapter 3

The morning crawls by, an endless tug-of-war between arousal and frustration. I cleaned up in the bathroom, but I swear that Mr. King's cum is still leaking out of me every time I shift in my chair. Yeah, it's probably just wishful thinking. After a trip to the copy machine, I kick off my heels—two of the lawyers saw me in them, and that's enough. My panties stick to my skin, the lace rubbing against my swollen pussy with each movement. I'm a needy slut, and it's barely past 11 a.m.

My instant messenger pings, providing a blessed distraction.

Come to the break room right now.

I try not to skip down the hall in excitement. Mr. Daniels is already there, leaning against the counter, arms crossed over his broad chest. He's not wearing a suit jacket, and I'm reminded again of how attractive he is. His rich, warm brown skin seems to glow under the break room lights, and he flashes me that amazing smile of his. His eyes, oh those eyes—crinkly at the corners and so full of lust—meet mine, and desire flutters in my stomach. After attending the conference with him yesterday, I'm looking at him in a new light. He's definitely grown more confident since he first joined the firm, which only makes him sexier.

"This is a delightful view," he says, his deep voice filling the room. His gaze travels over me, taking in my bra, my stockings, the way my nipples strain against the lace. "Come here."

I move closer, and he strokes my cheek with his fingers before trailing his hand down to my collarbone. His featherlight touch sends a shiver down my spine.

"I've been waiting for my turn with you all morning." His thumb tickles the skin on my breast just above my bra. "I hear you're being a good slut so far. So obedient."

"Thank you, sir." There's a fresh surge of wetness between my legs and I'm ready to worship his cock.

He chuckles, and turns me around, folding me over the break room table until I'm resting on my elbows. Oh, hello. He pulls my skirt up and presses up against my ass.

"I bet knowing that we can fuck you whenever we want today makes you wet."

"Yes," I whisper, and spread my legs in the hopes it entices him to take me right here.

His fingers slip beneath the lace of my panties, and he rubs my swollen clit. Jesus, if he doesn't fuck me soon, I'm going to go insane. He circles my clit slowly, his touch light and teasing. I clutch the side of the table and rock backwards.

When he inserts two fingers inside me and starts finger fucking me, I quiver as I try to hold back my orgasm. I'm peeping out in distress and the delight threatens to overwhelm me. "Oh, no, no. I'm going to come!"

He stills his hand and laughs. "No, you won't."

He removes his hand from my pussy and I almost groan. Fuck, this is worse.

"Come with me." He makes sure I can walk on my own, and I follow him to his office.

He shuts the door and sits at his desk. "Come over here and get on your knees. It's time for you to be a cockwarmer while I make a phone call."

Uh, fuck, that's hot. I sink to the floor in front of him, thankful I'm not wearing my heels any longer. He unzips his pants, freeing his cock, and I stare at his massive size. How did I get so lucky to work with four lawyers who all have impressive packages? Well, the real luck is that I have a husband willing to let me play with these gorgeous cocks. It's like winning the slut lottery.

"Open," he says firmly.

I part my lips, and he fits his cock into my mouth. I moan around him, the taste of his precum salty on my tongue. He presses on the back of my head, guiding my movements as I take him deeper. I relax, letting him fuck my mouth.

"That's it." He groans. "I always love using your mouth."

Always? Does he think about it outside of work? God, I hope he does. I moan in pleasure, the vibration making him twitch in my mouth. He twists my hair tighter, and suddenly, he holds my head still. His cock is still in my mouth but he's not thrusting.

He picks up his desk phone, dialing a number as I kneel there. I hear the ringing, and then a faint voice on the other end greeting him.

"Yes, this is Mr. Daniels," he says, sounding professional and calm, as if he isn't sitting there with his cock in my mouth. "I need to reschedule our meeting to next week."

My mind spins. I concentrate on not drooling on the cock occupying my mouth. This is humiliating, yet oddly exhilarating.

"No, Wednesday won't work." He shifts slightly, and I take the opportunity to change my position, trying to find a more comfortable angle. "I have a meeting scheduled with a client that day."

I curl my tongue around his shaft, and he grips my hair tight enough to make my scalp tingle. "Hold on a sec."

He presses mute on the receiver and looks at me. "Behave. You're just warming my cock. Don't even use your tongue."

Shit. I mumble, "Yes, sir," around his cock and then he unmutes the phone.

"I checked my calendar. Thursday works," he continues. "So, how have you been?" He now has a casual, friendly demeanor. "It's been a while since we caught up."

Oh god, what the fuck? I try to swallow, but some of my saliva runs down his cock. This is filthy, and I love it. I want to suck on him and clean him up, and just kneeling here while he chats as if he has no care in the world is the perfect blend of hot and annoying.

"That's great to hear," he says, laughing softly at something the other person says. "Yeah, we should definitely have lunch sometime soon." He ends the call and smirks down at me. "Okay, where were we?"

I hold still, waiting for him to give me instructions that I can move. He pushes my head down and I take that as a sign to start sucking again. I hollow my cheeks and get to work, but he takes over almost immediately and holds my head in one place as he flexes his hips to fuck my mouth. He groans at the moment his hot, salty release strikes the back of my throat. I struggle to swallow it all.

When he pulls me off his cock, I'm panting. He tucks himself back into his slacks. A mixture of cum and saliva spills down my chin. Quickly, I wipe it away with my fingers, then suck them clean, savoring every last bit.

He sighs, and I can tell he's pleased. My thoughts are jumbled. Jon is going to love hearing this part of the story.

He stirs and cups my face gently. "I think you've earned a reward."

I almost coo. Mmm, I like rewards. He lifts me to my feet and then boosts me up onto his desk. Oooh, is he going to fuck me? Can he even get it up again this quickly?

He forces me to lie back, but instead of fucking me, he sits down on his chair and drapes my legs over his shoulders. I gasp as he pulls my panties to the side.

His breath is hot against my pussy. "You're so fucking wet. I can see how much you need this."

"God, yes," I whimper.

He doesn't tease me and just dives in. I moan as he licks the length of my pussy and laps my clit. He devours me like I'm a five-star meal. My orgasm builds quickly, and I don't think I'll be able to stop it.

"Come for me." His voice is muffled against my pussy, but I'm still able to hear him. "Come all over my face."

As soon as he gives me permission, my orgasm hits. I'm drowning in a sea of bliss as he licks and sucks me through it. He's relentless and I'm almost too sensitive by the time he stops.

He stands up and wipes his mouth with the back of his hand. "You did so well, Miranda."

"Thank you, sir." I smile weakly, my body still buzzing with the aftermath of my orgasm.

He helps me sit up, and once he sees I'm steady, he says, "Now, clean yourself up. You've got more work to do today."

I hop off the desk and give him a little grin. "Yes sir, right away sir."

I sashay my way to the restroom. Thank god one of them let me come. I can think clearly after the orgasm, and my pussy tingles at the thought of what the next lawyer might do to me.

There's only five more hours until the party.

CHAPTER 4

I plop down into my office chair, my body humming like I've stuck my finger in an electrical socket. My bra feels too small, thanks to my tender breasts. Only one orgasm so far, and it's already past lunch. My bosses are playing hot potato with my libido, and I'm fairly certain all of them—except Mr. Daniels—are conspiring to keep me needy all damn day.

I peek at my phone, debating whether to shoot Jon a text. He's probably up to his elbows in work, but I know he'll want a status update. I unlock the screen and start tapping away.

Babe, I've only come once. I'm dying over here.

I can almost hear his teasing tone when he replies.

Aww, poor kitten. Being a good office slut?

The best. Oh, and they seem to be taking turns. Mr. Parks still hasn't fucked me.

Maybe he's got something special planned.

Hopefully it's his cock or fingers in my ass. As soon as Jon said he'd share my ass, I turned into my sluttiest self—well, let's be honest, I was mostly already there. But now all I can think about is having Mr. Parks' cock in my ass so I can drip cum from every hole.

Miranda:

> I don't need anything special, I just need more or-gasms.

I pout, wishing he was here to appreciate my pain.

Jon:

> I love it when you get all cranky.

Miranda:

> You're the best. Now stop distracting me. I'm trying to work!

Jon:

> You do that, and don't spend too much time imag-ining me sitting here stroking while thinking about watching you get fucked by your bosses.

A thrill zips through me. He always knows how to rev my engine, even from afar. I doubt he's actually stroking at work...right?

I text him some heart emojis and stash my phone in my purse. Dang, I wish Jon were here right now and watching all of this, but we'll have fun for days while I tell him everything that happened. First, I have to survive the rest of the day.

Right on cue, my instant messenger dings. It's Mr. Parks.

Mr. Parks:

> Come to my office.

Hell yeah. A delicious ache between my legs roars to life as I head for his office. His door is closed, and I knock.

"Come in."

Mr. Parks is at his desk, and his glasses perched on his nose give him a sexy, geeky look. My pussy clenches like she thinks she's going to get spanked, and I almost giggle from excitement. Okay, so yeah, I've been really looking forward to spending time with Mr. Parks again. He's the only lawyer who hasn't fucked my pussy yet this week.

"Lock the door. We don't want anyone walking in on this."

Uh, yeah...probably not. But is one of the other lawyers going to really walk in? I do as I'm told, and then stand there at the door, fidgeting. I'm so desperate right now, I could just lie down on his desk and beg him to do me. I'm not sure I have coyness in me right now.

"Come here," he finally says.

I step closer, my legs wobbling slightly. He leans back in his chair, eyes roving over me and I'm tempted to turn around so he can admire me from behind.

"Are you ready for me to fuck your ass today?" His tone is almost conversational, which makes this all dirtier.

Happy butterflies swirl in my stomach, and I keep my answer simple. "Yes."

"Good." He smiles, and I expect him to tell me to bend over.

He doesn't.

"But first there's a quiz."

Uh, what? "Quiz?"

"If you answer correctly, you can come when I fuck your ass. Answer wrong..." He leaves the rest unsaid.

My brain's scrambled from the day's festivities. But heck, maybe they'll be easy questions. "Okay. Ready when you are."

He motions me over to him. "One more thing. You'll be giving me a blowjob during the quiz. Now get on your knees."

Well, there goes my chance of an orgasm. No way am I going to be able to think with his cock in my mouth. I kneel between his legs and he pulls his cock out.

I'm a thirsty slut and he doesn't even have to tell me to open my mouth. I drop down onto his shaft, relishing the musky taste of his hard length. I really am in office slut mode, and if one of them told me to crawl naked to the break room to suck his cock, I'd do it.

I close my eyes and spend a moment familiarizing myself with his cock again, and savoring how it throbs in my mouth. He sucks in a breath when I flick the tip of my tongue along the veins, and then tugs on my hair to make me release him.

"What's the capital of France?"

Oh, this is easy. "Paris."

"Correct." He fucks my mouth again for a few minutes before pulling out. "Chemical symbol for gold?"

I try to think. "Um... Au?"

He thrusts back into my mouth, holding me there as he uses me. When he pulls out, I'm wooly-headed and gasping for air.

"Final question. What's 2,417 times 24?"

I hesitate, my thoughts sluggish like I'm wading through mud. Math? Seriously? The numbers jumble in my head. "I... I don't know."

"Two out of three isn't good enough. You don't get to come." He stands up, his chair rolling back with a soft squeak. "Bend over the desk."

I stumble to my feet and do as he requests, turning my head and resting my cheek against the smooth wooden surface. Knowing in advance I won't come pings the part of me that loves being a fucktoy. Using my ass for his pleasure only is the right kind of wrong.

He runs a hand over the fabric of my panties and pulls them down just far enough to expose my ass. He doesn't bother unhooking my garters.

"Such a pity you won't come. I wanted to make you scream while I fucked your ass. But rules are rules."

I imagine how much ecstasy it would take to make me scream and my nipples harden. I mean, I might come...Fuck it, I'm going to come if I can.

I hear the click of a cap opening, and then feel the cool lube. He takes his time, circling my entrance with a slick finger, making sure I'm prepared. This reminds me of years ago, that first day he brought me into his office and found out I'd never had anal sex. He just teased me with his finger, and made me eager to try it.

One of his fingers stretches me out. I moan as he adds more lube and a second finger. He pumps in and out while I adjust to having something in my ass. His cock is against my thigh, and he smears pre-cum along my skin.

"Maybe I should make you beg for it in the ass."

It sounds like he's talking to himself, so I stay quiet while pushing back against his fingers. The pressure is always a little uncomfortable at first, but it quickly turns to delight. God, I want another orgasm. He needs to just stick his cock in right now.

When he moves his free hand down to rub my clit, I quiver from pleasure and finally crack. "Please, Mr. Parks, I need your cock in my ass." I'm not above begging when I want something.

He chuckles. "That's more like it. I love it when you're a slut for an ass fucking." He removes his fingers, and a moment later the blunt head of his cock is pressing against my back entrance. He enters slowly, stretching me open around his thick shaft. The burn of the initial penetration gives way to pleasure as he eases inside.

"That's a sexy sight."

I look back at him, and his eyes are fixated on his cock sinking into my ass. I get naughty pleasure from imagining how dirty that looks from his view.

He grunts once he's fully seated and pauses, letting me acclimate. I flex my ass muscles for funzies, and we both moan as he pulls all the way out. He thrusts back in quickly and I squeal from the delight. Shit, fuck, he needs to keep doing that.

"So tight, so perfect," he grunts as he fucks me steadily.

I can only focus on the increasing ecstasy, and I don't know how long he drills into me. Everything is amazing. I jiggle my ass, trying to get as much pleasure as I can. I have to come before he does.

He picks up speed. "That's it, take my cock like the good little anal slut you are."

His words are punctuated by the slap of skin against skin as he pounds into me. His cock drags along my inner walls, and I'm so close to coming. My clit throbs, begging for attention,

"Yes, I'm an anal slut. Use my ass however you want." I'm babbling, too turned on to care about how desperate I sound.

He withdraws again until just the tip remains inside me before slamming back in. The force of his thrusts rocks the desk, and I have to brace myself against the surface to keep from being shoved forward.

"Please, Mr. Parks, I need to come. I'm so close." I'm practically sobbing now, and trembling with the effort of holding back my orgasm.

"No coming." He reaches around to rub my clit, and I nearly scream in rapture. He circles the nub mercilessly as he continues to fuck my ass.

"Please, I can't hold back. I'm going to come." My pussy spasms around nothing, and I'm going to explode any second.

"Too late," he groans as his cock throbs. Oh god, noooo. His warm seed coats my insides, and I'm twitching from the stolen orgasm.

He pulls out and sits in his chair. "Fuck, that was good."

I can only whimper in response as his cum drips out of my well-fucked hole. At least I got that, even if I didn't come.

He pulls a container of wet wipes from his desk and I sigh in relief when he cleans me up. After he uses one on himself, he puts his cock back into his slacks and then helps me to my feet. I stagger a bit, and I hold onto his waist while he pulls my panties up.

"Now thank me for fucking your ass and not letting you come."

His words immediately make me more submissive and I give him what he wants. "Thank you, Mr. Parks, for fucking my ass. And thank you for not letting me orgasm."

His eyes crinkle with satisfaction. "Anytime, Miranda. Now get back to work before one of the other partners comes looking for you."

I nod, and as I head to the door, he calls out. "And drink more water and eat a snack. Keep your strength up for later."

"I will."

His cum leaks out of my ass the entire walk back to my desk. There's only one cock I haven't had inside me yet today. Is Mr. Jacobs going to fuck me before the party?

CHAPTER 5

At about 3 p.m. Mr. Jacobs intercoms me and tells me to come to his office. I haven't done much work all day. Between the lawyers using me, I sat at my desk and blanked out while imagining being spit roasted by them.

When I get to his office, one glance from Mr. Jacobs has my heart racing.

"Shut the door," he orders.

My breath catches as I close it. If he didn't plan on using me, he'd leave it open, right? Cause really, closing the door is just for show—it's another way for him to control me.

He's sitting behind his desk, and his eyes devour me. I squirm under his stare and heat blossoms in my stomach.

"I heard you were quite the little slut today."

I'm not sure how to answer. I was a slut, and it was wonderful. But I'm not sure if that's going to get me what I want, so I try to deny it. "N-no, sir. I was a good girl."

Heh, a good girl at being a slut.

"Strip."

Mmm, oh yeah, I'm getting fucked, but just as added insurance, I take my time removing my skirt, since he still has my blouse. I lift my foot onto the chair, and toy with the clasps of my garter belt before I unhook one of my stockings. Mr. Jacobs stares at my legs. I know what he wants—and I'm more than willing to give it to him.

Slowly, I roll down the silk stocking, and the smooth fabric glides over my skin inch by inch as I reveal more of my bare leg. His gaze tracks the movement, and I get a zing of pleasure knowing I have his full attention. I finally slip the stocking off my foot, letting it dangle from my fingers for a moment before dropping it to the floor.

I switch legs, repeating the process with the other stocking. The room is silent except for the soft rustle of fabric and my own heartbeat pounding in my ears. I can sense the heat of his stare, the anticipation in the air.

Next, I remove the garter belt and it joins the stockings on the floor. Reaching behind my back, I unhook my bra and let the straps slip down my arms. I hold the cups in place for a moment, prolonging the reveal, before letting the bra fall away completely.

My breasts are full, yet perky, and I pull at the nipples while he watches with lust. Oh yeah, he wants me as much as I want him. I saved my panties for last because I know how to get him riled up. I turn around, facing away from him and hook my thumbs into the waistband. I slowly pull my panties down, leaning forward to give him a clear view of my ass as the fabric glides down my legs. Stepping out of them, I kick them aside with a playful flick of my foot. For the finale, I shimmy my hips before straightening up and facing him.

The desire in his eyes matches my raw need. He stands up and moves behind me. "Bend over. It's time for your spanking."

Fuck yeah. I position myself at his desk, resting on my forearms so I can look over my shoulder at him. I wiggle my ass to tempt him. My breasts are heavy, my nipples tight, and everytime they skim across the cool surface of the desk, it sends sparks of pleasure straight to my throbbing clit.

"Spread your legs," he orders, and I widen my stance.

His hand strikes my flesh, sharp and sudden. I gasp, the sting spreading like wildfire. He waits a beat, then strikes again. Each smack is a jolt of pain that melts into pleasure while my nerves sing.

As he continues to spank me, the tension increases in my core while my breath comes in short gasps. Each impact of his hand resonates through me.

"You're such a good little slut."

The praise makes me tingle and amplifies the delight. He changes his rhythm, alternating between sharp smacks and gentle caresses. The contrast drives me insane until I'm dizzy with need.

Each smack brings me closer to the abyss. A final, firm spank sends me spiraling. I cry with my climax, and pleasure radiates to my fingertips and toes.

His hand stills, resting gently on my heated flesh. "Good girl."

I am a good girl. I'm in a contented haze from the afterglow, and I barely register the rustling fabric as he takes his cock out. He positions himself behind me, and enters me with a single, powerful thrust. I moan as I almost come again. He was my first introduction to being a hotwife many years ago, and the fact that I'm allowed to fuck him again years later is surreal. I've changed since that first time—we all have—but somehow he still knows what I need.

He drives into me and each thrust creates waves of rapture. He reaches underneath me with both hands to play with my breasts, and he lifts me up slightly so he can roll my nipples with his fingers while fucking me.

"Ohhhh god," I moan as I try to fight against coming.

The tension coils again, but just as I'm about to come, he slows his movements. The change in pace leaves me teetering, the orgasm just out of reach. I moan in frustration as he continues to fuck me slowly.

"You don't get to come again," he growls.

Fuckity, fuck, fuck, fuck. He speeds up, and groans when he finally unloads. Pleasure zips through me, but it stops just shy of sending me over the edge. He fucks his cum back into me, and when he's done, it drips down my inner thigh. Oh yeah, I'm a mess, and going to get even dirtier soon.

I'm an odd mix of happy and frustrated when he says, "Work the rest of the day naked. No point in putting clothes back on."

Uh…other than I need my filthy panties to soak up his cum, but I don't argue. I'm not going to do anything that jeopardizes this party—especially knowing he just came and he might be willing to forgo the festivities if I get cranky.

I give him my best cutesy, "Yes, sir," and saunter out of his office, putting an extra sway in my hips for his benefit.

Is it time for this party yet?

Chapter 6

The clock hits 5 p.m. and my stomach flutters with excitement. Mr. Jacobs told me to bring Jon back to the conference room once he arrives.

I'm standing up and leaning against my desk when Jon enters the office and finds me. I'm going to keep my personal shame of sitting on a bunch of paper towels for the last hour to myself. They're in the garbage can, so he won't see them.

Jon's eyes widen a fraction when he sees that I'm naked. "Fuck, kitten. You're a goddamn vision."

His approval boosts my confidence. I'm a sexual goddess. "You like?" I turn slowly, giving him the full view.

"More than like." He steps closer, pulling me into a hug. "I'm obsessed. And I'm going to enjoy watching them fuck you before I take you home and remind you that you're mine."

Mmm, I love it when he gets all growly and possessive. He's going to be really worked up when this is over.

I blush with excitement. "They're waiting for us."

"Then let's go."

I lead him to the conference room, even though he knows exactly where it is. The door's open and as we walk into the room, I notice the lights are dimmed. The large table has been moved aside to create an open space. Mr.

Jacobs, Mr. King, Mr. Daniels, and Mr. Parks are perched casually against the table perimeter and all eyes are fixed on me.

"On your knees, Miranda," Mr. Jacobs commands, stepping forward.

Oh damn, they're not wasting any time. Jon moves over to a chair that is conveniently placed against the wall to give him a great view of the entire room.

I kneel down gracefully—I've had years of practice by now. Yeah, I'm on my knees often since I love sucking cocks. I lick my lips and study the bulge in Mr. Jacobs' slacks.

"Here's how this is going to go. You're going to suck on each of us, and then we're going to use you however we want because you're still our freeuse slut. You might orgasm, you might not, but you don't have to ask permission."

Okay, yeah, this sounds good. They use me and I can orgasm. I nod quickly and his eyes twinkle.

"And remember you can always use your safeword if this gets too rough."

I appreciate the reminder, but I already know from past experiences that I'm going to love everything they do to me. "Yes, sir."

Mr. King comes over, and takes his cock out of his pants. I guess Mr. Jacobs isn't going to go first like I assumed.

"Open."

My jaw drops down, and I welcome Mr. King's velvety-smooth cock into my mouth. I can see Jon to the side and he's leaning forward with his elbows resting on his knees, a rapt audience.

Being the center of attention, being used and desired, awakens every nerve in my body. I moan around Mr. King's cock as he fucks my throat. The tang of his precum is pleasant and I lick and suck on him, trying to see if I can make him come.

He pulls out before he does, and I pout. Yeah, my new goal is to make one of them blow their load in my throat when they didn't mean to.

Mr. Daniels is next, and I'm hungry for him. The men are only pulling their cocks out and not fully stripping, which somehow seems filthier. He barely has his out before I throw myself onto it with gusto. He grips my head firmly, forcing me to slow down as he guides me.

Again, the feeling of being used gives me a rush of delight. I know there is affection between us all—even me and Mr. King—but it's different from when Jon uses my mouth. Even though we've talked about boundaries, there's a tiny bit of uncertainty when I allow the lawyers to use me, which makes it even hotter. But having Jon here allows me to relax and really let go.

Mr. Daniels releases his grip to pull his cock out, and I'm left panting, my lips swollen and slick. Jon's gaze is on me. He's enjoying this and knowing that this is turning him on gives me an illicit thrill.

Mr. Parks steps up, his cock already hard and ready. He traces my lips with the head of his cock, teasing me. I dart my tongue out, trying to capture him, but he pulls back. "Eager, aren't you?"

"Please," I moan.

He holds my chin, tilting my head back before feeding me his cock. He's gentler than the others, his movements more controlled, but no less dominating.

My nipples tighten and my pussy spasms. I want more—need more. I ball my hands into fists and hold them against my thighs. Mr. Parks strokes my cheek softly before pulling his cock out without coming.

Mr. Jacobs is last. He puts his hands on my head, and guides me as he thrusts slowly into my throat. I gag slightly, but I'm able to take him. He fucks my mouth steadily, using me for his pleasure.

Jon's gaze is like a physical touch, searing my skin. It spurs me on, makes me want to take more, be more. I'm needy and aching to be fucked.

Mr. Jacobs pulls out, and a string of saliva sticks to his cock. I look up at the four of them, pleading. "Please fuck me."

They smirk and exchange looks. They know they have me right where they want me—aching, needy, theirs to use.

"I think the freeuse toy forgot that she doesn't get to decide how and when we use her."

It's Mr. King who speaks up and it takes all my willpower not to shoot daggers at him with my eyes.

"I'm sorry, sirs. Please, will you fuck me?" My words are soft and submissive, and I hope they're satisfied.

"That's a better attitude," Mr. King says. "On your hands and knees."

My heart thumps as I shift from kneeling to all fours. They circle me, and anticipation swirls in my stomach. I'm trembling by the time Mr. King kneels in front of me and Mr. Parks behind. Mr. Jacobs and Mr. Daniels lean against the conference table, watching.

Mr. King slides his dick back into my mouth while Mr. Park teases the entrance of my pussy with the head of his cock. I'm so desperate, I want to fuck myself on his cock, but I know better.

"Please," I whimper around Mr. King's shaft. I'm not sure which of them I'm talking to, but I don't care what they do as long as I orgasm.

Mr. Parks pushes inside me, and I'm so wet that he bottoms out easily. I moan as my body stretches to accommodate his cock.

Mr. Parks doesn't waste a second and he fucks me hard and fast. My pussy quakes as his balls slap against my clit.

He spanks my ass. "Don't move."

I'm so close, I'm not going to last much longer. I try to focus on sucking on Mr. King's cock, but it's impossible when Mr. Parks is pounding me so hard that it's shoving Mr. King's cock further down my throat.

"Look at our little office slut," Mr. Daniels says. "She's going to make you come, isn't she, Mr. Parks? It's amazing when her pussy flutters around me when I'm fucking her."

His filthy words make me moan. I love how degrading it is when they talk about me like I'm just a sex toy. I spent too many years wondering what was wrong with me for wanting this, and embracing this sluttiest side of myself is so fucking wonderful.

Mr. Parks' cock twitches. Oh god, yes, please fill me up. Every fiber of my being is focused on the impending ecstasy. My clit throbs and my nipples ache. I'm a live wire, the sparks threatening to ignite with each thrust.

"Come for me, Kitten." Jon's voice cuts through the fog of my lust.

That's all I need. I scream around Mr. King's cock as my orgasm crashes over me. Pleasure wracks my body, and I'm still coming when Mr. Park's hips stutter momentarily before he slams his cock into me one last time. His hot seed flooding me triggers a new wave of delight.

I'm lost in a sea of ecstasy when Mr. King explodes. I lose control and I can't swallow fast enough. Drool and cum leaks out of the sides of my mouth. I'm completely overwhelmed.

I'm still floating on a cloud of bliss when Mr. King pulls his cock out. The cool air of the conference room brushes against my heated flesh. I can't stop smiling. I'm a well-fucked slut, and it's not over yet.

Mr. Parks withdraws from my pussy, and his cum dripping out of me makes me shiver.

Mr. Jacobs speaks. "Clean him up."

Oh shit. I clamber to my knees again. Mr. Parks stands in front of me with his spent cock covered in our combined wetness. I lick from his balls up his shaft, tasting myself on him. He's still sensitive and I smile when his cock twitches.

Once I've given him a thorough tongue bath, Mr. Parks tucks his cock away and moves aside. Mr. Jacobs calls me over and then pushes me down on the table's surface. My nipples graze the wood as I rest on my elbows.

Mr. Jacobs slides his cock into my pussy. "Fuck, she feels so good."

He pounds into my pussy, and his cock drags against my inner walls. I moan loudly from the pleasure.

Mr. Daniels moves to stand next to my head, and he reaches out to stroke my hair. "You're such a good little office slut." He glances at the other partners. "I wonder how many times we can make her come."

That's it. Mr. Daniels is my favorite lawyer at the moment.

Mr. Jacobs grabs my arms and pulls them behind me. He holds them up and pivots, forcing me off the table so I'm facing Mr. Daniels. Mr. Jacobs picks up speed, and his hips slap against me. My pussy quivers, and I cry out and go limp as another orgasm skyrockets me to another plane of existence.

When I come back to earth, Mr. Daniels' cock is at my mouth, and I gurgle happily around his shaft. Mr. Jacobs grinds against me as he pumps my pussy full of his cum. I'm trembling, and I start wondering how much of this I can take. Can there be too much pleasure?

Mr. Jacobs pulls out, and Mr. Daniels withdraws from my mouth without coming. Mr. King takes over. I'm a rag doll as he moves me over to the table again, sitting me on top of it. Mr. King glides his hand up my thigh, his thumb circling my clit in delicate strokes. I melt against his hand and wrap my legs around his waist, hoping to draw him into me. He laughs and removes his hand and unhooks my legs.

"No you don't. I decide how I'm fucking you."

I rest back on the table while he folds my legs towards my chest. My ass is at the edge and he burrows into my wetness.

"Fuck, so good." He starts pounding me, his eyes fixated on where we're joined.

I'm still tender from my last two orgasms and it doesn't take long before I'm wound tight, my breath coming in shallow gasps.

"Oh god, I'm going to come," I cry out right before my orgasm washes over me. I'm lost in ecstasy, my fingers clawing at the table, seeking something, anything, to ground me. I can't hold on, can't fight against the wave of pleasure that consumes me.

Mr. King fucks me frantically, his cock swelling inside me and then exploding. He twitches as he pumps his cum into my well-used pussy.

When Mr. King pulls out, Mr. Jacobs moves between my legs. "One more," he says, sliding into me. "You can give us one more orgasm."

I can only moan in response. He's not wrong, and within minutes of him fucking me, I'm creaming all over his cock. I'm limp when Mr. Daniels picks me up and carries me over to a chair. He stands me up before sitting down himself.

"Ride me and fuck yourself on my cock."

I can do that. I face the room and lower myself onto his cock. Oh fuck. I'm not going to be able to walk straight tomorrow.

I'm so damn satisfied that it's hard to bounce on him, but I find a rhythm. Every nerve ending is pinged by his thick cock, and I'm not going to last long. He grasps my ass and lifts me up. Jon has a clear view of the chair and I play with my nipples while I fuck myself on Mr. Daniels' cock. Each tweak of my nipples sends a corresponding burst of pleasure from my clit, and my continual moans of "Oh god," are getting louder with every thrust.

"Come on, slut. You've got this." Mr. Daniel's voice is tight and he's clearly trying to hold back his own release.

He reaches down to play with my clit, and I shatter. My pussy quakes around him and I scream out. His cock pulses and he comes, adding to the collection of cum inside of me. I slump back against him, my head resting on his chest as I try to catch my breath.

I've lost count of my orgasms. I'm sweaty, sticky, and cum-filled. And I've never felt better in my life.

Jon pipes up from his chair. "One more time, Kitten. And guys, stuff all her holes."

Ooooh, god. Jon is nasty, and I love it.

Mr. King lies on the floor and they maneuver me over him. His cock is out and I sink down onto him. Fuck, my pussy is sore, but it still feels wonderful. Mr. King's cock stretches me again as I ride him slowly, enjoying the pings of pleasure and knowing there's more to come.

Mr. Parks produces a bottle of lube from his pocket and I lean down to give Mr. King a kiss while Mr. Parks preps me for his cock. My tongue twines with Mr. King's while Mr. Park works the lube into my ass. Within moments, he presses his cock against the tight ring and slowly inserts it. I moan into Mr. King's mouth from the intense pleasure. It takes a bit, but once he's inside me, I'm so fucking full, I feel like I could burst.

This is what happiness feels like, and that connection with Jon is unwavering even with me having two cocks in me right now.

"You good, Kitten?" Jon's voice is raw with emotion.

"So good."

When Mr. Daniels kneels next to me with his cock out, I swallow him down. This is the ultimate fantasy. Three lawyers in all my holes. The guys all fuck me and the pleasure makes my head spin. I didn't think I had another orgasm in me, but this is taking me to a place I've never been before. All my nerves sing in delight and it's heavenly.

"I think she needs all our cum at once," Mr. Daniels says, as he pulls out.

I don't know how they plan to do that, but at this point, I don't care what they do to me.

"Do you want to be covered in cum, slut?" Mr. Jacobs asks as he steps up next to me.

"Yes, please." I want it all. I want to be marked by them, to wear their cum on my skin. They have me so turned on that I might orgasm the moment they cover me in cum.

"Then beg for it. Tell us how much you want it." Mr. Jacobs commands.

I look up at him from under my eyelashes. "Please, I need your cum. Cover me in it." Begging the lawyers for their cum drops me into the darkest recess of my soul. A place where I'll do or say anything. "I'm a filthy office slut, and I'm here to be used. Please use me and paint me with your cum." I'm begging, the words pouring from me in a torrent of need.

Mr. Jacobs seems satisfied and says, "Open wide."

I obey, ready to take whatever he gives me. Mr. Jacobs eases into my throat, and as he thrusts into my mouth, the other lawyers focus on me. Their hands roam over my body, teasing and tweaking my nipples, stoking the fire that threatens to consume me.

Mr. Daniels stands next to me, holding his cock over my head while he strokes it. Mr. Jacobs fucks my mouth, and the rhythm of the thrusts in my ass are timed perfectly with Mr. King's cock in my pussy. I'm blissed out from the pleasure. Mr. Daniels' hand moves faster on his shaft and my skin tingles in anticipation of his hot cum on me. I'm so close, my orgasm is just within reach.

Mr. Jacobs' cock twitches as he nears his climax, his grip on my hair tightening. All the guys speed up their movements. Mr. Daniels' hot cum splashes on my face first. His release is the catalyst that triggers the others, and they're quick to follow. Mr. King and Mr. Parks groan and I feel my pussy and ass filled with cum as they explode deep inside me. It triggers my orgasm, and I cry out as my climax rips forcefully through my body. It's a soul-shaking orgasm that leaves me breathless and trembling.

Mr. Jacobs pulls out of my mouth at the last minute and aims for my chest. I shudder when his cum lands on my breasts, dripping down to my belly and thighs.

"Fuck," Mr. Daniels groans, his cock still spurting. His cum drips down my face and sends shockwaves of delight through me. I'm a filthy, cum-covered slut.

When Mr. Parks withdraws from my ass, he helps me climb off Mr. King. They leave me kneeling on the floor and they all step back, admiring their handiwork. I'm a canvas of desire, painted in their pleasure. It's glorious.

"Thank you." My voice is hoarse and I'm not sure if it's from all the cocks I had down my throat, or if it's from my moaning.

They chuckle, their gazes filled with satisfaction. "You're very welcome," Mr. Jacobs says. "We'll see you Monday, but unfortunately with Cindy back we'll have to be discreet if you want more fun."

Mmm, more fun. Jon and I will have to talk about that first. I giggle as the lawyers straighten their clothes. I'm tired and could lie down right here and sleep, but I force myself to stay on my knees.

The lawyers pause over by Jon, but I'm too addled to process what they're saying other than I hear them thank him for sharing me this week. Well, that's nice and respectful after such a filthy event.

Once they're gone, Jon kneels in front of me with a container of wet wipes that one of them must have given him. He cleans me up, and I giggle again as he wipes the cum off my face.

"You're a mess, Kitten," he laughs with me.

"Mmm hmm." I'm floating in my happy place, and indulging in the filthy sensation of their cum drying on me.

When Jon gets up and retrieves my clothes from a chair, I realize one of the lawyers must have put them there without me noticing. Jon dresses me like I'm a doll, all except my garter and stockings. It's sweet.

I'm a sleepy, happy little office slut, and I lean against Jon as we leave. "I love you, Jon."

He kisses the top of my head. "I love you too, Kitten."

Once we're in the car, Jon turns to me. "That was the hottest fucking thing I've ever seen in my life. Thank you."

"Mmm, I'm glad you enjoyed watching." I snuggle into the passenger seat. "I enjoyed the doing."

I close my eyes and drift.

CHAPTER 7

I blink and we're home. If someone had asked me back at the office if I was ready for Jon to fuck me, I would have said no, but the cool air as I step out of the car revives me, and just looking over at Jon's strained expression sends a bolt of desire straight to my core. I'm still humming from the aftermath of the office party, but there's a new energy inside me, one that's reserved only for him.

The moment we step into the house, Jon presses me against the wall and his mouth crashes onto mine. His kiss is demanding, and I melt into it, responding instantly. His tongue twirls with mine, and I can taste his urgency, his need to reclaim me.

"You're mine," he growls. "Mine to love. Mine to protect."

"Yes, yours," I whisper.

"I'm going to fuck you, Kitten. Hard. And you're going to take it because you belong to me."

"Yes, Sir. Please."

Oooh, hell yeah. Beast Jon came out to play. In my most honest moments, this is exactly why I love being a hotwife. I get railed by other men, and then Jon usually goes crazy and gives it to me hard.

He turns me around, pressing my breasts to the wall. His hands caress down my thighs and he hikes my skirt up. He grinds against my ass and I push back, trying to get him inside me.

He slaps my ass sharply, and I yelp from the pleasurable sting. "Who do you belong to?"

"You, Sir," I breathe out. "Only you."

"That's right," he growls while he moves my panties aside. He finds my clit and rubs it until I'm quivering from pleasure. My hands are flat on the wall and I use it as leverage to try and force his fingers inside me.

"Oh god, just fuck me. Please?"

"Oh, Kitten, I plan to," he laughs and pulls his hand out from between my legs. He quickly removes my clothes, dropping them in a pile on the floor. I step out of my heels as he continues. "But let's be clear on one thing..."

He doesn't complete his thought and he picks me up and carries me to the bedroom. He tosses me gently onto the bed and I watch as he strips.

Once he's naked, he crawls over me and nibbles on my neck. "I have two holes to reclaim."

Oh god, I'm about to have my ass stuffed full. "Yes. God, yes."

He sits back on his knees. "Spread your legs."

I eagerly part them and he nestles against me, his cock hard and thick, the tip already glistening with pre-cum. He teases me, rubbing the head of his cock against my clit before lining himself up with my entrance.

He pauses, holding back. He knows how to drive me wild, to make me ache for him, and I'm ready to explode by the time he finally slides inside me.

"Fuck," he groans, his cock stretching me open. He fills me perfectly, and having him inside me is a comfort.

He starts out slow, as if he's reacquainting himself with every inch of my body. I moan as he fucks me, my fingers digging into the sheets. I wrap my legs around him, urging him deeper.

Jon picks up the pace, and I cry out in pleasure from each thrust. He captures my lips in a searing kiss, and my tongue twirls with his. I'm lost in a sea of bliss as he trails kisses along my neck. I'm drowning in him—in us.

He reaches down to find my clit, his fingers working in time with his thrusts. "I want you to come on my cock, Kitten. Now."

It's all I need to fall over the edge. My orgasm crashes over me, my pussy clenching around his cock as waves of delight wash over me. I scream his name, my body quivering with the force of my climax. He continues to pound me through it, his own moans of pleasure mixing with mine. The rapture doesn't end, but just keeps climbing. I'm going to have another orgasm, and soon, and I'm not sure how that's even possible.

He pulls out, and before I can protest, he flips me over and tugs my hips up so I'm on my knees and elbows. His hands are on my ass, spreading me open. He has a bottle of lube. He obviously likes to be prepared. The gel is cold, and I jump as he coats my opening.

"Relax, Kitten," he murmurs as he pushes a finger into my ass. He moves it in and out of me before he adds a second. "You're taking my fingers like a good girl."

"Mmm, so good, Sir."

"I bet," he laughs as he adds a third finger, stretching my asshole to get me ready for him. "I think you're ready."

"Yessss." The word comes out in a long, drawn out hiss.

His lubed fingers leave my ass and the tip of his cock replaces them. "Breathe, Kitten."

I exhale and he pushes inside me. I'm so relaxed from being fucked all afternoon that his cock slides past the barrier easily. He doesn't stop until he's fully sheathed in my ass.

The pleasure is overwhelming. He tugs on my hair gently, and pulls my head up. I have to brace myself on the bed to stay steady. His other hand moves around to my front and he plays with my clit. I'm so sensitive that it hurts, but in the best possible way.

"Such a good girl," he says, his hips moving in small circles, his cock stretching my ass. "I think you can come like this."

I'm not sure I can, and I don't know if I could handle another orgasm. He's not giving me a choice, and I whimper as he thrusts and rubs my clit.

"Come again. Show me who you belong to."

His fingers are relentless on my clit, and I'm on the brink, the pleasure bordering on pain. I want to give him what he wants, but I'm not sure how much more I can take. I'm writhing, my breath ragged as the pressure increases.

"Please." I'm unsure what I'm even asking for, I'm so mentally fucked.

He slows down, but he doesn't stop. "You can do this, Kitten. I believe in you."

His fingers on my clit are short circuiting my brain. My body is on fire and I can't stop it. I don't want to stop it. I want to come apart, to surrender completely to him. I need to give him everything.

The pleasure crests and I scream his name as I come. Waves of ecstasy wash over me, each one more intense than the last. Jon's rhythm falters and he thrusts once, twice more and then stills inside me. He holds me in place as he comes, his cock pulsing in my ass as he fills me. The world fades away, leaving only the two of us.

I collapse onto the bed and he gently pulls his cock out and then lies next to me. He strokes my back gently. "I love you," he whispers. "You're always so good for me."

I'm floating in the haze, and I can't keep the smile off my face.

"You did such a good job today. You made me very happy. I'm so proud of you." He keeps telling me all the ways he loves me and I practically purr with contentment. He's always so sweet and loving after he reclaims me.

I'm drifting to sleep, his words wrapping around me like a warm blanket, his touch a gentle reassurance. He's the only man I love.

"You're mine, Kitten, no matter who I share you with."

"Mmm, yours," I murmur.

He kisses my shoulder. "Sleep a little but then you need to eat."

"Okay, love."

Everything is as it should be, and as my eyelids close, I know that Jon is my forever. Even if he decided to never share me with my bosses again, I'd still love him for all eternity. And I know he loves me the same way.

The End

ABOUT LACEY CROSS

Lacey Cross is a wife sharing erotica writer with over 100 short stories published since she started in 2021. Her stories emphasize the pleasure found from the wife living her best slut life and embracing the hotwife lifestyle. She explores themes of free use, submissive wives with dominant bulls, BDSM...and oh-so-many men.

9 781960 162403